AQUA TERRA IGNIS AER

ZODIAC ACADEMY

RUTHLESS FAE

CAROLINE
PECKHAM

SUSANNE
VALENTI

Zodiac Academy

Earth Cavern

Pitball Stadium

Saturn Auditorium

Uranus Infirmary

Aqua House

Neptune Tower

Luna Leisu

Water Lagoon

Pluto Offices

The Shimmering

Asteroid Place
Terra House
Hall
Mars Laboratory
King's Hollow
The Howling Meadow
The Wailing Wood
The Orb
Earth Observatory
Venus Library
rcury
nbers
Aer House
Fire Arena
Air
Cov

WELCOME TO ZODIAC ACADEMY

Note to all students: Vampire bites, loss of limbs or getting lost in The Wailing Wood will not count as a valid excuse for being late to class.

CALEB

CHAPTER ONE

The scent of a burning body still lingered in the air, catching in the back of my throat and making my scowl deepen. My heightened senses picked up every drop of blood which had been spilled tonight and I wondered again how such a thing had happened in the middle of campus with teachers all around.

I marched through The Wailing Wood with Max and Seth on either side of me. We travelled in silence, waiting until we could be sure of complete privacy before we discussed what had happened tonight with the Vega Twins.

The air between the trees was thick with tension and the darkness beneath their canopy almost complete. None of us summoned a light into existence though. Even in the dark we knew where we were going and we didn't want any chance of anyone following us tonight. Not after what had just happened. What we'd just done.

I strained my ears for any sound of Darius approaching. There had been no sign of him since he'd stormed out of the Lunar Leisure building and left us all to deal with Orion's wrath by the poolside.

My lip curled back as my mind landed on our Cardinal Magic Professor. No one had dared give me so much as a verbal warning since we'd arrived at this school yet he'd just seen fit to give us two weeks in detention. Who the hell did he think he was? Didn't he consider the fact that we would be his kings soon? Was he really so angry with us that he'd risk incurring our wrath?

He'll realise exactly who he's crossed once I've graduated this place. I'm more than an Heir to him; I'm the most powerful Vampire in Solaria and his superior in every way once I leave this academy behind.

My mind snagged on the way Tory had looked when he'd pulled her out of that pool and a sliver of ice trickled down my spine. I didn't want to think about that. I didn't want to remember the way her heart had been beating too slowly when I'd strained my ears to listen for it. I didn't want to think about the way she'd kept her eyes to the floor instead of glaring right back at us.

We'd needed to break them. It had to be done.

So why does it make me feel like a piece of shit?

It was cold in the woods and I drew on my fire Element to warm myself through. Flames licked along my limbs from the inside but it didn't do much to chase away the cold pit in my gut.

My energy was running low. I could feel the well of power within me straining to maintain the heat of my fire. I should have topped up on Tory's magic while we were at the dance. But I'd known the others were planning something for her and I just... hadn't.

I pushed a hand through my hair, my fingers catching in the curls as I messed it up.

It was her own fault really. I'd tried to get her to leave the dance with me before anything had happened. I'd done my best.

Keep telling yourself that.

Seth was toying with something in his hands and I glanced at it, spotting the coil of black and blue hair he had wrapped through his fingers.

He noticed my attention and smirked at me but I looked away without giving him a response.

His shoulder bumped against mine affectionately but I shrugged him off. Werewolf and Vampire natures were about as different as you could get when it came to tactile behaviour. And though I'd grown used to the way he pawed at me all the time and usually didn't mind it, I found it hard to tolerate when I was tense. And with what we'd just done, the dead body that had shown up, Darius going missing and my power running low, I was definitely tense.

I could see Seth pouting at me from the corner of my eye but I didn't care. I upped my pace a little and we turned off of the pathway, slipping between the trees towards King's Hollow.

We passed through a clearing and the light of the moon shone down on us for a moment. I glanced up, almost certain that I'd seen a shadow passing under the stars out of the corner of my eye.

I looked around curiously, wondering if Darius was flying above us in his Dragon form. Apart from a small patch around the moon, the sky was thick with clouds and even my Vampire eyesight couldn't pick out anything moving above us. It didn't mean he wasn't there though. Where else would he have gone? Darius wasn't quick to anger but when he did lose his temper he was always drawn to the release of transformation. His Dragon form was the perfect outlet for rage and as a Leo, his temper was fierce when it was unleashed.

The others didn't slow as I searched the sky for a sign of the fourth Heir but I didn't care about them leaving me behind.

I needed a moment away from them to think about what I was going to say when we made it to King's Hollow. I knew that what had happened tonight had been necessary in a way but it also didn't seem right to me. The Vampire Code forbade me from torturing my Source so I hadn't had anything to do with what they'd done to Tory; I hadn't even known what they had planned until it was underway. But even though I could claim to have been nothing more than a witness I still felt... kinda shitty.

I sighed.

There was no way to be sure if Darius was up there or not so I gave up on my hunt for him. If he wanted to see us then he knew where we'd be.

I put on a spurt of speed and raced between towering trunks, delving into the heart of The Wailing Wood until I felt the brush of magic against my skin.

The wards we'd placed around this place swept welcomingly across my flesh as I pushed through them, passing Max and Seth and making it to the Hollow first.

The ancient oak which housed King's Hollow towered above me as I made it to the entrance at its roots. Long ago, someone had wielded powerful Earth magic on this tree to create the place we called our haven. The four of us were always under so much pressure to portray the perfect image, to exude power and strength and command the attention of every Fae in the room, this one spot was the only place we had that we could call our own and truly be ourselves.

It was a sanctuary and an oasis in the maelstrom of our lives but for the first time that I could remember, I wasn't looking forward to entering it.

The huge door before me was woven from the very fabric of the bark and roots of the colossal tree. As I reached out to touch it, it welcomed the essence of my magic like it was greeting an old friend. Only the most powerful Fae could gain access to this place and as such, within its walls we could be free.

I didn't wait for Seth and Max as the door swung open to admit me. Instead I headed onto the staircase which was forged from the internal structure of the hollow trunk and began to ascend. Faeflies crawled across the wooden walls, glowing blue and green with their own little wells of magic and lighting the way for me.

The stairs wound up, curving around again and again until I reached another door made out of living vines. I reached out to them with my magic and they curled away from the entrance to admit me, white flowers blooming along their lengths as they took joy in the power I fed them.

My gut swirled uncomfortably as I tapped into my diminishing reserves again and I cursed the fact that I'd let myself run so low.

I released some more power, lighting a fire in the grate as I entered the huge treehouse which dominated the towering branches at the top of the oak tree.

I used the power of the flames I'd already created to aid me in making more so that I could light the lamps around the space too. Using one flame to create another took less magic than summoning one into existence from nothing but it irritated me that I was reduced to it.

An L-shaped grey couch was revealed at the heart of the room as the wooden walls were lit warmly by the firelight. To the right of the den was a ladder which led up to the higher level where beds awaited us should we decide to stay here tonight. I was torn between the desire to do that and avoid the curiosity of the members of my House and my desire to escape the other Heirs. I couldn't remember the last time I'd wanted to avoid them but right now, I didn't feel like lingering in their company.

My mother's words rang in my ears at that thought. *If you can love the other Heirs like brothers then your life will be all the easier for it, but either way, you are stuck together. Through the good and the bad you are united. Your individual feelings do not matter when it comes to the actions of the group. You are one. And you must never show even the slightest form of weakness to the outside world. The actions of each of you are the actions of all of you. You stand together. If you falter, the whole of Solaria will fall.*

With the Nymph attacks on the rise, I knew that that sentiment had never been more important than it was right now. Our kingdom was being thrown into turmoil, teetering on the edge of war. The last thing we needed at this moment in time had been the royal Vega Heirs turning up. And yet here they were, two girls with the potential to unhinge everything we'd come to know and trust about the world since The Savage King had died.

I dropped down onto the only armchair in the room. As soon as Seth arrived he'd be snuggling up to anyone sat on the couch and I wasn't in the mood for it.

I used the moment of solitude to let out a long breath as I ran a hand over my face.

I kept thinking about the look Tory had given me when I'd kissed her in that classroom. My heart had leapt with excitement when she hadn't pushed me away. And it wasn't just because I'd known I shouldn't be doing it. There was something about the twins that intrigued me to no end.

They'd grown up as Changelings in the mortal world with no knowledge of Fae or the way we ran our society. And yet somehow they kept on rising to the challenges thrown their way. It was like their birthright ran in their blood with all the ferocity of The Savage King himself, despite the fact that they'd never known they'd be expected to claim their power.

If they had grown up amongst the Fae, I had no doubt in my mind that they already would have secured their position above the four of us. And I supposed we wouldn't have balked at it if that was the way it had always been. If no one had ever thought they were dead in the first place, then we never would have expected to rule without them. But now they were just a problem; two powerful girls with no knowledge of our world or the ways of our people.

They couldn't be expected to lead us. They couldn't possibly hold us together in the face of war. If they claimed their birthright it would be disastrous for Solaria. Our parents were right to insist on us chasing them out of here. We couldn't let them graduate from the Academy. But what we'd done tonight...

"What are you moping about, Cal?" Max asked as he sauntered into the room.

I sat back, dropping my hands from my face to look up at him and Seth. The Werewolf crossed the room, retrieving some beers from the bucket of ice which had been created with water magic so that it never thawed, and tossing one into my lap. I sat the can down on the wooden floor without opening it.

"Nothing," I muttered, eyeing the half-smirk on Max's face. He was obviously pleased with how the night had gone and I didn't want to get into it with him. What was I even supposed to say? 'Good work tonight guys but now I feel like an asshole and I don't like it...' *Nice way to come off sounding like a pouty bitch there, Caleb.* No. It was probably best I held my tongue until I got over it.

"Look what I've made," Seth said, grinning as he held out Darcy's hair which he'd braided into a bracelet and placed around his wrist.

"That's sick," Max said enthusiastically.

I rolled my eyes without responding.

"Maybe she'll cut off your hair in revenge," I muttered, eyeing Seth's long, hazel locks.

"No chance. I broke her, I wouldn't be surprised to find out that the two of them have dropped out come morning," Seth said cockily, spinning his new bracelet around his wrist.

Max barked a laugh. "They should count themselves lucky to be able to walk out of here at all," he said, though I didn't buy it. He always fought against the image that Sirens were sympathetic by nature and he never wanted to admit that the fear and misery of others upset him when he fed on it. But I knew it did. He couldn't hide his true self from me or the other Heirs no matter how hard he tried. "For a minute there I thought we'd killed Tory - did you see how still she was when Orion snatched her out of the pool?"

"So you'd have been pleased with yourself if you'd killed her, would you?" I asked, my voice low with warning. I may not have bought into his shit all the time but in this instance he was acting too damn pleased with himself for what we'd done.

"It would have made things easier for us," Max said with a cocky smirk.

Before I could consider it, I shot out of my chair and threw him against the wall. Seth cried out in surprise as the wooden structure of the treehouse rattled with the force of our collision. Max swore as he aimed a punch at my side.

I snarled at him, the beast beneath my skin rising to the surface as I lost my temper and my fangs grew.

I lunged at his neck and Max ducked aside, snatching my face in his hand as he forced my canines away from him.

"Holy shit, Caleb, why are you *so angry?*" he asked, his eyes widening in surprise as his Siren gift got to work, feeding on my emotions and the remaining dregs of my power.

I lost control as he sucked at the shallow pool of my magic, my muscles flaring with the strength of my kind as I threw a punch into his face and he was thrown aside. Before he could recover, I leapt at him again, my fangs sinking deep into the flesh of his neck.

Max swore as he fell still beneath the weight of my power, my venom immobilising his magic as I drew it out of him and into myself.

I kept him pinned to the wall as I fed on him, draining much more from him than I would usually take from one of my friends. I couldn't remember the last time I'd taken power from any of them by force like this either but I was too angry and too empty to pull back.

"*Fuck!* Haven't you taken enough yet?" Max snarled as I refused to release him.

I growled low in the back of my throat, letting him know that I had zero intentions of stopping.

Seth laughed behind me like this was all some big joke but he wasn't stupid enough to approach. "Shit, Caleb, when was the last time you fed?"

A huge bang announced the arrival of a dragon landing on the roof and the whole treehouse shuddered beneath its weight.

A moment later, Darius dropped in through a hatch above us and I shoved Max away from me as I finally released him.

Darius barely even spared us a glance as he crossed the room butt naked, the stench of smoke and fire following in his wake. He opened a heavy chest and pulled out a pair of sweatpants to cover himself.

"Where the hell did you go?" I asked angrily as Darius continued to ignore the rest of us, claiming my former seat and my beer for good measure.

"You've got blood around your mouth," he said, ignoring my question as he opened the bottle and drained the whole thing.

I wiped Max's blood from my lip and sucked it from my thumb as I took the seat closest to Darius and pinned him in my gaze.

He scowled at me for several long seconds but I didn't back off so he finally gave me an answer.

"I needed to fly," he said with a shrug. "Or I was going to bite Orion's head off. Literally."

He still seemed pretty damn pissed off so I guessed that he was telling the truth about that. Everyone knew that if a Dragon Shifter really lost their temper with you they were likely to transform and eat you whole. Not that I'd seen Darius lose his cool like that very often. He'd learned the hard way how to keep his temper in check growing up with his father.

"And did you happen to accidentally barbecue someone on your way out?" Seth asked Darius casually, dropping down beside me and petting my arm. I knew he could tell that I was still riled up and he was looking to comfort me like I was one of his pack-mates, but I wasn't a damn wolf and the only thing I wanted right now was space.

"Of course I didn't," Darius replied dismissively like he thought Seth had been joking.

"Well *someone* did," Max said as he took a seat at the other end of the couch and healed the wound on his neck without looking at me. "There was a body all crisped up right outside Lunar Leisure when we left."

"Seriously?" Darius asked, looking between us like he thought we might be joking.

"If I'm honest, I thought you'd done it," Seth said as he shifted closer to me, pulling my hand into his like that would soothe me. "It certainly looked like Dragon Fire to me," he added.

I shoved him off of me and he whimpered a little before nuzzling against my neck.

"Piss off, Seth," I snapped, shoving him back again and eyeing that goddamn bracelet on his wrist as I leaned away from him.

"I don't like it when you're sad," he replied, reaching towards me once more despite the fact that I was clearly in no mood for it.

I got to my feet and stalked away, claiming another beer from the ice bucket just to give myself an excuse to leave.

"Why are you sad?" Darius asked me, his eyes following my movements.

"He's not sad, he's fucking raging," Max muttered, shooting me an irritated look.

"I thought we were discussing your sudden disappearance right around the time someone was burned to death?" I snapped in reply, refusing to let them turn the subject of the conversation around to me.

"I told you, I went for a flight," Darius snarled. "Or are you doubting me now too?"

"Who's doubting you?" Seth asked innocently, even though he'd just said that he thought Darius had killed someone.

"He means Orion. He's pissed we got detention from his buddy," Max supplied.

"He's not my *buddy*," Darius said. "He's a goddamn hypocrite."

"Well I think that detention is probably the least we should have expected after we nearly killed Tory," I muttered. I was still pissed at Orion for daring to give it to us but I guessed I could suck it up in light of what we'd almost done.

"I didn't see you doing much," Max replied. "In fact, if it wasn't for the Code you hide behind, I'd think that maybe you weren't standing with us on this. You didn't even help with the preparation of it."

"Well if this is what it takes to keep our positions then maybe I don't like being a part of it," I countered. As soon as the words left my lips I wished they hadn't. The three of them were staring at me like I'd just grown a second head.

Darius got to his feet and stalked toward me, his eyes narrowing to golden, reptilian slits as his Order tried to push its way out of his skin.

"Do you think I enjoyed doing that?" he demanded. "Do you think I want to be terrorising people and preying on their worst fears? You think I don't realise what that makes me? *Who* that makes me?"

I squared my shoulders, holding his eye. I shouldn't have said it but the words were out there now and I wasn't going to be forced into taking them back like a goddamn coward.

"How many times have we sat around this room and discussed all the things we don't like about the way our parents rule?" I hissed. "And yet at the first real test of our claim, we bow to their way of doing things."

"We don't have a choice," Darius said. "The Nymphs are already circling closer and the Vegas have barely been back a few weeks. They can smell weakness in the air. If those girls take the throne then we're all doomed."

"I'm not saying we shouldn't get rid of them," I said angrily. "But I *am* saying that I don't think becoming your father is the way to do it."

Darius's eyes flared with rage at my words but before he could lunge at me, I shot across the room and leapt out of the window.

With my Vampire speed, I was half way through The Wailing Wood before I even considered slowing down.

I didn't want to be around the other Heirs right now. Hell, I wasn't sure I even wanted to be around myself.

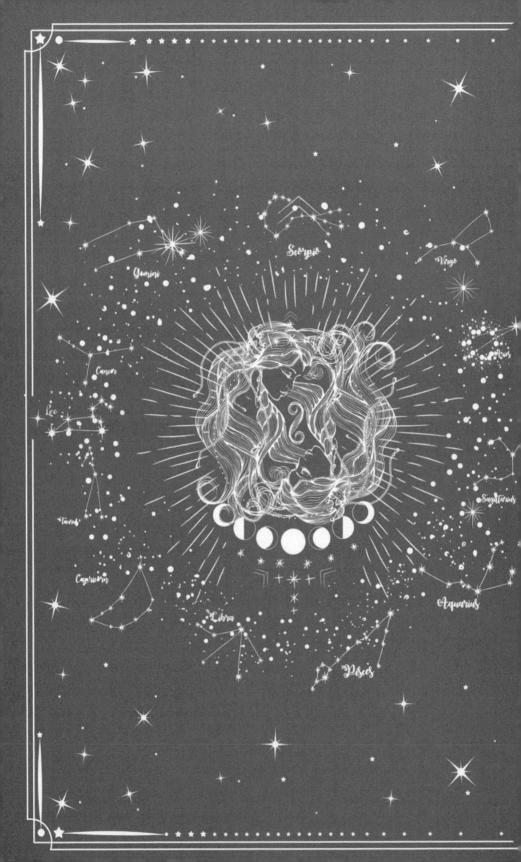

DARCY

CHAPTER TWO

I stood in the shower with my head bowed as a river of water cascaded over me. Tepid, barely warm at all. I hardly felt it on my skin as if I'd grown a thicker layer over night. A shield to the outside world. And I willed it to grow thicker still.

My heart was a fish on land, jerking desperately in my chest as it searched for a haven of safety to sink into. Somewhere the pain would stop.

I pushed a hand into my hair, assessing the damage. I still hadn't looked in the mirror. I'd walked straight past it through the en-suite. But I'd have to look soon enough. Uneven lengths were the least of my concern; where Seth's knife had sliced too close to the scalp was a hairless patch I wasn't sure the remaining length would cover.

I turned the water off and the pipes released a shuddering groan. I'd woken early, long before dawn, the memories of the formal playing on repeat in my mind. Over and over.

Tory and I had headed straight back to my room and locked ourselves in here. Diego and Sofia had come to check on us but we'd turned them away. I needed to be alone with my sister. And for once, I guessed she needed me as much as I needed her. What the Heirs had done to Tory...

My heart jerked again and tears jabbed at my eyes. I was long past letting them fall; my cheeks were red raw from them.

I could still smell the chlorine on Tory's skin when Orion had pulled her from the water. I could taste the heated air that had rushed up from Astrum's charred body. I could hear the Heirs laughing, taunting, jeering. And I hated them more than I'd ever realised it was possible to hate someone.

There was one thing that kept playing on my mind. Whoever The Shadow was, they'd won. Murdered one of the few people in Solaria who had tried to help us. And poor Astrum hadn't just been killed, he'd been obliterated, his body burned beyond recognition. If it hadn't been for the Tarot card he'd left us and the strange magical aura that had accompanied it, we would still be none the wiser as to who the body had belonged to.

I'm so sorry. I wish I could go back and change last night. I'd do so many things differently.

I stepped out of the shower, drying off before tugging on the jeans and black sweater I'd left slung over the basin. The mirror was fogged up and part of me wanted to leave it that way. But another, more stubborn part of me needed to see the damage.

Maybe it's not so bad.

Yeah and maybe the Titanic didn't sink.

I took a hand towel from the rail and quickly wiped it across the glass before I could change my mind. The mist cleared away to reveal a broken girl beyond it with hollow eyes.

My face was clean of make-up, but seemed somehow shadowed like the darkness of last night had seeped into my skin. Never to be washed away.

I lifted my gaze to my hair and drew in a sharp breath. It was longer at the front than the back, the dampness sticking it to either side of my face. I pushed my fingers into it, lifting up the choppy ends to feel the bald patch at the back. I pursed my lips and anger rose like the devil in my blood. A hiccough forced its way out of my lungs, promising more tears but I wouldn't let them out. Not again.

I hunched forward, bracing myself on the rim of the basin as rage and hatred built up in my throat like bile. My fingers locked tightly on the porcelain edges and my arms trembled with tension. I swallowed hard, forcing back the rush of emotions threatening to overwhelm me. I stared at my reflection, locked in my own gaze and refusing to let this unravel me.

I don't want to let them win. But I think they already have.

When I'd smothered the storm brewing inside me, I headed back to my bedroom, finding Tory standing by the tall, vertical window. The shutters were open and a fierce wind battered the pane beyond it. The turbine on top of Aer Tower roared and groaned under the onslaught, making it sound like the world was screaming.

Tory was framed by the dreary morning light, my room still cast in darkness. I flipped the light switch and she turned to me, blinking heavily as if I'd jolted her out of some cruel vision.

Her eyes skimmed over my hair and heat blazed along the back of my neck.

"It'll grow back," she said, her voice weaker than usual.

I nodded, dropping down onto the edge of the bed and drawing my knees up to my chest. *But my pride won't.*

Silence stretched on between us and Tory returned to gazing down at the campus grounds far below.

"What do we do now?" she asked eventually.

"I don't know," I answered, feeling more hopeless than I ever had in my life. "Nearly everyone in the Academy wants us gone. Maybe we should listen to them." It broke my heart to say it; this school had felt more like a home to me than any other place I'd ever rested my head. It was innate. I was Fae. I felt that in the deepest regions of my body. But I'd also never been as unwelcome as I was here.

Even our last foster dad, Pete, had put up with us being around without much complaint. Here, we were outcasts. Even the few who did accept us, like Geraldine and her followers, they didn't want *us*. They wanted their royal princesses. And we never intended on rising to that role. So what good did it do us by staying?

Tory sighed wearily. "I think you're right." She moved to join me on the bed, folding her legs up beneath her. The spark of resilience which always lived in her eyes had dimmed to a low-burning flame that desperately needed stoking. But I didn't think I had enough left in me to do it. "We're screwed back in Chicago though. Without money, we'll end up on the streets." Tory's brows tugged together as she thought over our predicament.

"We'll get by. We did before," I said, but even as I said it I knew it wasn't a great idea. No doubt our landlord had reclaimed the apartment we'd been renting by now and even if we had been able to go back there, how could we pay for the place?

My Atlas pinged and I reached for it on instinct, glancing at the message on the screen.

You've been mentioned in a FaeBook post, Darcy!

Sucker punch.

Maybe some dark part of me was a glutton for punishment because I went right ahead and clicked on the notification.

I won't shy away. How much worse can it get anyway?

Tory leaned forward to look as the post appeared on the page and my gut knotted and frayed as I read it.

Seth Capella:

Here's a play-by-play of Darcy Vega's life being destroyed. You're welcome. Let's hope she and her sister are booking a bus home this morning. But on the off chance that they decide to weather out another few weeks in hell, DO NOT assist Darcy with regrowing her hair. Anyone found to be helping her, student, faculty or otherwise will be moved into our firing line alongside the Vega Twins.

And if you hadn't realised it yet, we're untouchable. So don't be our enemy.

#kingsofsolaria #getoutofzodiac #gohomevegalosers

I cringed as the video Kylie had taken of me in Seth's lap began to play. Tory turned it off before I could relive my hair being cut off and my dignity being stripped away with it.

Tory rested her hand on mine for a moment and I gave her a sad smile. She dropped back onto the bed with a heavy breath and I went to toss the Atlas onto the mattress when another notification sounded.

"What now?" I muttered, glancing at the screen just to check I hadn't been tagged yet again. I frowned as I read the message from Principal Nova, evidently sent out to the entire Academy.

All students are required to attend an assembly from 8 to 9am in The Orb following the incident last night. Anyone who isn't present will lose their House one hundred and fifty points and be banned from all social clubs and societies for the coming week.

"The incident?" I hissed. "A man was *murdered*." I tossed the Atlas to Tory so she could read it and her brow furrowed.

"Screw House Points. They can dock as many as they want," she said. "I'm not going."

I nodded in agreement, not wanting to face a whole school of students

23

pointing and laughing because of my current appearance. I wasn't quite ready for that. I wasn't sure I ever would be.

It wasn't long before students exited their rooms and moved along the corridors; doors banged and people laughed and hollered as they headed out of the tower toward the assembly. It was as if last night hadn't happened at all. Half of them probably thought we were gone already. And if we'd had any sort of life to go back to, I had no doubt that we would have by now.

The tower slowly grew quiet and the chatter of students carried far away across campus.

I picked at the knees of my jeans, mulling over what to do. "I just wish we had some money. If Darius hadn't destroyed the cash we had when we came here at least we'd have something back in the mortal world."

Tory nodded sullenly. "Shame we can't magic up a big pile of-" she halted mid-sentence, launching herself upright. "Gold," she gasped, her eyes alight with some idea. She turned to me with a glimmer of her usual self shining out at me. "Darius has an entire room full of gold. And there's no way he'll miss that assembly and lose himself precious House Points for Ignis."

My mouth parted as I realised what she was suggesting. "But even if we could get into his room, how the hell are we going to get back to Chicago? We came here by stardust before and I haven't exactly seen any of the stuff lying around campus."

"No... but I bet Orion has some in his office," Tory said keenly and the fire in her gaze lit a flame in me too. Hope danced and skipped through my chest and gave me something to hold onto with all my might.

"We've only got an hour," I breathed, getting to my feet and hurrying to my closet. I wrenched open the door and grabbed a black baseball cap with ZA written in bright blue letters on the front of it. I put it on to cover my hair and rounded on Tory with an intense look.

"You get the gold, I'll get the stardust. We meet back here before that assembly ends."

Tory's hopeful expression fell away as I moved toward her. "So we're leaving," she whispered and the words wrenched at my insides. But it didn't look like the Heirs were ever going to stop trying to force us out of Zodiac Academy. And they'd almost killed Tory. How could we stay here after that? What if they succeeded next time?

"Yeah, Tor," I sighed, an anchor dragging my heart deep down into the depths of my body. "I don't want to go but what choice do we really have?"

For a moment she looked like she was about to cry, then she drew her shoulders back and stepped toward the door with a fierce expression. "Then let's hurry. No goodbyes."

I thought of Sofia, Diego, even Geraldine and my throat tightened at the thought of never seeing them again. But Tory was right. We needed to be gone before the assembly was over. And then we'd return to Chicago as if none of this had ever happened.

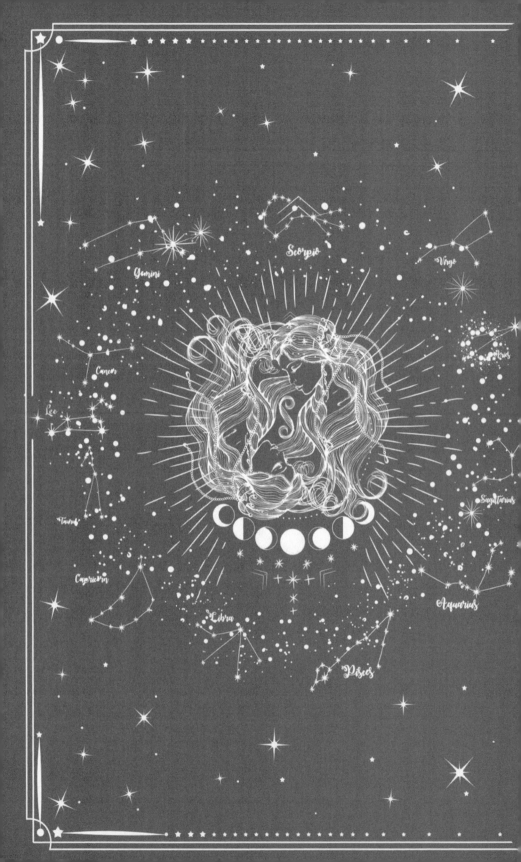

TORY

CHAPTER THREE

I watched Darcy as she walked away from me outside Aer Tower, heading for Jupiter Hall and Orion's office. The black baseball cap she'd pulled down over her ruined hair set a burning pit of rage blazing in my chest. She kept her head down as she walked, her shoulders a little hunched, though her stride was determined.

I wished we didn't have to split up to do this; the idea of her falling prey to any of the monsters in this school again made me feel so angry I could spit. But our plan was solid. They were all in the assembly about Astrum's death; no one would want to risk their precious House Points. Though I for one hoped they docked Ignis a thousand points for my absence and the shock of it gave Darius an aneurism.

Distant thunder rumbled overhead and I glanced up at the cloud-filled sky. It was dark enough to feel like dusk instead of mid-morning but I welcomed the lack of light; at least it would make it harder for anyone to see me from a distance.

Darcy moved out of sight and I released a long breath, psyching myself up for my part of our mad plan. I turned away from Aer House and headed south, taking a roundabout route to the Fire Territory which avoided the pathways while using my Atlas to stay on track. I walked along the line of the cliff which overlooked the churning sea. I kept my distance from the edge though, the sight of that fall and the tempestuous water beyond it making my throat tighten.

I tried to shake off the feeling of dread as the memories of last night surfaced again. So much had happened that it was hard to process all of it but it was almost impossible to shake the roiling terror that had filled me. I'd really thought that I was going to die in that pool. The kiss of the icy water, the frantic pounding of my heart... every time I'd closed my eyes last night the fear of it had crept in on me again. In the end I hadn't slept at all. I'd propped my back against the wall and waited while Darcy got some rest, trying not to flinch each time a nightmare caused her to groan in her sleep.

The Heirs had made it clear from the moment we met them that they wanted us broken and they wanted us gone. I'd been a fool to think we could stand in the face of that kind of power and hatred and survive it unscathed. This was what that naive belief had gotten me. We'd been humiliated, belittled, abused and beaten.

But not broken.

We were made of stronger stuff than that.

My sister and I had been moulded for survival since the day we'd been born. We'd escaped the Nymphs who'd killed our parents here in Solaria, then survived the flames which had destroyed our mortal family too. Together, we'd made it through countless foster homes, neglect, uncertainty, poverty and hunger. We'd always found our own way to endure it. We'd been born to survive. The fire that should have killed us when we were babies hadn't; it forged us into something stronger, cast our bones in steel and gave us strength in each other's company.

And if fire couldn't kill me then water sure as hell couldn't have me either. But I wasn't an idiot. If staying in this academy meant facing off against the Heirs at every turn then I knew we weren't equipped for that. Orion and Nova had tried to trap us here by holding our inheritance hostage but I wasn't the kind of girl to be held over a barrel. The stars might have guided us to this school but I'd been making my own luck and guiding my own destiny for long enough to know that I could take my fate into my own hands when I had to.

We needed money if we were going to get out of here and there was one way for us to get it.

I considered the insanity of what I was about to do for a moment and let myself focus on the thrill of the challenge instead of the wrath I could incur from Darius if he caught me.

There wasn't much more he could do to me at this point anyway. And the more I looked at this as a job, the calmer I became. This was what I'd done to survive for years; breaking and entering was my bread and butter. There was nothing quite like the thrill of the challenge when I had a job underway and a trickle of adrenaline ran down my spine in anticipation of it.

I checked my location on my Atlas, eyeing the little star which represented me before turning right and heading west towards Fire Territory.

The ground sloped down sharply as I descended the cliffs and I spotted the imposing structure of Ignis House ahead of me. Its jagged glass walls rose up towards the grey clouds in every shade of red, yellow and orange like a living flame. It was beautiful in a harsh kind of way, sort of like the Fae people.

Thunder rumbled overhead again and I glanced up at the sky as it grew even darker. There was still no sign of rain but the clouds looked pregnant with it, promising a downpour of epic proportions once they broke.

I upped my pace. Now that my destination was in sight, the call of the job had me in its grasp. I felt more like myself, shedding the feelings of inadequacy as I walked towards something I knew I could do. I'd spent the last few weeks trying to claim a new start here at Zodiac Academy but this was who I'd always been. So instead of striving to be something new, someone *more* I was going to embrace who I already was. And that, was a damn good thief.

I lifted my chin as I made it to Ignis House and summoned flames to get in. The heat in my palm flared into a ball of fire which crashed against the triangular symbol and unlocked the door. I tried to ignore the fact that I'd released too much power with that blast yet again. My fire magic didn't want to bow to my commands but I'd just have to keep practicing with it once we were away from here. I hoped that Darcy and I would be able to figure out how to control our powers without help, at least enough to get by in the mortal world. And though we obviously wouldn't ever learn to wield them in the way that we could have done by studying here, we would still be more powerful than any human who gave us trouble. That would be more than enough. Coercion alone should make life with the mortals a piece of cake; the first thing I'd be doing when we got back to Chicago was convincing some flashy hotel executives to give us a free stay in their penthouse. From there, the world would be our oyster.

I hurried up the stairs and into the common room, releasing a relieved breath as I found it empty. That notification had expressed that all students were required to attend the assembly but I hadn't been entirely sure that everyone would clear out like this. Apparently the threat of losing House Points was more than enough of a reason for them to attend. I guessed they'd face the wrath of the Heirs if they cost their House one hundred and fifty points and no one wanted to be on their bad side. I knew I certainly didn't; not that they'd ever given me a choice in the matter.

I crossed the open space at a determined march and headed for my own room first. I changed quickly, pulling on ripped jeans and a grey sweater before tying my long, black hair in a high ponytail.

At the base of my wardrobe was a large sports bag emblazoned with the Zodiac Academy crest for use in Physical Enhancement. We'd never even gotten around to taking that class yet and I guessed we never would now either. I tossed the sports kit out of it and threw it over my shoulder.

Next, I stepped into my en-suite and grabbed a couple of hair pins. They wouldn't be as good as the picks I'd owned back in my old apartment but I was sure I could work with them just fine.

I cast one last look over my room with a small flutter of disappointment whirling in my gut. For a little while I'd begun to think of this place as somewhere we could call home. But that had been a foolish idea. We'd never stayed anywhere long enough to make a home out of it before and I should have realised that this would be no different.

Bye bye room, it was nice while it lasted.

I closed the door with a sharp click then headed for the top floor.

My feet moved silently along the plush carpet even though I knew there was no need for it: there was no one here to hear me anyway. But skills honed from years of creeping, sneaking, breaking and entering wouldn't be forgotten out of a sloppy sense of safety. I'd stick to my own rules and get this done right.

I reached Darius's door and my heart thumped a warning tune in my chest. The last time I'd come here, he'd threatened me in no uncertain terms and after last night I had no question of just how ruthless he could be.

I reached out to test the handle and released a long breath to stop the trembling in my fingers.

He's not here. I'll never have to see him or any of those other assholes ever again after this. They can have their throne and we can have our freedom. And I hope all that power makes them miserable.

But if I wanted that to be true then we needed money. And who better to take it from than the king of dark and dangerous himself?

Unsurprisingly, the handle didn't turn when I tried it. The door was locked. He wasn't here.

I smiled to myself and dropped to my knees before the door, bringing the hair pins up to the lock.

I closed my eyes in concentration as I worked them into the small space, feeling the faint pressure of resistance from the metal pieces within it. It took me less than thirty seconds to align the pieces and with the right amount of pressure...

Click.

The victory dance was unnecessary but well earned. I grinned in satisfaction as I pushed the door wide and got to my feet.

Darius's room sprawled out before me and I hesitated on the threshold.

My boots skimmed the edge of his red carpet, my gaze took in the lavish decoration, the gold adornments everywhere.

That asshole had tried to break me but he'd failed. A broken girl would have turned and run for the hills with nothing and no one. But here I was, standing on the threshold of the Dragon's lair about to steal his treasure.

I may have been no match for his magic but my balls were as big as his any day of the week.

I stepped inside and pressed the door shut behind me with a flush of triumph.

I moved toward the chest at the foot of his bed and the scent of him surrounded me, smoke, cedar and raw power filling my lungs like a warning. But I was in my element now and I wouldn't be leaving without my prize. We needed this to start our lives away from this place. And a little bit of money was the least he owed us.

Warmth washed against my skin and I turned to see flames still burning in the grate. His bed covers were tossed aside haphazardly too and a glance at his lavish bathroom revealed wet towels on the floor and steam lining the walls. I guessed he'd been in a rush to get to the assembly as the rest of the room was immaculately tidy. In fact, it looked kinda like he was a bit OCD.

My gaze landed on a long desk beneath the red glass window beyond his bed and curiosity had me crossing the room to it before I gave it much thought.

Papers were lined up in neat piles and two stacks of envelopes addressed to 'Darius Acrux, Celestial Heir' sat to the left of the mahogany surface.

I wasn't sure why I was bothering to snoop on him but I couldn't help it.

I wanted to know what made that asshole tick. If I could understand him a bit better then maybe I could get a bit of closure about what he'd done to me. Or maybe I was just a nosey bitch. Either way, I wanted to see what dirt he was hiding in his fancy desk.

I picked up a pale pink envelope from the top of the closest pile and yanked the contents out.

On top of the wad was a letter written in elegant script and signed with a lipstick kiss. I skimmed the words, my eyebrows raising as I read over it.

> *Dear Darius,*
>
> *I recently read the interview you did for The Celestial Times and couldn't help but be overwhelmed by your poise and strength in the face of the trials you've been through. Only a true leader could see things as clearly as you do. I can't wait to follow more of your progress towards the throne.*
>
> *The photographs attached to the article only confirmed my suspicions about the pure, powerful man you are growing into and I will admit that I kept the one of you in your Pitball kit for my own personal collection.*
>
> *I find myself thinking of you in the dark, my body aching for the touch of your flesh against mine. The power you command and the strength of your nature combined with your chiselled features and temptation-worthy body have spurred me on to contact you this way. I know that you are duty bound to keep your bloodline pure with marriage but if you ever had need of a body to take pleasure in then I would offer mine without question, any time you wished for it.*
>
> *I hope with an ache of longing that you will accept my proposal and await your call on my flesh with eager anticipation.*
>
> *Forever yours Cindy-Lou Galaxa*

I raised an eyebrow at the grossly suggestive letter, feeling the urge to wipe my hand clean after touching it. A handful of photographs accompanied the letter and I glanced at them, finding a very flexible, very naked Cindy-Lou posing in a lot of hard to achieve poses which left nothing at all to the imagination.

Ewww.

I dropped the letter with a cringe, glancing at a few of the ones beneath it and finding a lot of the same stuff, from girls and guys alike. More than half of them hadn't even been opened and I wondered if that meant that Darius had no interest in them or if he was just saving them for later.

The other pile of mail was a little more interesting; letters from Fae asking him to give certain political matters his attention or use his influence to ask his father for help with various situations from crop growth to a Werewolf territory dispute to a suggestion about a politically motivated marriage or two.

I didn't have time to waste going through all of it though and it wasn't like it mattered anyway. I wasn't going to be living in Solaria after today so whatever way he chose to rule this kingdom had nothing to do with me.

I turned my back on the desk and headed for the chest at the foot of his bed instead. At least I'd be able to laugh myself sick every time I spent his money.

My heart pounded with a mixture of adrenaline, fear and exhilaration. This was probably one of the stupidest things I'd ever done but holy hell did it feel good.

Darius's treasure called to me like the whisper of darkest temptation and promised a hint of vengeance.

I dropped the sports bag beside me and pushed the heavy chest open. Gold coins mixed with gemstones and jewellery in a hoard worthy of a pirate king. I started scooping it into the bag, a wild grin capturing my lips as I made this small strike back at the asshole who had tormented me and my sister.

"Yo ho, yo ho and a bottle of rum," I murmured for my own benefit, snorting a laugh.

It didn't take long to fill the bag and I zipped it up, frowning into the chest which was still practically full.

I glanced around, wondering if there was something here that I could use to carry more of it but as I tried to move the bag I'd filled, I realised there was no point. I could barely lift it so there was no way I'd be able to carry any more.

With a sigh of disappointment, I heaved the bag into my arms, my muscles trembling with the effort as I dragged it over my shoulder.

Shit this stuff is heavy.

I was looking forward to pawning it and converting it into cold hard, American cash. The kind made of paper instead of heavy-ass bits of metal which would be a lot easier to transport. And spend.

I wasn't even sure if I'd be able to carry it back to Darcy's room but I refused to put any of it down. That bag was filled with our future and I wasn't going to put a single coin back.

I made it to the door and glanced back at Darius's room with a twinge of disappointment swirling in my gut. I wasn't even sure he'd notice this dent in his treasure and even if he did, it was hardly much of a blow against him. I'd wanted to take all of it from him but there was no way I could carry any more.

Maybe I could throw it out of the window or destroy it somehow...

My gaze fell on a chair which was sitting beside the fire. He'd tossed a pair of sweatpants over the back of it and they hung kinda close to the flames.

Dangerously close...

That may not have been strictly true, but it could have been.

I dropped the bag of treasure by the door with a heavy thump and stalked towards the fire. My heart started to pound a little faster. I wasn't really considering this... there was no way I'd actually-

I pushed the chair a few inches closer to the fire. The sweatpants swung back and forth above the flames.

My magic flared in response to the fire and I tugged on it, just a little.

My wayward control over my magic meant that just a little was actually a hell of a lot and I leapt back with a squeal of surprise as a tongue of flames licked its way over the sweatpants and quickly engulfed them. The chair went up next and then the carpet burst alight.

I backed up, caught between shock and laughter at what I'd done.

The heat of the flames licked against my skin but instead of recoiling from them, I felt like their power was filling me with energy and I wanted to join them in their destruction instead.

I backed up and bumped against Darius's huge bed, steadying myself on the bedpost which was made of solid gold.

The power of my fire magic was warring within the confines of my skin and beneath my heated fingers, the gold turned to liquid which ran down to the floor by my feet. I stared at my hands in surprise; I'd done that without even feeling a tingle of pain in my palms. The heat of my skin had been enough to melt gold, but my magic had protected me from it.

I stared at the puddle of melted gold beside me in shock for a moment before a crazed laugh left my lips.

That asshole tried to drown me... why not get a little revenge before I leave?

I moved to grab the next bedpost, melting that one too as soon as my skin made contact with the metal, quickly followed by the third and the fourth. The mattress fell to the floor with nothing to support the bed frame and the fire advanced on it for a new victim.

Smoke from the flames was beginning to fill the room and I upped my pace, resisting the urge to cough. I dropped down to my knees before the treasure chest and shoved my hands straight into it, drawing heat to my palms in a flood of magic.

Gold melted, gemstones sank into it, jewellery was destroyed and everything was reduced to a liquid lump of nothing. I twisted my hands through it like it was gold soup not boiling metal and marvelled at the magic I was managing. This little slice of revenge felt damn good.

When the contents of the chest had been reduced to a molten puddle, I withdrew my hands but something solid knocked against my knuckles.

I caught it in my grip on reflex, glancing down at the silver dagger in my hand as I backed away from the melted treasure. The handle was carved with strange symbols and it seemed unusually heavy.

For a moment I fell still, the dagger in my grip almost seeming to tremble with raw energy which wound its way through my own like a strange kind of greeting.

I ran my thumb over the sharp blade and the urge to press down pulled at me, an ache to spill a little blood coming over me for a moment.

I pressed the tip against my thumb, increasing the pressure slowly-

A loud crack sounded as one of the joists supporting the door to the en-suite buckled beneath the heat of the fire. I stared around in surprise as I realised I was standing in the only part of the room which hadn't yet been engulfed by the inferno.

The fire didn't come close to me, like it knew I was the one who had summoned it and it didn't want to hurt me, but I wasn't sure how long that would last.

The whole room was falling prey to the flames now and I had to leave.

I made it to the door and heaved the bag of treasure over my shoulder, looking at the room one last time as the fire raced to claim everything in it. Every piece of gold in the room had been reduced to a puddle of gloop. My heart pounded with adrenaline at what I'd done but there was no going back on it now. And I wouldn't want to even if I could; this was the least that psychotic douchebag deserved.

I shoved the door open and backed out, stopping to re-lock the door as quickly as I could. I had to drop the dagger to use the hairpins but I needed to do it if I expected anyone to believe the fire had been an accident. Not that it mattered too much; I hoped to be long gone before anyone ever came looking for a suspect, but years of dodging the cops made covering my tracks second nature.

As soon as it was done, I snatched the dagger back into my grip. There was something about it that spoke to me, awakening a weird urge in my soul which said it should be mine. Any why the hell not? He'd taken more than enough from me. I shoved it into my pocket before hoisting the bag of loot over my shoulder and jogging back out of Ignis House.

The scent of smoke followed me on the wind and thunder crashed in the sky above.

I kept my pace fierce, the weight of my haul driving me on as I raced out of Fire Territory as quickly as I could manage. I still didn't see anyone and I was more than pleased that they'd all been distracted by the assembly for so long.

As I made it back up the hill towards the cliff in Air Territory, I looked back down at Ignis House in the distance.

Flames had broken through the windows on the top floor where Darius's room sat, confirming that everything within it had been destroyed.

I stood watching the fire for several long seconds as the wind picked up around me and a savage grin pulled at my lips.

That asshole and his friends had gone way too far last night but this might just go a little way towards paying him back for it.

After all, they did believe in fate and destiny so why not a little kismet too?

Everyone knows, karma's a bitch. And today her name was Tory Vega.

DARCY

CHAPTER FOUR

I ran towards Jupiter Hall with the wind at my back and an electric energy humming through my veins. It felt good to be doing something useful, having a plan to hold onto even if it did mean we were giving up. That was the worst part about all of this: knowing the Heirs had won.

The second we went home, we would be giving them exactly what they wanted. And that sickened me like I'd swallowed poison.

But they were too powerful. They could destroy us and it didn't seem as if there'd be any consequences for it. *Just like Astrum had been destroyed...*

Guilt stirred inside me along with a wave of sadness. Who was to say *they* hadn't been behind his death? Darius had run off just before he'd shown up dead, and the burning remains were a bit of a giveaway. It had to be someone who possessed the Element of fire.

And hadn't Diego said something about Dragon Fire?

My thoughts scattered and I hurried to realign them onto the task at hand. I'd have to accept that we'd never discover the answers to all of the mysteries that surrounded us in Solaria. But it was better that than ending up in a body bag before term was out.

The campus grounds were eerily quiet as I jogged along the edge of The Wailing Wood, wanting to give The Orb a wide berth. The ruddy roof tiles of Jupiter Hall peeked out above the next line of trees and I hurried through them, circling around to the entrance.

I adjusted the cap over my head, hoping it might offer me some semblance of a disguise if anyone did happen to be looking out of Jupiter Hall. I crept into the expansive hallway of marble pillars and silence pressed in on me.

I waited a moment to be certain no one was here.

One heartbeat. Two.

I darted toward the stairs as quietly as I could, hurrying up to the next level and jogging toward Orion's office.

I slowed to a near-silent walk as I approached the door, just in case he wasn't attending the assembly and had decided to catch up on some work over the weekend. Our entire plan depended on him not being there. And even more so on there being stardust somewhere in his office.

We deserve a bit of luck for once.

Dammit, I should have read my Horoscope this morning.

I reached the door and gently pressed my ear to the wood, listening for any sounds beyond it. When I heard nothing, I tentatively turned the door handle.

Locked. Of course.

I didn't have the lock-picking skills my sister had mastered but I had another idea.

I let a soft breeze coil between my fingertips, willing it into the keyhole. I tried to extend my will to the end of the whip of air, reaching into the mechanism and praying I could somehow disable the lock.

I wiggled my fingers, sensing my power building against the barrier of my skin. Piling up and up. A loud bang ripped through the atmosphere and my heart leapt violently.

I swore between my teeth as a fist-size hole was punched through the door by the power of air. The door handle clattered to the floor on the other side and the door swung inward.

I glanced up and down the corridor either side of me, my blood pounding with adrenaline.

Okay, I seem to have gotten away with that.

I crept inside, pushing the door shut despite the fact it was damn obvious what had happened if anyone walked past. I didn't waste a second, fearing someone would have been alerted by the noise as I rushed across Orion's office. I circled his huge, crescent-shaped desk and dropped down behind it, surveying my next challenge.

I pulled at the drawers but every one of them was locked – *why are you such a security freak Professor!?*

My heart thundered like mad as I snatched a letter opener from his desk and jammed it into the small gap in the wood. I prised with all my might, but the golden blade only bent in my palm.

I stood up, backing away with a groan of frustration. I gazed at my predicament a few seconds longer before figuring I had no choice but to use my magic.

"Sorry Orion," I murmured, lifting my hands and directing a powerful blast of air at the top drawer. A hole smashed through it, but this time the entire front of the drawer fell off and clattered into pieces at my feet.

Oops.

I knelt down, tugging out the contents. Piles of papers, letters, leaflets. I tossed them all over my shoulder as I hunted for the silk pouch he'd had on him the day he'd come to our apartment.

Oh man I don't wanna go back to the mortal world. But the Heirs are such assholes and I've already destroyed half of Orion's office. He'd kick me out anyway after he finds this mess.

My fingers began to shake as I continued to rifle through the drawer, but there was nothing useful in it.

I moved to the next drawer, unleashing my magic once again and accidentally tearing a great hole in one side of the desk. The contents poured out of the jagged gap and I crawled around, wading through it as I hunted for the pouch.

Where are you? Come on, come on.

My heart froze into compacted ice as my fingers brushed silk. I pulled it out from beneath a large envelope and released a small squeal of joy.

I did it!

"-I'm always late, get over it, Washer." Orion's voice made my insides wither and die. "I'll be there in ten minutes, I have to send an email to the FIB first... because they're breathing down my neck since last night, of course!"

Oh holy shit!

I looked left and right, the mess of the room unable to be concealed in such a short time period. And the door was broken anyway. I couldn't do anything but stand there and get caught.

Crap crap crap.

The stardust!

I sprang to my feet, my heart in my throat as I fumbled with the silk pouch. I poured some of the glittering black dust into my palm, the magic contained within it sending a bolt of power into my veins.

"What the fuck?!" Orion bellowed a second before the door flew open and slammed into the wall.

He strode into the office, his eyes as black as death itself as they locked with mine. Horror, confusion and pure rage poured from him in a torrent.

His gaze darted from me to the stardust in my hand and I knew I had half a second to act.

I tossed it into the air, having absolutely no idea how to use the stuff but what else could I do? I thought of Aer Tower, desperate to get back to Tory so we could go back to Chicago, clutching onto that hope with all my might.

A swirl of darkness curtained my vision and Orion's office started to tumble out of existence. I saw him move in a burst of speed and before I knew it, strong hands were locked around my wrists. I yelped in alarm as the full weight of him collided with me. Then all at once, I was floating, gliding, travelling through an endless portal of stars, a million galaxies stretching out around me with no one here but me.

A sucking sensation dragged at my stomach and my vision was restored in a wave. I hit concrete on my back and half a second later a solid body landed on top of me, knocking the air from my lungs.

I groaned as my bones ached all over; my spine pressing into a cold, hard plain of stone and Orion weighing me down like another slab of concrete on top.

The force of the collision made my head spin and as Orion leaned back with the wind tugging at his hair and a fierce scowl fixed onto his face, I wasn't even scared. I was just horribly, horribly angry with myself for failing Tory.

"What the hell are you playing at?" Orion shouted at me, but I didn't answer, just shoved his immense shoulders to try and get him off of me.

He reared up and in a moment of clarity, I saw where we were. The huge plates of the turbine on top of Aer Tower reached high above us as they spun at speed in the raging wind.

Orion grabbed my hand which was still locked tightly around the bag of stardust.

"No!" I cried, throwing out my other hand to stop him. My voice was lost to the howling wind, but I'd felt it leave me with all the desperation of a dying animal. I needed that stardust. We were screwed without it.

Orion nearly had it from my grip and panic sped through me, refusing to let me give up.

A force like the propulsion of a jet engine left my body and Orion flew off of me, spiralling backwards through the air. I bolted upright and a gasp escaped me as he tumbled over the edge of the tower. I screamed, rolling to my knees and lurching upright to sprint after him.

Oh holy shit I've killed Professor Orion!

Before I reached the edge, he lunged back over it, propelled forward by his own magic and I cursed my idiocy for worrying about him at all.

I ran as hard and as fast as I could toward the stairwell, using every ounce of energy I had in me. I crashed into the door, sending it flying open as I practically tumbled down the stairs.

I just have to make it to Tory. Throw this damn dust, click my ruby shoes like Dorothy and fly us back to Chicago! There's no place like home... I just wish we had one of those.

Orion sent a blast of air into my back which flipped me around and slammed me into a wall. I struggled against the onslaught, desperate to lift my own hands and fight back but he had them firmly pinned to my sides.

He kicked the door shut at the top of the stone stairs and released a huff of relief. The droning noise of the turbines lessened and I tried to swallow the hard lump in my throat as he approached.

"Well that's one way to wake a guy up, huh?" For half a second I thought I sensed a lightness to his tone, a glitter of amusement in his eyes, maybe even a hint of pride. But all at once, it was gone. And I was totally certain I'd imagined it.

Orion strode down the steps with a demonic expression, not even a hint of mirth on his face. I wriggled against the ferocious power he'd wrapped around me but it was no good. He had me completely immobilised.

"Let me go," I demanded.

Orion slowed to a halt in front of me then casually flicked the cap from my head so it tumbled down the stairs. My heart crumpled like paper in my chest as he gave my hair a once over, scrutinising me but not belittling me like others had. He'd seen it last night, but this felt different. Like it was proof of my weakness. Of how Seth had broken me and made me want to flee. And I could tell Orion saw all of that with one, single look.

Him not saying anything was somehow worse than the berating I kept expecting to burst from his mouth.

"Get on with it then," I insisted, my fingers curling tighter around the stardust.

I should have hidden some in my pocket when I had the chance.

"Get on with what?" he asked coolly, his eyes narrowing.

He was so close and I could only think it was an attempt to intimidate me. Which for once, wasn't working. Because what the hell else did I have to lose right now? I was so far at the bottom of the food chain, I wasn't even worth eating.

"Whatever it is you're going to try and punish me with, sir," I said, breathless but miraculously keeping my voice steady. "Detention? I don't care. Because I won't be here. We're leaving."

Orion stepped even nearer and I couldn't do anything but stand there as he devoured the inches between us. "Is that what you were doing? Because it looked very much like you destroyed my office door, wrecked a custom-made desk and then transported us to the top of Aer Tower and threw me off the top of it, Miss Vega." His lips twitched and for half a second I thought he might laugh. But it didn't seem like he was going to crack a joke like he sometimes did.

"If I hadn't had a hitch-hiker, maybe I would have made it back to my room," I said, sensing my lower lip quivering. I didn't know if it was with anger or if I was just completely distraught. All I knew was that it felt like I was falling apart.

Orion eased off the air pressure holding me in place and my shoulders drooped. "Hand it over." He held out his palm and I clutched onto the pouch stubbornly. "Do you have any idea how much stardust costs? Dragon Fire is the only way to make it. They literally have to melt down meteors for this stuff, so unless you want to go and pay Darius Acrux for a bag, you're out of luck," he growled and I pressed my lips together, not answering. "That fun little trip to the top of the tower just cost the school a small fortune. So I hope you're pleased with yourself?"

"Obviously not," I muttered, glancing away from him. Tears burned the backs of my eyes and I refused to blink, glaring at the wall beyond Orion and begging him to just go away. Because I knew I was seconds from coming apart and I didn't want anyone to be here when it happened.

Orion reached forward and his hand wrapped around mine which contained the stardust. The warmth of his palm sent heat skittering through my body and I didn't know what to do as his hand remained there. Like he was going to take the stardust. But he still hadn't. He shifted closer and my body physically reacted, my muscles coiling and my heart galloping into a desperate rhythm.

I finally looked back at him and lifted my brows in a silent question.

What the hell are you doing? And why aren't I shoving you back?

His eyes scoured my face then shifted to my neck and I took in a slow breath.

Is he seriously going to bite me after everything I've been through? One last snack before I'm gone?

"I thought you and your sister were made of tougher stuff." He forced his fingers between mine and a noise of frustration escaped me as he prised the pouch from my grip. "You can go home, but you can't use this. Find another way." He released me, tucking the pouch into his pocket and my dreams stuttered and died.

He reached out again and I stilled entirely as his fingertips skimmed up my arm and charted a path to my neck.

"Say it then," he murmured and I frowned, my senses focused entirely on the line of fire his touch had painted across my skin.

I was still unable to move and I wasn't sure if he was keeping me in place or if I just wanted to be standing there now.

"Say what?" I whispered.

"That you give up your place at Zodiac Academy. That you weren't strong enough to stay. That you are not Fae."

"I am-" I started but his glare silenced me. He was so close, almost nose to nose. His scent skipped across me and the intoxicating aura he emitted seemed to slide through the walls of my skin, paralysing me.

"Fae fight for their place in the world, Blue. They don't ever bow out of a fight. If the Heirs have beaten you, then you're not one of us. And you never were." He stepped away and the heat of his body vanished, replaced with a cold wind leaking in from the howling storm beyond the door.

I stared at him for a long moment, his words cutting me to ribbons more than I ever thought words could.

If I leave, I'm not Fae.

I'm weak. I never belonged here.

I clenched my jaw, a deep well spilling over in my chest full of nothing but power. It pushed into every inch of my blood and swirled inside me like a hurricane.

"I am Fae," I snarled and Orion's brows arched as I pointed at him, a furious pit opening up inside me.

A smile spread onto his face and he folded his arms. "Oh yeah? Prove it."

Without another word, I turned away from him and ran down the steps. I took them two at a time, moving faster and faster, gaining momentum as I sprinted in the direction of my room.

I'm not going to be beaten.

I'm not going to bow out.

I can't. It's not in my nature, dammit.

The moment I reached the door, I yanked it open and found Tory on my bed, surrounded by a pile of gold.

"You did it," I gasped and she nodded, her eyes travelling over me as she hunted for the stardust.

I shook my head in answer, pulling the door firmly shut behind me. "Tory I..." I tried to get my words in order. How could I explain that Orion had made me see things so much clearer? That leaving didn't just feel like losing, it went entirely against who I was at my very core. And it must have gone against my sister's nature too. We were one and the same. Twins who'd shared each other's blood. Changelings, sisters, *Fae*.

"I think we should stay," I blurted and she rose from the bed with wide eyes.

"What?"

"We're Fae, Tor. Screw the Heirs."

A smile tugged at her mouth as she surveyed me. "What's gotten into you?"

Heat rolled up my spine and I almost said *Orion's gotten right under my skin and he knows how to pull my strings to get crazy reactions* but instead I diverted to, "Orion caught me and...well he took the stardust back - obviously. And then he just made me realise we were running away and we *don't* run away. We never have from anything. And no matter what the Heirs have done, I don't want them to beat us. Not like this at least. Not without a fight."

She chewed on her lower lip, glancing down at all of the sparkling gold on the bed. "You're right, Darcy. It felt so good getting back at Darius. But shit..."

"What?" I asked, sensing something was wrong.

"Well...I kinda set his whole room on fire." A laugh ripped from her throat and infected me too. We started giggling like kids, like our whole world hadn't been torn out from under us just hours ago. And I didn't ever want the feeling to stop.

"Please tell me you covered your tracks," I said at last, wiping the tears from under my eyes.

Tory nodded, a wicked grin gripping her features. "But I did steal this. He'll probably just think it melted along with everything else though." She scooped up a silver knife from my pillow and my brows arched. It was beautiful, slightly curved and shone like the moon itself.

"Wow," I cooed, reaching out to brush my fingers over the hilt. Magic coiled in my veins and drew right to edges of my skin as if it wanted to unite with the blade.

Tory tugged it away and dropped it into her satchel where it clinked against a handful of coins. "There's something weird about it," she breathed, taking her hand out of the bag as if she was struggling to part with the knife.

The strange tugging feeling floated away from my body and I frowned. "Do you think the teachers know students are keeping weapons?"

Tory shrugged. "The Heirs got two weeks in detention for nearly killing me, so I'm gonna guess they do and they don't care."

My heart grew heavier again as I thought about the Heirs. "What are we going to do about them? The thought of seeing Seth makes my skin crawl." I reached up to brush my fingers over my hair. It would take months for it to grow out enough to cover that bald patch. And *years* for it to reach the length it had been before. *Sonovabitch.*

Tory noticed me touching my hair and her eyes darkened. "We're going to get them back for what they did." The strength in her voice brought a smile to my lips. "But we're not trained well enough to face them with magic yet so we'll have to be clever about it."

"I like the sound of that," I said, a spark of excitement and a little fear igniting in my chest. "How are we going to get at them?"

Tory gave me a conspiratory look. "We'll have to work out their weaknesses. We'll take every opportunity we get to mess with them."

"Like Darius's gold." I grinned and she nodded keenly. "We hit them in ways they'll never suspect," I breathed excitedly.

"But we can't ever get caught," Tory said seriously.

"Never." My heart thumped madly at the mere idea of it. The four of them were the deadliest beasts in the Academy; if they figured out we were targeting them, who knew what fresh hell they'd conjure up to punish us?

Tory stood, yawning broadly. "I'm gonna have to bite the bullet and go back to my room. Shower...change. Hopefully Nova won't deduct points from us considering what happened last night but I wouldn't put it past her either."

I nodded. "Not much we can do about it now either way. What are we gonna do with all of that though?" I gestured to the gold.

Tory gazed at it for a moment then an idea glowed in her eyes. "We keep it. If we ever need to run back to Chicago, we have it as a backup plan. Plus I quite like knowing that we've got a big ass bag of Darius's gold smuggled away."

"Good plan, so where are we going to hide it?" I glanced around my room, unsure if anywhere was safe from the Heirs. If they ever caught wind of Tory stealing it, we were so dead.

Voices carried from out in the tower and I realised we'd run out of time to do anything about it right now. The assembly was over.

"We can keep it here for a while," I said quickly, gathering up a handful and kneeling down to hide it under the bed. Tory helped me, stuffing the gold chalices, coins and jewellery back into the sports bag and shoving it beneath the bed, as far in as we could push it.

When we were done, Tory got to her feet, giving me an expression which was laced with a little concern. "I just hope I can get back to Ignis House before Darius does because one of my biggest regrets leaving this place would have been missing the look on his face when he sees his room going up in smoke."

A laugh escaped me as she opened the door and waved goodbye. I didn't miss the way she checked up and down the corridor as she went and I knew it would be a while before we felt safe in these walls again. And perhaps we never really would. Not until we harnessed our powers. We'd been to the brink of hell and back and the Heirs could take us there again if they wanted to. But we'd be ready this time.

I locked my door and dropped onto my bed, releasing a slow breath as my heart rate finally settled. My Atlas pinged and I picked it up, wondering if there was a way to turn off my FaeBook notifications for good.

You have a private email waiting for you, Darcy!

I clicked on the banner with a frown and was taken to an inbox I didn't recognise.

Lance:
Location: Venus Library

Row: Epsilon

Text: Earth: The Power of Growth.

I read over the strange message, wondering if it had been intended for me. I didn't know anyone called Lance. But at least they weren't sending me hate mail. So I was counting that as a win.

Darcy:
Sorry, who is this? I think you might have the wrong person.

I hoped this wasn't going to be another Falling Star situation. If only Astrum had been upfront sooner, maybe... I didn't let myself finish that thought, my stomach knotting at the idea that his death could have been avoided if we'd acted differently. And now we'd decided to stay here, that meant we might be on campus with a murderer.

I started to wonder if the mystery man would reply. Maybe he had got the wrong person after all. But then another message came in and my heart tripped over itself as I read it.

Lance:

I think you know me better as the 'bourbon drinking Professor with a permanent scowl stamped on his face and a general air of failed dreams about him.'

Check out the book, Blue. You'll find it educational.

P.S

*Delete these messages **immediately**.*

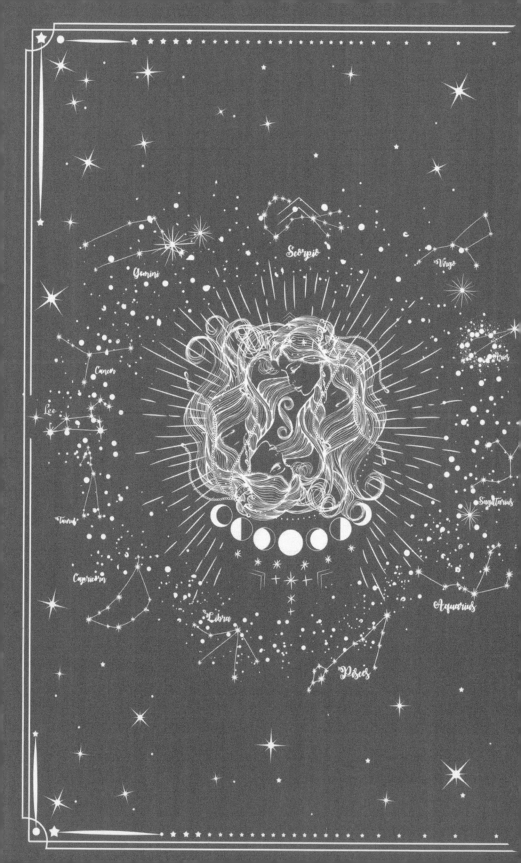

TORY

CHAPTER FIVE

I jogged down the spiralling staircase in Aer House, my heart pounding with exhilaration. We were staying. Leaving had seemed like the only option for a few bleak hours but the moment Darcy had said she wanted to stay, a weight had lifted from my chest.

I'd never run from any challenge in my life. And deep down in my soul, I'd known that I never would have forgiven myself if I'd ended up running from this.

I may not have wanted the throne or to rule over every other Fae in this academy, but I sure as hell didn't want to bow to the demands of a bunch of sadistic assholes either.

A couple of students noticed me as I passed, a few shouts coming my way like 'fancy a swim, Tory?' and 'did you enjoy your dip last night?'. I responded by holding my head high and moving beyond them without even bothering to respond. I had bigger fish to fry than a few hanger-on douchebags who were only concerned with impressing the Heirs.

I made it out of Aer House just in time to see lightning flashing within the dark sea of clouds overhead. Thunder boomed and I glanced up at the tempestuous sky, expecting rain at any moment.

I jogged back down the path that led to The Orb, my high ponytail swinging across my back from the fast pace. The wind blew a little fiercer and my hair whipped around me, the smell of smoke assaulting my nostrils. I gritted my teeth, hoping no one else had noticed that scent on my clothes when I'd passed them.

I kept up my pace as I passed The Orb and turned towards Ignis House, merging with other Fire Elemental students who were among the last to head back from the assembly. I wound my way between them, wanting to get back quickly and hurried forward as I spotted Sofia.

"Hey," I said as I fell into step with her.

"Tory!" She threw her arms around me and I stumbled back a step in surprise as I returned her embrace for a moment. "I was so worried about the two of you," she said. "I've seen the footage of what The Heirs-"

"I'm fine," I said quickly, wriggling out of her grasp as I spotted Darius prowling our way. The last thing I needed was for him to think I was moping about what he'd done to me. He was laughing with a bunch of his fan club and I resisted the urge to gag at their display. Milton Hubert was smiling at him so widely that I got the feeling he'd lick his boots if that's what Darius wanted.

Sofia followed my gaze as she released me and I gave her a nudge to get her moving towards the House again, turning my back on Darius as his gaze moved my way. I wanted to get back before him.

We walked on in silence and I encouraged her to move even faster as the crowd began to thicken.

The wind blustered around us, carrying the scent of smoke on the air just as a giant crash broke through the sky and the rain burst free of the clouds.

Several students cried out as the torrential downpour began and we started running toward the safety of the House. A lot of the older students created shields of hot air above their head to evaporate the rain before it could reach them but I didn't even consider attempting it. I let the rain drench me, releasing a laugh at my luck; now I didn't have to worry about anyone noticing the stench of smoke on my skin anymore.

Sofia looked at me like I was crazy and I grinned at her.

"I like the rain," I said by way of an explanation and she shook her head, clearly not agreeing.

As we made it to the doors of Ignis House, cries of alarm went up, people were screaming and calling for help and my heart quickened at the sound of it.

Inside, I took the steps two at a time, wanting a front row seat for when Darius made it upstairs and found out what had happened to his precious room. Sofia barely managed to keep up with me and I almost lost her more than once in the crowd of shouting, panicking students.

"Someone get Darius!" Marguerite screamed. "We need his water magic!"

I slipped into the common room and pressed my back to the wall where I could get a clear view of what was happening. The stench of smoke had filled the space and more than a few students were coughing and hurrying back outside.

"What the hell is going on?" Darius bellowed as he made it into the common room and a lot of the panicking voices fell quiet in response to his commanding voice.

"Upstairs!" Marguerite called desperately, running forward to grasp his hand. "It's your room - it's on fire!"

"WHAT?" Darius snatched his hand out of her grip and sprinted through the room.

The other students scattered to get out of his way as he charged up the stairs.

I caught Sofia's elbow and we made it into the crowd who followed him. She looked up at me with wide eyes and I shrugged in response like I was just as curious as her. I felt a bit shitty not telling her the truth but sharing what I'd done with her would only put her in danger. It was better for her if she remained totally innocent.

Milton Hubert elbowed me out of the way as we reached the top floor and I flattened myself against the wall to watch the commotion that broke out.

Darius's door had flames licking out from the top of it and a thick layer of smoke clung to the ceiling all along the corridor. But it didn't look like the fire had progressed beyond his room. I wondered if that was to do with my magic and the fact that I'd only wanted to target him or if it was just luck that it hadn't spread any further.

With a snarl of rage, Darius kicked his door hard enough to smash the lock and break it open.

The fire tried to explode towards him, hungry for the fresh supply of oxygen out here, but Darius already had his hands raised and he wrangled the flames under his control, forcing them back.

Students were crying out, the crowd thickening in the corridor while everyone gave Darius space to deal with the situation. I had to crane my neck to see over everyone's heads and I caught a glimpse of Darius commanding a great flood of water into existence before him as he stepped into the inferno.

"Who else holds the Element of water?" Marguerite shrieked in panic as Darius moved out of sight. "He needs help!"

Everyone looked around, someone said, 'I've got earth,' unhelpfully and then someone else noticed me.

"Help him!" the girl demanded, grabbing my arm and hauling me forward.

As the rest of the students noticed me, they shoved me through their ranks, crying out encouraging words and demanding I help the Ignis House Captain with his little problem.

I made it to the front of the crowd and came face to face with Marguerite, her bright red hair a mess for once and tears painted with mascara running down her cheeks.

"What are you waiting for?" she demanded, reaching out to grab my wrist. "Help him!"

I snatched my arm back out of her grasp. "No," I said simply, my voice firm and offering no room for negotiation.

"What?" she yelled. "You have to! You-"

"I don't have to," I said. "And after last night, I've had more than enough water to last me a lifetime. I don't feel like conjuring any more of it."

The sound of something heavy breaking was followed by a startled shout from Darius and a lot of the students behind us screamed in fear.

"Help him you bitch!" Marguerite lunged at me like she was thinking of forcing me down the corridor and I raised my hands, shoving her back with a smack of ice cold water which slammed her against the opposite wall.

"Oh, looks like I *can* manage a bit of water after all. That's enough though. I don't feel like summoning any more." I smirked at her and a few gasps of surprise came from the crowd.

Marguerite spluttered angrily, raising her hands to defend herself then seeming to think better of conjuring more fire in our current situation.

"Your House Captain needs your help!" she snarled.

"Well when I needed *his* help he told me I'd have to force it from him. So I think I'll be giving the same answer," I replied icily.

Marguerite shrieked, shoving herself off of the wall opposite me like she intended to attack me with her bare hands. Air magic built in my palms but before I had a chance to use it, a commanding voice filled the corridor.

"Move aside!" Professor Pyro's voice carried above all others and the crowd parted to let her and Principal Nova through.

They headed straight for the end of the corridor where Darius was still battling the blaze in his room and I offered Marguerite an innocent shrug as I joined the crowd who followed them.

The Professors headed straight inside and I caught a glimpse of the devastation within as I leaned against the wall to watch.

Darius was in the centre of the blackened space, panting heavily as he looked around at the remains of his bedroom. He'd managed to douse the flames but now everything was soaking wet as well as burned to a crisp. His jeans were singed, his shirt burned almost entirely off of his body to reveal the tattoos which marked his flesh and soot lined his face. I noticed a dark red symbol raised on his forearm which I recognised as the sign for Libra and wondered for a moment why he had someone else's star sign on his skin.

He looked angry as all hell, maybe even a little devastated and I couldn't deny the surge of triumph that ran through my veins.

Darius looked around as the Professor and Nova strode into the room, his dark hair falling forward over his eyes which were blazing with fury.

"What on earth happened here, Mr Acrux?" Principal Nova demanded sharply, her hands on her hips.

"I don't know," he snarled.

"First that incident with poor Professor Astrum last night and now this. What are the chances of two such major events being linked to fire magic within such a short space of time?" Professor Pyro muttered worriedly. "Perhaps we should be concerned that this was an attempt at a second attack?"

"Who would try and attack a Dragon Shifter with fire?" Nova replied dismissively. "I'd sooner believe this was an attempt to cover up evidence..." Her voice trailed off but her eyes narrowed on Darius.

"I hope you're not making an accusation against me, *Principal*," Darius growled, his voice menacingly low.

Everyone in the corridor had fallen silent in hopes of listening in.

A tense moment passed between Darius and the Principal.

"I'm sure the FIB will get to the bottom of this," she replied eventually. "*Whatever* the motivations for the blaze."

Darius clearly took that as an insinuation that he might have done this and his eyes flashed with the characteristics of his dragon form as his anger grew.

"We will arrange another room for you while this mess is sorted out-" Professor Pyro began, breaking the growing tension in the room.

"It's fine, I have somewhere to sleep," Darius snapped.

"Okay. Well, perhaps you can gather anything you can salvage here and..." She trailed off as she looked around at the complete and utter devastation in the room. It certainly didn't look like anything could be salvaged.

Poor little rich boy, all his pretty things are gone.

I had to fight the smile which was coming for my lips but I wasn't sure I was managing it.

"I just need my gold and..." Darius looked around at the spot where his chest of gold used to be and kicked aside some charred lumps of wood to reveal the puddle of molten treasure which had now cooled enough to fuse itself to the remains of the carpet and floorboards.

His whole body seemed to tremble with rage for a moment and the two Professors took a measured step away from him.

"Control your form, Mr Acrux!" Nova demanded in a shrill voice.

"Oh shit, he's losing control of the Dragon," a guy breathed behind me.

Darius rocked forward, bracing his hands on the floor as a growl of absolute fury escaped him which sounded way too deep for a man to make.

"Holy hell!" Pyro stumbled away and Darius managed to force himself upright as he started running.

He stumbled, half tripping and didn't quite make it to the window before the transformation began. Wings burst from his back, scales covered his skin and his clothes were shredded right off of him. He launched himself out of the shattered window half a second before his body exploded in size and a huge dragon burst from the confines of his flesh.

Darius released a powerful roar filled with absolute rage as he swept up into the sky and a little sliver of fear tracked along my spine. If he ever found out that I'd been responsible for this, he'd kill me.

Dragon Fire tore through the storm clouds and a deathly silence fell over the students as everyone strained to get a look at him as he flew away. More than a few people had been recording the whole thing on their Atlases and I was looking forward to watching the replay of my victory multiple times.

"Show's over, people!" Pyro shouted as she ushered the rest of us away. "Return to your rooms!"

"That's minus fifty points to Ignis for an out of control blaze!" Principal Nova called after Darius though he clearly couldn't hear her over all the crazy roaring and fire breathing. "And minus twenty for a student failing to control their Order form!"

I had to bite my lip to stop myself from laughing at that one. Darius Acrux had just completely lost his shit in front of everyone because of what I'd done and he had no idea that it was me.

The Principal noticed me before I could escape and she beckoned me over.

"I heard about the incidents last night," she said softly. "I'm glad to see you up and about."

"Oh, thanks," I said, surprised to hear the concern in her voice.

She reached out to squeeze my arm reassuringly. "Minus one hundred and fifty points for Ignis and Aer for the two of you missing assembly though," she said before releasing me and walking away.

My lips parted in surprise at the punishment. It wasn't like I gave a shit about House Points but that was cold. Maybe she wasn't so sympathetic after all.

I turned away quickly and followed the crowd downstairs. When we made it to my floor, I peeled off and retreated to the safety of my bedroom.

I pressed my back to the door as a shiver of adrenaline rocked through me. Setting Darius's room on fire might have been a terrible idea but *damn*, it had felt really good.

The next morning, I showered in my en-suite, with a small smile on my lips that just wouldn't quit.

While the hot water ran over my skin, I tried to make myself regret what I'd done from a self-preservation point of view at the very least but I was struggling to do it. It might have been reckless and impulsive but it was also pretty damn poetic. And it was the only way that I could strike back at Darius while I was still learning to take full control of my power.

I was absolutely done with just rolling over and taking shit from the Heirs. What they'd done to me and Darcy on the night of the party was beyond unforgivable. And if they wanted to make enemies of us then they had thoroughly succeeded.

Now we just needed to find ways to strike back at the rest of them.

I shut off the hot water reluctantly and headed back into my bedroom, running a towel through my hair.

I'd left most of Darius's treasure hidden in Darcy's room for now but a stack of eight fat coins sat in a tower on my desk where I'd left them last night.

I took a golden coin from the top of the pile and twisted it through my fingers. Looking at it made me feel stupidly happy. Like we'd won a point against *them* for once and they didn't even realise it. I inspected the coin for a few moments. A dragon was engraved on one side of it and a crown on the other. I pressed my thumb down on the dragon's face, drawing a little bit of heat to the surface of my skin until my thumb print blurred the features of the snarling beast.

I withdrew my thumb, smirking at the improvement to the coin before putting it down again so that I could get dressed.

I pulled on a pair of black jeans and a black tank top and did my eyeliner a little thicker than I usually would during the day. Today, I seriously needed to channel the badass chick who stole super bikes in her spare time and didn't take shit from any of the assholes at Joey's bar.

My Atlas pinged persistently from my nightstand and I sighed as I headed over to retrieve it. As I snatched it, my fingers brushed against the dagger I'd stolen from Darius and that funny sensation seemed to start up again like its presence was responding to me, urging me to take it. I grabbed it on an impulse and quickly took a seat at the foot of my bed as I opened up my Atlas.

Your daily horoscope is waiting for you Tory!

I pursed my lips as I opened up my horoscope, not really wanting to read yet another warning about watching my back today. But Darcy was adamant that paying attention to these predictions could help us avoid the bullies in this school so I would at least give it a read.

Good morning Gemini!
The stars have spoken about your day.
A shift in the alignment of your stars may just have a positive effect on your day. But beware of trusting in change too easily; if you want this to be a permanent situation then it will take hard work and dedication to your cause. You could find yourself on a collision course with a Taurus today but if you can keep a level head, the interaction may be better than expected.

I drummed my fingers against my thigh as I considered the words for a moment. I sure as hell wanted to think that our stars were about to change but the whole thing was so vague that I could hardly rely on it. The only Taurus I could think of off the top of my head was Caleb Altair and I had zero intentions of having any kind of interaction with him if I could avoid it, so keeping a level head probably wouldn't be an issue.

I dismissed the horoscope and decided to check in on the FaeBook homepage. It wasn't like I enjoyed seeing embarrassing stories and comments about me and Darcy but if I didn't know what was out there then I wouldn't be prepared to face it.

I bit my lip as I spotted all of the stories filling the newsfeed and couldn't help the breath of laughter that escaped me as a picture of Darius's livid face greeted me with a caption and plenty of comments.

Milton Hubert:

what a cruel world! The Fire Heir's room was burned to a crisp while we were all out of the House. Where will he sleep now? #anyoffersladies #worstluck #evenhisclothes

Marguerite Helebor:

Poor baby! You can always come and stay with me.

Comments:
Tyler Corbin:

Pretty sure he publicly dumped you Muffscruff, but way to go on looking desperate.

Marguerite Helebor:

We're on a break, loser, check your facts.

Tyler Corbin:

I really hope you have that chat with him in public again so that I can watch you get dumped twice. #bitchesbecrazy

Elouise Pirot:

There's plenty of space in my bed, Darius

Tilly Farbringer:

I'm in actual tears over this tragedy. Lighting a candle for Darius's loss tonight. #yourpainismypain

I opted to save myself from the need to vomit in my own mouth as I noticed the long line of sympathetic messages from half of the school and stopped reading, but my gaze was drawn back to that picture. Darius didn't just look furious, he seemed genuinely upset and I really hoped that there had been some things in his room he truly cared about. He deserved some bad luck and I wasn't the least bit against the idea of giving him some.

I scrolled on but all I found was post after post dedicated to Darius and his bedroom disaster. The posts about what the Heirs had done to me and Darcy had been buried by the new school drama and I was more than pleased to realise we were yesterday's news already. I grinned at a short video clip which showed the flames bursting from the roof of Ignis House and for a moment it was like the pain the Heirs had caused us had been banished.

A loud knock came at the door and I flinched, almost dropping my Atlas in surprise. I cursed myself for my frayed nerves but it wasn't that surprising; a couple of nights ago I'd almost drowned and now I was an arsonist.

I half considered pretending I wasn't here but that felt a little too like cowering in my room so I stood and moved towards the door instead.

I quickly scooped Darius's gold coins into my satchel and tossed it to the floor on my way to the door.

My fingers closed around the handle, I fixed a bored expression onto my face and I tugged the door open.

At the last second I realised I hadn't hidden Darius's dagger and my heart leapt in panic but it was too late to do anything about it.

Caleb Altair stood leaning against my doorframe with half a smile on his handsome face and a hand mid-way through messing up his blonde curls. *So much for avoiding him today.*

"Hey, sweetheart," he said as I full-on glared at him.

I didn't bother to wait for another word to pass his lips before slamming the door in his face.

He jammed his foot in the doorway to stop it from closing and I stalked away from him as the door bounced back open. My gaze snagged on the dagger lying on my bed so I flopped down on it like I didn't have a care in the world and one of the most vindictive men I'd ever met hadn't just intruded on my personal space.

"Can I come in?" Caleb asked, his voice softer than I would have expected. He hadn't set foot in the room yet and I couldn't help the surprise that flickered over my face.

"Well we both know I can't stop you if that's what you've decided to do," I said coldly.

"Which is why I'm offering you the choice," he replied. "I just want to talk. I swear I won't lay a finger on you, I'm not even going to bite you. I'd just like you to hear me out."

"Why?" I demanded, narrowing my eyes suspiciously.

"In private please, sweetheart, I'm drawing a bit of a crowd out here already."

I glanced over his shoulder and noticed a few of the other Fire Elemental students lurking beyond him like he'd said. I guessed the Terra House Captain didn't come to Ignis House all that often but he held the Element of Fire so he could get in easily enough. And it was probably even more intriguing to see him calling on me.

My magic built in my chest as I prepared to defend myself from him if necessary but he didn't make any move towards me. He genuinely seemed to want my permission to come in and despite myself, I was curious to hear what he had to say.

"Fine," I said eventually, beckoning him in. I scooted myself upright and pressed my back to the wall beside my bed, keeping my ass on the dagger.

My pulse spiked as Caleb stepped inside and his lips twitched a little as if he'd heard it. Which he probably had.

Damn vampire asshole.

The door clicked shut and Caleb waved a hand through the air. A wave of warmth slid over my skin and the hairs on the back of my neck prickled to attention.

"Silencing bubble," he explained as he noticed my confused expression. "Just to keep our conversation private."

I nodded vaguely, trying not to think about the fact that that also meant no one would be able to hear me scream.

Caleb moved towards me like he was going to come and sit beside me on the bed and I pointed at the chair by my desk instead. No way did I want him that close to me again.

He perched on the seat and ran his hand over his jaw as he surveyed me with his navy eyes.

"What do you want?" I demanded when he didn't seem inclined to enlighten me.

"It just occurred to me that you probably don't know much about The Vampire Code," he said slowly.

"The what?"

"Well, the different Orders of Fae all have their own governing body to guide the actions of their members while under the influence of their Order form. With so many different behaviours, natures, instincts and abilities to juggle, it's much easier to maintain control by having individual factions. And as my Source, I thought it was right that you know a bit about-"

"Caleb?" I asked, interrupting him. "If you're not here to bite me then maybe you just want to piss off? Because unless your latest form of torture is trying to bore me to death I've got absolutely nothing to say to you. I don't know if you've forgotten, but you and your twisted bunch of friends almost killed me the night before last so I have less than zero interest in spending any time in your company."

Caleb met the hatred in my gaze with a flicker of a smile. "Well I'm glad they didn't crush your spirit after all, sweetheart."

I bristled at the fact that he hadn't so much as flinched at my words.

I didn't miss the fact that he'd said 'they' as if he'd had no part in what had happened to me which was bullshit because I'd seen him standing right there beside them, a part of their group through and through.

Caleb continued to watch me with interest as I fought against the desire to start screaming at him.

What the hell was with this guy? He'd just barged into my personal space and started talking to me about the organisation of an Order I wanted nothing to do with.

"If you won't leave, then I will," I said firmly.

I shoved myself off of the bed, flipping the duvet over as I rose to conceal the stolen dagger.

I made it to the door but Caleb shot towards me in a blur of motion, pressing his hand to it beside my head and leaning close to me. I was pinned in by the masculine scent of him and the hard lines of his muscular body. My only choice was to meet his gaze as he trapped me in it.

"I just... wanted you to know that I had nothing to do with what happened at the pool," he breathed. "I knew the others were planning something, but I had no idea it would be so..."

I frowned up at him, wondering what the hell he wanted me to say to that.

"If you'd just left with me when I asked you to," he sighed. "Then we could have enjoyed a very different kind of evening."

"Oh so it's my fault because I didn't want to leave with you?" I asked, raising an eyebrow at him.

"No. But I did try to get you out of there, that's got to count for something."

"You tried to get me out of there so that you could get into my pants which really isn't heroic in any way. Did you make any attempt to get Darcy away from Seth before he hacked her hair off?" I growled.

"Well, no, but she isn't my Source. I have a duty to protect you from harm and I've sworn an oath which means I can't torture or torment you," Caleb said.

"Oh, how noble. I can't say I felt particularly protected in that pool though. I was half dead when Orion dragged me out of there."

"They wouldn't have killed you," he said, though his voice held a note of hesitation which made me think he wasn't entirely sure about that.

"Is that it then? Have you finished your half-assed attempt at an apology because I've got somewhere to be," I snapped.

"I'm not apologising," he said. "I'm just telling you it wasn't me. You don't need to be afraid of me doing anything like that to you. As my Source you can be sure of that."

"Well don't go to any special lengths on my account. I don't want to be your Source and if that's the only reason you have for not being a psychopath then it's nothing to be proud of. Why don't you just relieve me of your so-called bond and then you can have free rein to be as much of an asshole as the rest of your friends and I won't have to endure the feeling of your mouth on my skin again." I glared at him as he kept me pinned against the wall, refusing to back down. Magic tingled as it raced along my arms and pooled in the palms of my hands, ready to be unleashed.

Caleb held my gaze for several long seconds then sighed as he took his hand from the door and stepped back. "I didn't come here to argue with you, Tory. I want you to know that what happened the other night didn't make me feel good about anything. Fae have to claim their power and fight for their position but you're supposed to do that one on one. The way they ganged up on you... You know you broke through the ice while it was just Max controlling it? It took Darius's power combined with his to trap you beneath it."

"Well you already knew I was stronger than all of you. It's our lack of training that puts us at a disadvantage. It might be worth reminding your little friends of that, because just as soon as I get a lock on how to use my magic against the four of you, I'll be doing it. And I hear payback's a real bitch."

Instead of recoiling from that statement or getting angry about it, Caleb's mouth hooked into a smirk.

"I look forward to it." He took a step towards the door but I shifted in front of it to stop him from leaving.

"Just tell me why," I ground out. "Why can't you just accept us saying that we don't want the throne?"

"You say that now but once you're trained, and once your Order emerges you don't know how your minds could change, how you might embrace your Fae side and long for power like everyone else in this world. We can't take that risk." He smiled ruefully like that was just the way it was and I guessed for him it was the truth.

"Why can't we just stay here, learn to use our magic and gain our inheritance without it having anything to do with us ruling over a kingdom we know nothing about?" I pressed, refusing to give up on my point.

"Because that's not how Fae are. We're born with our magic but we have to work to harness it and wield it better than others. I might have been born an Heir to the Celestial Council but that doesn't automatically mean I get to sit in my mother's seat when she retires. I have a younger brother and a sister who are Heirs too and I'll have to prove that I'm stronger than them to take my place. I'll also have to fight off any outside challenges that come at me. I might even have to fight my mother for her place on the Council if she doesn't release it willingly. The Royal and Celestial families may be the most powerful in all of Solaria but it doesn't give us automatic rights to rule. Even here at school we're being watched, assessed, we constantly flex our magical muscles against the other students and make sure they remember exactly who we are and what we're capable of."

"That sounds exhausting," I muttered.

"It is. But it's also necessary. For the people to have faith in their rulers they need to see that we can hold our power without question. Unfortunately for you and your sister that also means we're either expected to keep you in

73

check or bow to you. You were born with more magic than us, not to mention the fact that you've both been Awakened with all four Elements. There are countless press articles being published every day calling for the Vegas to take back the throne. We have to ensure that everyone can see we're stronger than you if we don't want to let you have it."

"So what we want has nothing to do with it?" I asked. "And what about the fact that everyone called our father The Savage King? Surely no one would want his Heirs taking over if his reign was so awful?"

"People are fickle, there's always something to complain about when it comes to rulers and there are plenty of reasons for them to dislike the Celestial Council's rule even if it is immeasurably better than living under a tyrant. And you're not your father, many will wonder what changes the two of you might make to our kingdom. Plus they believe that if you're strong enough to claim the throne then it should be yours regardless."

"That's... really stupid," I said. "Power doesn't equal good leadership skills. Beating people into submission seems like a terrible way to choose a ruler. You could end up with a group of vindictive assholes for rulers who try to drown people who get in their way."

Caleb smirked at me. "Well if you ever take up your throne maybe you can try and shake up the way things are done. I don't rate your chances though, sweetheart. This is the way Fae are and that look in your eye says you're just the same as the rest of us."

"I'm nothing like you," I protested angrily.

"No? So you haven't daydreamed about giving us a taste of our own medicine? You aren't tempted to use your power to throw me across the room every time I bite you against your will?" He smiled knowingly and I shifted a little uncomfortably.

"Well I wouldn't have to think about doing any of that if you'd all just leave us alone," I protested.

"That's never going to happen," Caleb said with a shrug. "So what you have to decide is what you're going to do about it."

He stepped towards the door again and this time I let him leave. I stood in my doorway and watched Caleb as he walked away down the corridor. Other students scurried out of his path as he passed them and more than one nodded or even bowed their heads to him in deference. And it wasn't just fear that made them act that way; it was respect. Whatever I thought of the Heirs and their asshole ways, it was clear that the rest of the Fae didn't see it the same way. And although I had no intention of becoming like them, maybe it was time I accepted the fact that Fae did things differently.

If we were going to survive here then we needed to adapt. And I was ready to do just that.

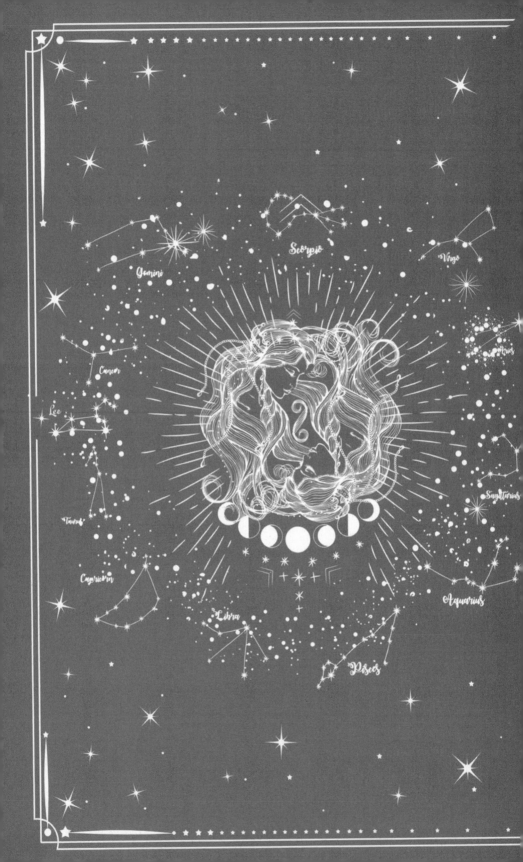

DARCY

CHAPTER SIX

Iheaded out of Aer Tower early Monday morning before most other students were even out of bed. It was barely past dawn and the coming light seemed to ripple through the sky. I was miles happier since Tory and I had decided to stay, though I couldn't help but fear the moment I ran into Seth. To see his sneering face, hear his mocking jibes. I wanted to get back at him in the way it hurt most; I'd hit his reputation. Wipe that constant owns-the-world smirk from his face and make his friends laugh at *him* like they had me. But I had no idea how I'd actually manage that. Not yet anyway.

I stepped out of the tower and a cool wind blew around me, holding a promise of the coming Fall. The sea air rolling over the cliff sent the long grass swirling and dancing like water before me. I followed the winding path toward The Wailing Wood where the faintest hint of yellow and orange tinted the tips of the leaves.

As I walked along the shadowy path, I recalled the feeling of being followed here, of the Heirs pouncing on me. But I wasn't going to avoid this place. At night it might have appeared to harbour my darkest nightmares, but that wasn't real. And in the day time it was one of my favourite places on campus.

I followed the track all the way around toward the main buildings, veering off of it as I approached Venus Library. I'd scribbled down the name of the book Orion had given me on the inside of my palm. I had no idea why he was suddenly helping me. Maybe he pitied me. But something about Orion told me he wasn't the sort of guy who pitied people.

Fae were strong, and the weakest of their kind naturally suffered. That was how Solaria worked. It was ingrained in everyone within Zodiac Academy's walls and beyond. I was kind of glad about that for once because I definitely didn't want to be pitied. Tory and I had been hurt deeply, ridiculed and no doubt made the butt of every joke in school. But I didn't need apologies and pats on the back. I didn't even want to run anymore. I wanted revenge, pure and simple. I wanted to claim my place back in this world and prove to everyone in it that I deserved to be here. That I was Fae and I wouldn't let anyone tell me otherwise ever again. And if that meant the Heirs came at us twofold, then so be it.

The library stood tall and imposing above me as I approached. I pushed through the doors and was greeted by the echoing clap of them closing behind me, sending a shiver darting down my spine.

The last time I'd been here had also been the last time I'd seen Astrum alive. I didn't want to consider the fact that he could have been killed because of his allegiance with Tory and I. But whoever 'The Shadow' was, they had been merciless when they'd discovered Falling Star's identity. And that could only mean one thing; he'd known something important. Something we may never now discover.

I crept through the expansive library, slipping into Row Epsilon under the glow of the large spherical lamp which hung from the ceiling. I checked the name of the book on my palm then ran my hand along the shelf as I searched for it. Not a wisp of dust coated my fingers when I took them away and I wondered if there was some magical janitor roaming the halls of Zodiac Academy or if it was all just enchanted to remain immaculate.

My gaze landed on a dark green, leather-bound book with golden lettering on the spine: Earth: The Power of Growth. My stomach swooped as I tugged it from the shelf and flipped it open. I ran my eyes down the contents page, hunting for what I needed.

Natural Growth:
Nails:
Toe...340
Finger...345
Claw...350

Hair:
Head...360
Legs...362
Armpit...364
Pubic region...368
Face...370
Body...372

A grin dragged up my mouth as I found exactly what I was looking for. I hurried to a circular wooden table at the end of the row and sat down, finding the chapter for hair growth. I skipped through a series of hair follicle diagrams and searched for the spell. Except it wasn't a spell at all. It was a potion.

Crap, I haven't learned anything about those yet.

I read a few pages of introductory text then scanned the list of ingredients. It wasn't long, just three items. But I had no idea where I'd find them.

3 Flakes of Dried Pepper Bark.

8 Scrapings of Mother of Pearl.

A Two Inch Yellow Crystal.

Mix together and leave in the light of the moon for two nights then wait until it turns transparent in the rising sun on the second day.

Face the North Star and drink 50ml per inch of desired hair growth.

Okay that seems simple enough, if not totally weird.

I jotted down the instructions, closed the book and headed back into the aisle to return it to the shelf. As I pushed it back into place, the book beside it caught my eye.

Earth: The Power of Summoning.

Curiosity got the better of me and I tugged the thick book out, turning to the contents page and reading the first section.

Summoning for beginners:

Insects:

Beetles and Cockroaches

Arachnids

Ants

Lice, Fleas, Earwigs and Termites

Moths and Butterflies

Locusts, Crickets and Grasshoppers

Flies and Mosquitoes

Bees and Wasps

My attention zeroed in on the word fleas and I flipped to that section, wondering if maybe…

I read through a few pages and my heart soared as my hunch paid off. A bubble of laughter escaped me as I discovered that something called an Aquarius Moonstone could call Werewolf lice under the control of the spell caster. *Now I just need to figure out where to get one.*

I started reading through more and more pages, fascinated by all of the crazy things summoning magic could do. In the advanced section of the book, there were ways to summon bigger animals then press your will into them to gain control over their bodies. It completely boggled my mind to think I might be capable of such a thing one day.

The school bell rang shrilly through the air and I stiffened in surprise. I checked an ornate silver clock on the wall and realised I'd been so engrossed in the book that I'd completely missed breakfast. I stuffed it back onto the shelf, adjusting my satchel over my shoulder as I headed toward the exit.

Students were swarming across campus, pouring out of The Orb and splitting off in groups down the winding paths in the direction of their first classes. I turned right toward Jupiter Hall, eyeing the crowd for any sign of Tory, Diego or Sofia. I'd lost the only hat I'd had in my closet after Orion had flicked it off of my head, so my hair was on show for everyone to see. I'd considered tying a scarf around it but figured that would only have drawn more attention. Besides, everyone had seen it on FaeBook anyway. The best I could do was front it out for now.

People snickered as I walked past them and they caught sight of the bald patch on the back of my head. My cheeks flamed but I held my chin up high, trying not to let it affect me, but it was pretty much impossible. I held onto the fact that once I located the ingredients from that book, I would be able to regrow my hair and this nightmare would finally end.

I headed into the wide foyer of Jupiter Hall and hurried up the stairs, joining the line of students filing into Orion's classroom. I craned my neck to look for my friends but before I spotted them I was suddenly crushed in a four armed hug.

"Darcy!" Sofia squealed, wrapping herself around me as Diego tugged us both into his chest.

"I'm so glad you guys decided to stay." Diego squeezed me tighter and I spotted Tory over his shoulder, observing the bear hug I was trapped in with a grin.

A girl a few feet away suddenly gasped, jumping up and down. "Ohmagod it's Caleb Altair."

I glanced over my shoulder in the direction she was pointing, pulling away from my friends. Caleb headed a line of Juniors as he strode down the corridor like he owned every ounce of oxygen in it. His friends pointed us out and my gut tightened as his stony gaze slid over us. His fan club were eyeing him hopefully and I knew in the depths of my heart he wasn't going to pass us by without comment.

He slowed his pace, breathing in deeply. "Do you smell that guys?" He sniffed the air and my scowl grew. "Smells like a bunch of Orderless Fae pretending they deserve a place in our prestigious Academy."

"Is it raining assholes today?" Tory commented, turning away from him and for a moment it almost looked like he was going to crack a smile.

"I have an Order," Sofia muttered under her breath but Caleb's Vampire hearing didn't let her get away with it.

"I wouldn't go around reminding people of that, blondie. Being a Pegasus is worse than not having an Order." His friend fist bumped him, nodding his agreement as he laughed. He was a tall guy with red hair and cold eyes.

"Yeah I dunno how there are so many of them on campus," the redhead jibed. "Only a freak would want to screw a horse."

Caleb chuckled at that, nodding firmly. "I think I'd rather give up my claim first."

His shitbag friends laughed their heads off as Caleb swept off down the hall to a stream of excited hoots.

"God he's awful," I growled. "Ignore him Sofia."

"If I ever bump into him as a Pegasus, I'll introduce him to my left hoof," Sofia hissed and I raised my brows at the fire in her eyes.

"I would so love to see that," Tory laughed, then lowered her voice as she looked to me. "I wonder if we can use his Pegasus hate against him?"

"Yeah, you should spread a rumour that he likes Pegasus ass," Sofia whispered, a manic gleam in her eyes. I kinda liked this crazy side to her and couldn't stop the laugh that bubbled from my throat.

Diego stared at her in shock, then nodded keenly. "That would be fantastico, Sofia. I doubt anyone would believe us *freaks* though." He winked at her and she blushed at his insinuation.

A chorus of shrieking laughter caught my attention and I turned with a crushing feeling in my chest as Kylie and her friends arrived.

"Looks like a half-plucked chicken is joining our Cardinal Magic class today," she said loudly, her pale eyes landing on me as a wicked smile pulled up her full lips. "Someone put it out of its misery." Her friends fell about laughing and I ground my teeth as I glared back at her.

"Looks like a fully plucked one has joined us too," Tory called back at her. "They haven't removed its huge beak yet though."

A collective *ooooh* sounded from our classmates and adrenaline slid into my veins.

Kylie's face turned red and her eyes swam with murder. Her dark-haired friend, Jillian, stared at us like a wide-eyed owl.

"What did you say to me, Princess Whore?" Kylie snarled.

I moved to Tory's side, not wanting her to fight my battles. "You heard her, Kylie. Why don't you run back to your supposed boyfriend? You know, the one who made you stand in a bush and film him while he kissed another girl." I didn't know where the fire in me came from, or if spinning my absolute humiliation into another tale would work at all. But Kylie's jaw ticked with rage and she stepped toward us like a predator. A circle formed around us and those who'd entered the class already poked their heads back out to see what was going on.

"Sethy only did that to destroy you, *Vega*," Kylie spat at me. "As if he'd ever kiss you out of choice."

"Well you can tell him I'd rather cut my tongue out than put it anywhere near his lying mouth again," I snarled and Diego took hold of my arm as if to pull me away.

"I see him kissing girls all over campus and none of them are you," Tory added mock-innocently. "If he does kiss you again, Kylie, you'd better be careful in case you catch an STI."

"You little bitch!" Kylie shrieked. Her entire head of blonde hair burst into streams of angry snakes, her skin shifted to a pale green colour and her teeth sharpened to points. I lurched back in surprise as the black and green vipers hissed at us, spitting venom. An Order rang in my head that Orion had mentioned – *Medusa*.

"Holy shit," Tory breathed, her shoulder knocking mine as she backed up. "She looks like a bird threw up a bucket of worms all over her head. I can't believe she tried to insult *your* hair."

Kylie's eyes narrowed to slits and she stepped forward, raising her hands as a storm of air circled between them.

Before she could so much as unleash a light breeze, she was lifted into the air by a vortex of wind, spinning wildly in circles so the vipers swung out around her head.

A laugh ripped from my throat as Orion walked into view, his hand raised as he cast the tornado.

"You should all be sat in my classroom waiting for me!" he bellowed, dropping his arm so that Kylie hit the floor, landing on her ass with a yelp. Her hair fell about her shoulders, returning to a sheet of gold and her cheeks flushed scarlet with embarrassment.

"Twenty points from Aer for losing control of your Order form," Orion barked then cast a gust of air which forced more students aside to let him through. He marched into the classroom out of sight and my heart beat frantically as everyone scrambled after him.

Kylie's friends left her in a heap, hurrying into the room without her. She flattened down her hair and tried to remain calm, but I could see she was totally knocked for six. A small part of me felt sorry for her but after what she'd done to me, I smothered that thought with a pillow until it suffocated to death.

My friends' laughter rang around me, mixing with that of our other classmates and infecting me until I joined in.

"Did you see the look in the snakes' eyes as they spun about her head?" Tyler Corbin roared a laugh as he re-enacted the whole thing at the front of the class.

Orion folded his arms, waiting behind his desk as the students fell into their seats and watched Tyler's display. A smile played around Orion's mouth and he met my gaze for half a second, making me grin even wider.

I dropped into my seat between Tory and Diego just as Kylie marched through the door. She drew her shoulders back as she hurried to her chair, but the moment she sat down, she sank low to try and hide, burying her face in her Atlas.

Excited chatter filled the room and Tyler was still spinning at the front of the class, waving someone's cardigan above his head. A tremendous bang made everyone fall deathly quiet. Orion had lifted his entire desk and slammed it down on the floor with a gust of air and the wooden floor vibrated from the impact. Tyler hurried back to his seat as Orion gave him a sharp look.

As quiet rang out, he turned to the board, picking up his electronic pen and writing across it in his slanted handwriting.

YOU ARE NOT PURE.

I took out my Atlas, navigating my way to the lesson notes. When I found them, I looked back at Orion, waiting on an explanation for his latest vaguely insulting start to a lesson.

He slowly walked toward Tyler Corbin who was frantically tapping out something on his Atlas, completely unaware of the danger which was lurking nearer. It wasn't until Orion's shadow fell over him that Tyler froze, lifting his gaze to meet the Professor's with an expression of apology.

"Are you writing a FaeBook post in my class, Corbin?" Orion growled and the amusement in the room was entirely disbanded by his terrifying tone.

"Yes but-" Tyler started but Orion snatched the Atlas and whacked it across the side of Tyler's head. He tossed it on the floor with a clatter then walked back to the board. "Ten points from Terra," he said casually, straightening his tie before tapping the board to bring up the first notes of the lesson.

Tyler rubbed his temple, reaching down and fishing his Atlas from the floor with a pout.

"Today we're discussing blood lines," Orion announced, pointing at the screen which contained a list of Orders and my curiosity piqued as I recognised the first one. It had belonged to The Savage King. My *father*.

Hydra.

Kraken.

Phoenix.

Arian Dolphin.

Empusa.

Ophiotaurus.

"Can anyone tell me what links these Orders?" Orion asked, gazing around the room as if he expected crickets.

"They're extinct, sir," Sofia said, her voice a little high.

Orion nodded firmly. "Five points to Ignis. And can anyone tell me why?" He turned back to the board, circling the Hydra Order in red.

"Because of impure blood lines?" a raven-haired girl called from the back.

"Precisely, Miss Abdul, five points to Aqua," Orion said. "The Hydra Order is the most recent to become extinct after King Vega died twenty years ago."

My gut knotted as I felt eyes drawn our way and I kept my gaze resolutely on the board.

"King Vega married outside of his Order, meaning his bloodline was mixed with that of a Harpy and whatever other genetics the Queen carried. As his daughters -" he gave us a pointed look "- haven't yet emerged in their Order forms, there is a possibility that the Hydra Order could arise once more. However...that will be down to various factors. Genetics, the stars they are linked to..." He tapped the board and a complicated tree of genetics appeared beneath a list of constellations. "The more genetics that are introduced to a bloodline, the less chance there is of a parent birthing offspring of the same Order. That is why some rarer Orders now try to keep their lines pure by only breeding with those of their kind. Can anyone give me an example?"

"The Dragons, sir?" Tyler offered and Orion nodded.

I shared a look with Tory as we both thought of Darius Acrux.

Orion continued, "Families of rarer Orders often implement arranged marri-" A loud BEEEEEEP sounded from Orion's Atlas, the high-pitched noise making my heart jolt.

He snatched it up immediately with a look of alarm, his eyes skating back and forth across a message he'd received. He ran a hand over his short beard, his forehead deeply furrowed.

"*Shit*," he hissed and everyone in the room sat up straighter.

He slowly placed the Atlas down on his desk, rested his palms either side of it and looked to the class with a grim expression. "It is my duty to inform you that the FIB have just announced that Professor Astrum's death was caused by a Nymph."

Gasps were sucked in around me and my heart stammered in my chest as I looked to Tory.

"A Nymph got on campus?!" Kylie shrieked and several of her friends started chatting animatedly.

"Aren't we supposed to have protection at this Academy?" another boy demanded, puffing out his chest.

"Have the FIB caught the Nymph?" another girl wailed.

Tyler began furiously tapping on his Atlas again and the noise in the classroom escalated.

"QUIET!" Orion roared and everyone obeyed.

My heart hammered as he bowed his head, his brow shadowing his eyes. "It seems the Nymph used their newly acquired Element of Fire which it had stolen from Astrum to try and destroy the Professor's body, but they didn't do a good enough job to conceal the evidence." He took a slow breath. "The Nymph in question has not yet been caught; Astrum possessed both air and fire so this creature will now be extremely dangerous. The FIB will be conducting interviews with anyone who may have witnessed something useful on the night of the murder. If you have any information and you are not called for an interview you *will* step forward regardless and offer it up willingly. Trust me when I say, you do not want to be interrogated by the FIB against your will." He fell silent but no one said anything. All I could hear was my heart jack-hammering in my chest.

A Nymph killed Astrum. So what does that mean? That it was a random murder? Or that the Nymphs cared about him giving us information?

The look in Orion's eyes said he was livid, his jaw ticking like a time bomb. "They have demanded that every student in the school be taught about Nymphs and though I normally don't teach that lesson until Junior year, we will be switching topics and covering it today instead." He tapped something on his Atlas then a minute later the notes on mine changed and a lesson title sprang up on the board.

The Physiology of Nymphs.

A heavy weight seemed to descend on the room. Everyone was waiting for Orion to speak, to offer some insight into the creature that had killed Astrum. And I was just as eager, leaning forward in my chair in anticipation.

"As anyone who has grown up in Solaria knows, Nymphs are creatures born without magical gifts, but they can acquire them from Fae. They are our sworn enemies. Their nature is one of destruction and death. But what you may not know is how they function, how their minds and bodies work. This knowledge is what will give you an advantage against them. A split second longer to escape death. And I will try to give you that advantage today."

Orion tapped the screen and a creepy image appeared of a tall figure with long, sharpened fingers. It looked almost tree-like, its body sinewy and brown. Its face was a demonic thing with red eyes and curling horns seemingly made from bark which twisted above its head.

"This is a Nymph in its true form," Orion explained and goosebumps fled across my skin. "They vary in size depending on age and gender, but that is the least of your concerns. Nymphs are gifted with an energy that is capable of disabling a Fae's magic. A Nymph can overwhelm Fae within less than thirty seconds at close range. The process has been described as a draining, sucking feeling that pulls at the well of magic inside you and immobilises it. This is accompanied by a rattling noise."

My throat constricted as I thought back to that night in the alley when we'd been meant to meet Falling Star the first time.

"Darcy, do you remember?" Tory whispered and I nodded, my mouth completely dry as I looked to her. *We were chased by a Nymph!? Holy crap.*

"Does anyone know where the Nymphs originate from?" Orion asked the class.

"The Shadow Realm," Diego offered, his face paling.

"Correct," Orion said.

"Isn't that where the fifth Element lives, sir?" Tyler asked excitedly.

"There's no such thing," Orion growled, glaring at him. "And I suggest you don't blow smoke up the ass of that particular rumour, Corbin, or you'll end up in detention with me for the foreseeable future."

Tyler slumped back in his chair with a huff.

"What's the Shadow Realm?" I asked, feeling out of my depth. A few giggles followed, but not as many as I'd expected. It seemed that there were plenty of people in the room who were eager to learn about it.

Orion turned to me with a heavy frown. "It's another mirror world. But it's not like ours or Earth. It's where dark magic originates. Nymphs are born of it, but they cannot wield it. Not unless they steal magic from Fae first." He moved to the board, pointing out the elongated fingers on the Nymph. "These pointed probes-"

"Butt probes!" Tyler blurted, bursting into laughter and several students joined in. A giggle escaped me and Tory snorted.

Orion flicked a finger and a torrent of water opened up above Tyler, pouring down on him in a ferocious wave. It abruptly stopped and Tyler spluttered heavily as water dripped into a growing puddle around his chair.

Orion continued on as if there had been no interruption at all. "-are razor sharp and can be inserted into the heart of a Fae to extract their magic. The process takes less than two minutes and once completed, the Fae will of course be dead and the Nymph will acquire the full power of the Elements that Fae possessed."

"So how can we defend ourselves against that?" Sofia begged, her eyes rounded with fear.

Orion tapped the screen in response, revealing a page entitled Shields and Defences. "The draining sensation is a tell-tale sign of a Nymph in your vicinity. A bluish flash often precedes the blast of energy," Orion said. "Before any other tactic is even considered, I highly suggest you run. You are freshmen, not trained Fae. You will stand little to no chance against a Nymph if they begin the draining process."

"And what if they get too close for us to run?" a guy asked, anxiously scraping a hand through his dark hair.

"Then you are most likely dead already," Orion said completely deadpan.

Way to give a pep talk, sir.

"But," Orion said with a dark grin that made his dimple pop out. "Most Fae are too tenacious not to fight to the bitter end. So here are a few tactics you can employ." He pointed at the first line on the board. "In light of what has happened, shields will no doubt take precedence in your Elemental Classes from now on. If used well, you may be able to shield yourself from the effects of a Nymph's draining power long enough for you to get away. The second tactic." He pointed to the next line. "Is to engage them in combat before they have a chance to start draining you. As you are not yet trained for battle, I would encourage you to blast the extent of your powers at the creature in one single, wide blow to increase the chances of you hitting your target. The third and most effective means of defence for you to use is to shift into your Order form. Nymphs cannot disable your Order abilities with their power so a Dragon can still breathe fire at them, a Vampire can still use their enhanced strength etcetera. At the very least, your Order form will make it easier for you to run."

I shifted uncomfortably in my seat. That bit of advice wasn't much help to me or Tory while we waited for our Orders to emerge.

"At least I'll see a ten foot tree monster coming at me from a way off," a girl in the row behind us said with a nervous laugh.

"Wrong," Orion chimed back at her. "Nymphs are chameleons. They can take the form of Fae."

"Great," Tyler groaned. "So *you* could be a Nymph for all we know." He pointed at Orion and the Professor gazed coolly back at him.

"The only thing I want to drain from you, Corbin, is a few pints of blood." He stalked closer with a manic glint in his eye and Tyler shrank in his chair.

A knock came at the door and before Orion could move to answer it, the door opened. My mouth parted at the sight of the beautiful woman I'd seen Orion on a date with in Tucana. But now she wasn't in a slinky dress that defined her hour-glass figure she was in a fitted black jumpsuit with a shiny silver badge on her chest labelling her as FIB.

"What the fuck?" Tory breathed in my ear and I nodded, unable to voice a single word on the matter. *Orion's hot date is part of the Fae Investigation Bureau??*

"Sorry to intrude, Lance," she said and something about the way she spoke his name made my hackles raise.

"Is everything alright, Francesca?" Orion asked, his voice velvet smooth. *They're definitely screwing each other. And I definitely don't care.*

"Some new evidence has come to light, I need to speak with a couple of your students." Her peridot eyes scanned the room and honed in on me and my sister. "Tory and Darcy Vega? You need to come with me."

Orion glanced between us with his lips pressing into a tight line. We stood up and I felt eyes burning a hundred holes in my back as I gathered my satchel and headed toward Francesca.

As I closed in on her, Orion darted forward and caught my wrist. I nearly stumbled into him from the force he used and had to steady myself against him. My hand landed right where his rolled-up sleeve met the crook of his elbow and I glanced down at a raised line of skin beneath my fingers. I frowned as I spotted a dark red tattoo branded there; it was a symbol I vaguely recognised and it took me half a second longer to remember it was the one for the star sign of Leo.

"You have detention with me on Saturday," Orion said in my ear, his voice a deadly purr that made my breathing quicken.

"I do?" I balked. "What for?" I met his eyes and my heart tripled its pace at the hungry look in them. He hadn't fed from me for a while and I half expected him to take advantage of me right then.

"Stardust, Miss Vega," he said and a lightning bolt seemed to hit my chest.

"Oh right...that," I muttered as he released me.

"Six am in the Jupiter Hall atrium on Saturday morning. Don't be late," he demanded.

"So long as you aren't," I said before I could stop myself and his eyes glittered as I stepped back and hurried out of the door after Tory and Francesca.

Francesca's heels clicked on the floor as she walked ahead of us at a fierce pace. She led us down a corridor past many more doors until eventually stopping outside one. She rapped her knuckles on it and a deep male voice answered.

"Just finishing up, one minute," he called.

Francesca took out a phone and started tapping on the screen.

"What is this about exactly?" Tory asked, folding her arms.

Francesca slowly dragged her eyes up from the phone, her long lashes casting a fan of shadow across her cheeks. "The interview will be conducted shortly. We're asking all witnesses to cooperate."

"I am cooperating, I'm just asking why you've singled us out," Tory pressed.

Francesca ignored her, returning to tapping on her phone.

I shared a look with my sister, fighting an eye roll at this woman's rude behaviour.

The door opened and Francesca looked up again as a tall man in a suit stepped out of the room. "All done, I'm heading over to Ignis House to check out the fire that started in Mr Acrux's room."

My tongue felt heavy and I fought the urge to look at Tory as he strode off down the hall.

"Wait here until I call you," Francesca commanded, stepping aside to let the last interviewee out of the room.

My gut took a dramatic dive and my blood ran icily cold as I came face to face with Seth Capella.

His eyebrows jumped up at the sight of Tory and I then a vicious smile cut into his cheeks. He casually lifted a hand, raking it through his long hair, giving me a clear look at the braid of blue hair he'd wrapped around his wrist. *My* hair.

Asshole!

My teeth gritted together as he sauntered toward us and Francesca disappeared into the room.

Tory stepped forward as if to place herself between us but I caught her arm to stop her, glaring at him. His eyes clawed over every inch of my mangled hair and that smile sliced deeper into his cheeks. "Oh shit, did a rogue lawn mower drive over you on your way to class, babe?" Seth mocked as he reached out to touch my butchered locks.

I heated my palm up with burning air and snatched his wrist before he could touch me. He winced, yanking his arm back with a snarl.

"*Hey*," he barked. "You wanna watch yourself, Vega. Next time it might be more than your hair you lose."

"Shouldn't you be off sniffing some dog's ass somewhere, mutt?" Tory asked coolly, placing a hand on her hip.

His eyes whipped to her like a loaded gun. He leaned in, breathing in her scent but not trying to touch her like he usually did. "You think this is all some game, don't you?" he growled, his eyes sharpening. "You're in over your heads and if that last warning wasn't enough for you, you're more stupid than I thought."

"I'm ready for you," Francesca's voice carried from the room.

Tory moved around Seth but as I went to follow he stepped into my path, sliding his hand onto my cheek in an almost loving gesture. I stood my ground, glaring at him, my fingers tingling with magic. But I knew if I tried to fight him he'd easily win. I wasn't a match for him. Not today.

My skin stung where his palm lay but I let him do it, refusing to run.

"I don't like the look of the fire in your eyes, babe," he growled. "Didn't I break you well enough?"

I stepped further into his personal space, my heart racing and my shoulders trembling. "Iron is made stronger in the hottest part of the fire, Seth. You didn't break me, you forged me."

He dropped his hand, his brows pulled together and a strange look entered his eyes as I walked away. My heart rammed into my throat as I darted after Tory and stepped into the room, unable to believe I'd gotten away with that.

All thoughts of Seth were forgotten as I spotted Francesca sitting at a table, her eyes two mossy chasms and her back as straight as a ruler.

"Sit," she ordered and Tory and I took chairs opposite her at the single table in the centre of the classroom.

Francesca pushed a tablet across the table toward us and tapped on the screen. "My name is Agent Sky. You're here because of the death of Professor Ling Astrum on the night of September twentieth. I am aware of your heritage and let me tell you that it means nothing in this room. You are witnesses to a murder and you will produce answers to my questions without fail."

We nodded and I knotted my fingers together under the desk. Even though I knew I hadn't done anything wrong, this woman was making me feel like a criminal. Tory looked more at ease in these surroundings; she'd bluffed her way out of more than one hairy situation with the law so this was a walk in the park for her. But I was not the coolest of cucumbers right then.

"One of you is about to offer me answers and I will give you five seconds to decide who." Francesca gave us a hard stare that made her beautiful face seem cut from stone. She pushed the tablet toward us and I leaned forward to look at the screen, finding all of the Falling Star messages Astrum sent to us.

"I'll do it," Tory blurted.

"Good." Francesca stood up. "That means you just volunteered your sister instead." My throat thickened as she moved around the table and reached towards me.

"What are you doing?" I breathed but she didn't reply. Instead, she pressed her palm flat against my forehead.

A fuzziness filled my mind and I blinked woozily as a strange aura floated over me. I tried to fight it off but it pushed deeper inside me, forcing me away on a dream. For a moment it seemed like Francesca only had one, glaring eye instead of two right at the centre of her forehead. It was a sea of green, drinking me in alongside all of my thoughts and worries. Before I could do anything to clamber my way back out of the hole I'd been sucked into, everything went dark.

"Darcy?" Someone was shaking me and I blinked heavily, finding Tory beside me. My cheek was plastered to the table and a roiling sickness twisted my gut.

"What happened?" I murmured, my thoughts slowly realigning.

Tory helped me sit upright and the horrible after effects of whatever Francesca had done to me finally ebbed away.

"That agent was a Cyclops," she said, looking mildly horrified. "She got in your head and took whatever answers she wanted. Sometimes you spoke about Astrum but I think mostly she just hacked directly into your memories." She frowned as a retch burned its way out of my throat.

I felt completely violated and she hadn't so much as warned me what she'd been going to do.

"She said she saw everything from that night and we're clear of suspicion so I guess that's...good," Tory added, clearly trying to cheer me up.

"Fantastic," I said dryly, rising to my feet.

"Oh and um..." Tory bit her lip as if she didn't want to say any more.

"What?" I urged, sensing she was about to drop a bomb.

"Well you've been passed out for a while. It's been almost twenty minutes since Agent Sky left. Orion sent Tyler here to tell you he can't make your Liaison tonight and well...he took a picture of you with your tongue lolling out and it's all over FaeBook." She said the last part fast like she was ripping off a bandaid and I groaned dramatically.

"I tried to stop him," Tory said half-heartedly. She pointed at the door where a smouldering burn mark was simmering at the top of it. "But I missed..."

"Well we're not under investigation anymore, right?" I said, hunting for the positives.

"Nope. I mentioned the Tarot card Astrum gave us but she didn't seem interested in it. I guess she saw it in your memories anyway. She knows we don't have any more information."

"Well that's something because I don't ever want a Cyclops in my head again."

"Yeah and I don't wanna watch that again either. Her boggly eye was freaking me out."

"How boggly was it exactly?" I started laughing.

"The boggliest eye I've ever seen. She looked like Mike Wasoswki from Monsters Inc."

I fell into fits of giggles and Tory burst out laughing too.

"That actually makes me feel a lot better," I said with a grin.

"Yeah if I emerge as a Cyclops I think I'd have to invest in some seriously big sunglasses to hide that freaky thing," Tory snorted.

We headed toward the door and I adjusted my satchel over my shoulder. I was pretty sure my skin was growing even thicker. Because if detention from Orion, being goaded by Seth Capella and a beautiful Cyclops tunnelling into my head wasn't enough to ruin my day, then what was?

DARIUS

CHAPTER SEVEN

I circled in the darkening clouds, flexing my wings as a cold wind hit my left flank and sent a shudder racing across my scales.

Heat blossomed through my chest, building in pressure to an undeniable crescendo which I released in a burst of fire. It rode on the back of an ear splitting roar, but did little to dispel the simmering rage in my gut.

I circled the sky once more before banking hard and tucking my wings close as I dove towards the roof of the parking lot at the north of the school grounds.

I hit the roof at speed, my claws scraping into the concrete with a satisfying screech of protest.

I withdrew into my Fae form as a figure stepped out of the shadows, shaking off the residual feeling of fire in my limbs and rolling my shoulders back as my bones realigned.

"Took you long enough," Lance muttered irritably as he tossed me a bag of clothes.

I snorted a humourless laugh as I started dressing myself. I was still pretty pissed at him over the whole detention thing but I'd decided to let it drop. We both knew no grudge between us would last and I didn't want to get into it with him.

"Well if *you're* the one telling me I'm late then I really must be. Besides you can blame Roxy Vega, she was out running later than usual and I was following her until she headed back into the House," I said.

"Aww did you have to fly in a few more circles, diddums?" he taunted. I zipped up my fly and he wrinkled his nose. "By the stars I've seen you naked *way* too many times."

"Many women would pay good money to have that problem," I teased, shrugging the shirt on. Not my shirt; his. I had no goddamn clothes left and though Lance was a pretty close fit for me, I didn't enjoy having to rely on charity to dress myself. It was a goddamn travesty.

"I still can't believe my room burnt down. This is the last place I want to be going tonight," I spat.

The unexpected visit to my family's manor wasn't something I was looking forward to but I didn't have much choice. I had already ordered myself a replacement wardrobe but it wasn't so easy to order in the amount of gold I needed to keep my magic replenished. I was too damn powerful to be able to make do with a few trinkets and bits of jewellery. Not that I'd ever had much reason to complain about the depth of my power before now, but this was infuriating. The only place for me to get enough replacement gold quickly was the family vault which meant an impromptu trip home.

"Well I don't exactly relish trips back there either but here we are," Lance said dryly. "Perhaps you can see Xavier while you're home anyway?"

At the mention of my brother, I perked up a little. He hadn't spoken to me in nearly two weeks, my messages had gone unanswered and my parents had refused to hand the phone to him when I spoke with them.

I knew something was going on with him but I wasn't sure what, and if only one good thing came from this trip then I would make sure that it was solving the mystery of why he'd been avoiding me.

"Yeah, it'll be good to see him," I agreed.

I hated leaving him alone in that house while I was away at the Academy. I knew that without me there as a buffer, our father's rages would fall on him more often and that knowledge sent a burning path of guilt through my veins.

Xavier was lucky though; he never got it as bad as me because he wasn't next in line. There wasn't the same pressure on him that I had to endure and so Father's gaze was more often turned my way. Which would certainly be true tonight. I had no doubt that he'd heard about the fire in my room already; things like that didn't stay private in our world. I'd already seen several stories in the local papers and a few pictures too. My classmates were always willing to sell me out for a juicy story and a wad of cash so it was no real surprise but what *was* a surprise was the silence I'd received on the subject since from my father.

Silence with him was highly unlikely to be a good sign. It either meant one of two things; he had bigger issues to deal with right now or he was so mad that he couldn't bear to talk to me at all. Both scenarios ended badly for me. I had no choice but to just press on with my trip to collect more treasure as planned though. It wasn't like this was a social call. And if my father was pissed at me he wouldn't just get over it. I'd have to face his wrath sooner or later regardless.

"You wanna take the highway and race there?" Lance asked, changing the subject and pulling me out of my tailspinning thoughts. We both knew what we were likely to be heading into but there wasn't anything that would change the fact.

"You wanna lose again so soon?" I taunted.

"You cheated last time."

"Overtaking you isn't cheating," I countered.

"It is when you cut me up and you aren't wearing a helmet. You know I can't put your life in danger," he said, rolling his eyes at me as he pressed his thumb to the brand on his arm which linked us to each other.

"Well it's not my fault that you're so obsessed with me," I joked.

"Yeah, maybe tonight's the night I'll finally pluck up the nerve to act on my undying love for you," he mocked, leading the way towards the door which led down into the parking lot.

"I sure hope so," I replied. "All the other girls will be so jealous if I'm the one who finally bags hot Professor Orion."

Lance barked a laugh and punched me in the bicep. I smirked at him in the dark stairwell. It sucked that we couldn't spend as much time together openly as we used to growing up. But since I'd arrived at Zodiac we'd had to downplay our friendship for more reasons than one. The amount of secret meetings we had together would likely make people believe we were having an affair if they ever caught wind of it.

"Actually, we should travel over there together tonight," he said slowly, glancing around like he thought someone might be listening to us. "There are things we should discuss."

"You're probably right," I agreed with a sigh of disappointment. I'd been looking forward to getting out on my bike and racing down the highway with the wind in my hair. I seriously needed some downtime to help me work through a bit of this rage that was eating me up, but we really did need to talk.

"I hear you broke up with the Sphinx," Lance said, opening the door to the parking lot and leading the way towards his car. The top level of the lot was reserved for the Heirs' vehicles and I'd pulled some strings so that he could park his Faerarri up here too.

"Marguerite? I was never officially dating her anyway. And she got... dull." I shrugged dismissively. There wasn't much point in me dating anyone so I never even attempted to have anything serious with any of the girls I was seeing. It was almost certain that I'd end up marrying my pig-ugly second cousin if my father got his way anyway. Not that I intended to let that happen without a fight. Either way, I'd need to find a pure blooded Dragon Shifter as an alternative if I wanted to marry someone else and there were very few of those available in this generation.

Lance unlocked his red sports car and motioned for me to climb in. I dropped into the passenger seat and settled back into the luxurious chair with a sigh.

Lance started the engine and I cast a silencing shield around us to make sure there was absolutely no way anyone could be listening in to our conversation.

"Did the FIB figure out how your room caught alight?" he asked, dropping the subject of my love life quickly in favour of what we really needed to discuss.

"They said it looks like an accident at the moment but they're going to carry out a full investigation before they come to a final conclusion. I did manage to get back in there though and I confirmed what I'd suspected about the draining dagger," I muttered.

"It's gone?" Lance asked worriedly as we took the spiralling ramp down through the centre of the parking lot to the exit.

"Yeah. I melted all of the gold again and sifted through it; the dagger isn't there. And if you're sure the fire couldn't have damaged it-"

"It would take a lot more than a house fire to destroy something that dark," Lance replied. "I don't even think Dragon Fire would do it."

"Well then, it appears we have a thief in our midst." Concern pooled in my gut.

"We can't risk anyone finding out what we've been up to," Lance said, his usual calm facade cracking just a little and letting me know exactly how much shit we were in.

"If someone has broken into my room and found that dagger then we could end up in serious trouble. But whoever it was clearly hasn't handed it over to the FIB or any of the Professors. I'd already be in a jail cell if that was the case. So they either took it to blackmail me or to use it themselves. Either way, we need to get it back."

"Francesca told me the FIB are going to be carrying out room to room searches of all the students' rooms. They think someone's got to be helping the Nymphs get on campus and are hoping to turn out some evidence."

"That's some pretty boring pillow talk, Lance. Maybe you need to work on your game," I teased.

"I haven't had any complaints," he replied with a smirk. "And I don't need advice on that from a kid."

I smiled widely. "I'll look forward to the wedding invite then."

He scoffed dismissively. "She's a Capricorn, we clash more often than we agree on anything. She's too stuck in her ways to work with me long term. We both know that's how it is and it's not an issue."

"Sounds just like all of my relationships whether we're compatible or not," I muttered. "Anyway, if the FIB conduct a search, that's not a good thing, is it? If they find that dagger, they'll trace it back to me."

"They need a teacher to assist them because the students are minors - I could volunteer to help. I'd be able to sense the dagger if I got close enough to it."

I grinned at the less than enthusiastic tone to his voice.

"What would I do without you?" I asked.

"Take more of your own beatings from your father for a start," he replied.

The smile fell from my face at that comment and I turned away to look out of the window instead of responding.

The silence stretched between us and Lance sighed dramatically.

"Forget I said that. You know I don't blame you for it."

"Doesn't make it any less true though, does it?" I asked.

I felt guilty enough that I had to drag him away from his life every time I had to go home and knowing that I was putting him closer to my father's rage only compounded my guilt. But if I showed up at home without Lance in tow,

Father would punish us both mercilessly for it.

His job was to protect me from any possible threats and Father seemed to think he'd have trouble doing that if we weren't within at least a mile of each other at all times. Not that we stuck to that rule when he wasn't around to check up on us but the damn bond certainly wanted us to.

I'd once gone to Northern Terania for a long weekend with a girl I'd been seeing at the time and had spent the whole vacation pining for him because of the distance between us. I'd ended up flying back to him in my Dragon form in the middle of the third night, leaving the girl there and effectively ending that relationship. I'd found him blind drunk in his apartment after he'd tried to drink away his longing for me and I'd ended up staying there for two nights in his bed. The damn bond was twisted and humiliating sometimes. Thankfully we'd managed to resist the temptation to spoon each other. And we hadn't spoken about it since. We hadn't risked going too far from each other after that though either.

The only exception to that weird rule seemed to be when Lance had travelled to the mortal world to collect the Vega Twins. It was like the bond couldn't sense that distance at all and for once I hadn't even been aware of the link connecting us. But as neither of us had the slightest desire to spend any extended time with the mortals, it didn't exactly help us.

"Perhaps the next time we try to break the bond it'll work," Lance suggested halfheartedly. It hadn't worked any of the other times we'd tried though.

The fact was that my father's magic was too strong and we weren't powerful enough to sever it. We kept hoping that that would change and I'd be able to free him from his bond to me but it never worked. As far as I could tell, Lance would be stuck protecting me for the rest of our lives and there was nothing we'd be able to do to free either of us from our connection.

I ran a thumb over the mark of his star sign on my forearm for a moment as I considered everything he'd lost for my father's desires. It wasn't like I would have wanted anyone else to be in his position; Lance was practically a brother to me, I more than trusted him with my life. But I never would have stolen his life from him like this to bind him to mine.

Eventually we made it to the outskirts of my family's property and Lance guided the car off of the road and onto the long drive. I nodded to the guards at the gate and they opened it for us. It took another ten minutes for us to make it up the drive to the sprawling manor. Lance guided his car into the underground garage and parked it at the end of the line of my family's vehicles. We exited into the echoing space and walked past the gleaming sports cars, immaculate four wheel drives and my own collection of motorbikes.

Silence fell between us as the weight of this place crashed over us. Most people enjoyed going home. I preferred being pretty much anywhere else.

We headed up the stairs into the main house and found my mother waiting for us in the atrium which was heavily decorated with golden ornaments. I could already feel my power replenishing itself just by standing in this house.

"How lovely of you both to visit," Mother cooed, not mentioning the reason for us coming here. She obviously knew but she didn't like to waste time discussing anything too interesting. She was a vapid creature, happy to amuse herself with pretty, petty things and leave the conniving to my father.

Her dark hair was perfectly styled as usual, swept into a neat bun at the base of her neck. She wore a deep purple dress which was so low cut that I squirmed uncomfortably as she pulled Lance into a hug, pressing her chest against him. He threw me a bemused expression over her shoulder and I grimaced in return. She descended on me next, enveloping me in a cloud of floral perfume as she air kissed me to avoid smudging her lipstick.

"I've missed you, Mother," I said, which was true in a sense; I missed the idea of having a mother who could be more than just a walking talking mannequin but I'd long since stopped worrying myself over it.

"Darius, darling, the house is so quiet with you gone," she said and I got the feeling that she meant that as a good thing. "Your father is just on a business call but he'll find you before dinner."

"Perfect," I said, my heart sinking. For the tiniest of moments I'd hoped that his absence might have meant he was stuck in the city at a meeting or something and I could avoid seeing him tonight. I was never that lucky though. "Is Xavier around?"

For a moment I could have sworn Mother's gaze darkened at the mention of my younger brother's name but she painted on a smile quickly enough that I couldn't be sure.

"He's been a little under the weather. Perhaps it would be best if you left him in peace tonight," she said smoothly.

I frowned. Xavier was the only member of this household who I actually *wanted* to see. There was no way I'd miss the chance to visit him while I was home, especially as he'd been weirdly silent in response to my calls and messages the last few weeks.

"I'll check in on him while I'm here," I said firmly.

Mother opened her mouth like she might object then shrugged dismissively. "I'm sure you'll do exactly as you please, no matter what I have to say on the subject. Lance, won't you join me for a glass of wine before dinner? I've hardly seen you recently."

"I'd be delighted, Aunt," Lance replied, letting her lead him towards the lounge. She wasn't really his aunt but our families always insisted on us addressing each other like we were related. It was an age-old tradition. The Orions and Acruxes were bound by more than the stars. We were bound by power and greed, our families' gifts used for each other's benefit.

I turned away from them and hurried up the stairs. If something was going on with Xavier then my best chance of getting to the bottom of it would be by talking to him alone before our father finished his call.

I strode down the second floor hallway into the east wing and passed my father's office. His voice carried to me and I hesitated a moment to try and gauge how long he might be occupied with the call.

"-told you what my decision is on this. I believe they could be of use in something very delicate so I want you to divert your attention from them for now. I'll make my move on that front when the timing is right."

I wondered vaguely who he had in his sights now but I wasn't foolish enough to hang around outside his office eavesdropping. If he caught me doing that he'd whip me bloody.

I passed further down the corridor, skirting the library before heading up the rear stairs to the east tower where Xavier's rooms kept company with mine.

I reached his bedroom door and rapped my knuckles against it loudly. I waited three seconds for a response before opening the door anyway.

My hand slipped on the door handle and I frowned down at my fingers as something gritty clung to them. Glitter caught the light, shining in a rainbow of colours across my skin as I looked at it in confusion.

"I'm surprised they let you come and see me," Xavier's voice came from the depths of his room and I moved inside, kicking the door shut behind me. The room was dark and I could hardly even see him in the wing-backed chair by the window.

"I'm a Celestial Heir; no one *lets* me do anything," I joked, because we both knew I was still firmly crushed beneath Father's thumb. At least as far as he knew; I'd been doing whatever I could to undermine his authority in secret for years now but I still wasn't even close to challenging him publicly.

Xavier scoffed dismissively. "How's school?"

"Fine. What's going on with you?" I asked, refusing to be diverted.

"Gotten rid of the Vega girls yet?" he asked, ignoring me.

"Not yet. Why is it so dark in here? You look like a damn Bond villain lurking in that chair in the shadows." I threw a few orbs of light burning into existence overhead and moved to stand before him.

"It got dark and I didn't see the point of turning on the lights." He shrugged and I frowned at him. Xavier was normally perky to the point of being damn irritating. I couldn't remember the last time I'd seen him without a smile on his face let alone the morose expression he was sporting now. He looked downright depressed and his dark, curly hair was dirty, his clothes dishevelled like he hadn't even showered.

"Tell me what the hell is going on," I demanded.

Xavier looked up at me, his lips parting, his eyes filling with tears. Acrux men didn't cry. Father had beaten that impulse out of us years and years ago.

I dropped down to my knees in front of him, catching his hand between mine. "You can tell me *anything,* Xavier," I said seriously.

He gripped me tightly, looking into my eyes like he was afraid to find a lie hiding there.

"My Order emerged," he breathed and the terror in his voice told me all I needed to about what had happened.

"You're not a Dragon?" I asked, my own voice cracking with fear for him. Father would have been more than furious to discover that his son was anything other than a full blooded Dragon Shifter. It was a matter of pride and respect; he ridiculed families with mixed blood, he believed wholeheartedly in the superiority of our kind. One of his sons being anything other was totally unthinkable.

Xavier shook his head slowly, trying to withdraw his hand from mine as footsteps sounded on the stairs behind me but I refused to release him.

"It doesn't change anything for me," I growled. "You're still my brother, I don't care if you're a Werewolf or a Vampire or a-"

"So he told you, did he?" Father's cold voice came from the doorway behind me and the hairs along the back of my neck stood to attention in warning.

Xavier snatched his hand out of mine, blinking away the evidence of the tears which hadn't even fallen. I stood before him, placing myself between him and Father.

"It doesn't matter," I said firmly, though the simmering rage in my father's eyes told a very different story. "I'm the oldest. I'm the first in line anyway, Xavier never wanted to challenge me for that role so-"

"Yes, I still have my Heir but I've lost the spare. Did he tell you *exactly* what Order he is?" Father snarled, his eyes changing to their Dragon form and a trail of smoke leaving his nostrils. He was so angry about this that he was battling against the urge to shift. I didn't think I'd ever seen him look so close to the edge before.

"Not yet. But surely it's not the end of the world if-"

"Shift," Father commanded, his gaze passing me to land on my brother.

Xavier got out of his chair and backed up, shaking his head in panic. His skin looked odd though, like there was light shining from within it, trying to break free.

"I told you, I'll get control of it; I won't shift *ever,*" he said anxiously. "No one will ever find out that I'm-"

"SHIFT!" Father bellowed, using fear to force the change on him.

Xavier cried out in panic as the light beneath his skin grew to a powerful glow and he bucked forward as his Order form took over.

I backed up as his form changed, giving him room to become-

"Fucking hell," I breathed, my eyes widening in panic.

"My thoughts precisely," Father hissed venomously.

Xavier had transformed into a lilac Pegasus complete with golden horn and rainbow patterned wings. His coat shone with glitter in the light of my magical orbs and his wide, horsey eyes looked back at us fearfully.

I stared at him with my mouth hanging open, scrambling for something, *anything* to say.

"I... didn't know we had any recessive Pegasus genes in the bloodline... maybe he's linked to the constellation," I muttered, unsure what else I could say.

Father hated the weaker, more common Orders. He was a Dragon through and through; he loved power, invoking fear and breathing fire. A Pegasus was about as far as you could get to the opposite end of the Order spectrum. They were flying horses who pooped glitter, granted wishes and were... *cute*. Xavier hadn't even been lucky enough to have a dark coloured coat, it was lilac. *Lilac!*

"I still think we should kill him to cover this up," Father growled and I flinched at the casual way he said it, like murdering his son was a genuine option. "But your mother has finally grown a backbone and won't allow it. She even came up with a backup plan in case I killed her too so that the information about this disaster would be leaked to the press the moment she died. So for now we've contained him here. This is a goddamn disaster. Can you imagine what the other Celestial families would say if they found out about this?"

I wanted to protest on Xavier's behalf but I couldn't think of a damn word to say.

"It's... he's... we can hide it," I said finally, feeling a rush of love toward my mother for finally standing against my father in something. She might have been a poor excuse for a woman but deep down inside she loved her children and this was better proof of that than I ever could have imagined.

"*Hide it?* If he ever expects to be able to wield his magic, he will need to fly in the clouds to replenish it. Even if we gave him stacks of gold and claimed he didn't like to transform for some reason, someone would see him *prancing about* at some point. There's no way we can send him to the Academy next year. I doubt he will ever be safe to leave the house again!"

I shook my head in denial but I was so shocked that I couldn't even think of anything to say to try and help my brother.

Father's hand closed on my shoulder. "I need to talk to you about *your* actions, Darius," he said, turning me away from Xavier. "This problem will have to wait and I can't bear to be in a room with this abomination a moment longer. Think of the shame he could bring to our family!"

Father steered me out of the room and I cast a look back at my brother before the door could close between us again. He shuddered back into his Fae form and crumpled down to the floor, burying his face in his hands.

The door clicked shut and Father dragged me away, leaving that heartbreaking image seared into the backs of my eyelids.

I didn't pay much attention to where we were going until we ended up in his office.

He closed the door and the sound of the lock turning drew me back to the moment as my heart leapt in response.

I made sure my features betrayed nothing of the inner turmoil of my feelings over the discovery of Xavier's Order though. My face was a flat mask, expressionless, patiently awaiting whatever Father had in store for me.

"So." He reached across the desk and swung the monitor there around to face me. Pictures filled the screen, my room on fire, the devastation following the blaze, my face filled with rage, me half-way through losing control of my Order form and leaping out the window as my clothes were shredded off of me. I silently thanked the assholes in Ignis House for leaking these shots to the press and made a vow to track each of them down and punish them for it. I glanced back at my father and spotted the simmering rage in his eyes.

I swallowed a lump in my throat.

"I'm told the FIB think the blaze was likely an accident-"

"I don't give a damn how it started," he hissed. Sometimes I'd have preferred it if he'd just yell at me. "What I care about is my Heir looking like a little fire just ruined his goddamn life. Like he can't even control his Order form when things go wrong."

"I..." I dropped my gaze from his and inspected the carpet by my feet. "You're right, I should have kept my emotions in check. I'd just found out that our efforts on the night of the dance still hadn't been enough to drive the Vegas out of the Academy and then all of my stuff-"

"Those girls are clearly tougher than we expected them to be after being raised in the mortal world. That approach isn't working as effectively as we'd hoped... We may need other ideas about the best way to deal with them."

My mouth fell open in surprise. He'd been hounding me into tormenting the twins. I'd been taking call after call from him to check on our progress with forcing them out. He'd pushed me to go to greater and greater lengths to chase them off. He'd made it clear that the Council saw this as a test of our strength and now they just wanted us to back off?

"Are you telling me to stop tormenting them?" I asked with a frown.

"Of course not. But it seems like you haven't gotten a clear read on them. I want to meet them to figure out exactly what we're dealing with."

I gritted my teeth at the implication that I couldn't manage this on my own.

"I don't understand what you want me to-" I began.

"You don't need to understand," he replied darkly. "You're my Heir not my equal, if I want you to do something then you will. I'm not interested in your questions on my methods."

I bit my tongue against answering back, knowing it wouldn't earn me anything good.

Father released an irritated breath, looking at the photographs on his monitor again. His jaw clenched as he scrutinised them.

"How many times have I taught you the importance of containing your emotions?" he asked quietly and my muscles tensed in anticipation of his next move. I knew what was coming.

The back of his hand collided with my face and I was knocked back a step as my lip split and blood coated my tongue.

I flinched a moment before the next blow landed and he snarled with rage at that minor failure. He closed his fist for the third strike and the force of his punch knocked me back into the bookshelf which stood against the wall and stumbling down to one knee.

The door crashed open and Lance ran in shouting out in anger as my pain called him to my aid through our bond.

Father snarled at him, throwing out a hand as he cast magic to hold him back.

Lance hurled his own magic into action, a powerful wind blasting into the room aimed directly at my Father. Before it could do what he'd intended,

Father summoned his own air magic, catching Lance's power in a net of his own and turning it back against him.

The maelstrom grew flaming talons as it whipped around my friend, slamming his arms down to his sides to immobilise him and halt his magic in its tracks. The flames grew into cords which tightened around Lance, burning through his clothes and searing his flesh as they held him in place.

Lance cried out in pain as he fell to the ground and my Father's magic continued to burn him.

"Stop it!" I yelled from my position crouched on the floor, flames bursting to life in my right hand while a dagger formed out of ice in my left. I got to my feet and took a step towards the man who was responsible for everything bad in my life.

Father turned his steely gaze to me. "Are you sure you're ready to challenge me, *boy?*" he spat dismissively. "Because I'd think long and hard about your next move if I were you."

I glared at him, my gaze flicking to Lance and back again as I struggled with the fire which ached to be set free in my veins and the knowledge that I couldn't win this fight. I wasn't strong enough to face him. Not yet.

I shook my head slightly, lowering my eyes as I extinguished the flames in my palm and the icy dagger spilled through my fingers as nothing more than a puddle of warm water.

It took less than half a second for my father's power to slam into me. I was thrown backwards, tumbling across the floor.

"You goddamn motherfucker!" Lance bellowed at my father's back.

"Sometimes this bond I put on the two of you is such a nuisance," Father snarled in response to his continued insults.

His boot collided with my ribs and the air was forced from my lungs.

I clenched my fists and bit down on the cries of pain which wanted to tear their way out of my throat. I knew each noise I allowed free would only earn me another kick. Another punch.

Lance continued to swear at him as his punishment progressed.

When he was finally done with me, he stepped back and straightened his tie as he healed the wounds on his knuckles. I lay panting on the floor before him, agony searing through my body and the Dragon in me warring beneath my flesh, desperate to escape. I held it in check though; if I transformed he would too and I'd be no better off.

"Clean yourself up before you join us for dinner," Father said coldly as he strode from the room.

He was half way down the corridor before he released Lance from the hold of his magic and my friend cursed as he scrambled towards me.

I dragged myself upright using the edge of the desk and he caught my arm to steady me.

I spat a wad of blood from my mouth and he started healing my wounds without bothering to ask my permission. I knew they hurt him almost as much as they hurt me anyway and he wouldn't take no for an answer.

I didn't look at him while he worked, fixing my gaze on the photographs on my father's computer instead. There was something about that fire that didn't add up. Someone had taken that dagger which meant it was almost certainly set on purpose. They'd come at one of the most powerful Fae in the Academy, hell in the *country*, but *why*? Who would be that stupid? Who would risk my wrath when I caught them? The only people I could even think of who hated me enough to want to come at me like that were the Vegas, but the idea of them striking back at me was ridiculous.

Whoever it was had already marked themselves for the full force of my vengeance. And I was sure as shit going to catch them. When I found out who the fuck had done it, I'd make them pay for the issues they'd caused me in blood and misery.

My fist clenched with determination and anger burned deep in my chest.

"Did I miss any?" Lance asked as he finished healing me.

I shook my head; every injury was gone as if they'd never been there at all. They only ever scarred me in ways that weren't visible.

I glanced at Lance, though I didn't thank him. He didn't want me to. It made things more awkward whenever I tried. The bond forced him to help me when I needed him to whether he'd choose to or not. Though I'd like to think he'd want to regardless, but the fact that his choice in the matter was taken away meant I could never be sure of that.

There were bags beneath his eyes and I could tell his magic was running dangerously low after his altercation with my father and his efforts in healing me.

"Here," I muttered, offering him my wrist.

He hesitated. We'd both agreed not to do this too often; whenever he fed from me it felt like the bond between us sharpened, grew to something more tangible and harder to resist. But he needed blood and I had power to spare in this gold-infested house. Even the door handles were solid gold.

Lance's teeth slid into my flesh and I waited patiently as he took what he needed from me. An ache grew in my chest as he drew my power into him and I had to fight against the urge to pull him closer, to run my hands over his hair - I clenched my teeth.

This bond is so screwed up in so many ways.

"He's getting worse," I muttered. "Something will have to be done soon."

Lance groaned as he forced himself to release me and took a measured step back even though I could tell it was a struggle for him to do so.

"Maybe we should escalate our plans," he said, holding my gaze.

"Yes," I agreed. "Maybe we should."

"If you're ready to push back harder, I can double my efforts in training you. Take it to the next level." His gaze was wary as he suggested it, we both knew that what he was offering was dangerous, possibly even deadly.

But if I wanted any chance of facing my father and winning then I needed every advantage I could get.

I squashed the flicker of doubt that rose in me and completely ignored the sliver of fear that trickled through my blood.

"I'm ready," I said firmly. And even if we both knew that might not be the truth, neither of us mentioned the fact. It *was* time we started pushing back harder.

"We will need to be particularly cautious with the FIB on campus," Lance warned. If we were caught then we both knew that even my family name might not be enough to protect us from the consequences.

I nodded firmly but didn't back down. "I know. But it's time we did this."

Lance offered me a dark smile. "Then as soon as we get back, we'll begin."

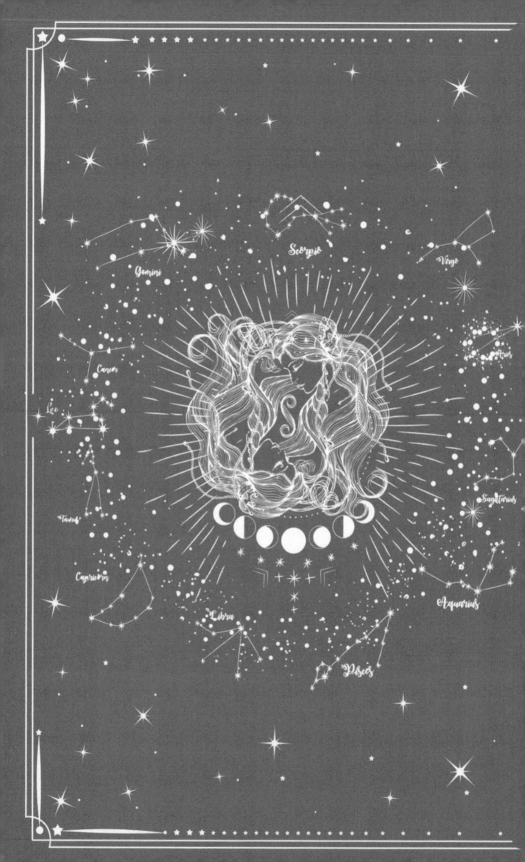

TORY

CHAPTER EIGHT

I stood in the locker rooms outside our Water Elemental class with my bathing suit clenched in my fist as I tried to stop my limbs from trembling. Darcy was watching me from the corner of her eyes as she got herself changed into the skimpy outfit required for the class but she didn't say anything. She knew I was trying to work through this on my own but I wasn't totally sure if I could.

I kept hearing the sound of water rushing in my ears, imagining a ceiling of ice forming above my head, my lungs were burning for air but my next breath would be the end of me...

Darius and Max had prowled into class ahead of us and I knew the two of them would be waiting out there once I left this room. I wanted to believe I was strong enough to face them, but in all honesty I wasn't sure if I was.

The last time I'd been near a large body of water with the Heirs close by it had almost been the end of me. And while Orion's reaction and punishment had reassured me that they weren't allowed to murder me, I wasn't sure what else was off the cards.

The locker room emptied out until only my sister and I were left.

"I could tell Washer you're not feeling well," Darcy said softly. "And you can just go back to your room while-"

"Run away?" I asked hopelessly. "And what about the next lesson? Or the next? Do I stop running at some point or just give up any hope of learning water magic at all?"

"Maybe there's a class you could take without the Heirs-"

I shook my head fiercely. I couldn't do it. If one thing terrified me more than heading out into that class then it was running away from it. Because if I backed down now then I might as well admit they'd won. And if I was beaten then I'd never come back from it.

"I'm going to walk out there with my head held high and show those assholes that you can't break a Vega," I said, determination lacing my tone.

"Hell yeah you are," Darcy said with a grin.

I stripped out of my uniform before my nerves got the chance to change my mind again and pulled on the bathing suit.

I took a deep breath and gave Darcy a nod as we walked toward the door. If she could face the school with her hair hacked to bits then I could take part in a lesson by a pool with a couple of douchebags.

I stepped out into the beautiful hidden lagoon where our lessons were held and kept my chin high as I strode towards the students gathered around Washer.

My throat tightened as the warm water lapped over my feet but I ignored it, refusing to so much as slow my pace.

"Cutting it fine, Little Vegas," Max Rigel called as soon as he spotted us. His dark skin was mostly concealed by the navy scales of his Siren form and it gave him a kind of unearthly beauty, but it also highlighted the fact that he was a beast for all the world to see. "I was beginning to think you weren't going to show for some reason."

A few girls tittered.

"Now, now," Professor Washer chided. "No need to start teasing the lovely ladies the moment they show up." He grinned at us before slapping Max on the ass in the weirdest display of teacher discipline I'd ever seen. Max flinched away from him and Darius barked a laugh at his expense.

I couldn't help but release a laugh in response too. But it quickly died as Washer strode towards us in a pair of green Speedos so tight that I could see every detail of his anatomy clearer than I could have if he'd been nude.

"Ten points to Ignis for being willing to get wet with me after your little incident the other night, Miss Vega," Washer purred, throwing me a wink.

I tried to smile gratefully but in all honesty I was having trouble stopping myself from throwing up all over my bare feet.

Darius was eyeing me with way too much interest for my liking, his inked arms folded over his muscular chest.

"He looks like an angry bouncer who's seen way too many fake IDs," Darcy whispered in my ear and I couldn't help but smirk.

I wanted to glare right back at Darius but I settled for keeping my chin high and ignoring his existence.

Washer moved around the class, giving instructions to different students on what he wanted them to work on today. My heart sank as he headed away from us and the Heirs approached.

The water lapping around my knees started to grow colder as they closed in on us and I took half a step back as the surface began to freeze over.

Fire magic flared in my veins as panic threatened to come for me and the water closest to me hissed and sizzled as it boiled.

"It's getting chilly around here," Max purred as he stalked closer, the ice thickening.

I looked up at them, drawing a little closer to Darcy but refusing to back away.

I exchanged a look with my sister which said we were in this together even if that might not be enough to save our asses.

But before Darius and Max could make it to us, Geraldine approached, striding through the water, her face set with determination. At her side was a pretty, dark haired girl with a fierce look in her eyes and her fingers curling into fists. The two of them had *Ass* badges pinned to their skimpy bathing suits which was quite impressive considering the lack of room in the things; I was surprised they hadn't speared a nipple when pinning them on.

"Your majesties!" Geraldine called as if she hadn't even noticed the two Heirs closing in on their prey. "Good golly, I just realised the darndest thing: neither of you have seen my Order form!"

"Err, what?" Darcy asked with a frown.

I wasn't sure whether it was safe to turn my back on Max and Darius so I only spared Geraldine a glance which was enough to give me a view of her large breasts as she yanked her bathing suit down.

"This is Angelica, the latest member of the Almighty Sovereign Society," Geraldine said just as Angelica started to strip too. I offered Angelica a smile but Geraldine ploughed on before we could exchange words. "And her Order form is equally impressive in the water. Professor Washer agreed that it would be educational for you to spend this lesson with us so that you can see how some of the most powerful Orders adapt their powers to the water."

"I'm not actually sure what your Order is, Geraldine," I admitted.

"She's a great big guard dog," Max said dismissively but I noticed that he'd stopped his advance on us and his eyes were glued to Geraldine who was now fully nude.

"A guard dog with poisonous teeth which can kill even the strongest of Fae in less than fifteen minutes," Geraldine said in a matter of fact tone which couldn't really be counted as a threat but still made Max's frown deepen.

"And my bastard cousin is a smaller version of the king of beasts," Darius added, throwing Angelica a dismissive look.

"My mother may have been foolish enough to engage in an affair with your uncle," Angelica replied coolly. "But I don't think I've ever heard you call me *cousin* before, Darius. And I see no need for you to start recognising my existence now."

"Well if you'd rather throw your lot in with the Vegas then my family were obviously right to ignore your relationship to us," he replied.

Angelica smiled and I gasped as her teeth lengthened and sharpened. She dropped her bathing suit at her feet and lunged forward, transforming into a glimmering red dragon before releasing a roar which made the water shudder around my feet. She was much smaller than Darius's Dragon form, about the size of a large horse, but the delicate beauty of her reptilian body still took my breath away.

"It will be my unwavering pleasure to guard you in my Order form for this lesson, majesties." Geraldine bowed to us, pointing her bare ass at the Heirs before the transformation ripped through her.

I lurched back a step as her body expanded and two more heads grew from her shoulders, complete with shining white fangs which no doubt held that poison she'd mentioned.

Holy crap on a cornflake.

The three headed dog which was Geraldine was almost as big as a goddamn elephant and I craned my head back to look up at her in astonishment.

Three huge pairs of jaws bared three sets of fangs and she growled low in the back of her three throats.

I looked beyond her to the Heirs and found the two of them striding away. They didn't seem to be in a particular hurry but they'd obviously decided that it wasn't worth facing off with a Cerberus and a Dragon to get to us.

"Holy shit, Geraldine," I muttered as I looked over her brindle coat in astonishment. "Who knew you were a straight up badass underneath the sweet raisin bran exterior?"

Cerberus Geraldine tilted her three huge heads like a happy puppy and wagged her tail in response to my words before striding out into the deeper water with Dragon Angelica at her side.

"Wow," Darcy breathed as we moved after them and I found my panic over this lesson had been driven away.

I couldn't say we'd ever really done anything to earn such unwavering loyalty from the A.S.S. but in that moment, I swore never to take them for granted ever again.

I woke in the middle of the night to the sound of music flowing through the walls and winding its way into my skull. I shook my head to clear it as the eerie tune continued on. It was hauntingly beautiful and yet achingly sad at the same time. Something about it set my heart racing. It was unlike anything I'd ever heard before and I couldn't even begin to imagine what kind of instrument could play such a tune. No. It wasn't an instrument; it was a voice. But instead of a voice which would give words to the world, this felt like the voice of a soul.

As soon as the idea entered my mind I tried to dismiss it. The voice of a soul? That was insane. And how would I have the faintest idea of what that would sound like anyway?

I shook my head, trying to clear it of the strange thought and the endless music.

I lay back down again, closing my eyes with every intention to go back to sleep but before I knew it, I found myself on my feet.

I walked for the door and paused with my fingertips on the handle.

What's going on? Why am I trying to head outside in the middle of the night?

The song wound around me again, my heartbeat seeming to find a rhythm with it.

I placed my hands over my ears to block it out but somehow it sounded even louder than before.

A small piece of me was aware that I should be terrified of whatever new magic this was. Someone was casting a spell on me. But I didn't feel afraid; I felt eager to follow the music and find out where it led.

I was only wearing a pair of dark green silk shorts and a matching cami but it had been a fairly warm day so I hoped it wouldn't be too cold outside even though it was the middle of the night.

I caught a grey hoodie from the hook by the door just in case and pushed my feet into my sneakers. It was all I could manage before the song nudged me out of the door.

A smile was tugging at my lips but I wasn't sure why.

I headed along the corridor outside my room and down the stairs into the Ignis House common room as I pushed my arms into the hoodie and left the zip open. One senior had fallen asleep studying at a desk in the corner but no one else was up at this hour. The fires still burned of course, lighting the room enough to see by and I crossed the space quickly.

My heart continued to pound to the rhythm of the song and as I stepped out into the night, it grew even louder.

Why is no one else awake? Surely they can hear it too...

I picked up my pace, following the music into the dark. It was pitch black out here and cold too but I knew exactly where I was going - even though I didn't actually have a clue. My feet kept moving to the lulling rhythm of the music and I was powerless to resist following it wherever it led.

I still wasn't afraid. Was that a part of this magic? To keep me quiet and subdued while the song led me... where exactly? I didn't know. But I was going to follow this trail until I found out.

I passed The Orb which glimmered a little in the starlight and turned west into Water Territory. I'd never been out here at night and the sound of water running all around me in brooks and streams stirred up memories of my fears. Of drowning in that car. Of drowning in the pool while the Heirs all watched...

Even though those memories surfaced at the sound of the water around me, I still didn't react in any way. My heart kept thumping to the rhythm of the music. My feet kept treading the path it led me down.

I was afraid but I wasn't. I was trapped but willing.

Suddenly my feet veered off of the path and I pushed my way through a trailing swathe of mossy vines. I found myself in a clearing surrounded by curtains of creepers filled with white flowers which were in full bloom despite it being night.

In the centre of the clearing, moonlight shone down on a large rock, highlighting a figure sitting on top of it. He had his back to me but I could pick out shimmering scales which lined his flesh. A prickle of recognition flooded me and I inhaled sharply, sensing a noose closing around my neck. I'd just walked straight into a trap and the hairs along my arms rose as I felt a cage of magic springing to life around me.

The song stopped abruptly and the Siren on the rock turned to look down at me. Max's dark features fell from relieved into a scowl the second his gaze landed on me in my open hoodie and silk pyjamas.

"Oh for the love of everything that's destined," he growled. "Why the hell did it have to be *you*?"

"Why the hell did *what* have to be me?" I demanded, folding my arms and holding his eye despite the fear licking down my spine. "And why the hell am I here?"

Max scowled at me for a moment that stretched so long I shifted my weight onto my other foot.

When he continued to uphold the silence I decided to make a break for it. I turned my back on him and made to push my way out of the clearing. But when I did, my hand met with a solid force instead of sinking into the curtain of vines.

Max sighed loudly and I spun back to face him.

"Let me go," I demanded as coolly as I could manage. The last time he'd had me at his mercy he'd tried to drown me and the dark blue scales which lined his exposed body only reminded me of his affinity to water.

"It's like I've summoned a goddamn mortal," he cursed.

"What?"

"You *can't* go. Not until you've kissed me," Max said, using a tone which suggested I was stupid.

"What the hell are you even talking about? I would sooner kiss a horse's ass. Let me out of here," I snapped.

"That's not up to me. You were drawn here by my Siren song so you have to kiss me if you want to go. I don't control it. It picks someone who the magic thinks needs to feel my power. For some unknown reason, it picked *you."*

"Why would I believe anything you say?" I demanded.

"Well you can't leave, can you? And neither can I. And no offence, little Vega but I can find girls who want to kiss me easily enough without resorting to something this elaborate. This is part of what my Order does. When the stars align right we're compelled to release our song and wait for the arrival of the person destined to hear it. I don't get any say in who that is, *obviously.* And neither of us can leave until we get this over with."

"Why would your power require me to kiss you?" I demanded.

"Because when you hear the call of a Siren you have no choice but to answer it. You're Song-Spelled. And when you follow the song, you have to kiss me. For the duration of that kiss, my power will be reversed so that instead of me feeding on your emotions, you'll feed on mine. And believe me, I couldn't think of anyone I'd less like to give a peek into my mind. But here we are." Max raised his eyebrows at me expectantly and I couldn't help but believe him. There wasn't any other explanation for the song that had led me here and as far as I could tell, there was no trap waiting to be sprung.

I pursed my lips, trying to think of some way out of this. I pushed my hand against the barrier beside me hopefully but it was just as solid as before.

No such luck there then.

"This is ridiculous," I muttered, taking a step towards him. "A few weeks ago I was hanging around a biker bar and trying to figure out how to keep me and Darcy fed this winter. Now I'm in a freaking magic school looking at a Siren on a rock who lured me out of bed in the middle of the night with a pretty song like a goddamn pied piper for sleeping women."

"Well if it makes you feel any better, sitting on a rock isn't all it's cracked up to be either," Max replied dryly. "My ass is cold and numb - you took your damn time in coming here."

I rolled my eyes. I was the one who'd been 'Song-Spelled' out of my bed in the middle of the night and had traipsed half way across the school grounds in the dark.

"Well I'm not forcing you to sit on a rock," I replied.

"That's kinda how it goes though isn't it? Siren sits on a rock and lures unwitting people to them."

"I think you mean victims," I said, remembering the stories from Sinbad the sailor where the Sirens lured men to them and drowned them.

"They outlawed Sirens killing the Song-Spelled over a century ago," Max said in a tone that suggested he thought I was stupid. "But I can imagine why so many Sirens killed those who they kissed; they didn't want their *victims* as you call them running off with all of their secrets."

"So I'm going to learn your secrets, am I?" I asked, wondering what the hell kind of depraved things Max Rigel kept locked up in his mind.

"I'm too powerful for that," he assured me. "But a less powerful Siren might lose control of the flow of their thoughts and feelings if they kissed someone stronger than them. They might feel compelled to murder to protect themselves if that happened."

"Lovely," I said, my tone flat. I hadn't thought that I would be able to dislike the Siren Order any more than I did already but it had happened.

"Shall we do this then?" Max asked, standing and hopping down from the rock to land before me.

He was only covered by a small pair of swimming trunks and his navy blue scales concealed the flesh from his ankles to his wrists and neck, leaving only his face, hands and feet clear of them.

He stepped towards me and I held up a hand to halt him.

"You seriously expect me to kiss you?" I asked. After all the horrendous things he'd done to me and my sister since we'd arrived at this academy I couldn't think of many things I'd like to do less.

"Unless staying trapped here alone with me for the rest of time is preferable?" he asked, seeming unimpressed with how reluctant I was.

I glared at him as I weighed up my options. Both choices seemed equally awful but if he was telling the truth then I'd have to kiss him eventually either way. We couldn't stay here forever.

"On the lips?" I checked, hoping for a way out.

"No, on my ass," he joked. "Want me to bend over?"

"That might be preferable to your face," I deadpanned.

"Come on," he said, moving closer again, clearly wanting this over with.

"Just wait!" I insisted, raising my hand a bit higher, he was almost close enough to touch and I could feel the warmth of his body radiating half an inch from my outstretched palm.

"What for?"

"Can you *not* talk for a few minutes?" I asked.

"Why?"

"Because if you shut up, then I can try and focus on your looks and forget about the personality that goes with them," I said. It didn't matter that I was admitting I found him attractive, it wasn't like I desired him no matter how gorgeous he was; the beast inside was easily enough to repulse me. And he knew what he looked like anyway.

Max scowled at me but did as I requested and stayed silent.

My gaze swept over his handsome features, strong brow and deep eyes. He was captivating and all masculine; the scent of the sea washed toward me from his skin and his scales hugged every contour of his toned abdomen. Yeah, if I could forget the asshole that lived within his flesh then I could summon up the motivation to kiss him without puking.

I dropped my hand. Released a breath. Stepped forward.

Max moved too until the space dividing us was almost gone.

"If this is some trick, I'm going to kick you in your scaly balls," I warned.

For half a heartbeat Max actually smirked at me, like he'd found that funny and then his mouth was on mine.

I froze, meaning to pull back the moment our lips had brushed against each other's but something wound its way around me and I found myself caught in that moment.

The power of the Siren's Song drew me closer and instead of wanting to pull back, I found myself leaning in.

Max's mouth moved against mine slowly and I gasped as I felt a sliver of lust trickling beneath my skin which didn't feel like my own. It was quickly followed by an image of me from a few minutes ago when Max had first seen me in the clearing. He'd looked over my silky pyjamas, noticing the curves of my body and the way my flesh was exposed. The moonlight shone on my dark hair making it look like a spill of ink and he was filled with irritation and a little anger, countered by the strange desire to take this kiss from me.

I flinched internally at the tide of his emotions as they danced across my mind. It disoriented me and for a moment, I felt like I was falling. I reached out, my hand landing on the firm line of his hip as I tried to steady myself.

My touch ignited a flare of lust in him which washed into me again and lit a fire of excitement in my veins. This was wrong. I should have been pulling away from him but his hands caught my waist and he dragged me against him instead, cementing the connection between us.

A soft moan escaped me as his kiss deepened and his lust fed into mine, creating a whirlwind of it which I couldn't escape. He pushed his tongue into my mouth and I tasted salt water as I devoured his kiss.

A small voice in the back of my head was shouting at me to remember what he was and as I focused on it, I drew on the well of power within me to help me resist him.

But instead of doing what I wanted, it flung me further into his psyche, beyond the lust he'd been allowing me to see and into the untold corners of his mind.

He kissed me harder, his grip on me tightening as my hands travelled up his broad chest, the scales silky smooth beneath my palms.

I was vaguely aware of him trying to push things away from me but it was like I'd been handed the key to his mind and everywhere I looked were open doors.

I wondered if this was what he felt when he was feeding on power and emotions from other people. Had he been looking straight into my mind when he'd drawn my greatest fear from me?

The moment that thought crossed my mind, Max gripped me harder; he was kissing me like he would die if he didn't and while one part of me was caught in the heat of his arms and the feeling of his lips against mine, another started to notice flashes of memory.

I could hear a man's voice and I knew it was his father. His tone was kind, understanding while Max was swamped with fear and loss.

"There was nothing anyone could do for her. By the time anybody realised she was sick, it was too late. I don't know why she hid the symptoms from me. I could have done something..."

Max looked up through tear-blurred eyes as the loss of his mother overwhelmed him and saw another woman looking into the room. The corner of her mouth lifted into a sly smile for half a heartbeat and he *knew* that she'd been responsible for causing his mother's death. His stepmother had wanted her gone for as long as he could remember... his mother was a dirty little secret.

What secret?

At my direction, the answer came to me between the taste of his lips and a groan of longing that escaped him.

No one outside of the family had ever known it, but Max was a bastard. His father had married his wife through an arrangement to keep his bloodline pure but he'd been in love with another woman. He'd kept seeing her in secret and had gotten her pregnant before his wife. To cover it up they'd hidden her and his wife had pretended to be pregnant rather than face the scandal. He was still an Heir because his power came from his father's side but if anyone ever found out he was illegitimate they could push for one of his half-siblings to take his place.

His father had always stood firmly beside him but his step-mother was devious and wanted one of her own children on his throne.

I could feel the tension in Max's body but he didn't seem to be able to pull away from me. Instead the heat of his kiss was increasing, his hands moving beneath the hoodie I wore and skimming the flesh at the base of my spine.

I almost drew back, not liking this insight into his mind despite the fact that my body was begging for more of him and my hands had moved behind his neck. But before I could withdraw, I felt a flicker of his fear again. The sensation of his emotions skewing my own sent a shiver down my spine and I couldn't help but wonder why the hell he liked the taste of other people's fear.

Because I know that taking their fear from them makes them happier.

I jolted in surprise at that revelation but I knew it was true. I could feel what he felt and I could see memories of him absorbing fear from others. It wasn't the fear he enjoyed; it was the sense of peace and calm he left them with as he removed it. He only claimed to like the fear itself as a way to seem more intimidating and cover up the fact that he preferred using his power on softer emotions.

I was given a flicker of more memories as he took joy and hope from people too and how that lit him up from the inside. But if he took too much joy from someone it left them sad and he hated that.

My gut squirmed. I was looking into the soul of a monster and I didn't like the fact that I was finding out so many opinion-altering things about him. He was an asshole. Through and through. And I didn't want to feel bad about his mother's murder or sympathetic to the way he fed from people's emotions.

With a wrench of determination, I drew back and broke our kiss.

My lips felt bruised and were tingling from the intensity of it. His eyes burned with desire for a fleeting moment and all I could do was stare at him in utter shock.

What the hell just happened?

He'd been pushing at my clothes, trying to get closer to me as he was lost to the passion of our connection and I could feel the heat of his palm as it splayed across my lower back beneath my cami. My hoodie had been knocked back off of my shoulders and his other hand cupped my cheek. My own fingers were fisted in his mohawk and our bodies were pressed together so that I could feel the hard contours of his muscles against my flesh.

We were both breathing heavily like we'd done a lot more than kissing and I fought to shake off the lust that had grown beneath his touch.

With a shake of my head, I moved my hands to his chest and shoved him back a step as I broke away from him.

"What the hell was that?" I demanded.

Max's hands fell limp at his sides and he looked almost panicked for a moment.

The spell holding me here had gone and I could feel the air moving around us again in a cool breeze but I didn't leave. I wanted answers.

"You just..." Max scowled at me as he sifted through what had just happened and a dark accusation flashed in his eyes. *"Fuck!"* He advanced on me suddenly. I couldn't help but back up a few steps even though I wanted to hold my ground. "Who the hell do you think you are to go poking around in my head?" he demanded.

In the blink of an eye his rage turned to panic and he whirled away from me again.

"You're the one who drew me out here in the middle of the night," I reminded him angrily. "So whatever the hell that was, it's on you!"

He turned back to look at me again, his hand shifting beside him and drawing a stronger wind to rustle through the clearing at his call. I braced for some kind of attack, summoning my own power even though I knew I was outmatched.

"My song has never called anyone more powerful than me before," he muttered, almost to himself. "Hell, there never *was* anyone more powerful than me before... normally I can control what the Song-Spelled get to see of me but you took control..."

"I used your own power on you?" I asked, putting the pieces together.

"What's it going to take for you to keep your mouth shut?" he snarled.

"What's the big deal?" I asked. "Where I come from every other person has a step parent or a single parent, half siblings or a foster family. Why would anyone give a shit about your daddy fooling around?"

"Because the Celestial families don't just marry any old street trash they take a liking to," he growled. "We keep our bloodlines pure and our power intact. Half of our marriages are arranged for us. And my step-mother's family just so happen to be some of the most powerful people in Solaria outside of the Council. Offending them would have massive consequences. Not to mention the fact that my real mother had a Minotaur for a Grandfather."

"A Minotaur?" I frowned at him. "What does that have to do with-"

"Because that means there's a chance that I'm carrying goddamn Minotaur genes! Which could make it a lot harder for me to find a wife. Who wants to risk muddying their blood like that? The Siren Order is much more powerful than-"

"So you're telling me that if you fell in love with a... Medusa or a Pegasus you wouldn't marry them?" I asked with a frown.

Max's lips parted. He stared at me for a long second then released a breath of laughter.

"A fucking Pegasus? Even if I found out I was *Elysian Mates* with a Pegasus I doubt I'd be allowed to consider marrying them! Can you imagine?!" He ran a hand over his face in exasperation.

"What's an Elysian Mate?" I asked with a frown.

"Gah you're so ignorant it kills me! It's like your one true love. Point is I couldn't marry them if they weren't a Siren."

"Well that seems pretty damn stupid," I replied. "What's the point in having all of your power if you can't even have happiness with it?"

Max shook his head. "If you want to go and marry a Cyclops then please be my guest. I would love to see you weaken your claim like that. It would make things even easier for us."

"No one will be having any say in who I marry," I replied scathingly. "If I fall in love with a Cyclops or a Pegasus or even a damn mortal, then I'll be with them regardless."

"You're an idiot," he said, looking up at the sky. "But I couldn't give two shits what you do with your love life anyway. Go back to the mortal world and marry Big Bird for all I care. It'll make things a lot easier for us anyway."

"Well I'd sooner choose happiness over worrying about a stupid scandal," I bit back. And Big Bird sounded like a much better option than a lot of the assholes in this school anyway.

"If anyone finds out about my parentage, it will cause a hell of a lot more than just some *scandal,*" Max replied. "It could cause a divide amongst our supporters. It could tear a hole in the foundation of our government and leave us vulnerable right as the Nymphs are gaining power. Why do you think my step-mother has never told anyone? In public she acts like the doting mother she should be but behind closed doors she plots my downfall. If something were to happen to me then my half sister Ellis would be the Heir. That's what she's hoping for, but my father stands in her way."

He said the words so matter of factly that I almost felt a hint of pity for him. But then I remembered what a dickwad he was and quickly squashed that thought.

"Fine. Whatever," I said. "I couldn't care less about your mommy issues anyway."

"No one knows about this," he said, his voice low. *"No one."*

"Not even the other Heirs?" I asked in surprise.

Max clenched his jaw which was confirmation enough. This really must have been a big secret if he'd even kept it from them.

"Fine," I said, taking a step back. "I'll keep your dirty little secret."

"Just like that?" he asked disbelievingly.

"Unlike *you*, I don't take pleasure in causing other people pain," I replied. "Just don't go serenading me out of my bed again any time soon."

I gathered the hoodie closer around me and headed out of the clearing. Max didn't follow and relief flooded me as I made my way back to Ignis House as quickly as I could.

That encounter had been weird as hell and I was just glad it was over.

DARCY

CHAPTER NINE

Tory's run-in with Max last night was all we could talk about over breakfast. He might have been a total asshole, but that Siren song thing was kinda screwed up. And though we may have had his deepest fear in our grip now, we weren't gonna stoop to his level and exploit it. Besides, the knowledge that Tory knew his darkest secret was probably enough to torture him psychologically.

When the bell rang, I headed to Tarot with Tory, Sofia and Diego, my gut knotting over revisiting Astrum's classroom. The stark reminder of his violent death made my neck prickle as we passed by the patch of ground where he'd been found. It had now been covered with wildflowers by someone with the Element of earth and I supposed that meant the FIB had taken whatever evidence they needed from the area.

We soon arrived in Mercury Chambers and as we filed down the gloomy staircase to the classroom, Kylie's voice carried to me from behind. "You'd think she'd just shave it off. Every time I see that ugly bald patch I'm tempted to do it for her."

I clenched my jaw, determinedly ignoring her and giving Tory a shake of the head. When she flexed her fingers anyway I gave her a look that said *she's not worth it.*

"Do you think she knows it's even there?" Jillian whisper-giggled.

"Maybe not," Kylie said loudly. "Hey Darcy!" she called, her voice sugary sweet. I still didn't turn around. "Do you know you're missing a chunk of hair on the back of your head?"

"Now now, settle down."

My blood chilled at the sound of Professor Washer's voice and as the crowd parted ahead of me, I spotted him in Astrum's place at the centre of the Tarot room. The large, circular table ringed around him and though he was thankfully not half naked like he usually was in our Water Elemental Class he still made my skin crawl fully clothed in a white shirt and floral tie. He swept his hazel locks out of his eyes, shooting me a lopsided smile as I dropped into my seat.

He spread his hands on the table before me, lowering his head to speak just to me. "Don't worry about your hair. There's still plenty left to run your fingers through."

I shuddered as he walked away.

"Maybe you *should* shave it off," Tory whispered.

I released a laugh and Washer looked back over his shoulder, glancing between us hopefully as if we'd been checking him out.

Unlikely Professor Pervert.

Washer clapped his hands to get everyone's attention. "Now, although we are all deeply saddened by losing our exceptional Tarot Professor, I have taken on the role temporarily until the Academy hires a replacement. I am not quite as adept at reading the cards as he was, but I assure you I know how to use my hands. So today's lesson will focus on palmistry."

A low current of groans sounded from a few of the girls who were gifted with the Element of Water and I shared the sentiment. Kylie sat up straighter, seemingly unaware of Washer's overly familiar behaviour with his students as she tossed him a bright smile.

He swept a hand over his hair again, making his shirt ride up to reveal the tanned skin beneath.

"Heave," Tory said under her breath, faking a vomit beside me.

I covered my mouth as she continued the act and Washer's eyes slid onto her. "Is everything alright, Miss Vega?" He moved toward her and the brush of his Siren gifts tickled me like feathers against my skin.

Tory drew away, quickly nodding. "I'm fine."

"Good," he purred deeply, but he didn't leave as he reached out to take her hand. "I'll start with a few palmistry demonstrations."

Tory grimaced as she let Washer take her hand and he started painting his finger across the lines on her skin. Her eyes unfocused a little and a dreamy smile pulled at her mouth as she stared at him. I wanted to slap the guy for forcing emotions on my sister. What the hell was wrong with this creep?

"You have quite the exciting taste in lovers, don't you miss Vega?" he purred seductively and a faint frown pulled at Tory's features.

Sofia had explained that the most powerful Sirens could actually look at your memories and apparently Washer was strong enough to peek inside Tory's head. I grimaced at him, prodding Tory in the ribs to try and help her snap out of his hold.

When he drew away and his eyes fell on me, I hurriedly dropped down to rummage in my bag, pretending to search for a pen.

"Your hand, Darcy," Washer encouraged with a devilish note to his tone.

Ergh- no no no.

His influence rushed into me and I felt him stealing away my resistance, replacing it with perfect willing. I stared up at him as I held out my hand and lust dripped through my body, tugging at everything inside me. How could I have thought he was so disgusting just moments ago? His face was so rugged...

his hands so smooth...his skin such a perfect golden hue.

"Your love line tells me there's a forbidden romance in your future," he whispered, his finger circling on a small break in the line on my palm. "A stormy sea is coming, Miss Vega, but you will ride it well."

I sighed softly, but something niggled in the back of my mind. *He's a Siren. And a lecherous pig.*

I shoved back against his influence with all my might, channelling power into my veins and the strength of his hold started to recede. He chuckled, stepping away. "Who's next?"

Diego folded his arms, glaring at Washer with a *stay away* expression but it didn't matter, Washer only had eyes for the muscular guy beside him, leaning in with a predatory grin.

"God," I whispered to Tory. "How does he get away with it?"

"I heard he gets a lot of sway because of his Order," Sofia breathed, leaning past Tory to speak to all of us. "He's allowed to use his powers on us because he needs emotions to regenerate."

"I guess so long as he doesn't actually screw a student that's alright then," Tory said sardonically, pursing her lips. "I'd rather cut off my nose than lay a hand on him or any other teacher in this school for that matter."

"Even Orion?" I blurted before I could stop myself.

Tory looked at me, her eyes widening in surprise. "Yes, *especially* Orion, Darcy. Are you serious?"

"He's just got that you know...brooding thing going on."

"You mean the holier-than-thou assholeness factor?" she asked.

"That's the one. I wouldn't *actually* go there. Obviously." I blew out a laugh, turning to look at the notes on my Atlas to try and hide my blush.

"Teachers wouldn't dare lay a hand on students really," Sofia said quietly. "I read the rule book when I arrived here-"

"Of course you did," Diego chided and she threw him a mischievous grin before going on.

"Any teacher who crossed that line wouldn't just be fired, they'd be power-shamed by the Celestial Council. Stripped of their rank in the whole of Solaria. Can you imagine?" She shuddered and genuine goosebumps raised across her arms.

"Maybe I can, I don't think we could sink much lower," I said with a half shrug.

Sofia shook her head seriously. "No, Darcy, it's worse than you think. The whole Fae world would turn their back on you."

"I'm kinda with Darcy here," Tory piped up. "That sounds very familiar already."

Sofia shook her head again. "Trust me, if you were power-shamed, you wouldn't have a place in this school. You'd have to work your way up from the very bottom, try to earn respect back from even the weakest of Fae-"

"So!" Washer called out to the room, stepping back to the centre of the round desk. "I want you to all pair up, use the notes on your Atlas to do a palm reading of each other's life lines. If you discover you are doomed to die tomorrow, please take your wailing into the hallway where I will come and comfort you."

I turned to Tory, finding the same disgusted expression on her face as was on mine. "I would *rather* die tomorrow than be comforted by Washer in the hallway." I whispered and Tory released a bark of laughter that made Washer look our way hopefully again.

We pointedly ignored him and Tory took my hand, starting to follow the line curving along the top part of my palm.

While she worked, my eyes drifted across the room to the large mural on the opposite wall. The Zodiac constellations were painted beautifully in splashes of silver with swirling names marking each one. Pisces, Aries, Libra, Leo, Capricorn, Taurus. Straight lines linking each star highlighted the shapes they created between them. Whoever had done the mural was incredibly skilled and I wondered vaguely if Astrum had painted it himself. At that thought, my heart weighed heavier in my chest and I looked to Tory with a frown.

"Do you think we'll ever work out what Astrum wanted us to know?"

She kept her eyes on my palm but her brow furrowed deeply as she considered my words. "Probably not."

"*Tory*," I pressed and she looked up with a teasing grin. "Maybe I should show the card to Orion. He might know what it means."

Tory considered that a moment then nodded. "I don't trust him exactly, but after he saved my ass from the Heirs, I've warmed up to him by one-percent."

"Okay, I'll do it."

We studied the life lines a while longer and it seemed like Tory and I didn't have much to worry about in that department, although we had a worrying amount of 'potential deaths' which Washer pointed out could occur at any moment in time. *Good to know.*

"Now, let's mix things up," Washer said keenly. "You will re-pair then interpret your love lines." He started directing people towards different seats and my heart sank dramatically when he paired me with Kylie.

Perfect.

I grabbed my things, moving over to sit in Jillian's vacated chair as she headed over to take mine next to Tory. Kylie leaned away from me like I carried rabies, her upper lip curling back. Her hand shot into the air as she turned to Washer. "Sir! I'd like to re-pair with someone who isn't trying to steal my boyfriend's throne."

"Now now, do be civil, my dear." He looked between us. "You make a lovely pair." My insides churned as he surveyed us too long and I sensed Kylie recoiling from him too.

"Total creep," I whispered when he moved away, hoping to at least make it through the class without this being completely unbearable.

She stared at me for a moment with a tight pout in place, then finally nodded. "Yeah, you got that right." She snatched my hand, turning it over and studying the love line, her nails pinching my skin.

The silence between us became so uncomfortable I simply had to break it. "So you're a Medusa-"

"And?" she went on the defence and I sighed, giving up on this already.

"And I've never seen a girl sprout snakes out of her head, that's all."

"Well I bet you wish you could so they could cover that ghastly bald patch," she said promptly and I scowled darkly, pulling my hand out of her claws.

"Why do you hate me so much?" I whisper-shouted, furious that she continued to treat me this way. Wasn't it enough that I'd had my hair sheared off by her heartless boyfriend? And she'd damn well filmed the whole thing.

"You're a threat to Sethy's throne," she said, her eyes flashing and her shoulders squaring.

"I don't want his throne," I said for what felt like the thousandth time since I'd arrived in Solaria.

"Swap hands," Washer called out and I took Kylie's hand. She reluctantly uncurled her fingers to let me see her palm, but I couldn't concentrate to try and do a reading.

"I thought Fae fought their own fights," I said, staring determinedly at her hand as angry energy burned through my veins.

"I *am* fighting my own fight. I'm fighting to keep his eyes off of you," she blurted, then froze as if she hadn't meant to say it.

I looked up at her, shocked that she would still think Seth gave a damn about me. Or that he ever had. "He pretended to like me, he cut my hair off and you recorded it. How can you possibly think I'm a threat to you?"

She blinked heavily and for a moment I thought she was going to cry. "Because you're beautiful and every time you're in a room he stares at you. And when you're not there he can't stop looking at that disgusting bracelet of hair he made. He wants you to bow to him, but given half a chance he'd have it both ways and have you under his arm too," she said nearly all of it through her teeth and turned bright red as she did so. Tears splashed down her cheeks and I was left in complete and utter shock as she sprang from her seat and ran from the room.

I suddenly noticed how close Washer was standing and felt his power radiating through the air. He'd fed on her pain, her sadness, and drawn it all out for me to hear and him to feast on. Was everyone in this school just hunting for their next goddamn piece of meat?

He hounded after her toward the door and it only took half a second longer for Jillian to sprint after them, calling her name.

My mind reeled from what she'd said and I had to conclude that she was completely deluded.

"Ha! Posted. Kylie's gonna flip." Tyler started laughing as he finished posting something on FaeBook. A tell-tale ping told me I'd been tagged and I took in a breath to ready myself for an impending earthquake as I tapped on the notification on my screen.

Tyler Corbin:
Just witnessed a Major Meltdown after Washer sucked out two truths and a lie from @Kylie Major's mouth.
Truth: @Darcy Vega makes @Seth Capella drool
Truth: We've all seen him sniff the bracelet (no one blames you, bro)
Lie: He wouldn't actually have a Vega Twin under his arm, but he might take one under his sheets once or twice.
#majorfail #suckedbyasiren #majorenvy

"Bastard," I breathed as laughter rang out around the room. I looked up to find Tyler smirking at me while pretending to casually massage out a kink in his shoulder.

Fury crashed through my chest in a wave. "Seth Capella does not-"
Ding!

I glanced down at my screen, discovering that Seth had replied to Tyler's post. And that was saying something as the Heirs rarely ever replied to anyone's posts.

Seth Capella:

FUN game. Let's flip it around and play two lies and one truth @Tyler Corbin.

Your mom was the best lay of my life.

Your dad was the second.

Your face is going through a brick wall the next time I see you.

(hint: both of your parents suck in bed).

My heart pounded out of tune as I sensed the anger behind his words. Tyler turned as white as a sheet as he placed his Atlas down on the desk and stared at it without blinking.

When class was finally dismissed, I was more than glad to make my escape from the room and head back to Aer Tower. The day was finally over and I fully intended on doing nothing but lazing in my room all evening with my friends and practising some Elemental magic.

As we walked along the circular path around The Orb, a notification pinged on my Atlas. I was half tempted to ignore it, sure it would be nothing but another FaeBook post designed to ruin my day. But curiosity got the better of me and I took it out, finding an official message waiting for me.

Your Liaison has been rescheduled for 7pm tonight with Professor Orion.

A small smile crept onto my face and I hid it quickly before the others could see, rearranging my features into disappointment. "Looks like I can't hang out all night. Orion's rescheduled my Liaison."

"You can show him the card," Tory reminded me. "Maybe he'll know something."

"Are you sure that's a good idea?" Diego asked uncertainly.

"He helped them before," Sofia said. "Besides, the worst he could do is dismiss it and then you're in the same position anyway."

"I suppose that's true," Diego said with a shrug, shifting toward Sofia and wrapping his arm around her shoulders. She leaned into him, turning a pastel shade of pink as he ruffled her hair. The two of them hadn't defined things since the formal and I wondered if Diego was ever going to pluck up the courage to officially ask her out.

Tory looped around them to my side, rolling her eyes at their backs. The sun was already low on the horizon and bathing the campus in a dim amber hue. My horoscope had said today was going to be the start of a deep, undying love and I had the feeling it had meant my love for this Academy. It might have been filled with cut-throat Fae and have danger lurking around every corner, but it was also the most wonderful, spell-binding place I'd ever been. And it was starting to feel like home.

Seven pm and Orion was predictably late. I'd even dragged my heels on the way to his office to account for it, but he still hadn't arrived.

I sighed, on the verge of giving up as another few minutes ticked by. The hole I'd cut through his door was now fixed and I wondered if the desk was intact too. I wasn't looking forward to my Saturday detention this weekend. Whatever way Orion disciplined students, I imagined it was no fun at all. *Didn't he once say corporal punishment is totally legal here? Holy shit, I hope it's not that...*

It was almost half past when I gave up, heading back through the corridors of Jupiter Hall with a frown etched into my features. Astrum's card was burning a hole in my pocket and I so longed to ask Orion about it. Amongst other things. And okay, maybe I'd been half a percent eager to see him. I didn't know what it was that drew me to him. He was obviously good looking. Like slap-you-in-the-face hot. He was also a mega asshole most of the time. But those two things tended to be a dangerous combination and I was definitely a sucker for it.

I headed out of the building, following the curving pathway around The Orb, the fresh night air brushing against my skin. I wandered along, soaking in the quiet as I wondered whether the others would still be hanging out in Diego's room like they had been when I left.

"Look who it isn't," Seth's voice hit my ears.

My blood ran cold as I spotted him with Kylie and a group of his wolf pack standing under the light of a lantern. On the floor between them was Tyler Corbin with a bloody face, his nose skewed to one side and his hand raised as he tried to hold off the junior who was cupping flames in his hand.

I halted in my tracks, feeling like a deer in headlights as they spread out across the pathway to stop me from advancing.

Seth moved to the head of the group with a smirk wrapped around his beautiful features. "It *isn't* the queen of Solaria. It *isn't* the object of my affections and it *isn't* a girl with blue hair."

Kylie puffed up her chest at his words and I scowled, my eyes falling on Tyler. He might have brought this on himself but I still pitied him; he was a warthog about to be ripped into by a pack of lions.

"Leave him alone," I told Seth, my hands beginning to shake as fear took a violent hold of me.

"He got what he asked for," Seth snarled. "Just like you did, Vega." His eyes were two frozen lakes and I fought the urge to back up as he took another step toward me.

"Hey wolves?" he called to his pack, jerking his head to beckon them forward.

Kylie stepped aside to let them pass and the group closed in around Seth, nuzzling his arms, his neck. He smiled hungrily at me, pawing at the backs of his friends. "Who wants to go hunting?"

Fear raced through me as the wolves started howling to the sky, cupping their hands around their mouths. Seth stalked forward and in an act of fury, I raised my hands and drew magic to my palms. Fire flickered and I threw all of my energy into it, casting it out of me in a ferocious wave. It tumbled out of control, a huge flame bursting toward them as if it was fuelled by gasoline.

Seth threw up his arms and a glimmering blue shield arced around him and his friends, dissolving the fire as it touched it. I lost sight of them all behind a sheet of smoke, my pounding heart crashing against my ribcage.

A piercing howl tore through the air and Seth's huge white form burst out of the smoke, making me scream in alarm. I fled. It was the only logical thing to do. I wasn't trained. I couldn't fight so many at once, but could I outpace a damn Werewolf?

No chance!

I veered sharply right, the snap of jaws sounding dangerously close to my ear. I sprinted toward the nearest building, half falling into Venus Library and running down the first aisle.

The doors banged open behind me and I cursed as the sound of heavy paws bounded through the cavernous room.

"Mr Capella!" the librarian shrieked. "Take your games outside, there are ancient texts in here that don't need your drool all over them. If you're looking for the Vega girl, she went that way. But please continue your hunt in Fae forms."

I mentally called the librarian a million names under the sun as I hurried to the back of the library. *Continue your hunt? You bitch!*

An emergency exit glowed up ahead and hope beamed through me as I ran toward it, pushing the bar.

An alarm bell rang out and panic tore through me as howls cut the air to shreds.

"In Fae form!" the librarian begged but the rush of paws was all I needed to hear to know they weren't obeying.

I ran out onto the grass, turning left and tearing along into the shadows, half blind as I raced for the cover of the next building. I ran my hand along the back wall of Mars Laboratories, desperately searching for a way in.

"Awoooo! Get her Sethy!" Kylie's voice sailed after me followed by her laughter and I had the feeling she was riding one of the wolves.

My hand scraped nothing but stone and I picked up my pace again, though every second I wasted brought me closer to being caught.

Come on, there must be a way in. Please please.

I wasn't fast enough. And there was no way in. Nowhere to run.

A hand shot out of nowhere and dragged me through a door just up ahead of me. I was plunged into absolute darkness and a scream bit at my throat just before a palm slammed down over my mouth. I was dragged against a hard body as the door clicked quietly closed, my back to their front.

The scent of cinnamon stoked a fire in my belly and I stiffened as I realised who had come to my aid.

"Absolutely silent," he breathed in my ear and I nodded against his hand.

"Look over there," Kylie's voice was muffled beyond the door and my mouth dried up.

I recoiled against Orion, barely breathing as I waited for that door to be found. For the wolves to tear me from his arms and rip me apart. Professor or not, he surely couldn't take on a whole wolf pack if they were determined to sink their teeth into me.

The sound of heavy paws padded loudly beyond the building and my heart beat like a rabbit's in a cage, so loud I feared they'd hear it. Orion probably could with his enhanced senses. But the wolves hadn't found me yet, so that had to be a good thing.

My skin prickled with heat where the press of his chest and stomach met my back. I shut my eyes, willing my thoughts onto why I was hiding and nothing else.

"She's not here," Kylie sighed in frustration. "Try down near Jupiter Hall." The sounds of the pack headed away and the breath fell out of my lungs in a shuddering tumble as Orion removed his palm from my mouth.

The muscles in my legs twitched as I prepared to move but Orion's hand suddenly sailed around my waist and stopped me from stepping forward. My heart beat a forbidden tune and I stilled entirely, frozen in place.

We were flush to each other. And I only realised how intimate this was now that I was no longer in fear for my life. Yet I didn't try to move again and he didn't either. I wasn't sure if I was holding my breath or if the air was simply stuck in my lungs and refusing to come out.

The most rational reason for him holding onto me was that he was about to bite me. He'd saved me from facing an Heir so I guessed I owed him. The other reason though...*oh holy shit the other reason...*

His fingers found my skin between my shirt and waistband and heat weaved a frantic whirlpool through my belly, pushing lower into the deepest regions of my body.

So against the rules.

Must move. But I want to stay.

I felt his breath in my hair, the heat, the desire. My instincts told me he wanted me, but that was pure insanity. I just couldn't come up with any better reasoning though. He made my thoughts hazy and my morals fray. He was my teacher. And I knew he'd lose his job if anyone saw us like this. Maybe more. And maybe I could lose my place at Zodiac too.

Move, Darcy, move!

I turned around, finding my resolve but his arm remained in place so it lay on my back instead. His fingers curled into a ball, keeping me close, not letting me escape. It was dark, but a slit of light was cast from a door further down the hall to our left. Just enough to see by.

If I look up at him, I think I'll burst apart into a million heated fragments.

But if I don't, I'll never see the answer to my question in his eyes.

I forced my gaze up to meet his and felt the spell break, dashed to pieces on the hard look in his eyes. His face morphed into something stony, distant. His throat bobbed and he pushed me firmly back.

"They're gone, so move," he growled, sending a jolt through me at the sudden loudness.

I backed up, staring at him as my anger began to grow. I hadn't done anything. He was the one who'd wrapped his damn arm around me.

You definitely ground your ass against him.

Maybe for one single second but that was it!

"Sir-"

"Don't you dare talk back," he snarled, shoving the door open. "MOVE!"

I scampered out onto the grass, furious with myself, with him. With this stupid academy. With Seth for driving me in here like a fox chased by hounds.

Tears burned my throat, my eyes but no *way* were they gonna fall until I was locked in my room without the chance of anyone seeing them. And even then I knew it would be better if I just swallowed them down, never letting another tear out until one day I choked on them all. A Siren would have had a field day if they found me now, sucking up all this emotion coursing through me.

"Where the hell do you think you're going?" Orion snapped and my spine straightened as I glanced over my shoulder at him as he stood in the doorway. He wore a shirt and smart trousers but his hair was suspiciously damp, speaking of a recent shower.

I raised my hands, giving him a stumped expression, completely baffled by his question. "Er, back to my room?"

"We have a Liaison session to complete."

"Which you didn't show up for," I pointed out, incredulous that he was suddenly acting like I was a misbehaving student. He definitely initiated that ass to crotch hug- *jerk!*

"Pitball practice ran over. And besides, I'm here now aren't I? That counts as showing up." He turned his back on me, heading across the grass in the direction of Jupiter Hall as if he expected me to follow.

"That doesn't count. And what were you doing lurking around the back of Mars Labs anyway?"

He glanced back over his shoulder, cocking an eyebrow at my tone. My heart stuttered but the berating I expected didn't come. "I wasn't lurking, Miss Vega, I came to check out the commotion. Now if you're done questioning me, let's move."

I remained in place, both furious and flustered by his crazy mood swings. "I'm not coming," I hissed, knowing he'd hear me no matter how quietly I said it. I turned in the opposite direction, folding my arms as I marched toward the path, wanting to get back to my room before Seth showed up again.

A blur in my periphery alerted me one second too late as Orion swept me off my feet and tossed me over his shoulder. I yelled in alarm, smashing my hand into his back on instinct. "Let me down! Are you insane?!" I kinda hoped another teacher would hear, but as he marched me onto the pathway under the full light of the lamps, I sensed he didn't have any worries about being seen. But surely this was against the rules?

"Professor Orion put me down this second!" I demanded, my cheeks flaming. At least I'd had the foresight to put some damn jeans on in place of my school skirt. Or this would have been a hundred times more embarrassing right now.

"Good evening, Professor. Having a little trouble with a student?" Principal Nova's voice carried from ahead and my mouth fell open in disbelief.

"Nothing to worry about, just Miss Vega skipping Liaison."

"Well I'm glad to see you rounded her up." Nova tutted, passing us by without a second glance.

I gasped in horror and Orion released a low laugh.

"I'll walk, alright? Just put me down," I ordered.

He didn't say another word until we stepped into his office a couple of minutes later and he dropped me into the seat in front of his desk.

I flattened the choppy ends of my hair which were now sticking up all over the place, shaken to my core. Orion yawned broadly, lowering into his Ottomon on the other side of the desk and casually taking out his Bourbon, pouring himself a glass.

I laced my fingers together to stop them from shaking, staring at him with a mixture of rage, frustration and absolute embarrassment. I wanted to demand he tell me what the hell he was playing at by running his hands all over me five minutes ago and then turning on me like an enemy soldier. But my lips simply wouldn't part. My vocal chords were on lock down so I just stared, waiting for an explanation that I probably wasn't going to get.

Orion sighed contentedly as he drank most of the measure he'd poured then planted the glass down on his desk. "I think it's best we talk about the Nymph situation in Solaria. You were pulled out of class before the end of my lesson the other day so I'll catch you up."

I narrowed my eyes, wondering if maybe he had some sort of personality disorder I wasn't aware of. He'd gone from volcanic hot to glacial cold in the space of five seconds and apparently he'd forgotten all about it.

"Sir..." I started, unsure how to phrase this in a way that was actually going to get a response.

"Miss Vega?" he asked, his expression totally innocent as if he had no idea what I was going to say.

I changed tact at the last second, realising I had another way to approach this. "I thought Fae weren't supposed to intervene in other people's fights."

He scratched his beard then shrugged. "That was a wolf pack. It's different."

"Is it?" I narrowed my eyes. *At least he answered.*

"It's my duty to protect you as your Professor." He said *professor* extra loudly like that was supposed to make a point.

He pushed up his sleeve, his brow wrinkling as he scratched the red tattoo of the Leo sign there. "So Nymphs," he said firmly and I sensed that was the end of my line of inquiries.

I sighed, resigned as I sat back in my seat. Maybe there had been some unbidden connection between us for a moment but rules were rules. And apparently now he was abiding by them.

"Everyone needs to be vigilant on campus. You shouldn't travel around alone. If a Nymph were to absorb the magic of a powerful Fae like you, it could be disastrous for all of Solaria."

Dread inched into my gut. "Surely there's something you can do? Can't you stop them getting on campus?"

"Obviously we have protection spells in place, but how the Nymph got in is still a mystery to the FIB. Which means we can't be sure it won't strike again."

A bead of fear rolled down my spine and I nodded.

"So you and your sister will walk around campus with at least one other student from now on, especially after dark, understand?"

"Sure," I agreed, more than happy to comply. I didn't want to be caught off guard if a Nymph showed up. The idea was terrifying.

He drained the last of his bourbon and checked his watch. "Well, that's the end of the session."

"Are you kidding me?" I breathed.

"It's eight o'clock," he said with a shrug, rising to his feet.

"No – wait." I got up too, reaching into my pocket and pulling out Astrum's card.

He frowned as I placed it down on his desk, my heart juddering madly as I pushed it toward him. "Astrum gave this to me and Tory and I wondered maybe...if you might know what it means. He said you never really saw eye to eye but I don't know, maybe I'm wrong?"

Orion's lips pressed into a sharp line as he fished the card from the desk, examining it. "Astrum never thought much of me and my family," he muttered, mostly to himself.

"Why was that?" I asked gently as his eyes remained fixed on the message inscribed on the card.

"He taught me when I was at Zodiac. He was a royalist and I was outwardly against them. And he hated me because of my own beliefs… amongst other things."

"Oh," I whispered, nodding.

Orion looked up from the card, seemingly dragged out of a daze. He frowned in a way that told me some deep hurt was concealed beneath all of those hard layers he hid behind. He stepped around the desk, holding the card out toward me. "I don't know what this means. And I highly doubt I'm the man he would have wanted you to seek answers from."

He remained close to me as I reached for the card and pulled it from his fingers. "What aren't you saying?" I asked, sure he was holding back on something. A tightness grew in my chest like his mere presence was capable of sucking the air from my lungs.

He leaned in close, his breath a delicious cocktail of bourbon and danger. "There's many things I'm not saying and for good reason. But I'll tell you this… I've spent most of my life hating The Savage King and anyone associated with him too. Including you and your sister when you first came here." His eyes flickered with shadows that threatened to tear me apart. "But I learned a long time ago that blood doesn't define a person, so I shouldn't have judged you so quickly. You're unlucky to bear the title that you do. And I would never bow to either of you for many reasons. But you aren't bad people. That being said…" His eyes travelled down me, the sensation of a zip opening along the line he cast with his eyes. "I will do whatever it takes to ensure Darius and the other Heirs sit on the throne of Solaria. And I urge you to *never* underestimate that vow."

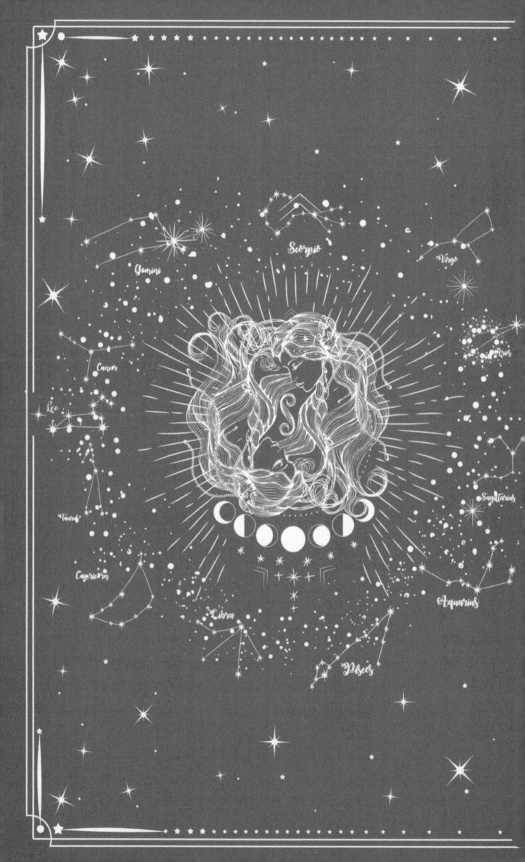

TORY

CHAPTER TEN

I sat in the Ignis common room with Sofia on Thursday evening, practicing my defence against Coercion with varying degrees of effectiveness. I'd basically mastered the art of maintaining a mental shield against attacks while I was concentrating on it. But if I was distracted, she was able to slip commands past my defences. At least she was kind to me; only demanding I draw a line on my arm each time she Coerced me. So far, I had nine lines marking my forearm, one for each time she'd gotten past my guard.

I was trying to keep her commands out while creating ice cubes with my water magic at the same time and concentrating on the two tasks was frustratingly difficult.

I swilled the ice around the glass I was using to contain them, releasing a breath as I tried to focus again. Sofia was trying not to smirk at me and failing. I knew she got a kick out of it every time she got past my defences but I wouldn't begrudge her her fun. Besides, I needed the help and at least she wasn't making me dance on the table or strip for everyone.

The doors opened and I looked around as a group of six FIB agents dressed in black filed into the room alongside Professor Orion.

"Everyone shut up!" he yelled, bringing the room to silence. "As a part of the investigation into Professor Astrum's murder and the fire in Darius Acrux's room, the FIB will be carrying out searches of everyone's rooms. This is not optional. I don't want to hear any whining. You will be docked ten House Points for every complaint that reaches my ears - and I have *exceptional* hearing. None of you are to return to your rooms from this point on until they have been searched. You will remain here in the common room until further notice. Questions?"

Marguerite got to her feet. "Sir, I don't understand why I'm being treated like a-"

Orion cast a gust of wind at her that sent her flying over the back of the couch she'd risen from and crashing onto her ass on the far side of it. A smattering of laughter broke out as she shrieked in surprise.

"Good. No questions then. The agents need to conduct a final check of Mr Acrux's room and then the searches will begin." Orion motioned for the agents to head for the stairs and my mind began to whirl with panic. My heart was thundering an unsteady rhythm in my chest, my palms were slick and a little voice in the back of my head was very unhelpfully screaming *no, no, no, no, no, no!*

If they searched my room they'd find those coins and that dagger. There was no way I could explain having either which didn't involve me being caught out for setting that fire. And death by supremely pissed off Dragon asshole was not what I'd envisioned for my evening. Hell no. I needed a plan. And fast.

"I think we need to try something a bit more motivating," I announced to Sofia, looking away from Orion and the two agents who were still standing in the room as if they didn't interest me in the slightest.

"Oh?"

"Yeah, why don't you Coerce me to drench myself with freezing water and I'll see if I can fight it off?"

"Are you sure?" she asked hesitantly but I could tell she was a little tempted to try.

"Why not?" I said with a smirk which probably covered my panic. Hopefully. "What harm can a little water do anyway?"

Sofia frowned, clearly thinking of what the Heirs had done to me the other night but I smiled encouragingly until she relented.

"Okay then. *Drench yourself with freezing cold water.*"

Her command slid over me and I made no attempt to shield myself from it. My arms instantly lifted into the air and I conjured a torrent of water to slam down over my head.

I leapt up with a shriek in response to the icy kiss of the water and my teeth began to chatter at once. Every head in the room turned my way and I stumbled away from the table we'd been working at as Sofia started babbling apologies. I waved her off, muttering that it was my own fault.

Now for some class A acting skills.

"Holy shit that's s-so cold!" I exclaimed.

"Miss Vega, what the hell is going on over there?" Orion demanded.

I headed straight towards him without hesitation, shivering as the icy water plastered my uniform to my body. The white shirt had turned transparent and a puddle was forming beneath me.

"S-sir, can I please go and get changed?" I asked, giving him an imploring look.

"You command the Element of Fire, I'm sure you can dry yourself out," he said flatly.

Damn.

I nodded slowly. This was about to get a lot more embarrassing, but needs must. I called on my fire magic and let it heat my skin until the water began to steam out of my uniform.

Orion offered me a hard smile that seemed to say *see* and I smiled back before ramping up the power I was exerting. My shirt burst alight first and I shrieked as my long socks followed suit. I held enough control over the flames to stop them from burning me but I screamed like I didn't.

"Oh for the love of the moon!" Orion exclaimed before dousing me in water again with his own magic.

I gasped as my heart lurched with terror for a moment as I found myself at the mercy of someone else's water magic again but Orion stopped the torrent as quickly as it had begun. A hole had burned right through the front of my shirt and the hem of my skirt was a kind of blackened glob of synthetic goo.

"Maybe you should just let her get changed," muttered the agent closest to me. He offered me a friendly smile and I returned it, simpering just a little. Damn I was a good actress when I had to be.

"Fine," Orion snapped, clearly not falling for my damsel in distress act quite so keenly as the agent. "Lead the way, Miss Vega."

He motioned for me to go ahead and I scurried in front of him, heading to my room. I pretended to fumble with the key as we arrived, dropping it to the floor and apologising as Orion sighed impatiently.

"I need to assist with the search, get moving *now*."

"Right. Sorry." I managed to unlock the door and headed in, unhooking my remaining shirt buttons as I went.

Orion moved to follow me inside and I raised an eyebrow at him. "Are you coming in here while I get changed, *sir?*" I asked. My shirt was already unbuttoned and I was guessing him seeing any more of me would be a pretty bad look for a teacher. He narrowed his eyes at me as he stepped back out of my personal space.

"Hurry up," he demanded before closing the door between us.

I ran across the room and lifted my mattress to reveal the coins and dagger I'd taken from Darius's room. I quickly snagged a black sock out of the drawer beside my bed and shoved them all inside it before moving to the window and throwing it open.

I took a deep breath and focused all of my attention onto my magic as I pulled it to the surface of my skin. I called on the power of air and tossed the sock out of the window, catching it on a breeze and guiding it down to the ground outside Ignis House. Next, I drew on the power of earth, aiming all of my attention on the ground around the black sock as I begged everything and anything around it to grow. The brown grass which grew throughout the Fire Territory thickened and grew taller to hide my stash and my thundering heart quieted a little as the sock and its contents were hidden.

As quickly as I could, I wrenched my ruined uniform off of me and changed into a pair of leggings and a grey sweater.

"What's taking so long?" Orion demanded from outside and I jammed my feet into my sneakers.

"Just coming!" I called back.

My gaze caught on the black jacket which still hung on the back of my door from the other night and I grinned as I snatched it into my grasp.

The door opened and I came face to face with a rather angry looking Orion.

"I was just getting this," I explained, holding his jacket out to him.

He frowned at it for a moment before clearly remembering draping it around me after he'd pulled me from the pool the other night.

"So... thanks, I guess," I added as I stepped into the corridor and closed my door again.

Orion took the jacket from me, raising an eyebrow at my tone. "You guess?"

"Well, you dragged me out of the water and all so I'm grateful for that. But you did only give those assholes a few weeks detention for attempted murder... so I'm not exactly falling all over myself with gratitude to you. It's kinda obvious where your loyalties lie." I shrugged as I turned away from him but he moved with his Vampire speed and caught my wrist to stop me.

"You and your sister don't have a lot of friends around here. Maybe you should think a little bit about your attitude if you're wondering why that might be," he warned.

I stepped closer to him, smiling sweetly. "Thanks for the advice, Professor, but we've never needed anybody else to look out for us before so I'm not going to start expecting it now."

I pulled out of his grip then turned away. He let me go but I could tell he was half tempted to say something else. I kept going until I made it back to the common room, concentrating on breathing normally and slowing my heart rate. The last thing I needed was Professor Grouchy Vampire catching onto me before I could retrieve that stash.

The other agents returned from their latest inspection of Darius's destroyed room and the whole group of them including Orion headed upstairs to start searching rooms.

Sofia began working on a Cardinal Magic assignment and I feigned interest in it as I let the seconds tick by. I scrolled through my FaeBook feed, smirking as I noticed a few posts mentioning Caleb Altair's secret Pegasus fetish. Our plans against him were starting to take shape. Sofia had started spreading that little rumour amongst the Pegasus herd and we'd been stoking the flames of it through the A.S.S. whenever the opportunity arose.

Once fifteen minutes had passed, I got to my feet.

"I just realised I have a parcel waiting for me in the Pluto Offices," I said casually. "I might as well go and grab it while I think of it."

"You want me to walk with you?" Sofia offered and I could tell she was a little worried about me wandering around campus alone after what the Heirs had done the other night.

"I'll be fine," I said, waving her back down into her seat. "What's the worst they can do to me anyway?"

Sofia looked at me like she was about to start a list and I shrugged as I headed for the exit.

As soon as I was out of sight I practically sprinted for the door that led out to the Fire Territory, forcing myself to slow my pace once I was outside again. I skirted Ignis House as casually as I could, wandering off of the path to the area of land around the back of the building that my window overlooked.

I hesitated, leaning my back against the cool, glass wall of Ignis House as I looked towards the spot where my stolen goods were hidden. Every nerve in my body was begging for me to race forward and snatch it but I refused to obey.

I'd been in too many tight situations to let my nerves get the better of me. I needed to be sure I hadn't been followed. I needed to know no one was watching me.

I pulled my Atlas out of my satchel and started scrolling through FaeBook posts like I didn't have a care in the world.

I gave it a few minutes and was about to give it up and move to retrieve my loot when a prickle travelled down my spine. I suddenly had the very real belief that someone was watching me.

I resisted the urge to look around for the source of my discomfort and continued to scroll through the FaeBook feed. There wasn't much to catch my interest today, a few bits of gossip about an earth student who had been cheating on her girlfriend. Some conspiracy theories about Astrum's death. I noticed a group dedicated to finding a way to cheer Darius up after the fire in his room. It looked like they were going to throw him a party... and quite possibly offer him an orgy too by the looks of it.

I scoffed in disgust. I guessed I couldn't have expected to have ruined his fun for long but at least I could look back at that photo of him literally bursting with anger any time I wanted to.

A harsh wind gusted down on me and I flinched in surprise as my hair was blown back and the light of the moon blotted out for a moment.

My heart leapt in panic as I spotted the golden Dragon diving from the sky towards me and I pressed my back against the wall of Ignis House, almost dropping my Atlas in fright.

I fought to keep my features as neutral as possible as Darius landed in front of me, the ground juddering beneath his weight.

A deep growl emanated from his throat and he swivelled his reptilian head so that one, huge, golden eye could survey me.

I swallowed thickly, looking over his enormous body in awe. He towered above me, forcing me to tilt my head right back to look up at him. I couldn't help but appreciate the beauty of this beast, the way the moonlight glimmered on his scales and his eyes flashed with untamed power.

He spat something from his mouth and I glanced at the wad of material just as his body retreated back into his Fae form.

"Oh for the love of crap," I swore as he stood before me butt naked. Again. "You could have landed anywhere you liked, why did you choose to flash your goods at me?"

Darius smirked at me as he prowled forward, apparently not the least bit embarrassed by his body being on show. Not that he should have been, he had sculpted muscles and shoulders that just screamed *touch me*. His skin was tanned and kissed by his tattoos and just looking at him had heat rising across my body.

Bad Tory. Don't look at the jackass like that. He might look good enough to eat but he'd sure as shit give you indigestion.

"Why are you hanging around out here?" he asked as he stooped to gather the clothes he'd dropped. He stepped into his pants while keeping his gaze fixed on me.

"Well, I *was* enjoying some time away from assholes, but we can officially count that as being over."

Darius shrugged his t-shirt on, covering up that beautiful body and allowing me the clarity of mind to look away from him.

"It kinda looks like you were reading about me," he countered, pointing at my Atlas which was hanging loose in my hand.

I glanced at the screen and spotted a picture of him which had been posted by the girls organising his party. It looked like a posed shot for a photo shoot and he was gazing wistfully off of a bridge without his shirt on.

"Oh yeah, you caught me. Secret fangirl right here. I just love to stand about staring at photos of you, daydreaming about your oh so dreamy body and imagining what it would be like if you had a halfway decent personality."

Zero truth to any of those comments.

Darius actually quirked a smile in response to that remark and my bottom jaw practically hit my sneakers. Or at least it would have if I hadn't perfected the art of resting bitch face and stuck it into place with superglue at the start of this interaction.

He glanced up at the sky and held a hand out like he was checking for rain.

"Well, don't hang around out here too long, Roxy," he said, using that irritating as hell nickname for me. "We wouldn't want you to come close to drowning again."

I scowled at him as he strode away from me towards the House, my heart skipping a beat as he moved past the clump of scraggy grass which concealed the sock of stolen goods from his bedroom.

Darius didn't so much as hesitate as he passed right by it and I waited for him to disappear inside before finally moving forward to claim it. I shoved the lot deep into the bottom of my satchel and took off across the grounds towards Aer House.

It was getting late but that was alright; we'd need the cover of night to move the stash of stolen goods from Darcy's room.

As I hiked up the hill, that prickling sensation ran along my spine again and I paused, certain that someone was behind me.

I dropped down, pretending to re-tie my sneaker and looked through a curtain of my hair back towards Ignis House.

It didn't take me long to spot Darius lurking on the track. He was vaguely trying to blend into the shadows but beneath the light of the full moon his broad frame was pretty impossible to hide in the open, rocky landscape of Fire Territory.

My heart started pounding a little as I wondered what the hell he was doing. He'd only just arrived at Ignis House and he'd seemed intent on heading inside a few moments ago. It was like he'd waited for me to walk away and was now following me.

A shiver of unease ran down my spine at that thought. I was confident he hadn't seen me reclaiming the treasure outside because he would have confronted me already if he'd figured out I'd stolen from him. So he must have had some other reason to follow me. While I walked alone. In the dark. At night.

I'm not going to let him spring another goddamn attack on me.

Just ahead of me, the path split in two directions, one towards The Orb and the other to Aer House. I wasn't going to lead him to my real destination and the open meadows of Air Territory weren't going to help me lose him so as I straightened, I turned towards The Orb.

I pulled my headphones out of my satchel and placed them over my ears but I didn't actually turn any music on before I started jogging. I was tempted to sprint, wondering if the Dragon asshole could keep up with my top speed but I decided that would look suspicious.

I didn't look back again as I ran but I could feel him following me, his gaze on my body feeling almost like a physical sensation.

The Orb loomed ahead and I darted straight inside. It was fairly empty, but several students were around having a late dinner or enjoying a coffee and slice of cake with friends.

I snagged a bottle of water from the frozen ice cooler as I passed it so that I had an excuse for coming in here then crossed to the exit on the far side of the room. I glanced over my shoulder before I stepped outside and saw Darius striding through the room. I caught his gaze for a fleeting moment then slipped out into the dark again.

I sprinted to the right of the exit and into the shadows surrounding Mars Laboratories, pressing my back to the wall as soon as I reached it and ducking behind an arch in the brickwork.

I looked back at The Orb just as Darius stepped out and he fell still, looking all around with a frown on his face. I smirked to myself as I waited silently in the shadows. I'd given the cops and several security guards the slip more than once and I was sure Darius Acrux wouldn't be much of a challenge.

He looked left and right, swearing beneath his breath as he tried to figure out where I'd gone.

"Have you seen Roxy Vega?" he snapped at a group of girls as they appeared from the direction of Jupiter Hall.

"No," they replied, lingering in case he wanted anything else from them.

Darius snarled irritably and headed the other way, moving closer to me as he searched the shadows.

As he stalked past me and on towards Earth Observatory, I slipped along the wall and kept going until I reached the far end of the building. The Wailing Wood spread out beyond me but I'd have to make it across another path and a long stretch of grass before I would reach the trees.

I glanced around to see if Darius or anyone else was close enough to see me then made a run for it. My heart pounded as I sprinted for the trees and I passed between two huge trunks before making it into the darkness beneath them.

There wasn't an official path here but I kept running until I came to one deeper into the trees. I pulled up short on the dirt track and caught my breath as I listened for the sounds of pursuit. Silence greeted me and I grinned to myself as I turned in the direction of Aer House. Whatever Darius had had planned for me, he was going to be disappointed.

I started running again and didn't slow until I reached Aer Tower. I threw a gust of air magic at the lock to let me in and jogged up the curving stairwell to Darcy's room.

I hammered on the door and she opened it with wide eyes. I stepped inside without waiting for her to ask why I was here.

"Has something happened?" she asked nervously, looking me over like she expected to find something had been done to me.

"Not yet," I said. "But Orion just turned up in Ignis House with a bunch of FIB agents and started searching every room for evidence to do with Astrum's death. They're bound to start on the rest of the Houses once they're done there so we need to move Darius's gold, like yesterday."

"Oh crap. Okay," Darcy agreed. "But what the hell are we going to do with it?"

"Bury it I guess?" I offered, having no other ideas.

I dropped down onto my knees and started dragging the gold out from under her bed, checking inside the huge sports bag and making doubly sure that I hadn't missed so much as a single coin. Darcy checked it all too and once we were sure that we had every piece, we moved towards the door again.

"I'll go ahead and check that no one's lurking outside," she said. "I'll send a message to your Atlas if there is. If not then follow two minutes behind me."

"Okay." I heaved the heavy bag over my shoulders and waited as she disappeared into the hall.

I counted two minutes and no message came through so I slipped out after her. I tiptoed down the stairwell, careful not to jostle the bag and make a sound. When I finally reached the bottom, I found Darcy waiting for me in the shadows by the door.

We headed outside and moved north into The Wailing Wood. The trees were thick and ominous around us, their branches whispering in a soft breeze overhead that set my skin crawling with anxiety.

"I vote we bury it in here," I said. "We can set some kind of marker to find it again if we need to but at least this way no one will be able to prove it had anything to do with us if it's found."

"Good plan," Darcy agreed. "Look, there's a few animal tracks that lead through the trees away from the path. If we follow them they'll probably lead us to the heart of the forest."

I followed her as she led the way further into the trees and took the route off of the path. When she was sure we'd gone far enough, she stopped and I dropped the heavy bag of treasure between us.

"Now what?" I breathed. Our Earth Elemental lessons had all been about the power of growth so far. We'd created flowers and vines, even encouraged trees to grow new limbs, but we'd done nothing with the actual earth yet. I imagined we had the power to dig a hole in the soil by our feet with magic but I wasn't really sure where to begin.

"Let's just try and create a hole and see what happens," Darcy suggested.

I didn't have any better ideas so I followed her lead and aimed my hands at the soil by our feet. I imagined a hole in my mind, the soil parting to create the perfect hiding place for our treasure...

Nothing.

Darcy was clenching her teeth so hard in concentration that it looked like she might burst a blood vessel.

I dropped to my knees and pressed my palms flat to the ground to see if that might work better instead.

A faint tremor marked the path of magic flowing into the dirt around me but no hole appeared and without a shovel we were going to really struggle to get this done.

"Crap," Darcy cursed. "We could just throw it in the lake?"

I balked at the idea of all this pretty treasure sinking to the bottom of the lake. "The Sirens might find it again," I reasoned, though part of me refusing was just because I couldn't bear to part with this hard won prize so easily.

"Well I guess we'd better start digging then," Darcy said, sounding resigned.

I nodded my agreement and began to claw at the dirt around me.

Darcy joined in and I continued to try and throw my earth magic at the task. Sometimes it seemed like the clump of soil I broke away was bigger than I'd expect and I wondered if my magic was aiding me a little even though it clearly wasn't doing everything I wanted from it.

Darcy was breathing heavily beside me and sweat was lining my brow alongside the smears of mud from the countless times I'd swiped my hair away from my face. Heaven only knew what the hell I'd look like when we were done here but I'd have to worry about that once our job was complete. The hole was still only half dug and we needed to get the treasure into it yet.

I was so engrossed in our task that I didn't even notice the footsteps approaching until it was too late to hide what we were doing.

"Holy guacamole, your majesties!" Geraldine exclaimed and Darcy squealed in fright.

"Shit Geraldine! Don't sneak up on people, like that!" I barked as my heartbeat thundered in response to her arrival.

"What in the name of Santa sunbathing in a thong are you up to?" she asked, her eyes wide and wild.

I couldn't help but laugh in response to that. She'd caught us red-handed anyway. We had no choice but to come clean and hope for the best.

"Well, I didn't want to drag you into this, Geraldine," I said slowly. "But I think I'm going to have to trust you with our secret."

Darcy shot me a look to say 'are you sure about this?' but I could only shrug hopefully.

"The honour of keeping your secrets would be the single greatest accolade I have ever achieved," Geraldine gushed. "I will take it to the grave. I would hold your confidence even if I was tortured on the rack, fed alive to starving rats, boiled in a vat of week-old gravy, beaten by the fists of-"

"We get it Geraldine, we can trust you," Darcy said to stop her. "What are you doing out here in the middle of the night anyway?"

"I was just replenishing my magic," she explained, brandishing a basket of purple flowers at us while still peering at our half-dug hole curiously. "I'm of the Cerberus Order. We have to eat aconite, which you might know better as wolfsbane, to replenish our magic. I was just gathering fresh supplies of it which is easier to do at night. It's deadly poisonous to most other Orders though, so no snacking! What are *you* doing?"

"I'm guessing you heard about the little fire in Darius Acrux's room?" I asked her quietly, glancing about in case any more late night wanderers were in the woods. "Well, that was kinda... me."

"Well pull my tail and call me Miss Whiskers!" she exclaimed. "So this is *his* gold?"

"Yeah."

"And we need to bury it before the FIB or the teachers find out," Darcy added.

"Look no further! Geraldine Grus is a firm friend and trustworthy protector of the true Heirs to the throne of Solaria. Your scandal is my scandal, your war is my war and your enemy is my enemy. Darius Acrux should burn in the fiery pits of the afterlife for what he did to you. If he was on fire and I was in my Cerberus form I wouldn't even extinguish the flames with my urine. Please allow me to assist you with my earth magic, your highnesses."

"Please do," I begged as she stepped forward.

Geraldine raised her hands, commanding her magic to do her bidding and a deep hole sank into the ground. She grabbed the bag of loot and threw it into the hole like it weighed less than nothing.

"Wow, Geraldine, you're ripped," I commented.

"Thank you," she said, flushing red in the moonlight. "I do like to dally in the Pitball arena in my spare time. It would be my absolute pleasure to introduce you to the sport some day."

"I'd love that," Darcy said enthusiastically.

"Well that would just be the toad's pyjamas," Geraldine squealed excitedly. "Would you perhaps like to come and watch me play at the next match this Sunday? I just know I'd knock your diamond encrusted socks off if you did!"

"It's a date," I agreed. Anything to pay her back for saving our asses here.

I snatched the sock from my satchel and took the coins from it before tossing them into the hole too. As I held the dagger out over the hole though, that weird presence it seemed to hold begged me not to release it and I paused.

"What are you waiting for?" Darcy hissed.

My grip tightened on the blade instead of loosening.

Why should I have to toss it away? I like it, it's mine now... I want to keep it.

I exhaled slowly, all of my instincts warring against the insane idea to keep hold of the dagger. I'd been in enough scrapes to know that wandering around with a stolen dagger while an investigation into who stole it was taking place was an absolutely terrible idea. I shook my head fiercely, shrugging off the desire to keep the blade and flinging it down on top of the bag.

That thing is really weird.

Geraldine raised her hand before her and with a surge of movement, the soil covered the stolen treasure and the ground flattened out above it. She encouraged a patch of pink and gold flowers to bloom over the spot and I dropped a pin on the map on my Atlas at our location so that I could find it again if necessary.

"X marks the spot," I joked, feeling like we were a bunch of pirates.

Darcy released a breath of laughter.

We all grinned at each other as we moved away from the scene of the crime and Geraldine reached out with her magic to remove every speck of dirt from our clothes and bodies. She even managed to drag the dirt out from under my fingernails and I marvelled at her power.

We kept quiet as we made it back to the path and paused within a clearing where the moonlight spilled over us.

"We keep this secret among the three of us," I reiterated just in case Geraldine got any ideas about telling the rest of the Ass Club about what we'd done.

"I swear on the sanctity of our friendship that I'll never breathe a word of this to another soul," she agreed seriously.

I couldn't help but smile at the strange girl who had offered us her loyalty so completely. I'd found her disturbing and downright annoying at times but I couldn't help but feel the truth in those words as she spoke them. We *were* friends. The kind who met up and buried secrets in the depths of the woods in the middle of the night and never told another soul about them. The kind who trusted in each other's motivations and forgave their worst behaviours no matter what.

"Here's to a long and beautiful friendship," I swore, holding my hand out between us.

"To friendship," Darcy agreed, placing her hand on top of mine.

"Friendship," Geraldine agreed, completing the pile with a sniff that announced the arrival of her tears.

We smiled conspiratorially at each other one last time before parting ways and heading back to our individual Houses. I hadn't expected to spend my evening burying evidence in the middle of a forest. But it wasn't the worst way to spend a night either.

DARCY

CHAPTER ELEVEN

The FIB had been searching Aer Tower for the past two hours and I sensed from the banging and clattering sounding from the floor beneath mine that it wouldn't be long until they checked this corridor.

Even though Tory and I had hidden the gold in the woods last night, I kept looking under my bed in case we'd missed a piece. It would be just our luck to decide to stay at the Academy and then be kicked out for stealing from an Heir. I was dog tired, but at least my corridor hadn't been the first on their list to search this morning. They must have been here since before dawn.

"Room searches! Get your doors open and stand in the corridor!" I recognised Francesca's voice out in the tower and my heart turned over. I'd tried to go back to sleep for a while but it was impossible while knowing the FIB were on their way here.

I moved to my door, drawing my shoulders back and schooling my expression into indifference as I stepped out of the room in my PJs of black shorts and a tank top. *I'm not guilty, so why do I feel like a criminal?*

I let my door swing wide and placed my back against the wall beside it. Francesca and a team of FIB marched along the hallway led by Orion. He had a savage look on his face that made my heart pound a little harder. The closest room to him wasn't open and he immediately marched up to it and bashed his fist against the wood. I didn't know much about the girl whose room it was, only that I'd seen her hanging out with Kylie a few times.

"Out!" he demanded, then produced a strange looking key from his pocket. A slim, silver thing with multiple prongs on the end. He slid it into the lock and a girl squealed the second he threw the door open.

A boy darted out of the room, tugging up his pants and laughing his head off as he veered around the FIB and out of sight. The girl emerged a second later hugging a sheet to her chest.

"I need five minutes!" she yelled at Orion, but he released a blast of air from his palm that shoved her out of his way before he marched into her room. A member of the FIB headed after him while Francesca directed units to the other rooms.

Diego exited his room down the hall, looking to me with a frown. "You good?" he mouthed and I nodded, offering him a playful eye roll. He took out his Atlas, tapping something on it and a second later mine pinged. I leaned back into my room, plucking it off of my nightstand and reading the private message Diego had sent me on FaeBook.

Diego:

FML.

Wanna grab breakfast from The Orb after this?

I tapped out a reply with a smile.

Darcy:

Sure, I need to stop at the Mars Labs on the way though.

I looked up as I sent the message and Diego gave me a questioning look. I'd done a little digging and discovered that the items I needed for my hair regrowth were kept in stock rooms at the labs. I pointed at my hair then tapped out another response in explanation.

Darcy:

Operation: Hair Repair.
Your mission, should you choose to accept it, is to watch out for teachers while I borrow some ingredients.

Diego snorted a laugh as he wrote out a reply.

Diego:

Borrow?

Darcy:

;)

Someone yanked the Atlas from my hands and I jolted, glancing up to find Orion thoroughly in my personal space. "Something funny, Miss Vega?" he asked lightly.

I couldn't seem to wipe the smile from my face so I bit down on my lip to try and hide it. I shook my head in answer to his question. He cast an eye down my messages and that was enough to stifle my amusement.

"*Hey.*" I grabbed it back from him and his eyes flickered with dark shadows. Why was he always nosing into my private life?

"Have you got any contraband in your room?" he asked.

"No, sir," I said honestly while a member of the FIB barrelled inside and started rifling through my things.

"Not yet anyway," he murmured so only I could hear, then walked away toward the next room.

I fought a grin as I watched him in my periphery. *Well you put me up to it, Professor.*

I locked my fingers around my Atlas, watching Orion as he weaved in and out of the rooms, his brow furrowed in concentration. *What's he thinking?*

"Ah – give me that!" Diego's voice caught my attention and I spotted him wrestling a wooden box out of the arms of an FIB agent. He hugged it to his chest and Orion came at him with the speed of a charging rhino.

I gasped as he raised a hand, casting a force of air that slammed Diego back into the wall, lifting him off of his feet. The box clattered to the floor and laughter broke out around me as the other students grouped together to watch. I hurried forward to help, horrified that he'd attack Diego like that.

"Let him go!" I caught Orion's arm, yanking backwards and he cast a gust of air that swept me off my feet and sent me flying back down the corridor. I crashed into the legs of several students who only laughed harder. None of them offered me a hand to help me up.

I ground my teeth, pushing myself upright and marching back toward them.

Orion scooped the box from the floor while Diego kicked against the wall to try and get free.

"Don't touch that you asshole! It belonged to mi abuela!" Diego roared, but Orion ignored him, smashing the box against the wall full force, making my stomach lurch in surprise. It cascaded into a hundred broken shards and amongst the debris was a bunch of photographs of Diego tucked under the arm of an elderly woman. Between it all was a red journal which Orion promptly snatched off of the floor.

"Let me down! Tu eres un pedazo de mierda, Vampiro escoria!" Diego bellowed, making the walls shake. I'd never seen him so mad and whatever the hell he'd just said, I sensed it was not *please can I get down, sir.*

"Anyone care to translate that?" Orion asked the corridor, flipping the first page of the book open. "Although your tone is enough to land you in detention already, Mr Polaris."

Diego's eyes flared with hellfire as he stared down at Orion with more hatred than I'd ever seen in someone's eyes. "You want a translation? I called you a piece of shit Vampire scum, because that is *exactly* what you are."

"Diego," I gasped, begging him to stop with my expression as he met my gaze. His fury melted away and desperation took its place as he turned back to Orion.

"Don't read it," he begged as Orion cleared his throat loudly.

"*Sir*," I said firmly, walking toward him a little more warily this time.

"Oh good it's in English." Orion smiled cruelly.

"I just write journal entries to practice the language that's all," Diego growled. "You don't need to read it!"

"September first," Orion said loudly. "I found The Awakening to be even better than expected. I think I may have made my first friend-" He paused for effect and laughter carried from the other students. Even a few of the FIB joined in. My stomach churned and anger burned in my gut at him humiliating Diego like this.

Francesca leaned against a doorway, watching Orion with an expression that suggested he was telling a lovely bedtime story.

Orion flicked over a few more pages, grinning darkly. "September third." He was getting cold, hard revenge on Diego for insulting him, but wasn't pinning him up against a wall and breaking his prized possession enough? "I think I'm becoming attracted to someone of the Pegasus Order. Is it the way she glides through the sky, leaving trails of glitter in her wake? Or maybe it's the way the glitter remains in those alluring eyes of hers even in her Fae form. Sofia Cygnus gets more than my heart throbbing-"

"*Lance*," Francesca chuckled in the gentlest of warnings. And I imagined that was mainly because she wanted to get on with her job.

"We're just getting to the good bit," Orion said with a smirk as he looked to Diego. "Or are you going to stop me?" There was a challenge in his tone and I had the feeling he genuinely wanted him to fight back.

Diego struggled harder, casting air in his hands but it wasn't nearly enough to force off Orion's binds.

"No? Well I'll continue." He gazed down at the page, his brows jumping up as he silently read the next line.

I stalked forward before he could read it aloud, furious at Orion, at everyone in this Academy for being such cruel, unforgiving bullies.

"Stop it!" I yelled as he opened his mouth.

Magic twisted through my veins, tangling together in a way I hadn't experienced before. Vines flooded from my hands and fire of deepest blue swept down them in a blazing line of fury. Orion immediately whipped a hand out, tugging the oxygen from the air and dousing the flames. I gritted my teeth, willing the vines to wrap around him as he wielded the air with expert skill to keep them away. Through sheer determination, I managed to lock one around his throat, ripping him backwards so he smashed into the ground.

The vines slithered away in an instant as shock jarred my heart and made my magic die in a wave. Diego hit the ground with a groan, gathering up the pieces of his broken box and stuffing the photos into his pocket.

Orion was still clutching onto the journal as he sat upright, rubbing the back of his head. I tentatively moved forward and crouched down before him. A heated lump burned my throat as I reached out and prised the book from his hand, passing it wordlessly behind me to Diego. I couldn't drag my gaze away from Orion as he stared at me unblinkingly.

The FIB were moving again, ordering the students out of their way as they continued their search.

Orion's mouth tugged up at one corner and his dimple punctured his cheek. "I was hoping you'd do that," he said in a low voice.

I frowned in confusion, unsure what to say to that. "I just attacked you," I said in disbelief. "I'm waiting for my punishment here."

I moved to stand and he caught my wrist, using my momentum to help himself up. I glanced at Diego to see if he was alright and I could tell his pride was injured more than his body.

Orion suddenly fisted his hand in the short ends of my hair and I yelped in alarm as he dragged me forward and dug his fangs into my throat. I was too slow to react and my magic was immediately immobilised. He released a feral noise as I went slack in his arms and a deep shiver gripped my bones.

People barely even glanced our way as if this was a completely normal occurrence. And though I was starting to get used to seeing Caleb bite Tory's neck instead of her wrist, nothing quite compared to being in the jaws of a beast myself.

Diego was muttering to himself in Spanish as he marched back into his room and kicked the door closed.

Oh thanks, buddy.

Orion's arm slid tightly around my waist and my eyes drifted closed as the pain ebbed away, replaced by something much more delicious. And definitely, definitely forbidden. I clutched onto his arm and his muscles flexed beneath my fingers, eliciting a soft, barely perceptible moan from my lips. His bite deepened and though I knew he must have heard me I prayed he'd mistake it for a whimper of pain.

I don't like this I don't like this I don't like this.

If I kept telling myself that it would definitely stop my veins from sparking and my head from spinning.

He finally extracted his fangs, but his mouth lingered on my neck a second longer than was appropriate. His lips pressed against the bite for what could only have been a millisecond but I felt it in every corner of my being, like the ground had just dropped away beneath my feet.

He stepped back and I tried to process the mad power play that had just passed between us.

He wiped the corner of his mouth with his thumb and I sensed he was hiding a smile. "Don't forget you have detention with me on Saturday." He strode off, just like that and I didn't move for several long seconds.

I finally turned around and found the corridor emptying out. The last of the FIB were walking away empty handed, but I spotted Francesca lingering by the exit as she waited for Orion. He joined her as they walked away and I didn't miss the way she rubbed her shoulder against his, or slid her hand possessively onto his arm.

Some deep, animal instinct inside me made my upper lip curl back as if I was about to snarl like a beast.

A door banging beside me tore me out of that strange sensation and I found that Diego had returned, tugging on a dark green coat. "Are we still going to the Mars Labs?" he grunted, adjusting his beanie hat with a heavy grimace.

I felt a pang of annoyance toward him for abandoning me to Orion's teeth after I'd stuck my neck out for him. "I can manage," I muttered.

He sighed heavily. "Sorry chica," he said gently, stepping closer. "I flip out sometimes. I knew it was best to just put some distance between me and Orion for a moment. Didn't mean to run off on you... Thanks for what you did." He nudged me and I broke a small smile, the weight in my chest lifting. "Come on, let me make it up to you by helping you sort *this* out." He rubbed my head, messing up my hair – which didn't mean much considering the current state of it. But my mood brightened by a mile as I realised that might well be about to change.

"Let's go soon then." I beamed.

"Put on something warm, it's raining out there," Diego said, pointing out my PJs.

"Sure, gimme two mins."

He laughed. "You'll be longer than that when you see what they've done. Knock for me when you're ready."

He headed back to his room and I hurried away in a panic, speeding through my door. My mouth fell open as I found the place completely torn apart. The contents of my drawers were turned out, my clothes had been pulled haphazardly out of the wardrobe, the mattress was flipped up.

I scowled, hauling it back into place and shoving things back into my drawers. I knelt down and pulled out my nightstand drawer which was remarkably in order except-

I sucked in air, rummaging through the few items I kept in it, but it wasn't there. Astrum's card was gone.

My heart thumped heavily in my ears as if I was hearing it under water.

Francesca knew about it already, why would she or her agents take it?

Maybe they just need to double check it.

But then why didn't they tell me?

Surely I would have been questioned if they thought it was suspicious?

"Death," a voice rolled over me which made my spine turn into a pillar of ice. I looked up from where I was kneeling on the floor, finding Seth in the doorway twirling Astrum's card between his fingers. "Do you know what this card means?" he asked slowly as if he was playing with his food. After I'd unleashed my power on Orion and he'd drunk from my source, I wasn't in a position to even attempt to fight Seth off. Crying out for help was pointless and humiliating. So I rose to my feet and faced him, trying not to let my hands shake.

I didn't answer his question, but he went on anyway.

"Finality," he purred. "The end." He stepped into my room, his aura filling the air with poison. "Do you think it's about us?" He flipped the card over, mock pretending to find Astrum's inscription for the first time. But if he'd stolen it from my room while the commotion went on in the hallway, he sure as hell had had time to read it. "I made a mistake and now my time is up. The Shadow has discovered me and there is no hope for me to escape their wrath. The answers you seek are hidden between Leo and Libra. Don't trust the flames. Claim your throne." He spoke the final words like they were a curse on the world. "*Tell me who wrote this.*"

His Coercion was powerful and I was completely unprepared to block it. The name tumbled from my lips before I could even attempt to hold it back. "Professor Astrum."

Seth mulled that over for a moment. "So this *Shadow* topped off a teacher? They must be someone very bad." He stalked closer and I fought the burning instinct to recoil, refusing to let him see me intimidated. "But no one's badder than me," he said in a wolfish growl that made my heart jolt.

"What do you want?" I asked in an even voice, reaching for the card but he lifted it above my head out of reach. *Bastard.*

He puckered up his lips. "A kiss. That's the price for getting it back."

"I'd rather cut my tongue out," I spat.

He laughed darkly. "That would be a shame. I was looking forward to feeling it wrapped around mine again."

"You're deluded," I said, swiping for the card once more, but he was so tall that he just flipped his hand up to keep it away from me.

My hands balled into fists and I tried to figure out a way to get him out of my room and take that card from him in the process.

"Come on, one little kiss. I'll even give you back your hair." He twisted his wrist to taunt me with the blue braid latched around it.

Anger burned through me like acid. "What's your problem?" I snapped. "Why the hell do you want me to kiss you?"

The hard wall in his eyes lowered a fraction and he dropped his hand, flipping the card between his fingers with expert skill. "Maybe make up sex is what we need to dispel all of this tension," he said, conjuring a lustful smile.

I eyed the card, knowing lunging for it was pointless. So I really only had one choice.

"Get out." I turned my back on him; it was one of the biggest insults you could offer in Solaria. He growled deeply in his throat, pure wolf.

Fear gripped my spine. I shut my eyes, willing myself not to move, not to run, not to do anything, even though I'd just offered myself up as an open target.

"You live in my house, babe. That makes you a part of my pack. And I'm your Alpha."

"I'm not a part of any pack. So go alph-uck yourself," I hissed, my voice shaking a fraction as I pushed out the words that surprised even me.

He snatched my arm, forcing me around to face him. His eyes glowed with danger and my throat tightened with fear as he glared down at me.

"You don't choose the pack, the pack chooses you. And so long as you're in these walls and I say you're in my pack, you adhere to my wolf hierarchy. Which, if you hadn't realised, you are at the bottom of, babe. So if your Alpha says howl, you ask how loud."

I yanked my hand free and in the same movement, snatched the card from his grip. I tucked it straight down the back of my skirt and his eyebrow cocked.

"Is that an invitation?" He smirked and I raised my hands warily, fear dripping through me.

"If you touch me I'll blast every ounce of energy I have at you," I whispered, my voice lost to fear.

Please don't touch me, I don't have much power left.

His brows knitted sharply together. "I'm only joking, Darcy." He surveyed my expression and took a step back, his features skewing.

"I don't know *what* you and your vile friends are capable of." I pointed at the door. "Get. Out."

He backed up again. "What does the riddle refer to? What answers are you looking for?"

"That's none of your business."

"I could just Coerce you again," he said, though it didn't sound like he was keen on the idea.

I ground my teeth, not wanting to be forced, but volunteering the information equated to the same thing. "We have a thousand questions since we arrived in Solaria," I said, my tone accusing. Because he knew we were clueless in this world, and he and his friends had still tried to destroy us over a throne we didn't want. "Astrum could have been referring to anything."

"Leo and Libra," he murmured, running a hand into his hair. "Well if Astrum was referring to Darius and Orion you're gonna be in the dark forever. The day they answer your questions is the day hell freezes over."

I frowned, momentarily distracted from the fact that there was a hungry wolf in my room. "Orion is my Liaison, he has to tell me about my past."

"Pfft," he laughed coldly. "Do you actually think he tells you everything?" He leaned closer, lowering his voice. "Even *I* don't know what shit he and Darius get up to. Their lies run so deep even their friends get kept in the dark." He released a low, doggish whimper, rubbing the back of his neck like that fact deeply upset him. I was surprised when he kept talking and wondered if he was actually trying to offload on me right now.

Arrogant jerk.

"I mean don't get me wrong, I love Darius. But I know he lies straight to my face sometimes. Whatever he and Orion are up to, it's pure sin."

"Seth?"

He looked to me, smiling as if we were best friends and I wanted to rip his face off for it. "Yes, babe?"

"Get the hell out of my room. And don't ever come back here again."

He pressed his tongue into his cheek, moving to the door and stroking the band of blue hair around his wrist. I hated him so viscerally it hurt. He was wearing my wound, brandishing it for the entire school to see. It wasn't like I could ever reattach it, but I still wanted it back.

"See you soon, weakling." He headed away and a ragged breath left my lungs as the fear inside me finally gave way to relief. I leaned against the wall for a moment, catching my breath, replaying the conversation in my mind. Perhaps I hadn't won, but I hadn't lost either.

When I felt strong enough to move, I shut the door and headed to the bathroom. I showered quickly then changed into my uniform, tugging on a black rain coat over the top of my navy blazer. I pulled on my boots and headed to the door, my fingers hovering above the handle.

He's not out there, just move.

I lifted my chin and stepped outside, walking to Diego's room and knocking. He answered a second later and some of his dreary music carried to me from his Atlas. He turned it off, seeming depressed as he stepped into the hall after me.

Breakfast would be ready at The Orb by now and I wanted to meet Tory there to tell her about the crazy couple of hours I'd had. And I seriously wanted to discuss new theories on this Tarot card. It didn't seem right that Astrum would point us toward Darius and Orion for answers. He'd openly stated how much he disliked the two of them.

My mind spun as Diego and I headed out of the tower into a sheet of rain. I pulled up my hood and Diego did the same, following me along in silence as I led the way towards Mars Laboratories.

Rain splashed up from the stone path and when we reached the track that cut through The Wailing Wood, we found it had turned into a muddy bog. I tip-toed along the edges of it while Diego slogged through, his hands stuffed in his pockets and his eyes on the ground.

"Are you alright?" I called to him, using the jutting roots of trees to make a careful path over the mud. My foot slipped more than once but miraculously I didn't fall on my ass.

"Yeah," he said glumly.

"You sure?" I pressed, giving him a hopeful look to see if he might open up.

He huffed heavily. "It's that Vampire," he growled. "Screw Orion, who does he think he is?"

My heart twisted weirdly in my chest and I looked up at the canopy

189

above, blinking as raindrops dotted my cheeks. "He's not all bad."

"Are you serious?" he snapped.

"I mean, he's a total dick but like...I think it's his teaching style."

"Darcy Vega please tell me you're not standing up for the guy who just broke mi abuela's carved trinket box." He blinked and for a moment I was sure tears were swimming in his eyes.

"Oh Diego, I'm sorry, I didn't mean it like that." I balanced precariously on a root as he came to a halt ankle deep in mud at the heart of the path.

He sniffed heavily and I gave up on keeping my boots clean, dropping off of the root into the mud and squelching my way toward him.

He sniffed again. "Your shoes are getting ruined," he murmured.

"It's okay," I said. "You can buy me a new pair," I teased and he snorted a laugh.

"You really are becoming Fae, chica." He pushed my shoulder and I released a small laugh.

"Tell me about your er, abuela? Was she the woman in the photo?"

He nodded. "My grandmother," he said thickly. "She was the only person in the world who ever really cared about me, you know?"

I frowned, rubbing his arm as the rain cascaded down on us through the canopy, the scent of the damp rising in the air.

"Was?" I asked gently.

"She died last year," he choked out. "Now I'm all alone."

"I thought you had family," I said, gazing into his soft, pale eyes.

"I do, they're just not that proud of me. They sent me here to prove my worth. And I feel like I'm failing them."

"You're not," I promised. "We've only been here a few weeks, what more can you do?"

"I don't even have my Order yet," he muttered.

"Neither do I." I prodded his shoulder and he cracked a smile.

"Guess you're as useless as me then, huh?" he teased. "But from the way you knocked Orion on his ass earlier, I'd say you're gonna be just fine in this place. You belong here. I'm just...a misfit."

"We're all misfits," I said as we started walking again, trudging along in the puddles. "Every freshmen in this place is just trying to make it through in their own way. You've got a good heart, Diego. That doesn't mean you don't fit in here. In my opinion, this place could use a few good hearts."

Diego took hold of my hand and my mouth opened and closed. I didn't know what to do so I just left it there, my icy fingers cupped in the warmth of his.

Okay this is weird.

As we exited the trees, I pulled my hand free, pretending to adjust my hood. An awkward silence descended as we closed in on Mars Laboratories, but the closer we got, the more my mind swung to the task at hand.

Students were darting into the shelter of The Orb as the rain beat down harder and I quickened my pace towards the labs, keeping my head low as I ducked into the red brick building.

The walls were painted a murky blood-orange and murals of the planet Mars were splashed across them. I quickly realised I had no idea where exactly I was supposed to locate these ingredients and I only really had one way of finding out.

I took my Atlas from my satchel as Diego started admiring the artwork on the walls. I navigated my way to the private email service and tapped out a message to Orion.

Darcy:
Quick question...I'm in Mars Labs.
Could you give me a little clue as to where I might find a certain set of ingredients?

I went to put my Atlas away, wondering if we'd have to head to The Orb for a while until he replied, but before it even touched my bag, a notification flashed up on it.

A stupid grin bit into my cheeks as I found a message waiting from Orion. AKA Lance. Which I simply could *not* imagine ever calling him.

Lance:

Floor 3

Lab 306

6633211

Will the ends still be blue?

I reread the last line several times, unsure why the hell he would ask me that and why on earth he cared. I didn't have time to answer so I stuffed the Atlas in my bag and jogged over to Diego, grabbing his arm and drawing him into a stairway.

We headed up to level three and I checked that the coast was clear through a window in the door.

"Right, you keep watch. Text me if anyone heads this way," I said. "If anyone asks why you're here just say you're waiting for someone."

"Okay," Diego agreed, looking miles happier than he had when we'd left Aer Tower. "Good luck."

I nodded, my heart pounding madly as I stepped into the long corridor and walked along it at a casual pace. My coat was still dripping wet, leaving a puddle behind me as I went so I hurriedly unzipped it, stuffing it in my bag as I closed in on room 306.

Will I dye the ends of my hair blue again?

I hadn't thought beyond regrowing it, let alone ordering dye to the school to return the colour to my hair. I'd had it that way to remind me of the past. To never trust anyone again. But did I really need the reminder these days?

192

I found the lab which was split into rows of long worktops. The door was unlocked, but the second I stepped inside, I spotted a professor at his desk. I froze, waiting for him to rebuke me, before realising he was asleep. His head was craned back as he dozed in his chair and his moustache fluttered as he released a snore.

My gaze locked on the metal door behind him.

I could run, bolt. But I'd come this far already.

Screw it.

I plucked up my nerve and moved as quietly as I could across the room. I stepped past the desk, adrenaline pumping as I approached the door. It was locked by a keycode and I silently thanked Orion as I took out my Atlas and tapped in the number he'd given me.

A low beeeeeep sounded it opening and I glanced over my shoulder in a panic.

The professor snored loudly and I breathed a sigh, hurrying into the room. Shelves and shelves of ingredients, potions and magical items stretched out ahead of me, but luckily for me they were alphabetised with labels under each row.

I moved into the first aisle, finding several jars of Aquarius Moonstones starting off the As. They glittered like diamonds and my heart leapt with excitement at finding exactly what I needed to implement the first stage of my revenge against Seth Capella. I grabbed one of the stones, pocketing it with a wide grin on my face. After my run-in with him this morning I was doubly ready to exact a bit of vengeance on him.

I checked my list and hunted for the first item: three flakes of Dried Pepper Bark.

It wasn't long before I located it. The bark came in a little tub and I carefully wrapped a few of the flakes in a tissue before tucking them into my satchel. A thrill danced through me as I moved down a few aisles, searching for Mother of Pearl. I found tiny pots of it alongside large mollusc shells where the scrapings had come from. I bagged one of the pots and moved on to the next aisle, hunting for my final item: a two inch yellow crystal.

I searched the Y section and the C, but couldn't see any sign of it. When I was on the verge of giving up, a glint caught my eye. I headed to the far end of the room where a window overlooked a dark room, but something seemed to glitter within it.

A red switch beside me was labelled *lights* so I flicked it and my mouth parted at the beautiful sight unfolding before me. A long, tubular room swept out ahead and on rows of long tables, seemingly growing from various tubs, jars and glass tubes were hundreds and hundreds of crystals. Every colour under the sun twinkled back at me, segregated by their unique hue.

Excitement sped through me as I opened the heavy door and stepped inside. An icy gust swept over me and my breath puffed out as I walked down one of the aisles, hurrying toward the section of glittering yellow crystals. They were all in jars, some in clusters and others so big they'd been segmented into huge glass vats of their own.

A measuring rod lay at the end of the row so I snatched it up and sought out a two inch crystal amongst the cluster of yellows. When I found one, I plucked it from its jar and turned it over in my palm, admiring its beauty.

My Atlas pinged loudly and my gut clenched sharply. I snatched it out, expecting to find a warning from Diego but instead it was another message from Orion.

Lance*:*

Maybe green this time? Although 'Green' as a nickname isn't quite so catchy. The suspense is killing me.

A laugh escaped me as I tucked my tablet away with the crystal. I put the measuring rod back and hurried to the end of the room. I headed out of the door, shutting it behind me and switching off the light.

I strode toward the next door with a skip in my step but before I reached it, it swung open. My heart lurched wildly and I dove behind it as the Professor walked into the room. He yawned broadly, moving down an aisle and humming to himself. I caught the door before it swung closed, adrenaline surging as I rushed out of it then broke into a run through the lab.

I shoved the door open into the corridor, my eyes locking with Diego's where he stood at the far end of it.

I grinned, waving my satchel at him triumphantly as I charged in his direction. After my classes tonight, I'd head straight back to my room, brew this potion and be myself again!

My foot slid out beneath me as I hit the puddle my coat had formed earlier and my heart lurched into my throat as I fell backwards and my butt impacted with the ground.

"Ow," I groaned, pushing myself upright and finding Diego there to pull me up.

"You alright?" he asked, starting to laugh.

"Yeah." I rubbed my ass, hobbling along as I shook out my sore ankle, refusing to let anything dampen my mood right then. "Thanks for looking out for me."

"No problem," he said brightly. "Next time I need a lookout, I know who to ask."

"To be honest, Tory's probably a safer bet when it comes to this sort of thing."

"No way, you were doing great until you slipped over and nearly broke a leg," Diego taunted, releasing another few notes of laughter.

"That's the problem," I giggled. "Whenever I try to pull off something impressive, I always end up on my ass."

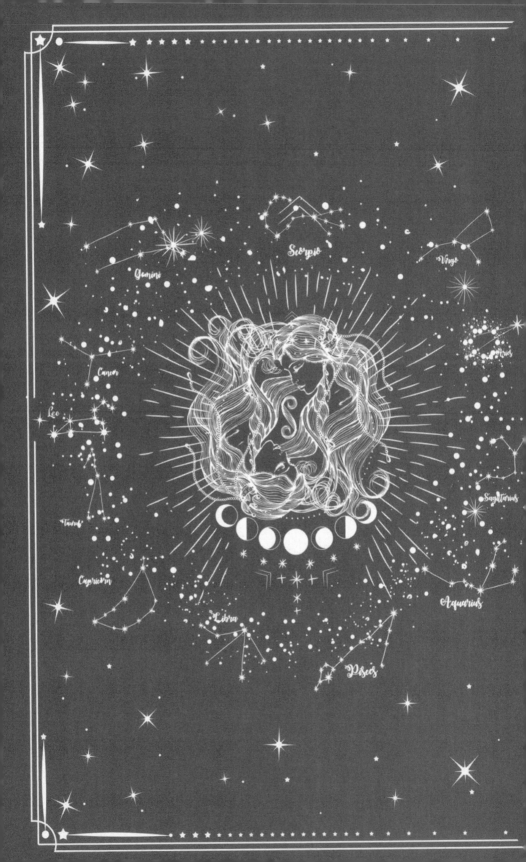

TORY

CHAPTER TWELVE

My Fire Elemental class had been yet another disastrous combination of over flamboyant flames and out of control infernos. I just couldn't wrangle it into my control, especially while wearing the protective suit that was required for class.

I'd tried to speak to Professor Pyro about it. I'd even told her that when I practiced without the suit on I had much more control but she'd dismissed my theory as nonsense, telling me it was all in my head. She'd also docked me twenty House Points for failing to practice with Darius yet again. The Fire Heir had smirked in response to that, flexing his muscles at me in a clear challenge, the words *make me* ringing in my memory as I scowled at him.

I half considered asking Caleb to help me instead. He held the Element of Fire too and even though it wasn't his primary power, he was still likely to be capable of assisting me. But even though he seemed slightly less abhorrent than the other Heirs at times, I still didn't trust him as far as I could throw him. And I got the feeling that he wouldn't undermine Darius's decision about helping me even if I begged. Which I absolutely wouldn't do.

So I was left with the infuriating option of practicing alone every night after my evening runs. I ended each run in the Fire Arena wearing my running stuff rather than the flame-proof outfit and I was definitely managing to do more with my powers when I did that. I could control the size of the flames and even get them to move in basic directions. But Professor Pyro didn't believe that had anything to do with my outfit and claimed it had more to do with stage fright. I might have believed her if it weren't for the fact that I was steadily improving in all of my other lessons.

To prove my point, I'd asked Darcy, Sofia and Diego to join me in the Fire Arena after dinner so that I could show them the improvements I'd made and get them to confirm I wasn't insane. Darcy had been having similar troubles with her Fire magic and I wanted her to try wielding her flames without the suit too. Maybe I was onto something.

To make sure I had time to do that, I'd headed out on my evening run early and I ran through Water Territory with my headphones on and my heart rate up.

I loved running here. Back in Chicago it had been all back alleys and concrete jungle. I'd been dodging cars, pedestrians and trash cans at every turn. In the Academy grounds I was more likely to come across a herd of Pegasus, a swooping Griffin or a shimmering waterfall. It was beyond beautiful here and the differences between the four territories always took my breath away.

I headed over a small bridge and began to circle the lake, adjusting my breathing as the hill elevated beneath my feet.

A prickle ran along my spine as I reached the top of the hill and I stumbled to a halt as a Nemean Lion leapt out of the trees in front of me.

My breath caught in my lungs as the huge lion roared excitedly and shook his mane before bounding into the trees on the other side of the path. The student was obviously enjoying stretching their powerful legs in their Order form and I stared after them in surprise.

Shit I don't think I'll ever get used to that.

"You should pay more attention to your surroundings," Darius called and I turned to find him leaning against a tree like he had nowhere else in the world to be. He was wearing a mud stained sports kit with the Ignis symbol emblazoned across his chest so I guessed he'd been at Pitball training, but that didn't explain his sudden appearance here.

This wasn't the first time I'd seen him while I was out running and I was starting to get the feeling that he was following me. His reasons for doing so couldn't be anything good so I'd changed up my route every night this week but I still kept bumping into him regardless.

I glanced about in case the other Heirs were going to spring a trap at any moment but there was no sign of them. I pointed to my ears, shrugging like the heavy bass of the music in my headphones prevented me from hearing him then ran on.

He didn't make any move to follow me but I upped my pace regardless, turning from the main path and heading back towards The Orb. The last thing I needed was to go head to head with an Heir right now. I was all for bringing them down covertly but I wasn't ready to confront them directly... yet.

I made it back to The Orb and slowed as I used my Water magic to clean the sweat and spattered mud from my skin and clothes. Professor Washer had taught us how to do it last week and even though his description of reaching 'every little nook and cranny' had made me vomit in my mouth, I had to admit that it was a damn handy bit of magic.

One of my favourite tracks came on over the headphones and I smiled to myself as I walked into The Orb, giving my attention to the song as All The Small Things blasted in my ears.

I stepped through the door without really looking where I was going and crashed straight into a hard body.

"Sorry," I muttered, stepping back and glancing up to find Professor Orion looking down at me with a super unamused expression on his face. He was wearing a sports kit splattered with mud too and I vaguely remembered that he was the Pitball coach.

"And there was me thinking that Blue was the clumsy twin," he said dryly.

"Just thought I'd mix it up a bit," I replied with a shrug, shifting one of my headphones off of my ear so that I could hear him properly.

"Well I think I prefer it when you're predictably different to each other," he said, making a move to walk away from me. His sleeves were pushed back and my gaze fell on the red symbol for Leo that was raised on his forearm. It didn't really look like a tattoo, it was more like a brand.

"Isn't Darius a Leo?" I asked quickly, snagging his attention before he could walk away. My mouth always did run away with me and apparently even Mr Grumpy's best death stare wasn't enough to make me back down. But if their connection could help us figure out what Astrum's message had meant then it was worth annoying him over.

"Why would I have any interest in discussing Mr Acrux's star sign with you in my free time?" he asked dismissively.

"Because you're a Libra," I said. "And you've got matching *best friends forever* tattoos, I just thought it was a bit strange."

Orion's bored expression dipped into a scowl which warned me in no uncertain terms to back off but I raised my chin as I waited for his response. I may have just stepped into the arena with a pitbull but I couldn't back out now.

"Perhaps if you spent as much time studying as you do inspecting other people's bodies then you might not have so much trouble keeping up in my class," he suggested.

Before I could respond, he turned and walked away. I watched him leave through narrowed eyes. Something weird was going on between him and Darius and I had the feeling it involved me and my sister.

"Your majesty! We've brought a selection of meals to the table for you to choose from!" Angelica called.

I turned as another enthusiastic Ass member waved me over to our table in the centre of the room and moved forward to greet all of them while firmly reminding them to drop the royal titles. Again.

I smiled as I spotted Sofia, Diego and Darcy chatting together on their way towards the food too and I slipped between the crowd to join them as we dropped into chairs in the middle of the Ass Club.

"Did you have a good run?" Darcy asked with a smirk.

"Yeah. You should all join me next time," I said.

"Ew," Sofia commented. "I prefer to exercise in my Order form or not at all."

"Yeah, I'm really not built for running. Or any kind of physical activities," Diego added, tugging his beanie hat a little lower like he was imagining it blowing away.

I rolled my eyes at them. "Your loss."

Geraldine appeared and took the seat beside me. I smiled warmly at her as she offered me a slice of pizza from her plate. She was wearing a white Pitball kit too with the symbol for earth emblazoned on her chest but she'd taken the time to remove the dirt from hers.

I relaxed back into my chair as I took a bite of cheesy goodness.

"I overheard you talking to Orion about his tattoo," she said as she began to eat too. "And I followed him to take a closer look at it out of interest."

"Look at you, Geraldine, I'm beginning to think I'm totally corrupting you," I teased.

She blushed a little but went on. "Did I hear you say that Darius Acrux has one that matches?"

"He does," I agreed. "And I've seen the two of them... hanging out." I shrugged, it hardly sounded like the conspiracy theory of the year but I knew in my gut that they were up to something.

Darcy overheard our conversation and leaned in to join our discussion too.

"Do you know something?" she asked, obviously noticing the fact that Geraldine looked about fit to burst.

"By golly, I think I do. From the looks of that tattoo and what you've told me... I mean, hot, gooey oat cakes, I can't believe I'm even *thinking* this but..."

"But..?" I urged.

"Well it looks like they've undergone a protection bond," she said dramatically, looking around at us with wide eyes like she'd just informed me she was pregnant with fourteen kittens.

"Sorry Geraldine but we'll need a bit more explanation there," I said and Darcy giggled.

"Oh, of course. So, a protection bond is an ancient piece of magic which links two souls together. In generations past, members of my family were selected to be guardians for members of yours," she added proudly.

"Oh, wow," Darcy said as that was clearly the response Geraldine wanted.

I shifted a little in my seat. My soul was perfectly content not being bound to anyone else's, thank you very much. Geraldine leaned forward conspiratorially to continue her explanation and I was glad she wasn't making a suggestion to bond herself to us.

"In effect, magic is used to fuse the two of them together by linking their souls. Its purpose is to protect the life of an important person AKA the ward - in this case, Darius - by making sure that the guardian - Orion - will always place themselves between him and danger. So in effect, if Darius were to come under attack, Orion would feel it and be duty bound to come to his aid. It was said that guardians could even feel the pain of their wards if they were injured and would give every last drop of their magic to protect and heal them."

"So a guardian would die for their ward?" Darcy asked, her voice dropping to a whisper.

"Absolutely, if it was necessary to save their ward's life. Apparently the bond does more than just make the guardian protective though. It also draws the two of them together, their souls aching for each other's company if they spend too much time apart. It's supposed to be very intense. It is quite an outdated practice though. Years ago, the powerful families used to force people to be their guardians against their will. So laws were put into place to stop that from happening. Now, a guardian must volunteer to take up the position and complete various assessments and trials before they can be bonded to their ward. Orion must care very deeply for Darius to have agreed to such a role. It's not something that can be undone once the magic is cast; being a guardian is for life. Only death can release either of them from the bond."

"So Darius is bound by this just as much as Orion is?" Darcy asked in an undertone.

Geraldine nodded seriously. "Oh holy pop-tarts! Speak of the devil," she muttered, looking over my shoulder.

I turned to see Darius striding into the room with Seth, Max and Caleb at his side. They were still in their dirty Pitball kits which seemed to be drawing even more attention to them than usual and I couldn't deny how good they looked in them. Caleb's shirt had even been torn over one shoulder and my gaze lingered on the toned muscles of his chest which it exposed. Several girls called out to try and snag their attention, a few more of them waving and whistling. The Heirs absorbed the attention like they were owed it and I tried not to stare along with everyone else.

I swallowed thickly, hoping not to draw their attention.

Max's eyes shifted over to us and I stilled as he pointed our way.

"Oh crap," Darcy breathed as the others followed his gaze and the four of them cut straight through the crowded room towards us.

Students scrambled aside as they moved, a few even leaping out of their chairs to give them room to approach.

The A.S.S. bristled around us, some of them standing, others raising their hands like they might cast magic. I should have felt reassured by their show of solidarity but I knew it didn't really mean anything. Fae had to fight for their own position, if the Heirs came against us one on one no one would intervene.

"Hey, little Vegas," Max said as the four of them came to stand over us. I'd hardly seen him since he'd Song-Spelled me and I'd begun to hope that he was avoiding me because I knew his secret. Apparently not.

"What do you want?" I asked coldly.

"Just checking in with our favourite twins," Seth cooed, reaching forward to stroke my hair. I slapped his hand away from me and glared at him. "Maybe I should make myself a Tory bracelet too."

Silence had fallen all around The Orb as everyone waited to see what was going to happen.

My gaze slid to Caleb and he smiled lightly which wasn't all that reassuring as I didn't trust him one bit.

"Perhaps we weren't clear enough the other night at the dance," Max growled as he shifted forward to the front of the group. "But that was a gentle warning for you to leave this place. Maybe you should take it before things escalate."

"Escalate?" Darcy demanded. "How could they possibly escalate?"

"Oh I'm sure the two of you have more fears you'd like to share with the group," he purred and I could feel the pull of his magic as he used his Siren powers against us.

A pool of warmth and trust grew in my gut, a soft smile pulled at my lips. Max was kind, he was a good listener, why wouldn't I want to let him help me deal with my fears?

Max grinned triumphantly and grabbed a chair, turning it so that he could sit on it backwards as he leaned close to me.

"Tell me about the boyfriend who left you to drown in that car," he urged, reaching out to touch my cheek. "Did you give him your V-card too?"

A flicker of fear shuddered through me as I remembered sinking to the bottom of that river. But he'd been wrong about the V-card guess. I'd given my virginity to a wholly different asshole.

"No," I breathed. "I didn't."

"You wanna tell the group who did then?" Max asked with a grin, his power wrapping me in thick cords and refusing to let go. In place of the fear that had been pulling at me, I felt lust building in my veins and my flesh heated at the memory of a dark room, roaming hands-

Oh hell no, you psychotic asshole!

I shoved all of my will into fighting off the pull of his gift and my fist snapped out with every inch of rage I was harbouring against this douchebag. My knuckles collided directly with the centre of his throat. Max fell back off of the chair with a cry of pain and hit the floor with the chair on top of him. The Siren spell was broken and I was on my feet half a second later, flames springing to life in my hands.

I spared half a glance at the other Heirs but they only looked on in surprise. This was between me and Max and they weren't going to get involved for once.

"You crazy bitch," Max wheezed, his voice strangled with pain.

"I *am* a crazy bitch," I agreed, glaring down at him. "And if you try that screwed up Siren shit on me ever again you'll find out just how much of a bitch I can be."

He hissed a curse and raised a palm, throwing a wave of water at me. I unleashed the fire in my hands, throwing a torrent of power into the blow and the two Elements collided in the space between us, cancelling each other out with a hiss of steam.

Max scrambled backwards, preparing a second blow and adrenaline shot through my limbs. I was outmatched here and he knew it.

I may not have been able to fight him with magic but I'd grown up in the shittiest part of town and I sure as hell knew how to brawl like a cornered alley cat.

Before he could cast another spell at me, I aimed a kick at his balls.

Max grunted a curse as he doubled in on himself, clutching his manhood. I leaned down to speak to him in a low tone.

"I'd think long and hard about trying to pull any more secrets from my lips," I hissed. "Because some of the ones I'm keeping aren't my own."

His eyes widened in surprise as he looked up at me.

"If you tell anyone what I said when you were Song-Spelled then I'll-"

I interrupted him before he could threaten me with anything, my voice low and cold. "It won't matter what you do to me after. Your secret will be out there. So I think you were just about to agree to keeping your leech powers to yourself."

Max scowled as he propped himself up on one arm, the pain in his balls obviously easing off.

"Fine," he spat, as if he was going to get up but I wanted to really make sure he got the point.

I lifted my palms at Max as Darcy cried out in encouragement and I sent a wave of air crashing into him. It caught him in its grip and sent him flying into the air and tumbling away from me across the room.

I didn't wait for him to recover and come for me again. I caught Darcy's arm and we turned and headed for the exit. Diego, Sofia, Geraldine, Angelica and the rest of the A.S.S. got to their feet and swarmed around us as we walked away. Darcy linked her arm with mine and she grinned triumphantly as we made it outside.

"That's another point to us," she said in a low voice.

"And man did it feel good."

Before we could get very far, Caleb shot through the crowd and came to a halt in front of me. He dropped his kit bag on the floor beside us and pushed a hand through his curls in a way that drew attention to his flexing bicep and didn't seem to be entirely accidental.

"Can I have a word, sweetheart?" he asked casually, like I hadn't just gone head to head with one of his friends and come out on top.

"Why?" I asked, my tone unfriendly.

"You're breaking my heart with this ice queen act," he teased, stepping into my personal space.

"If you're going to bite me then just get on with it. Toying with your food is so unattractive."

"No biting. Just come and talk to me," he said, turning puppy dog eyes on me and damn if Caleb Altair didn't look cute as hell when he was begging.

I glanced at Darcy and was surprised to find her eyes sparkling with excitement. "It's fine," she said. "We can wait for you here if you want some privacy."

I almost asked her why the hell she'd think I'd want privacy with one of the assholes who'd tormented us but her gaze slipped from mine to Caleb's kit bag on the ground for the most fleeting of seconds and I realised this just might be the opportunity we'd been waiting for to get some revenge on the Terra Heir. And I could be the distraction.

"Fine," I said, sighing in a defeated way.

Caleb smiled like I'd just made his day and caught my hand, pulling me after him as he led me around the side of The Orb, leaving his bag on the ground.

He drew me along until we were alone at the rear of the building, the light of the setting sun blazing orange across its golden surface.

As soon as he was sure we couldn't be seen, he caught my waist and pushed me back against the bronze structure. Thanks to my run I was wearing leggings and a sports bra so his hands were warm against the bare skin on my stomach.

"What are you doing?" I asked before he could move any closer.

"Hoping to convince you to kiss me again," he murmured and my pulse hitched at the confidence in his tone.

"Not likely," I said dismissively.

Caleb groaned like I was torturing him and I couldn't help but smile a little. "I can't believe you just sucker punched Max," he said.

"Of course I did, he was being a dick. And I'm not going to give him details of my sex life to jerk off over."

"You're a straight up badass Tory," Caleb joked, drawing a little closer to me. "Were you worried that people might have found out what I did with you in that classroom?" He reached out to touch my cheek but I fought off the temptation to be sucked in by his rugged looks.

"Well it would be pretty embarrassing if anyone found out I had such terrible taste in men," I replied.

Caleb chuckled darkly and a little shiver ran down my spine but I refused to acknowledge it.

"Are you going to tell me Max's secret then?" he asked, changing the subject.

I frowned at him a little. I'd thought that part of my interaction with Max had stayed private because of the noise the crowd was making but Caleb obviously used his Vampire hearing to listen in.

"Oh you know, he gets a hard on for Pegasuses just like you," I teased and a thrill of satisfaction ran through me as I saw anger flashing in Caleb's navy eyes at that taunt.

"That rumour is a load of shit," he snapped and my smile widened.

"Touchy," I teased.

Caleb released a breath before flashing me a dazzling smile which said he didn't give a shit but I could see through it.

"So. You're not going to tell me Max's secret then?" he pressed. "I could Coerce it from you, you know."

"I'm sure you could. Or you could just ask him yourself." I shrugged.

I wasn't entirely sure why I was keeping Max's secret apart from the fact that I'd seen the honesty in him when he'd said that revealing it could hurt Solaria as a whole. And as much as I didn't want to take on the responsibility of ruling this kingdom, I didn't want to give the Nymphs an advantage against it either.

Caleb seemed to consider that and I guessed loyalty to his friend won out over curiosity because he dropped the subject.

"So how did you enjoy being Song-Spelled?" he asked mischievously.

"Being forced out of my bed in the middle of the night to spend time with one of my least favourite people? I've had better evenings," I said dryly.

"Yeah but you did get to make out with him," he said with a grin.

I rolled my eyes and didn't dignify that with a response.

"So are you going to tell me who's the better kisser?" he pushed, leaning in so close that his breath mingled with mine.

"Hmm." I bit my lip as I made a show of considering it and the hunger lighting Caleb's eyes made my pulse hitch. "Neither of you really stood out so it's hard to say."

Caleb pushed his tongue into his cheek as he tried to stop me from baiting him. "Maybe you need a reminder then?"

He moved forward but I turned away so that his mouth hit my cheek instead of my lips.

"You're really going to make me work for this aren't you?" he growled as his mouth shifted down to my neck and my skin lit up beneath him.

But I wasn't ready to let him off the hook for everything he and his friends had put us through. He needed to be punished and I hoped that I'd given Darcy enough time to advance our plans against him.

I cleared my throat to cover the racing of my heart and pushed him back.

"I actually have things to do tonight so if you're done with your questions and you're not going to bite me then I'm going to leave."

Caleb stared at me in surprise as I slipped out of his grip.

I turned away from him and headed back around The Orb to find my friends again.

"You're killing me, you know that right?" he called after me.

"I'm sure you can find a nice Pegasus girl to help you work through some of that frustration," I replied without bothering to look back at him.

As I returned to Darcy and the others she grinned at me conspiratorially. Caleb's bag was exactly where he'd left it as if nothing had happened in his absence.

We walked away and I glanced back at him as he retrieved it. His gaze was fixed on me and I smirked at him as he watched me leave. I knew I was playing with fire when it came to him but I just couldn't help myself.

Once we were far enough from him to be sure that he wouldn't overhear, I turned to Darcy expectantly.

"So?"

"I got his Atlas. Caleb Altair just joined a lot of Pegasus appreciation groups on FaeBook," she said with a grin. "And he also sent a few suggestive messages to some Pegasus girls on campus."

An excited laugh fell from my lips and I high fived my sister. "Those assholes won't know what hit them when we're through."

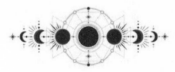

It was pretty late by the time I made it back to my room but the satisfied smirk hadn't left my lips since I'd sucker punched Max in the throat.

I amused myself by sorting through my latest online shopping orders while listening to some seriously cheery music which I'd selected from a playlist I'd found on my Atlas. I was intermittently dancing and singing along and I couldn't keep the smug ass smile from my face as I did. I was guessing a Pegasus had put the playlist together and it suited my mood just fine right then because I was every shade of happy after beating down Max Rigel in front of all of his friends.

Of course, I was sure I'd suffer the consequences of that interaction soon enough but it was worth whatever he'd throw at me next just to know that

I'd well and truly humiliated him for once.

The weather was having mood swings again and it had swung back to stupidly humid tonight. I'd thrown my window open and dressed in a tiny pair of shorts and a thin cami but I still felt hotter than a polar bear at the beach.

I was waiting for Sofia to join me for a study session but she was running late. I was happy enough to sort through my latest online shopping purchases though. Darcy seemed to think I had an addiction and as I rifled through a box of lacy underwear I was beginning to think she might have a point. But I didn't care, I'd never had a disposable income before and the stipend we'd been given was stupidly generous. I didn't mind flexing my plastic muscles to their limit as a hobby.

A loud knock sounded at my door just as Taylor Swift's Shake It Off started and I upped my dance moves as I called for Sofia to come in.

"You're just in time," I said as I grabbed a red bra from the box. "Diego would go nuts over you in this."

I turned to face her and my mouth fell open as I found a brooding Dragon asshole in my doorway instead of my friend. Weirdly, he was smiling at me like I amused him instead of scowling like I'd just pissed on his grandma but I wasn't going to trust in this strangely friendly visage.

I stopped dancing instantly and tossed the bra back in the box.

"Don't stop dancing on my account," Darius urged, his eyes dripping over my shorts in a way that made my blood heat.

"What do you want?" I demanded.

"I had no idea you were such a huge Taylor Swift fan," he said, leaning against the doorframe like he owned the damn place. Which I guessed he thought he did as the almighty House Captain.

Taylor belted out another chorus and I tilted my head as I regarded him. "She makes some very good points which I happen to agree with."

"It suits you," he said.

"What does?" I asked.

211

"Smiling."

I scowled at him in response. "It's hardly surprising you haven't seen it very often." I tapped my Atlas and killed the music as I folded my arms. "Back to my original question though: what do you want?"

Darius released a breath and the amusement left his eyes as he adjusted to the new tone in the room.

"I have an invitation for you and your sister to come to a party at my family's house to meet the Celestial Council," he said.

I raised an eyebrow at him, waiting for the punchline as he offered me a thick envelope stamped with swirling golden script.

"No thanks," I replied, not taking it and swinging the door shut in his face.

His boot landed over the threshold and the door bounced off of it. Why did these assholes think that was okay?

"It's not the kind of invitation you can refuse," he said through gritted teeth.

"I beg to disagree," I said dryly. A night at his house sounded like a very specific flavour of hell and I had no interest in tasting it.

"What makes you think that you can say no?" he growled. "It's next Saturday night. I'll come get you at six. Wear something nice." He eyed my shorts and tight shirt with disapproval and I raised an eyebrow at him as he turned to walk away, tossing the invite at my feet. He hadn't seemed to hate my outfit so much when he'd been watching my dance moves.

"Yeah, that's not going to work for me," I called, leaving the invite on the floor. "But feel free to rock up here any time you like next weekend, I won't be here anyway."

I swung the door shut and headed to my bed, flopping down and tapping my Atlas back on as the cheery beat of my music resumed. I plugged my headphones in and slapped them on, selecting some old school Eminem to suit my new mood and smirking at the change in pace.

I lay back on the soft mattress for half a second before the door flew open and Darius stalked in again, all testosterone and flexing muscles. But I wasn't afraid of him for once; this was an argument he couldn't win. I wasn't going to his stupid party no matter what he did to me.

I pretended not to notice him and cranked up the volume as he began laying into me and his voice was lost to Eminem suggesting the real slim shady please stand up.

My heart was pounding a little harder but I ignored it as I forcefully ignored him.

After about five seconds of me pretending there wasn't a six and a half foot lump of muscle standing over me with a scowl deep enough to get lost in, a torrent of water slammed into me.

I flinched back and cried out just as Darius ripped my headphones off and tossed them aside.

"You are walking on damn thin ice with me, Roxy," he growled. "If you keep pushing me you're seriously going to regret it."

"Screw you," I spat. "You treat me like shit every day of the week so what difference does it make if you threaten to do it more? You want me to go to your stupid party? Then you're going to have to find me and drag me there kicking and screaming and I'll spend the entire night embarrassing the shit out of you just for the hell of it. It's not like I give a crap what Mommy and Daddy Acrux think of me anyway."

Darius snatched my wrist into his grasp and dragged me upright so that he could snarl in my face.

"This is your last warning."

"Warn away, asshole," I hissed. "You can't do any more to me than you have already. And I notice you haven't tried to drown me again since your little pal Orion gave you a dressing down so I'm guessing you aren't actually allowed to kill me."

His grip on my arm tightened painfully and I couldn't rein in my flinch quickly enough to stop him noticing. He released me suddenly and I drew my arm against my chest, fighting the urge to massage the pain away.

"Of course I'm not going to kill you," he muttered and I scoffed in response. So he had one line which he wouldn't cross and that was murder. Great to know. He let out a long sigh before continuing in a softer tone. "What will it take to get you to come with me willingly?"

I narrowed my eyes at him. "To quote you when I came to your room needing help; if you want me to help you, you'll have to make me. And as I'm sure you can't control my smart mouth or preference for crop tops and leather jackets I doubt you'll be able to force my cooperation in this at a level which you would find acceptable so I suggest you just give up."

Darius eyed me curiously for a moment and the difference it made to his features was almost breathtaking. I wasn't sure he'd ever *really* looked at me with anything other than a scowl in place before. He really was devastatingly good looking. Every inch of his face looked like it had been carved from stone, all strong lines and perfect angles. My heart thumped unevenly for a moment and I swallowed down the traitorous glimmer of attraction I felt to him, holding myself firmly in denial over it.

"How about a trade then?" he suggested, lowering his voice and leaning closer to me like we were sharing a secret. "I'll tutor you like I said if you and your sister come to this party willingly, make nice with my father, wear a pretty dress and make some attempt to behave like you're civilised."

I was so shocked by his suggestion that for several seconds I could only stare at him.

"*And* I'll promise to be... nice to you," he added, reading my silence as hesitation instead of surprise. "For that night only."

"I doubt you know how," I replied flatly, plucking at my wet shirt which was plastered to me. I was going to have to impose on Darcy tonight if I wanted to sleep in a dry bed.

Darius pursed his lips and reached out towards me. I took a step back, expecting him to turn angry again but instead his fingers skimmed against the soaked material which clung to my stomach as he drew the water back out of my shirt. My heart fluttered a little in response to his touch and I cursed my terrible taste in men for the millionth time.

I watched him in silence as every drop of water was removed from my clothes, hair and bed until a ball of liquid hung in the air between us. Darius directed it into my bathroom and I watched as it dropped into the basin and disappeared down the drain.

"See, I can be nice," he said as if he'd just done me a favour even though we both knew that he'd been the one to drench me in the first place. He withdrew his hand from my waist and I ignored the ache I felt as the point of contact between us was broken.

"You must really care about impressing Daddy Acrux," I muttered, twisting my long hair between my fingers just to give myself something to do.

Darius gave a noncommittal noise in response and I realised my guess was off the mark.

"*Or* you're really that afraid of disappointing him," I added.

Darius's dark eyes flashed with some deep emotion for half a second before he squashed it back down.

"You don't know anything about my family," he growled, that anger rising in him just as quickly as it had disappeared.

"Well if they're anything like *you* then they're obviously a bunch of assholes."

A wave of heated power slammed into me, knocking me back against the wall as Darius surged forward, leaning down to glare right into my eyes.

"Say that again," he challenged, the threat in his voice clear.

My heart pounded with fear but I knew I'd been right before. He couldn't kill me. And I was sick of feeling like I just had to roll over and take his bullshit. If he was determined to torment me then fine, there was nothing I could do about it. But I wasn't going to let him break me.

"Well at least I know where you get it from," I breathed.

His eyes flashed with the reptilian slits of his Dragon form, the irises turning golden for a moment as he glared at me. "Fuck you." He was gone as quickly as he'd arrived, his power releasing me so that I was left slumped against the wall while he stalked from my room.

For a few seconds, I couldn't move, my heart raced and fear trickled through my veins but I forced myself to follow him to the doorway. He'd almost made it to the end of the corridor when I called out to stop him.

"I'll meet you in the Fire Arena after dinner tomorrow. If you can stick to your word and help me harness my magic then I'll come to your stupid party and I'll even wear a pretty dress like I'm a nice girl."

Darius stopped and looked over his shoulder at me in surprise.

"Just like that?"

I shrugged. "Maybe I wanna see how the other half live," I teased.

For a second he actually seemed amused but I must have been imagining it. "I'll have dresses sent over for you." Darius walked away before I could tell him that I was perfectly capable of dressing myself and I rolled my eyes as I shut the door.

Looks like we'll be having dinner with the devil next Saturday night then.

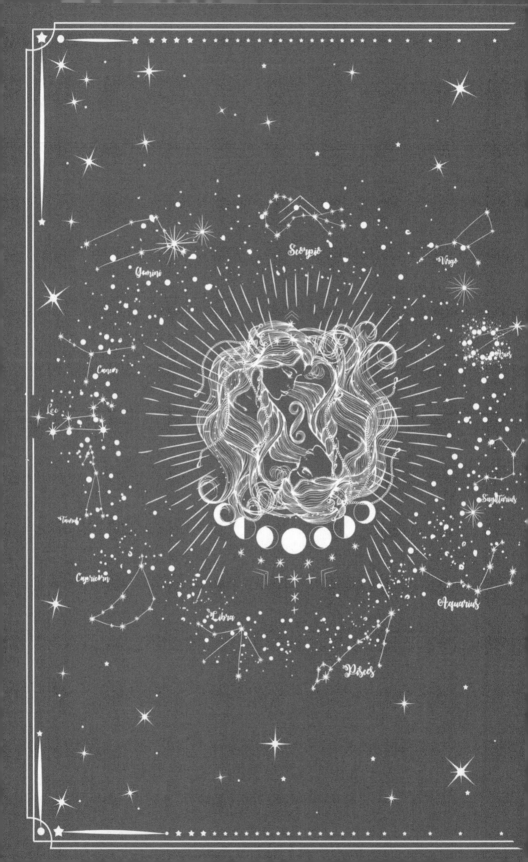

DARCY

CHAPTER THIRTEEN

I woke to the sound of wind chimes jingling on my Atlas and joy beamed through me as I shot out of bed.

Today is the day!

My heart jumped excitedly as I raced across my room to the bottle which sat in the light of the morning sun before the window. The yellow crystal emitted a bright glow where it floated at the bottom of the liquid. It had turned entirely clear just like the instructions had said it would. *Yay!*

I used the star chart on my Atlas to angle myself toward the North Star then sat down on the floor with the bottle, taking a steadying breath. I prayed with all my heart that this would work as I unscrewed the top and the scent of something heavenly sweet reached my nose.

Here goes nothing.

I tipped it into my mouth and was delighted by the delicious taste, swallowing a small mouthful before stopping. I didn't want to risk the chance that I'd gotten the recipe wrong and was about to accidentally poison myself.

I reached up to touch my hair, hope burning through me like a shining star.

Come on. Please grow.

My eyes watered as I waited, tugging at my locks, begging it to extend. "Grow out dammit."

I skimmed my fingers over the bald patch at the back of my head and the tears burned more keenly, threatening to fall.

Soft, luscious hair pushed into my palm and a squeal of excitement escaped me as a new inch grew all over my head.

"Yes!" I stood up, tipping the bottle into my mouth and pouring it all down my throat.

I ran to the bathroom, whipping the door open and hurrying to the basin to look in the mirror. It was already longer, down to my chin, then my neck, my shoulders.

I whooped my delight, jogging on the spot as I ran my fingers through the dark, silky locks. They tumbled all the way down my back, perhaps even a little longer than I'd had it before. I wound it around my fingers and reached beneath it to check for bald patches. Nothing. I was whole again. And I felt stronger than I ever had.

I hurried back to my room with a fire roaring in my heart.

I snatched my Atlas, tapping on my horoscope with a wide smile on my face. I had to endure detention with Orion today whilst stuck in the company of the Heirs, but even *that* wasn't capable of dousing my mood.

Good morning Gemini.

The stars have spoken about your day!

You'll find yourself at the mercy of a Libra today, but take heart, Libras tend to offer fairness in everything they do. If you follow the natural push and pull of your signs, you'll find the day flows much more smoothly. Beware though, as Mercury moves closer to retrograde in the coming weeks, the stars are

feeling more volatile. A simple flip of a coin could change your day for the
better, or for much worse.
Your actions will decide which way the wind blows.

Okay so that sounded *fairly* positive. The smile was still stamped on my face and I was going to ensure the stars kept it there for the remainder of the day.

I didn't have long before I had to meet Orion in Jupiter Hall to commence my detention – *please don't be a beating!* - so I hurried to The Orb to grab some breakfast beforehand.

Campus was peacefully quiet, the only sound the chirruping dawn chorus and the rustle of leaves in the wind. Shadows shifted overhead and I cupped my hand with my eyes, gazing up to spot a group of Harpies sailing under the light of dawn.

I hadn't seen any in their shifted form before and I marvelled at their beauty. Apart from their bird-like characteristics, they still looked mostly Fae. Their wings held a silvery hue which flashed pink in the rising sun. Their bodies were plated with bronze and copper armour and their feet had morphed into sharp talons.

Laughter carried down from them as they cartwheeled and twisted through the air and for a moment I was captivated watching them. My mother had belonged to their Order. And the sight of them playing in the sky made me hope I might emerge as one of them too. Her blood ran in my veins but so did my father's. A Hydra. I shuddered at the idea of it. I certainly didn't want to be a fifty headed giant beast roaming around campus like an extra in Jurassic Park. *No thanks.*

When I walked into The Orb, I found the place predictably empty. Not even Geraldine was up this early to put on her usual breakfast feast for us. Though that was probably because she'd finally figured out Tory didn't show her face for anyone before nine am on the weekends. And even that was a rarity.

I headed to the pristine buffet of shining pastries and vats of cereal which were ready and waiting as always. I never saw a single member of staff in the Academy outside of the faculty so I wondered if this kind of work was done by magic.

I helped myself to a croissant and a cup of coffee, glancing around the large room and wondering where to sit. My eyes fell on the Heirs' curved red sofa as I took a large bite out of my pastry.

I can't sit there.

Can I?

Feeling high on the buzz that invaded me, I weaved through the tables and found myself standing before it. I glanced around to double check I was alone then dropped down at the heart of it, placing my coffee on the table. I felt the same rush I imagined Goldilocks had felt in the three bears' house and a giggle escaped me as a few crumbs cascaded down onto the seats either side of me.

My gaze kept flipping to the door. I knew I was playing with fire; the Heirs had detention with me today and they would surely grab some breakfast before it started. But it felt too good defying them for me to stop.

When I'd swallowed the last bite of my croissant, I picked up my coffee and jerked it toward me a bit too hastily, splashing it across the plush surface (and okay a bit on my knees).

Oh shit.

I stood up, heading back to the breakfast table to grab a few napkins when the door opened. I moved like the wind, dropping into the closest chair, my heart pounding wildly as the four Heirs strolled in one after the other.

I refused to look over at the coffee stained sofa, instead focusing on finishing my drink with my head angled away from them and my hair creating a curtain between us.

"Get me a pan au chocolat, Max," Seth demanded, dropping into his seat before immediately springing back up. "Ergh! What the fuck?"

"What?" Darius asked, yawning as he moved to join him.

"Someone spilled coffee on my seat."

Haha sucker.

Max headed over to the breakfast table, throwing a glance my way, his scowl deepening. But thankfully he didn't utter a word.

"I thought your sister was the one joining us in detention?" Caleb suddenly purred in my ear and I jolted in alarm. He leaned in close to my neck, shifting my hair away so he could gain access to my throat. His lips brushed gently over my skin and I jerked away in horror.

"I'm not Tory," I blurted, pushing him back and lurching out of my seat in the same movement. *And does he always touch my sister so freaking intimately?*

Caleb stared at me with a crease on his brow. "Is that supposed to be a joke?" He grinned playfully but I shook my head, sensing all of the Heirs looking my way now.

Seth rubbed the back of his damp pants, stalking toward me with his eyes narrowed. "Who helped you?" he growled, his voice void of warmth.

I stood my ground, my hand clamped tightly around my coffee cup. "I helped myself. I can read a library book, Seth. It's not rocket science."

His eyes narrowed to even sharper slits as he glowered at my full head of hair. I slowly brought the coffee to my lips and took a sip, desperately trying not to show how intimidated I felt. But that feeling wasn't as powerful as the song spilling from my heart in response to his expression. Because I'd won. And that tail of blue hair around his wrist didn't mean as much as it had yesterday.

His gaze fell to the coffee cup in my hand and my heart juddered. A dark grin pulled at his mouth and he folded his arms. "Hey guys, it looks like this Vega was trying out the throne this morning." He stepped closer and the shadows of the other Heirs drew in.

My mouth dried up as my eyes flicked between them, fear slithering through my body.

"Did you sit on our couch?" Max asked like I'd done a whole lot worse.

"You don't own it," I blurted before I could stop myself.

The group closed in tighter and the hairs raised on the back of my neck.

Crap crap crap. I should not have pissed off the bear family. Goldilocks definitely got eaten in the original version of that story.

"Actually, sweetheart, we do own it," Caleb said. "This place would be nothing without the Celestial Families funding it."

"So apologise," Max whispered close to my ear, but he didn't use his Siren powers against me.

I pressed my lips together, refusing to say it. If I did, I'd be giving in. Bowing to their display of power. And even if I suffered the consequences for it, I had to stand my ground.

Just please don't take my hair again.

Darius toyed with a small sphere of flame in his palm. "Why did Orion give you detention, Gwendalina?"

I glowered at the name, watching as the magic in his hand twisted and writhed.

"That's between me and him."

"Oohh secrets with Orion," Seth taunted. "You always did give him the fuck-me eyes. Are you in trouble for trying to spread your legs for a teacher, babe? Guess the students aren't interested so you had to look elsewhere. I'll make sure to ask him for all the details later."

The poison in his words slid into my veins and I dug deep for my courage, hunting for a response to his vicious question. "Well I guess that's the difference between us Seth. I'd spend the rest of the afternoon vomiting if anyone gave me details about *your* sex life. But you seem awfully interested in mine." My heart thumped an erratic tune as I latched onto the one insult that I knew had gotten under his skin. The beating Tyler had taken for suggesting Seth was interested in me was a clear indicator of how much it bothered him. And though I knew I wasn't going to come out of this altercation unscathed, I also knew that standing my ground was the only way to survive this Academy. Besides, after reuniting with my hair I was still determined to stay on top of the world today. No matter what.

"Maybe that's why she's here," Max chided and I turned to him with a questioning frown. "So Orion can spread them again."

"Screw you," I hissed, blood thumping against every inch of my skin.

"Back off," Darius said, surprising me. "Orion wouldn't lay a hand on the daughter of The Savage King. He's got more class than that."

Caleb knocked his shoulder into Darius's. "I forgot you two were little buddies."

"We're not little buddies," Darius said flatly but broke a smile when Caleb turned away.

"No we are definitely not, Mr Acrux," Orion's voice cut across the room and the group split apart to look for him. He stood in the doorway in a t-shirt and jeans, looking like one of us with his casual clothes and youthful appearance. I wondered how much older than us he actually was; it couldn't have been more than a few years. "Especially since you all left me waiting in Jupiter Hall. You've all just added an extra two hours to your day which means the sun will be long gone by the time you head to eat whatever scraps are left for dinner this evening."

"For fuck's sake," Max huffed and my heart sank a little.

Dammit, why is this day trying to ruin my mood?

Darius checked his watch, frowning at Orion. "You picked today to be on time for the first time in your life?"

"Yup," Orion popped the P, grinning darkly. "I have plenty in store for you and I just can't *wait* to get started." He looked to me with a frown. "Where's your sister?" he asked sharply.

"Um here?" I said and his frown deepened. "I pushed a hand into my hair. I'm Darcy, sir."

"Oh," he whispered, his throat bobbing. "Well, follow me." He headed

225

out of the door with a dark smile that made my stomach knot.

Max shouldered roughly past me, followed by Seth shoving into my other shoulder. *Douchebags.*

I left a few yards between us as I followed, leaving my coffee cup down on a table as I went, wondering whether I was really going to get away with the sofa incident.

Orion strode off at a brisk pace ahead of the group, making a beeline for The Wailing Wood. From the carefree aura hanging around the Heirs I assumed we weren't about to be beaten and left to die in the forest.

I relaxed a little as we headed into the trees and the Heirs paid me no attention. Orion cut a path all the way through to The Howling Meadow and I frowned as he halted in front of a set of shovels. He turned to face us, his eyes sparkling with one of those grins that said he was about to do something wicked. "The first half of your detention will be spent digging an eight foot deep hole in the meadow."

My heart clenched uncomfortably. Was he for real? I wasn't exactly built for hard labour with my puny arms and small stature.

Caleb snatched up a shovel and Orion caught hold of it the end before he walked off. "You will be digging the hole as a team, Altair."

Caleb groaned. "You know our Order work better alone."

"So do the Dragons and I don't hear Darius complaining. Now get to work. No magic." Orion folded his arms, his expression saying the time for questions was over.

I arched a brow at the way he'd casually called Darius by his first name. And when he passed him a shovel, Darius even thanked him. It seemed like Geraldine's theory about them was spot on. They were a lot more than *little buddies.* They were bonded by those marks on their arms.

Darius stalked off with the other guys and I moved forward to collect my shovel. Orion scooped it up, holding it out for me. Before I took it he caught my hand, brushing his thumb across my palm and sending a shiver through me. He repeated the process on the other hand then pressed his index finger to his lips. "That'll stop your skin chaffing," he whispered.

I stared at him in complete surprise as he passed me the shovel and moved aside.

"Thank you," I said, confused as I stepped past him, making my way through the high grass and colourful array of meadow flowers as I walked toward the Heirs. The four of them had formed a circle and were already getting to work digging the hole.

My chest compressed as I drew closer, expecting them to look up and hurl abuse at me at any moment. It wasn't abuse that got hurled though, a shovel full of mud flew my way and slapped me right in the face.

"Ah!" I yelped, spitting out mud as they all roared with laughter. "*Jerks*."

"DROP AND GIVE ME FIFTY SETH CAPELLA!" Orion boomed and I wiped the mud from my eyes, spotting him climbing up onto a high chair that looked more fitting for a lifeguard than a vampire in a field.

Who the hell put that there?

Seth was already half way through his set of push-ups as I joined the circle, pulling back my new hair which was now speckled with mud as I took a band from my wrist and tied it into a knot. I placed myself between Caleb and Darius, wanting to be as far from the other two as possible. Not that Darius and Caleb were much of an improvement but neither of them were the guy who'd cut off my hair or the one who'd drawn my deepest fear from my lips.

Darius worked like a machine, throwing his weight into the shovel and slamming his boot down on the rim to dig it deeper. I tried to mimic his style, forcing the shovel as deep into the earth as I could manage before tossing the dirt behind me into a pile.

My pile was noticeably smaller than the others' as they worked together, taking a deep slice off of the earth already.

I soon had to catch my breath, desperate for water as I wiped sweat and mud from my brow.

"Vega!" Orion beckoned me and I was grateful to put the shovel down. I was a little dizzy as I walked up to his high metal chair where he was sitting a few feet above my head. He now had a large umbrella set up over it and a flask of coffee in his hand which he'd apparently brought with him. His Atlas was propped on his knee and he looked like he was thoroughly enjoying his morning as he gazed down at my mud stained skin with a bright smile. Thanks to his magic, at least I didn't have any blisters on my hands.

"Water." Orion waved his hand and water gathered in the air before me, circling into a glistening sphere. Orion tossed me a cup and I caught it at the last second. The water dropped straight into it with a splash and I guzzled it down greedily,

"That's favouritism, sir!" Caleb called.

"You're right, how rude of me!" Orion shouted back, lifting a hand and a torrential waterfall poured down on all of the heirs. Max crowed like a cockerel, pounding his chest, seemingly spurred on by the downpour. The others didn't seem quite as happy as the water continued to fall down on them.

A laugh rushed from my throat and Orion threw me a wink. "So I'm having a little trouble, Miss Vega."

"With what, sir?"

"Telling you apart from your sister," he said in a low voice that I imagined only I could hear through the torrential storm he was still casting over the Heirs. "And you never did answer my question. Blue or green?"

A smile twisted up my lips and I shrugged, deciding to leave him in continued suspense over that question, walking back to join the group.

"I want an answer by sundown," he called after me and my grin grew even wider.

Never gonna happen, Professor Two Personalities.

I headed into Orion's downpour as it eased to a localised rain shower. I sighed as it cooled my heated skin and washed away the mud coating my clothes. I stooped down to pick up my shovel but Darius got there first, whipping it up and tossing it to Seth. Seth threw it to Max and he threw it to Caleb. I darted forward to take it and Caleb launched it over my head back to Darius with a bark of laughter.

"For god's sake," I huffed, not buying into their game as I folded my arms.

Darius held it out to me and I moved to take it. I wrapped my fingers around the end and he tugged sharply to draw me toward him. My foot slipped in the mud and someone's foot shot in front of me to finish me off. I landed on my back with a loud splat and laughter rang out around me.

"GIVE ME FIFTY ALTAIR!" Orion bellowed so I guessed Caleb had been the one to trip me. I got to my feet with a grimace, wiping my muddy hands down my jeans.

"He's gone full Pitball coach. It was only a bit of fun," Caleb muttered, stepping out of the rain and dropping down to do his set. I couldn't help but notice the swell of his muscular arms as he moved up and down at a fierce pace. I turned away, internally berating myself as I dug my shovel into the ground. The water made the mud easier to shift and I threw a huge scoop over my shoulder with relief.

"Argh!" Caleb cried and I gasped as I realised I'd thrown the load all over him.

He jumped to his feet, his mouth skewing into a grin and my heart slowed a fraction as I mirrored his smile. "Better watch it, Vega," he said as he passed me but it didn't hold any of the nastiness the other Heirs kept flinging my way.

Seth started singing Raindrops Keep Falling on my Head by Burt Bacharach full pelt. His white shirt had turned entirely transparent to reveal his muscular body and water dripped from him in streams.

"Shut the fuck up!" Orion shouted. "I'm trying to concentrate here."

"Watching porn again, sir?" Seth shot at him with a smirk.

"Yeah, your mom's really improved since the last edition," he answered without missing a beat and Seth's face dropped into a scowl as a laugh tore from my throat.

"Do you know who *is* always watching porn?" Max chipped in.

"You?" the three other guys answered in unison.

They all burst out laughing and I fought the urge to join in.

"Hilarious," Max said dryly. "I meant Washer. He snuck off in class the other day to rub one out."

"Liar," Darius laughed while I wrinkled my nose.

"Psh," Caleb waved down Darius. "I don't even have water magic, but every time I go into their territory I hear Washer watching porn. That guy has got a lust addiction I swear."

"I believe that," I said to myself, but everyone turned to me, brows raised as if they couldn't believe I'd dared to join in on their conversation. I tucked a loose lock of hair behind my ear, feeling awkward under their scrutiny.

"Oh yeah, how come?" Caleb asked, giving me a bemused look.

"He's taken over my Tarot class," I said, feeling a little uncomfortable with them all looking at me. "But we're not even reading cards, he made us do palmistry so he can paw at everyone."

"Ha, no way," Caleb laughed. "Sucks for the girls."

"Not just them, bro," Darius said. "Have you seen the outfits the guys have to wear for Water Elemental class? That creep wants to see my junk every time I show up there."

"I know, and could the bathing suits be any more low cut on the girls?" I said, rolling my eyes.

"Don't say that in front of him or he'll find a way to make it happen," Darius joked with me and I laughed along a little nervously.

Holy shit, the Dragon is actually talking to me like an equal for once.

I noticed Seth watching our interaction with a glower. He flipped a glance at Orion then continued working, the sight of the braid of hair on his wrist setting me on edge again.

It was midday by the time the hole was dug and we stood at the bottom of an eight foot pit, ankle deep in mud, soaked to the bone and tired as hell. Well *I* was anyway. The past few hours, I'd lost my footing so many times I was covered in filth but I'd done my bit. My aching arms were a testament to that.

"Right I hope you all enjoyed your morning as much as I did," Orion called down to us. "Up you get."

Caleb created a slim platform of earth which spiralled up beneath him so he could jump out at the top. Max propelled himself up with a blast of air from his palms and Darius scored a path into the wall of the pit with fire, creating a passage up to the top. Seth propelled himself out with air too and I rubbed my fingers together, my mouth dry as all five of them stared down at me, waiting expectantly. I knew I could have just used Darius's path but I wanted to do it myself and prove my competence.

Max sniggered, elbowing Darius beside him who broke a grin.

I was getting better and better at controlling my air powers and as I shut my eyes to block out the four mocking faces angled my way, I felt for the pressure of air in my body, pushing it out of my hands.

I shot up to the top at high speed and triumph soared through me. I realised a heartbeat too late I'd forgotten to aim and crashed into Seth full force, taking him to the ground. He stared up at me in shock and I scrambled off of him with my cheeks flaming. Someone held a hand out for me and I looked up, finding Darius there.

"Poor effort," he said with a smirk and I reluctantly took his hand as he dragged me upright.

Orion gazed at us with a flicker of amusement in his eyes then pointed at Caleb. "Altair, fill in that hole."

Caleb stepped forward, wielding the mounds of dirt around him and forcing it all down into the hole we'd wasted the entire morning digging. Although, as I glanced between our group and thought about the way a couple of the Heirs had treated me like an actual human being a few times today, I wondered if it wasn't wasted after all.

Orion led us back to the centre of campus and all the way up to Jupiter Hall. We headed inside and followed him across the atrium to a stairwell beyond a large marble archway. He climbed up several floors at a brisk pace and we jogged after him, soon arriving in a long corridor and stopping beneath a hatch in the ceiling.

Orion jumped up, catching hold of the tab, his shirt riding up as he did so and giving me a glimpse of his tightened abs. My cheeks flushed hot and desire unfurled in my belly. I noticed Seth's gaze lingering on him too and was only mildly surprised to realise he clearly swung both ways.

As I turned away from Orion to hide my blush, I spotted a row of metal trowels and large black gloves laid across a cushioned window seat. I frowned as I tried to work out what we were about to do.

Orion pulled down a ladder and I stared up at the clouds above, the sound of the wind whipping by overhead.

"Up," he instructed as we stared at him. He passed out the trowels and thick gloves to the Heirs as they went ahead and disappeared onto the roof.

"You're all wet," he pointed out, his eyes raking down my body. I nodded in answer, unable to make my tongue work as he passed me a trowel and a pair of gloves. "Have they not taught you to dry yourself in your Air Elemental class yet?"

"No, sir."

He looked so inviting, his expression tugging me in and his eyes lighting a blaze that swirled in my chest.

"Useless. Well up you go then," he said and I moved toward the ladder, taking hold of the first rung.

Orion stepped up close behind me and his fingers brushed my waist, barely perceptible but I felt it everywhere. It scored a line of goosebumps across my back and a heavenly shiver fluttered up my spine. Heated air pushed under my clothes, drying them out almost instantly.

"Thank you," I whispered for the second time today. *What's gotten into him?*

He took hold of the ladder either side of my hands. "Up," he breathed against my cheek and hot wax seemed to pour down each of my legs, making it almost impossible to move. But somehow, I managed it.

I climbed up to the hatch, my breath stalling as I arrived on top of Jupiter Hall. The roof was covered with red tiles, dropping into a gentle slope on either side of me and reaching toward a sheer drop below. Orion jumped up beside me and turned me around to face the other end of the roof where the Heirs were grouped together, looking grim.

Coating the tiles was a thick, grey substance which resembled cement.

"A Griffin who shall not be named came up here the other day," Orion announced. "Drunk and in his Order form. Apparently whatever he'd just eaten didn't agree with him."

"Oh my god," I breathed, realising what the mess was.

"Griffin shit is seriously nasty," Orion continued brightly. "It dries as hard as rock and can give you a burning, blotchy purple rash for days if you get it on your skin."

The Heirs immediately started pulling on their gloves, all except Max who folded his arms and shook his head. "I'm not doing that. I've got sensitive skin. I'll get ten times more of a rash than anyone else who touches that shit."

My ears pricked up at that. *That sounds like something I'd love to see.*

His friends started laughing and Orion gave him a weary look.

"If you refuse, you can forget about playing in the match against Starlight Academy next week."

"But sir! My dad's coming to watch that game," Max complained.

"So get cleaning," Orion growled and his tone sent a quiver through me. When he wasn't directing his harsh tone at me, it was super hot.

Max pulled on the gloves, muttering curse words under his breath as he knelt near a pile of the Griffin excrement and started chipping away at it. The second he worked a lump free, a sickly smell rose into the air like rotting cabbage.

Caleb bent over and retched and Orion wrinkled his nose.

"Down wind Altair," Orion encouraged, covering his face as he walked to the other end of the roof.

Caleb pulled his shirt up over his nose and changed positions so the wind was blowing away from him. I moved to kneel beside my own pile of poo and released a sigh as I started scraping it off of the tiles with my trowel.

I soon had to lift my own shirt up and cover my nose, the stench becoming too much as more and more of the stuff was broken away. When no one was looking, I pocketed a lump of it, hoping Tory and I might be able to use it in revenge against Max. *Imagine if we could get it all over him somehow, his beautiful face would be all splotchy and purple...*

Orion provided some large buckets and I shared one with Caleb as we filled it while Max took on the role of carting it back and forth to dump it in The Wailing Wood.

As the sun sank lower in the sky and I started to daydream about food and a hot shower, I noticed Darius was slacking off, sitting on the far edge of the roof with Orion. Their backs were to us and they chatted in low voices. Occasionally their laughter drifted our way. Caleb and Seth would look up and glare at them, then get back to work.

Max reappeared from his last trip to the woods, floating up from the ground using the power of air and hovering above us all as he wasted some time gliding along.

Orion was too engrossed chatting to Darius to notice and the other Heirs took it as a signal to stop working. I concentrated on my work, turning my back on them and hoping Orion would call time on this detention soon. The sun seemed to be taking longer than ever to reach the horizon today.

"Hey peaches," Max said, dropping the bucket near me and making me jump. "What was the reason you got detention again?"

"She didn't say," Caleb replied for me, dropping down beside me.

Max rested his hand on my shoulder and I jerked away in panic, lifting a palm to defend myself. Before the magic even tingled my fingertips, his influence took over, sending a flood of trust and calm right through to my bones.

"So?" Max pressed.

"I stole stardust from Orion's office," I breathed and I spotted Seth moving closer, his interest clearly piqued. He'd tied his hair up in a knot atop his head which highlighted the razor sharp angles of his cheek bones.

"Stardust?" Seth questioned. "What for?"

"We were gonna go home," the words escaped my lips and a small, internal voice screamed at me for revealing that.

The three of them shared a look and a calculating expression crept onto Seth's face. He raised a palm, painting lines in the air and a strange trickling sensation swept over me.

Max grinned, glancing at Orion and Darius who were still facing away from us as they sat on the roof's edge.

"Hey Professor Dickshit!" Max shouted and my mind reeled when neither Orion or Darius responded, clearly unable to hear him.

"Perfect," Seth said coldly. "Let her go, Max."

"Dude, Orion is right there," Caleb hissed, shaking his head as Max released me.

The pressure of his power slowly ebbed from my chest and fear found me instead. Seth yanked me to my feet, drawing me into the cage his body created.

"Get your hands off of me," I snarled, drawing magic to my fingertips. Fire flared and I grabbed his arms in a moment of pure adrenaline, searing his flesh. Seth gritted his teeth, hauling me toward the edge of the roof and refusing to let go. "Why didn't you leave?" he demanded, his eyes flashing with something that almost looked like fear.

"Stop it!" I snapped as Max's laughter hit my ears. Caleb looked between everyone, his jaw set and a dark frown on his face.

The scent of singed skin carried to my nose, but Seth was wild, his eyes flaring as he refused to release me. "Why?!" he shoved me into Max's arms and the second he touched me, I was putty in their hands again.

"Why?" Max repeated in my ear as his power coiled around my tongue and made me give the answer they wanted.

"Because this feels like our home. We belong here."

"I knew it." Seth threw an accusing finger at me. "They do want the throne."

All three Heirs suddenly went flying backwards through the air and I gasped in surprise as they were thrown over the edge of the roof. Instead of falling they were flipped upside down, dangling as if held by their ankles above the sheer drop below.

Orion stormed past me, his sleeves rolled up and his expression a fiery pit of rage. "You cast a fucking silence spell behind my back? Are you *asking* to get expelled?!" he roared.

Darius moved to my side, tucking his hands into his pockets as he gazed up at his friends with a tight-lipped expression.

"ANSWER ME!" Orion bellowed and I spotted students down on campus pointing up at the Heirs dangling above the pathway below.

"No sir," they spoke in unison.

Seth's hair had come free of his man bun and was flying around him in the breeze. He tried to hold it back but I was pretty sure Orion increased the wind pressure to place him in an even stormier gust.

"Is that the Celestial Heirs?" a voice carried to me from below then laughter and gasps followed.

I imagined FaeBook was blowing up right about now and a bubble filled my chest, replacing my anxiety at their threatening behaviour.

Max stared down at the ground angrily as the students started taking photographs. "You've made your point, Professor. Let us down."

"Fine," Orion growled, waving a hand and his magic released them.

I gasped in shock as they plummeted towards the ground, running to the edge with my heart hammering like crazy.

Seth flipped himself upside down, landing lightly on his feet with all the grace of an angel, while Max spun through the air, making a show for the onlookers on a magical breeze. Caleb caught himself on a pillar of land, creating steps to descend down to the pathway and taking a bow for the students standing there.

I pursed my lips as their fan base fell about them, clapping and giggling.

"Damn," Orion muttered, moving to my side. "I hoped at least one of them would go splat." I didn't know whether he was joking or not but Darius barked a laugh. So apparently he was.

"They're untouchable," I whispered, unable to take my eyes off of the group below as my hands curled into tight fists.

"No one's untouchable," Orion said in a rumbling tone that struck a deep chord in my heart. "You just have to find the right buttons to push, Blue." He lowered his voice to a secret whisper, leaning in close. "Or is it Green?"

TORY

CHAPTER FOUTEEN

I ran south through Air Territory with the long grass trailing around my knees as I carved a path through the overgrown meadow towards the Fire Arena where I was due to meet Darius once he'd finished up detention with Orion.

I'd reached the last section of my playlist and the beat had urged me into a sprint, my long hair blowing out behind me in the wind as I raced downhill, the end in sight.

I was close to a new P.B., I just had to keep up this pace and I'd smash my ten km record.

I wondered if Darius was really going to show. He'd seemed pretty damn set on me and Darcy attending his fancy party but he'd also lied about meeting me enough times that I didn't trust his word for shit.

I crossed into Fire Territory and the ground evened out, getting harder beneath my sneakers. I upped my pace a final time as I sprinted for the Fire Arena and skidded to a halt on the gravel outside it with seventeen seconds to spare.

I whooped in triumph, smiling to myself at my win then took a moment to use my water magic to clean the sweat and dirt from my body as my heart rate slowed.

A blur of motion shot towards me and I gasped as Caleb Altair appeared beside me, running his hand through his golden curls and grinning at me like I was his best buddy.

"You still couldn't beat *me* though, could you?" Caleb asked casually, jamming his hands into his jeans pockets.

"I could if you didn't use your bloodsucker powers," I replied, panting a little as I caught my breath.

"But why wouldn't I use my superpowers if I have them at my disposal?" he teased.

I cracked a smile despite myself. Caleb had a charm about him that was difficult to resist even if he *was* a parasitic jackass.

"Let me guess, you've come to bite me?" I'd enjoyed the few days of freedom from his teeth but I'd known it wouldn't last. He might have felt a little guilty over what had happened to me in the pool the night of the party but he wasn't going to let me off the hook forever.

"Nope. I've been taking advantage of the other Heirs in payment for my participation in your misery the other night so I'm still pretty full on Seth's power at the minute," he said and I couldn't quite hide my surprise at that.

"If you want punishment then shouldn't *I* be the one to dole it out?" I asked, cocking an eyebrow at him. No need to mention the fact that it just so happened we'd already started on our plans for him.

Caleb smiled darkly. "Depends what you have in mind, sweetheart. Maybe I'd like your brand of punishment."

I stepped a little closer, breathing in the sweet scent of him as I tilted my mouth close to his and lowered my voice. "But if you like it, it's not going to teach you a lesson, is it?"

I stepped around him and started heading towards the Arena.

Red flowers blossomed to life all around me as I walked and I bit my lip to stop myself from smiling at his display of magic.

"I'm not really a flowers kind of girl," I said, without looking back at him, though I couldn't resist the urge to taunt him a little too. "Perhaps a Pegasus would like them better?"

"I don't want a fucking Pegasus," he said with enough grit in his voice to let me know how much that had pissed him off.

I laughed and kept walking.

"Tell me what you do like then," he called after me.

"Oil and engine fumes," I replied.

I glanced back just before I headed into the Arena and found him grinning at me like I was a challenge he wanted to rise to.

"You still need to pay though," I warned.

"Whatever you desire, sweetheart." He flashed me a dazzling smile complete with dimples before shooting away from me with the speed of his Order.

I rolled my eyes as I headed inside the Arena for my meeting with the Fire Heir. I got the feeling that this interaction would be a lot less amusing than that one had been.

I strolled straight through the locker rooms without getting changed and made my way out onto the wide, sandy arena.

To my surprise, Darius was already there, a herd of fiery horses galloping around him in a circle as he wielded his magic in a display which had drawn a group of fans clamouring around him.

I wandered closer, eyeing the five horses with interest and noticing the differences between each of them. I knew how much more difficult it was to maintain individual details when shaping magic like that and I couldn't help but be impressed: I couldn't even form two different basic shapes at once. Though I was hoping that would be different with him to help me take control of my power. If I could figure it out then Pyro wanted me to pass on what I learned to Darcy too so it was doubly important I got the most out of this lesson.

Darius spotted me approaching and he flicked a hand in my direction, sending the horses galloping towards me.

I flinched as they didn't slow, throwing a crude shield of water in front of me to protect myself at the last moment.

The horses smashed against the shield, sizzling out of existence as Darius released his hold on them and let the magic disperse. The crowd of students watching him applauded excitedly.

"Aren't you going to get changed?" he asked as he strolled towards me, eyeing my leggings and sports bra combo.

I shook my head. "That suit makes my fire magic go all haywire. I have better control over it like this," I said, refusing to back down on this point.

Darius shrugged. "You're the one risking your skin if you lose control," he warned. He was wearing the skintight grey outfit provided for the class and I tried not to look at the way it clung to his muscular frame.

"My magic won't hurt me," I countered.

"Whatever you say. Don't expect me to heal you if it does."

"Oh no, I'd fully expect you to let me burn to death," I assured him, my tone flat.

Darius frowned like he didn't much like that assessment of him but said nothing to challenge my assumption. "Are you ready to start?"

I nodded, though I didn't really have any idea what this would entail.

He cast a look at the gathered students who were still watching him like he was the most interesting thing in the world.

"Come on." Darius beckoned me to follow him and I fell into step with him as he crossed to the far side of the arena where there wasn't anyone else practicing. The other students seemed to get the hint and dispersed, though I noticed a small group of girls slowly trailing behind us.

"Must be nice being Mr Popular," I commented.

Darius grunted in a way that didn't really give me any insight into his feelings on it. "You and your sister get your own share of attention."

"Well we're the shiny new toys on campus," I reasoned. "No doubt everyone will get bored of us soon enough. My general persona is pretty off putting to most people."

"I'd noticed," Darius replied but his tone was more teasing than outright hostile so I let it slide. "How are your magic reserves?" he asked, coming to a halt. "Am I going to have my hands full with you or are you running low?"

"Oh I'm always a handful," I said challengingly and his gaze swept over me like he wasn't sure what to say in response to that.

"Let's find out if that's true, shall we?" Darius held his hand out to me and I eyed it suspiciously for a moment. Professor Pyro had explained to me that we had to maintain physical contact if we wanted to combine our power but I had more than a few reservations about it.

I slowly reached out to take his hand, my palm fitting right inside his before he curled his fingers around my hand, encasing it completely.

I bit my lip against the sensation of his skin against mine as I waited for him to tell me what to do next.

"Just concentrate on the well of your power," he murmured. "Imagine it's a pool inside your chest and I'm going to push my magic to join with it. When you feel it, squeeze my hand."

"Okay," I agreed.

"It helps if you close your eyes," he added.

I shot him a suspicious look but he'd followed his own advice and had shut his eyes so he didn't see it. For a moment I couldn't resist the urge to study his face while unobserved and I only realised I was staring when I felt a strange tingling in my chest which had nothing to do with my own magic.

I snapped my eyes shut and squeezed his fingers as I focused on the new sensation. I could feel his magic brushing up against mine and it set something

243

burning with satisfaction deep within my core.

"Try to let me in," he said. "I can force it if you can't but we'll work better together if our magic is in harmony."

"How do I do that?" I asked. I could feel his magic as a separate entity to my own, our powers were dancing around each other but they weren't merging.

"You have to trust me," he said softly.

I cleared my throat, not bothering to justify that with a response. I'd sooner trust a fox in a chicken coop.

We stood like that for a few more moments and I tried to find a way to let his magic join with mine but it was no good.

"You'll have to force it then," I said eventually. "Because I can't even pretend to trust you."

"Try not to fight back at least," he muttered, seeming annoyed by the fact that I couldn't do it.

But what did he expect? I was hardly going to just greet his magic with open arms after everything he'd done to me.

The touch of his magic grew more powerful alongside mine until it was cloying, overwhelming, working to smother my own. In response, my own power grew stronger, burning brighter within me as it fought against the confines he was trying to place on it. I realised that this was the way Professor Pyro had guided my power: with brute force. Which meant that Darius had tried to do it differently on purpose, like he cared about making it more pleasant. But the idea of that was so ridiculous that I quickly pushed it aside. No doubt he just wanted to gain full control over my magic so that he could use it to humiliate me or something.

"Stop fighting me," he ordered, his grip tightening on my hand.

"This feels like going against my nature," I muttered.

"Power sharing is the most natural thing in the world when you trust someone," he countered. "But it's an intimate thing to do, it always feels strange with someone new. Especially if you don't particularly care for them."

I snorted at that statement. Yeah, I didn't particularly care for Darius Acrux, that's exactly how I'd put it.

"Are you going to stop fighting or am I going to kick the doors down?" he asked as the strength of his power increased again.

"I..." I frowned in concentration as I tried to soften the shields around my magic. It was harder than I would have thought, my power clearly not wanting to open itself up but I finally managed it.

Darius's power slid inside my own and I gasped as his raw energy filled me. My muscles tensed and my back arched involuntarily. When Pyro had pressed her power against mine I'd barely even noticed the brush of it in comparison to my own magic. But Darius's power was like a living beast crawling beneath my skin and nuzzling against my own inner creature. There was no chance of me being unaware of its presence within me.

My breathing grew heavier as I adjusted to it, energy racing down my spine and my grip on Darius's hand tightening.

My eyes fluttered open and I couldn't help but look up at him. The point of contact between us felt like it was too much and not enough at the same time. He shifted his thumb across the back of my hand and electricity darted up my arm in response.

"Is it supposed to feel like that?" I breathed.

Darius's lips parted and his eyes roamed over me for a moment before he spoke. "We're both incredibly powerful," he hedged. "Power craves power."

I wanted to say something in response to that but the magic inside me flared with the desperate need for an outlet and I gasped as it pushed against the confines of my skin.

Darius's gaze darkened as he looked at me, his eyes dropping to my mouth for a moment before he cleared his throat.

"Try and conjure a ball of fire," he said.

I did so instantly, the relief of using some of this magic making my arm tremble for a moment before I managed to get control of it.

Darius's magic swam with mine and I could feel his will lending me strength as I urged the flames into the shape of a perfect sphere.

I glanced at Darius, expecting some praise but I instantly realised that was a stupid expectation to have with him.

"Bigger," he commanded, not looking at me.

I obeyed, growing the sphere to the size of a small car.

"Smaller."

I did as I was told again.

"Square. Triangle. Rectangle. Smaller. Bigger-" Every time he made a command I focused on it and the fire did as I wanted.

I bit my lip to stop myself from grinning as I completed more and more challenges and our combined magic bled from me in a trail of flaming ecstasy. It was the most intense rush I'd ever gotten from wielding my power and I knew it was because it was combined with his.

When I'd created countless shapes in varying sizes, he got me to create more than one at once. Then to change their shapes, make them move, merge them together and peel them back apart. My head was spinning with the orders he barked my way but I managed to keep up through pure force of will.

My limbs were practically trembling with the energy I was channeling and he suddenly called a halt, releasing my hand.

My skin felt oddly cold without his and I folded my arms just to give my hand something else to do.

Darius looked me over without making any comment on my performance. "Do you feel drained?" he asked. "Do you need to stop?"

I reached out to the well of power in me but I couldn't sense any difference in it than before. "Nope. I'm good," I said with a shrug.

Darius narrowed his eyes at me. "You don't need to lie if you're running low," he said. "I'm not going to take advantage of the fact that your power is depleted if you admit it."

I rolled my eyes at him and cast a huge fireball into existence a few meters away from us. The flames warmed my skin and I smiled at them.

"Still good," I assured him.

"Fine. I need a top up though," he muttered irritably, before turning and stalking away from me.

"Did I burn you out?" I teased as I followed him despite the fact that he hadn't invited me to.

"No but I can feel my power waning. It's harder to lend magic than wielding it anyway," he said dismissively.

"Ohhh that explains it then," I said, my tone holding just enough falseness to it to make sure he caught on to my mockery.

Darius reached a sports bag that was waiting at the edge of the arena and sat down beside it. He scooped handfuls of gold coins into his lap and leaned back against the wall as he took a long drink from a bottle of water.

I took a seat beside him and he looked at me from the corner of his eye without saying anything else.

"So you managed to save your pirate gold from the fire?" I asked innocently as he ran a few coins through his fingers.

"Unfortunately not. I had to go home for more," he muttered.

"Oh. Handy that you have piles to spare then," I said, reaching out to snag a coin from his lap.

His hand snapped out and snatched my wrist, a deep growl emanating from within his chest. A sliver of fear raced through me but I refused to acknowledge it as I raised an eyebrow at him.

"Did you just *growl* at me?"

"Why do you insist on baiting me?" he asked, his voice low, his grip on me unrelenting.

"Why do you make it so easy?" I flicked the coin back into his lap and he released me.

His posture relaxed a little as I returned it and a small smile tugged at my lips as I realised something.

"That treasure means a lot to you, huh? Must have really sucked to have lost so much of it."

"Accidents happen." He shrugged, refusing to rise to the bait this time.

"How exactly? Did you leave your scented candles burning too close to your silk pyjamas?" I asked.

I knew I was treading the line of stupidity by asking him about the fire but I really wanted to hear just how much the whole thing had gotten to him first hand. And with the right amount of prodding, I might have been able to get him to open up about it.

"It was actually my curling iron too close to my bondage gear. The oil makes those suckers flammable as hell."

I wasn't fast enough to stop myself from laughing at that and his mouth twitched in amusement too.

I schooled my expression quickly, returning to my point.

"Well at least all of your poncy asshole clothes burned up, this is a good chance for you to purchase a new wardrobe that makes you look like less of a douchebag."

"Every cloud," he said calmly. This line of taunting clearly wasn't going to get a rise from him so I decided to drop it.

Infuriatingly it sounded like he really was putting the fire down to an accident and if that was the case then it was all too easy for him to move on from it. My mind whirled with ways that I could make him suffer more over this. Maybe I could use the treasure against him somehow? He was clearly possessive over it. If he realised that some of it had been stolen I was sure it would drive him insane. A plan was beginning to form in the depths of my mind but I kept it there to work on later so that he didn't see any guilt written across my face.

"Ready to go again?" Darius asked as he swept the gold back into the sports bag.

"It wasn't me we were waiting on," I reminded him as he got to his feet.

He offered me his hand and for half a second I thought he was being polite as he pulled me to my feet but he didn't release me and I felt the brush of his magic flooding inside me a moment later.

A gasp of surprise escaped my lips as he didn't even offer me a warning and his eyes flashed excitedly for a moment in response. If it wasn't an absolutely insane idea, I almost would have thought he was enjoying this. And I had to admit it was kind of a rush.

"You've got a handle on basic shapes and control. So now I want you to make something more complicated," he instructed and I got the feeling he liked bossing me around.

"Like what?"

"Something you're familiar with. An animal or object you know as well as your own face. Something you'd recognise in the dark," he suggested.

"Okay," I said hesitantly, trying to picture something like that in my mind's eye. At first I scrambled for what to create but when the idea struck me it was the obvious choice. "I'm ready," I confirmed.

I held my free hand out before me and tried to conjure what I needed to create my illusion. Pieces of it started to come together but they fell apart as I tried to merge them.

"Again," Darius commanded.

I did as I was told but after three more attempts I was ready to give up. I just couldn't manipulate the magic in the way I needed to.

Darius suddenly released his grip on my hand and moved behind me, catching my waist between his palms. The feeling of his skin against mine sent a jolt of energy racing through me and I tensed, trying to tug out of his grip.

"What are you doing?" I hissed, shifting forward again but he didn't let go, the pressure of his fingers increasing on my waist.

"You need to use both hands to perform the magic properly," he said, his tone suggesting he was amused though I couldn't see his face to read his expression. "Don't flatter yourself."

My heart pounded faster as he shifted his hands on my skin, his fingers pressing against my hip bones and skimming the waistband of my leggings. For a moment my brain completely scrambled and the only thing I could think about was the way he was touching me.

I threw every inch of my focus into the magic and tried with all my might to ignore the feeling of his hands on my body.

Damn super-hot asshole. He knows exactly what he's doing.

I released a long breath and conjured the flames to life in my hands again. I focused on their form, imagining the way I wanted them to look. Darius's magic danced alongside my own as I channelled it and with his help, I managed to mould the fire into what I wanted. The ball became a wheel which split in two to create a second then a chassis, saddle and handlebars all sprung to life until a sleek super bike sat in my palms.

I stared at it for a moment, a breath of laughter escaping me as I took in exactly what I'd managed to do.

"Can you ride one of those?" Darius asked curiously as he looked over my shoulder at my work.

I snorted a laugh. "That's an understatement. If you really want to get rid of me then just give me a bike and an open road and I'll be gone."

"That's... interesting."

He didn't add any further comment and I reminded myself that I didn't care what he thought anyway. With a nudge of my power, I sent the bike flying out of my hands and racing through the air in front of me.

Darius's grip on my waist tightened a little as I drew more power from him but I didn't try to hold back. Our magic was burning through me, aching for this release and I was smiling like a damn idiot as it did what it was told for once.

As I turned the bike in a sharp circle over our heads, Darius shifted forward, his hands sliding across my stomach and down a few inches so that the tips of his fingers pushed beneath my waistband.

I inhaled sharply as a spike of energy ripped right through my core and my concentration was shattered, tearing the bike apart so that little flames tumbled out of the sky all around us.

"You need to work on your focus, Roxy," Darius teased, maintaining the new position of his hands.

I almost jerked out of his grip but I knew that that was what he wanted. He was winding me up, trying to get a rise out of me by abusing this situation.

But if he thought he could throw off my magic with his touch then two could play at that game.

"Maybe I should try something bigger?" I suggested, not giving him the satisfaction of mentioning the way he was touching me or the fact that he kept moving his fingers instead of just staying still. His touch danced across the delicate skin beneath my waistband sending a flood of heat to my core and making a sultry, amorous part of me ache for him to shift lower still and I had to bite my tongue to distract myself from it. I refused to give any recognition to the fact that my skin was coming alive in response, desire unfurling in me like he'd woken a sleeping beast.

"If you think you can manage it," he said in a tone that suggested I couldn't.

"I'm pretty sure I can handle more than you think," I replied dismissively.

I conjured a much bigger ball of fire this time, shaping it into the beginnings of a huge bird while drawing at least four times as much energy through the bond that connected us as I had the last time.

Darius tried to cover up his sharp intake of breath as I tugged on his magic and I took a step backward so that I was pressed against him, his arms tightening around me.

The movement of his hands stilled as my body pushed back against his, the lines of his muscular build moulding to my curves, my ass pushing into his crotch. I refused to let the game I was playing with him distract me as I spun the ball of fire into a huge falcon. It took more effort than the bike because I

251

wasn't as familiar with the shape and it was so much bigger. In turn I had to use Darius more to control it and as I yanked on his magic, I shifted my hips so that my ass ground against him.

Two can play at this game.

A deep growl resounded in his chest and I smirked in satisfaction as I made the falcon soar overhead. From the corner of my eye I could see members of his little fan club staring at us and hear them whispering but I ignored them; Darius was the one who'd started this game and I wasn't going to let him beat me.

Darius recovered from his surprise fairly quickly, holding me firmly as his fingers pushed down a little further, brushing against the top of my underwear.

Heat pooled in my core and my heart thundered like a jackhammer in my ears but I worked to hide the reactions of my body to his.

I conjured a second falcon and sent it up to fly with the first, frowning at the effort it took to maintain the two creations. I could only make them fly in circles, their movements mirroring each other but it was so much more than I'd ever managed before that it made me want to jump up and down with excitement.

With a wicked grin, I did just that, bouncing on the balls of my feet and clapping excitedly as my ass rubbed up and down against Darius's crotch.

"Fuck," he muttered and I felt the evidence of his arousal pressing against me as his grip on my waist tightened. His concentration broke and the falcons shattered above us.

My skin flared with heat and energy raced through my body, aching for him to move his hands again. I wanted to turn and claim his mouth with mine. I wanted him to keep up the torment he'd started on my flesh and give my body over to his mercy.

I gave myself half a second to indulge in the fantasy of making use of Darius Acrux's perfect body and I turned my head to the left so that I could look up at him.

His endlessly dark eyes found mine and for a moment no words passed between us, just heat and need and aching desire.

"Darius?" I breathed, biting down on my bottom lip.

His eyes dropped to my mouth and he pulled me against him even more firmly. I could feel every inch of his desire for me pressing against my ass and I couldn't deny the fact that certain parts of my body wanted to do more than just indulge in this fantasy. But the fact that he was disgustingly attractive didn't change any of the things about him that made him utterly repulsive.

"Mmm?" He leaned closer to me, our breath mingling as nothing more than a few millimetres separated our lips.

I hung in that moment with him, reaching up to brush my fingertips across the dark stubble which lined his jaw. A dark thrill ran through me as I toyed with this beast, the danger in him calling to me in a way it really shouldn't have if I had better sense.

"Don't flatter yourself." I pushed out of his hold and walked away from him across the Fire Arena.

I didn't look back but I could feel his eyes on me the whole time I went, urging me to. I wondered if he'd had much experience of rejection before now and somehow I really doubted it. The idea of that made me want to do a happy dance all the way to the dinner table.

"I'll come and get you and your sister from your room at six on Saturday before the party with my Father and the other Councillors," he called. "Your dresses will arrive that morning."

"Whatever you say," I replied without looking back.

I walked straight outside and started heading for The Orb where I was meeting Darcy and the others for a late dinner. I wasn't really sure what I'd say to them about how my training session with Darius had gone but the shit-eating grin on my face probably said it all.

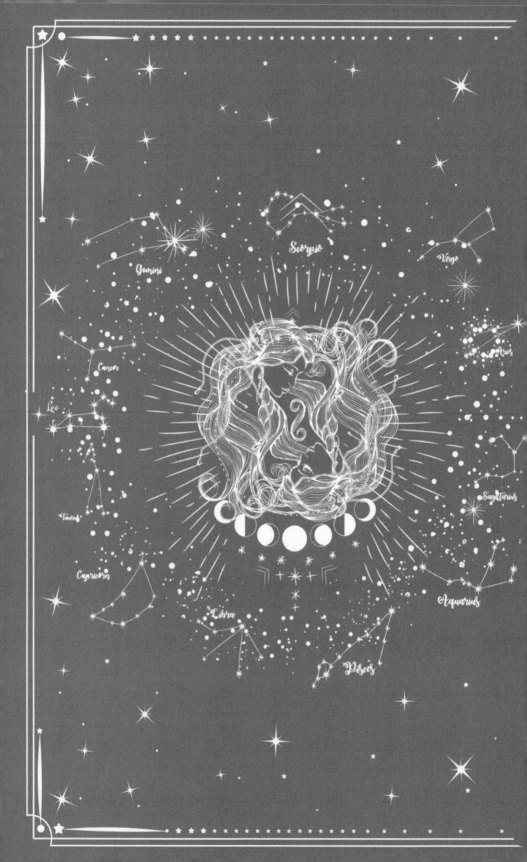

DARCY

CHAPTER FIFTEEN

Monday night marked our first Astrology Class in the Earth Observatory. And it didn't start until eight o'clock. I was distracted during my Liaison while Orion sat across his desk from me, attempting to explain Nymph anatomy in greater detail while I tried not to wonder what those lips would feel like against more places than my neck.

I bet his kisses taste like bourbon and power.

"Miss Vega?"

I blinked, snapping myself out of my latest dirty daydream as Orion rose from his seat.

"Time's up," he answered my questioning expression. "I'm so glad I didn't waste my time tonight. You've been listening so attentively." His narrowed eyes told me that was sarcasm and I gave him an apologetic grin. *Well I had fun anyway.*

I gathered up my bag, wishing I could head back to my room, have a shower and change out of this uniform. But according to the email I'd received when the class had been added to my timetable, we had to turn up dressed in the Zodiac uniform even for lessons after hours.

"I'll walk you back to your House," Orion said. "And maybe on the way you can tell me exactly what you've spent the last hour thinking about." He strode toward the door with a smirk and I followed him across the room, my heart pitter-pattering.

"No thanks, I've got Astrology now, sir," I said, saying absolutely nothing more about my daydreams. *Those can never see the light of day.*

"Then I'll take you to Earth Observatory." Orion stepped out into the hall, waiting for me as I followed.

I frowned at him. "I think I can manage a ten minute walk alone."

"Well I'm heading in that direction anyway so we may as well go together." Orion headed off and I fell into step beside him, fighting an eye-roll.

We headed onto the path beyond Jupiter Hall and a yawn pulled at my mouth as we turned in the direction of Earth Observatory. Students were spilling out of The Orb heading back to their Houses, but I wasn't jealous. Despite the long-ass day I'd had, I was excited to attend my first ever Astrology class. Supposedly our schedule was going to fill up even more once we passed The Reckoning. Or *if* we passed it. *God I hope we do. We might end up back in Chicago after all. Even Darius's gold doesn't make me feel much better about that.*

I spent most of my free time practising Elemental magic with Tory and the others in preparation for the exam. Orion was still refusing to teach us anything practical in class, and I half wondered if his vague promises of practical lessons would really ever come to fruition.

I stole a look at him as we walked in perfect silence, finding it surprisingly not awkward. I noticed the deep set of his eyes, the way his shoulders were slightly tense and his fingers were flexing a little.

"Are you expecting an ambush?" I teased and he glanced my way, his expression deadly serious.

"You should always expect an ambush, Miss Vega."

"Oh," I breathed, figuring he was probably right considering the way the Fae world carried on. I'd not really thought about what it might be like to live somewhere beyond the walls of the Academy. Would it be just as cut-throat out there as it was in here?

"Darcy!" Sofia's voice caught my attention and I spotted her up ahead with Diego, standing outside the observatory. She beckoned me over and I stopped walking, looking to Orion to say goodbye. He turned to me too and a strange energy passed between us as we simply stood there for much longer than was necessary.

Why are we even stopping to say goodbye? Why am I not just walking away now?

He half tipped his head then shot away at high-speed, disappearing back the way we'd come.

So he hadn't been heading this way. I knew *it. His casual stalking was clearly to do with his worries over a Nymph getting its probes into my magic.*

"Daaarccccyy!" Sofia sang and I turned back to them, finding her on Diego's back, waving her arms.

I snorted a laugh in surprise, hurrying over to join them.

Diego dropped Sofia with a grin. "Did Orion walk you here?" he asked in confusion.

"Er-" I started but Sofia danced around me, flicking my hair and giggling. For a moment her skin seemed to shimmer like diamonds. *Weird.*

"Darcy luuuuurves him. Look at her face."

"What's got into you? And are you sparkling?" I stared at her as she spun in circles a few times, smiling from ear to ear.

"Don't you feel it?" she sighed, coming to a halt as she smiled serenely at me.

"Um...no?" I said, beginning to laugh.

Sofia started spinning again, her skirt twirling around her thighs.

Diego shifted closer. "She flew through a rainbow just before sunset. She's been like this since."

"Is that why she wasn't at dinner?" I asked with a laugh.

"Yep," Diego said. "All of the Pegasuses are high on rainbow juice."

"Hey guys!" Tory jogged over to join us, wearing jeans and a blue crop top. She looked down at our uniforms in surprise. "Oh, were we not supposed to change?"

"Nope," I said in a teasing tone. "Didn't you read the email?"

Tory gestured to her clothes. "Does it look like I read the email, Darcy?"

I started laughing. "Let's hope the Professor isn't an asshole," I said, giving her a look which suggested that was very unlikely.

I spotted the class filing into the observatory ahead of us and we moved to join them. The imposing building was built from shining onyx stone, reaching high up above us to an enormous black metal dome which crested the top of it. My heart skittered excitedly as we headed inside, arriving in a low-lit atrium where a large elevator awaited us. The doors slid open as someone pressed the call button and the fifty or so freshmen filed into the enormous space.

I shuffled in beside Tory who glanced at everyone's uniforms with pursed lips.

"Maybe I should have gone and changed, your detention sounded like hell the other day," she whispered in my ear.

"Too late now," I said with half a shrug.

The doors parted again and we all moved out into the huge dome at the top of the building. A circle of chairs ringed a stage at the heart of it, the seating area sloping down toward it. On the stage was a massive bronze telescope angled up toward a hole at the very top of the roof and beside it were two cushioned velvet seats.

A prickling kind of quiet descended on everyone and anticipation scored through me as we moved to sit down.

I dropped into a chair in the back row beside Tory and just as I pulled out my Atlas, a blinding spotlight fell over the two of us. I raised a hand to cover my eyes, squinting against the harsh light.

"The Vega Twins are in our midst! Bow down to their glory!" a powerful female voice rang through the room.

"Oh no," Tory breathed and my heart burst like a dodgy firework.

Great.

As my eyes adjusted to the glaring light, firstly I saw a sea of staring students and Tyler Corbin's Atlas raised to film the entire thing. Second, I spotted the Professor who had conducted our Awakening weaving through the chairs toward the stage. Her long raven hair fell all the way down to her waist and her sharp features gave her the vague appearance of a bird.

She pointed to the plush chairs set up on the stage. "Come girls, rise to your feet. Take your rightful place at the centre of the room."

"Um, we're fine actually," Tory called down to her.

"*Nonsense*, get down here this instant." Her eyes turned volcanic, her voice terrifyingly fierce and offering no room for negotiation.

Tory and I stood and my skin tingled from all of the eyes on us as we descended the sloping floor toward the stage.

"I am Professor Zenith," she announced as we arrived then curtsied low, pulling out the skirt of her long dark dress. "Your humble teacher and proud sponsor of the Almighty Sovereign Society."

Oh man, I think I would have preferred an asshole to an Ass. Now everyone is glaring at us.

She stood upright, gripping each of our arms and guiding us firmly toward the armchairs. Her nails dug into my skin as she placed me firmly down into it.

"Forgive me, I'm a little over excited," she whispered, her eyes roaming over us as she stepped away again. She turned to the room where people were staring at us with looks of outright hatred, some snickering, while others whispered to each other.

My cheeks burned and I shifted awkwardly in my chair as Zenith stepped behind the telescope and returned a moment later with a huge hamper. She placed it at our feet, flipping open the top of it to reveal an entire picnic of strawberries, cheese and bread complete with a bottle of champagne.

"Please, help yourselves," she encouraged, bowing again as she moved to stand before the class.

I wanted to curl into a ball and vanish as a few jeers rang out around us. But if Zenith heard it, she didn't let on.

The loud pop of the champagne cork sounded like a claxon and Tory shrugged as she filled two glasses. "Everyone hates us for this anyway," she murmured to me. "So we might as well have a drink."

I snorted a laugh, accepting the glass she offered me and drinking it quickly.

"Now," Zenith said in a deep tone, her eyes shadowing as she waved a hand before her. The room darkened immediately so all I could see was her and the pale blue glow of magic she wielded in her palms. She spoke directly to Tory and I as if no one else in the class existed.

"Today, girls, it will be my honour to teach you about Star Bonds." She coaxed a beautiful light into her hands and it spread out, rising higher and higher. Mine and Tory's chairs started reclining and the humming noise in the room told me it was happening to everyone else's seats too.

The domed roof came alive with magic, the ceiling transforming into an endless night sky.

"The constellations define everything about Fae nature," Zenith explained and I was glad that the class's attention was no longer on us.

Silvery lines appeared between the stars, marking out the arrangements and swirling handwriting named each one. "First, the Zodiac constellations," Zenith said in a tone that set my heart pumping. She might have been a bit overenthusiastic, but she certainly knew how to spark interest. One by one the constellations lit up above us and my mouth parted in fascination. It was beautiful, a speckled sea of lights, intertwining to form incredible shapes.

I picked out the twins of Gemini amongst them nestled between Cancer and Taurus.

"Although some Star Signs may cause Fae to clash in day to day life, it is possible for all signs to form friendships and relationships. However, a Star Bond is something very special indeed that is much more powerful than any normal connection." The stars faded away a little and our lecture notes appeared across the canvas in silvery writing.

The Three Types of Star Bond:

Nebula Allies

Elysian Mates

Astral Adversaries

My brows lifted as I read the words, my curiosity rising even further.

Zenith started to explain, "Your Nebula Allies are the most abundant of the Star Bonds, but still highly special. They are friends who seem to understand you almost from the first point of contact. Someone who makes your energy soar and always seeks the best for you in life. Nebula Allies are the deepest kinds of friends you can find. To know you have found one, you only need to assess the bond between you both." The constellations came back into focus and the words faded away. I thought of Tory and wondered if that bond applied to us, and if being twins meant we automatically had it.

"A Nebula Ally occurs when your are both born under the same conditions of the Cosmic Calendar," Zenith went on and the image shifted above to show the star signs Aquarius and Scorpio moving into focus. "For example, if an Aquarius and Scorpio are both born with Jupiter in their eighth House, they may form a Star Bond as Nebula Allies. You will tend to gravitate towards these people, sensing they are a kindred spirit. And once they are in your life, it is unlikely they will ever leave."

"What's a House?" Tory muttered to me, but Zenith jumped on the question immediately, evidently hearing her.

"The Zodiac constellations create a celestial clock between them, Miss Vega." The sky changed above us, showing the Zodiac symbols in a circle. Creating an inner ring between them were twelve boxes. "The planets, sun and moon are all constantly moving and as they conduct their cycles, they move between the twelve Houses. To discover the exact positions of these celestial beings when you were born, you only need the specific time, date and year of your birth."

"Well we were never told the time of our birth and we were Changelings anyway so there's probably no way of knowing for sure. Even our birthday could be wrong come to think of it," I said and Zenith sucked in air.

"But my sweet princesses, you are forgetting that I am your loyal follower. I of course memorised the exact moment your lives began in this plane of existence. I charted the stars right through the royal pregnancy to the exact millisecond you each arrived."

"Oh god," Tory whispered and I fought a laugh as I craned my neck to try and get a look at Zenith in the room. It was so dark, all I could make out was a shifting shadow a few feet away from us.

She moved closer, leaning down between us. "Roxanya Vega was the first to be born at exactly three minutes and eleven seconds past midnight on the eleventh of June." She darted toward me. "And Gwendalina was the second born, at eleven minutes and three seconds past midnight. Do you have any idea how powerful these numbers are? Three and eleven are the strongest numbers in the universe and you were both born with them etched into your celestial DNA."

"So that's er...good?" I asked, glad our birthday was the same as it has been in the mortal world. I didn't mind adopting the surname of our birth parents but anything more than that seemed like too much change. I didn't want to lose who I'd been before.

"Good is not the word. Incredible, inconceivable, inexplicable. Because that is not all. Not even close. The sun rules the House of Gemini, girls. The most powerful celestial being in the solar system." She rested her hands on the backs of our seats as if steadying herself. "By the stars, I am beside myself with excitement to find out which Order you will emerge as. Even *I* cannot predict it." She moved away and I found my mouth dry from her words. I knew we were strong, but sometimes it felt like we were the weakest Fae in the school because we hadn't harnessed our powers. It suddenly sank in that when we did manage it, we would be a force to be reckoned with. *Then the Heirs won't* dare *lay a finger on us.*

"Now, back to the lesson," Zenith called and a few grumbled mutterings reached my ears. Words like 'favouritism' and 'Vega whores' were amongst them. The second one had definitely come from Kylie.

The image of the sky shifted once more and I forced away my irritation as I gazed back at the ceiling.

"Elysian Mates are the most unpredictable of all the Star Bonds," Zenith started. "An Elysian Mate is your absolute perfect match. Your other half, your soul mate, your twin flame, your one true love. It has many names. But in Solaria we call it this. Your Elysian Mate is Star Bound to you somewhere in this world. And if you come into contact with each other, the Zodiac will draw you together like two ends of a rope bound to a turning wheel. And the more time you spend together, the more you will be pulled magnetically and inescapably toward one another. But..." She trailed off and my heart pounded harder as the sky turned blood red above us. Two stars sailed across the heavens from opposing ends of the ceiling, tearing toward each other on a collision course. "The stars will test you. The longer you are in each other's company, the more volatile the universe will become. And if you pass all of the tests the stars throw at you, you will be presented with your Divine Moment."

"I had a Divine Moment in the shower this morning," Tyler called out.

"Quiet, you insolent child!" Zenith snapped at him I suppressed a giggle. "Your Divine Moment is the moment the fate between you and your Elysian Mate is decided. You will both be called under the night sky and be presented with the choice to seal your bond forever more. If you choose to stay together, your love will be branded on you, forming a ring of silver around your irises. But if you choose to part..."

The stars collided in the sky above us and a fiery display seemed to rain down on the class. I flinched and some people screamed as the flames tumbled down over us, but they fizzled out before they reached our heads. "You will be Star Crossed and a black ring will form around your irises, marking your love as doomed by the stars themselves. From that day forward, every celestial being in the universe will work against you, forcing you apart."

My mouth fell slack at that.

"What kind of tests will come before a Divine Moment?" Kylie asked. "Mine and Sethy's is probably coming any day now and I want to be prepared."

"Seth Capella?" Professor Zenith questioned, speaking his name like it was dirt.

"Yes," Kylie said excitedly.

"Ha," Zenith scoffed. "Well *if* such an event is on its way to you, then I cannot enlighten you. No star-given tests are the same. One of you may be required to save the other from death itself, or perhaps temptation will come in the form of another woman designed to draw your other half away from you."

I sensed Kylie's eyes on me across the room, narrowed to the thinnest slits. "Maybe my latest test has already begun," she whispered loudly to Jillian and I rolled my eyes.

"Although many actively seek their Elysian Mates, many also do not," Zenith said darkly. "The risk is too high for some, and for others it is a matter of blood lines. One cannot choose their Elysian Mate. So if a Fae hopes to produce children of the same Order, they may avoid their Mate at all costs. The chances of them being the same Order is unlikely as the universe doesn't care for such things, but once they are found they will be impossible to resist."

"How can you tell if you've found them?" Sofia asked shyly.

"Your love will burn with the intensity of a Supernova," Zenith answered. "You will be drawn to them beyond all explanation, they will burrow so deep under your skin that you won't ever remember a time that they weren't there. But passion can be deceptive. You may think you have found the one when in fact you have found a Nebula Ally who also has sexual chemistry with your Star Sign."

"I hope I'm Elysian Mates with Max Rigel," a girl whispered, giggling with one of her friends.

"So do I," a guy added on the other side of the room.

"Silence!" Zenith demanded. "We now move onto our final Star Bond. Astral Adversaries."

A shiver rushed over me and I glanced at Tory in the low light, the two of us clearly thinking the same thing. *If anyone are our Star Bound enemies, it's the Heirs.*

"An Astral Adversary forms a bond of intense hatred between both parties. Though they are rare and not everyone possesses one, some are unlucky enough to have several. The Astral Adversaries tend to be of a Star Sign which clashes violently with your nature. On top of this, their Natal Charts will oppose yours in many ways. If you were born at night, they will have been born in the day. If you draw your spiritual energy from the sun, they will draw it from the moon. Light and dark, night and day. Collisions between Astral Adversaries often end up fatal. Unfortunately, unlike the Elysian Mates, they are bound to clash with you again and again until one of you is destroyed. So if you have one, beware."

Dread slipped into my gut as I thought about how close the Heirs had come to killing Tory. Could we really be bound to those four jerks, doomed to clash again and again until it ended in disaster?

I really hope not.

The rest of the lesson was spent sitting upright in our chairs while we worked out our Natal Charts on our Atlases. Zenith barely paid attention to the other students as she fussed around Tory and I, explaining what it meant to have certain planets in different Houses when you were born. It was all a lot to take in, especially with her continually refilling glasses of champagne for us (but who was I to turn down a free drink?).

My head was swimmy by the time she dismissed class and we headed back down to the atrium in the elevator, filing out onto the path beyond the Observatory.

Kylie was talking animatedly up ahead and her voice drew my attention. "It's amazing that I've found my Mate so young. Sethy and I will probably start planning the wedding soon."

"But doesn't he have to marry someone of the Werewolf Order?" Jillian asked her.

"No *Jillian*," Kylie snapped. "I've known his family my whole life. I grew up next door to him. His mom is practically family already. She wouldn't care if Sethy didn't marry into his Order. We're in love, she'd want us to be happy."

Their voices carried away and I spotted Tory rolling her eyes as we came to a halt to say our goodbyes.

"See you in the morning. Watch out for Astral Adversaries on your way back to Air Territory," Tory called, laughing as she and Sofia peeled away from Diego and I.

Sofia seemed to have come down from her rainbow high, yawning broadly and giving us a sleepy-eyed wave.

Diego and I headed off toward The Wailing Wood and I mulled over what we'd learned as we walked. As we approached the trees, I reached into my bag to use the flashlight on my Atlas. Until I got my fire magic under control or learned how to create the light orbs I often saw students casting, I was happy to rely on good old fashioned technology.

"Dammit," I swore when I didn't find it in my satchel.

"What?" Diego asked as we drew to a halt.

I sighed in frustration. "I have to go back, I forgot my Atlas."

"Oh chica, you'd lose your head if it wasn't screwed on."

I gave him a slanted smile, jabbing him on the shoulder. "I'll see you tomorrow okay?"

"I'll go with you," he said, glancing over his shoulder into the dark wood. "It's not safe out on campus alone."

A group of students headed past us, chatting merrily as they went.

"It's fine, there's loads of people still around. Plus the FIB were crawling all over the Academy just days ago, they're probably still lurking about somewhere keeping an eye on us."

He frowned but finally nodded. "Just be quick, okay? No pit stops."

I agreed and he waved goodbye as he headed into the wood. I started jogging back to Earth Observatory and was soon hurrying through the door into the atrium. I headed to the elevator, pressing the button to call it and wondering if Zenith was still in the classroom. I'd have to face her over-the-top flattery again if she was and all I really wanted to do was go back to Aer Tower and practice some magic in preparation for The Reckoning.

I didn't like being the centre of attention at the best of times, and though I'd grown used to Geraldine's ways, I definitely didn't want it from a teacher in front of all the other students. The next time we had Astrology, I was going to sit in the back row and refuse to move. And I imagined Tory would feel the exact same way.

The doors slid open and a huge labrador-sized eagle swooped out, rushing over my head in a fan of bronze feathers. I ducked in alarm, my heart battering against my ribcage as I turned to watch it soar out of the door with a tan handbag clutched in its talons.

Oh I guess that's Zenith.

I headed into the elevator, my heart slowing and a laugh bubbling out of my throat as I ascended into the observatory. *This place never gets dull.*

I arrived on the top floor and stepped out into the room. The doors slid closed behind me, extinguishing the light from the elevator so I was plunged into darkness. I swore as I fumbled for a light switch but found none as my hand trailed across the wall.

As my eyes adjusted I could just see the moonlight cast through the circular hole in the middle of the roof. The stage was lit in the vague silvery glow and I felt for the first row of chairs, making my way between them toward it.

I stumbled over something and cursed as I caught myself on the back of a chair, moving more carefully to the front row. I headed to where I'd been sitting, brushing my hand across the seat and finding my Atlas wedged down the side of a cushion. I tapped the screen to turn the flashlight on but the power was dead. I stuffed it into my bag with a sigh.

Dammit. I guess my lucky stars aren't shining today.

The doors to the elevator slid open and I stiffened, gazing up to the top of the observatory where light flooded out of the elevator.

"Hello?" I called, my heart climbing into my throat. There was no one inside it. Maybe I'd just pressed the call button when I searched for a light switch...

A scuttling noise turned my blood to ice and a flickering shadow was cast across the elevator walls just before the doors slid shut. Darkness prevailed once more as white ghosts floated before my eyes. I blinked to try and clear them, hurrying forward to get the hell out of there as fast as I could.

I made it halfway up the aisle before a horrible, rasping, rattling noise sounded from behind me. Terror clawed at my veins and tore at my heart. *Nymph!*

The well of my power seemed to be blanketed under a thick cloak and I found it harder and harder to draw it to the surface of my skin. Horror devoured me from the inside out. I ran as fast I could, speeding toward the elevator and managing to force magic to my fingertips in the same moment.

A sucking, clicking noise sounded horribly close to my ears and I pounded on the call button to open the doors.

Come on come on.

I turned around, raising my hands, ready to fight with everything I had. The doors slid open behind me and I stumbled right up to the back wall. A shadow loomed on the verges of the light cast by the elevator, huge and terrifying, sending a spiral of fear through me.

I thought of Orion's class, his advice tumbling through my head all at once. *If you can't fight, then run.* I lurched forward, jabbing my finger on the button for the ground floor, smacking it again and again.

I threw all of the magic I could wrangle from my body and vines spanned across the doorway, blocking the creature's path to me while the doors closed.

My power was almost entirely immobilised. I was weakened from the inside out.

I crumpled to my knees, gasping in fear as I tried to hold onto what remained of my magic. The lights flickered above me and the sound of the elevator doors closing caressed my ears.

A sigh parted my lips as it started descending and I regained control of my power. It filled me up like a balloon then ran smoothly back into my veins.

The doors reopened on the bottom floor and someone immediately disintegrated the vines I'd cast. He shot to my side, pulling me into his arms.

"What happened?" Orion barked, his eyes desperate as he gathered me closer.

"There's a Nymph up there," I gasped, gripping onto his arms as he pulled me upright.

His face paled and fear flashed through his eyes; it was the only time I'd ever seen him look afraid. He guided me out of the elevator and stood me against the wall. "Stay here," he growled, stepping back into the elevator.

"Wait!" I gasped, but the doors closed before I could stop him. It wasn't safe. We needed to get help.

I gathered my wits and ran out of the observatory, looking for anyone close enough to call upon. All was quiet and before I could even think about who to look for, Orion shot back to my side in a blur of motion.

"There's nothing up there," he growled and I turned to him, shaking my head.

"You're wrong," I breathed, hugging my arms around my body. "I felt it."

Orion gave me a hard look then turned to gaze up at the top of the Observatory with a terse frown. I followed his line of sight, realising what he was thinking.

"It got out of the roof?" I whispered, chilled to the bone as I gazed up and down the path which headed away in either direction.

Had that thing been on campus since Astrum's murder, or had it found a way to sneak beyond Zodiac's defences again?

Orion took out his Atlas and called someone on it, tapping on the speakerphone. Nova answered and he started hurriedly explaining what had happened.

"Good gracious," Nova gasped. "I'll call the FIB immediately and send a team out to hunt it. Get Miss Vega back to her room before you join us."

"Yes ma'am," he said then hung up and grabbed my arm, suddenly hauling me along at a frightening pace.

"Hey," I protested, trying to tug free of him but he didn't let go. "You're hurting me," I snapped, trying to prise his fingers off where they dug painfully into my arm.

Instead of loosening his grip he tightened it.

"Do you think I follow you around campus for fun, Miss Vega?" he barked and my heart convulsed.

"What?" I blurted as I basically had to start jogging to keep up with his crazy fast stride.

He didn't answer until we delved into The Wailing Wood and the chilling silence of the place pressed in on all sides. He stopped me beneath the amber light of a lantern, dragging me close by the lapels of my blazer.

"Sir!" I yelled, drawing magic to my fingertips in my desperation to make him stop.

"I told you not to go anywhere alone, especially after dark."

His voice ignited a deep and pulsing fire in my belly and I stared up at him in fury. "Get off of me." I threw air into my palms and he was shoved back a few paces. A lock of his perfectly styled hair fell loose and he slowly pushed it into place, his face set in a deadly scowl.

He ran at me in blur and the air was nearly knocked out of my lungs as he threw me over his shoulder and locked his arms around my legs, speeding off along the path at a terrifying pace.

In mere moments, he planted me down again and I stumbled back, hitting a wall and grasping onto it for support. I looked around, discovering I was outside Aer Tower, the wind turbines high above us groaning in the wind.

"Start walking around campus in pairs or I'll assign you a personal escort," he barked.

I couldn't believe how angry he was getting. "I thought that's what *you* were doing. You keep following me everywhere and you already made it clear you don't want the Nymph getting their hands on my powers."

"Exactly, kid."

"Don't call me *kid*." I pushed off of the wall, rage slithering through me. "This Academy might make me wear a uniform like a high school student, but I'm eighteen and I've looked after myself most of my life anyway. You think it would have been any different back there if I'd had a friend with me? We're freshmen. We're not trained to fight Nymphs."

Orion's jaw ticked as he absorbed my words. Eventually, he nodded, his eyes moving to look up at the tower. A baying howl sounded in the distance and he glanced over his shoulder. "The hunt's started, I should go and join them."

"Be careful," I whispered.

He looked back at me with a frown and something broken and desperate shone from his eyes for a moment. He blinked firmly and his expression morphed into a fierce scowl. "Stop looking at me like that," he snarled and I fought the urge to recoil from his terrifying tone.

"Like what?"

"You know what," he snapped. "I'm your teacher."

"I *know*," I balked, horrified at what he was suggesting. That he could somehow read how much I wanted him.

"Do you?" he stepped forward.

I nodded firmly, though I wasn't sure my body was getting the message because I had the urge to wrap myself around him and kiss him goodbye. It was absolutely crazy. But him running off after a Nymph made me dread the idea that he wouldn't come back.

"Then stop looking at me like *that*."

Embarrassment poured through me like a tsunami, but I fought it away, elbowing aside my shame. Because how dare he accuse me of being inappropriate? He'd had his hands all over me the other day and he'd shouted at me for that too. I was so done with his bullshit. So I stepped forward, looking him square in the eye as my hands began to shake. "Then stop looking back, *Lance*."

I left him with a gobsmacked expression on his face as I turned away, casting air at the symbol above the door. It unlocked with a loud clunk and I darted inside, slamming it behind me without a single glance back.

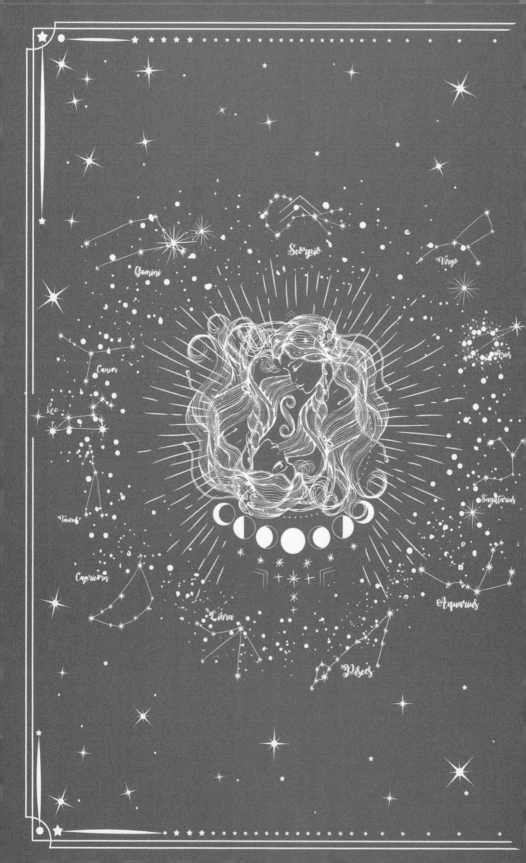

TORY

CHAPTER SIXTEEN

I stood by my open window, looking out over what I could see of the grounds beyond as a sheet of drizzle fell from the thick clouds above and saturated everything. It was five in the morning and every inch of my body was protesting this early venture but my latest plan demanded it be done.

Darius's room had been fixed up by the maintenance crew over the last few days and an announcement had gone out last night to say that he'd be returning to Ignis House tomorrow morning once the paint on his shiny new walls had dried.

If I wanted to implement my plan then I needed to do it now.

I was a little nervous about heading outside after the attempted Nymph attack on Darcy last night but the FIB and teachers had been crawling over every inch of the grounds until very recently and I was sure the thing had either been caught already or had gone deep into hiding again.

I shivered as the cold wind blew in around me and pulled my window shut. I wasn't looking forward to going out in that weather but at least it should mean that no one else would be out there either.

A ping drew my attention to my Atlas and I opened it up to cast an eye over my horoscope.

Good morning Gemini.
The stars have spoken about your day!
Today will be a day of two halves, you will face great highs and turbulent lows. Beware a run in with an Aquarius. Their wrath is unavoidable today and you will have to weather the storm with your head held high. A Pisces may present further obstacles but the way you handle them will determine the outcome of that interaction.
Try to keep heart though, in the end this day may see your plans falling together if only you manage to persevere.

I frowned at the super negative predictions. *Today sounds like it's going to be a shitstorm then.* And if an Aquarius was going to unleash their wrath on me then I had the feeling I'd be seeing Seth today. Peachy.

I pulled on the thick black jacket which had arrived as part of my latest online deliveries and zipped it up to my chin before adding gloves to the mix. The waterproof boots I'd purchased were warm and comfortable on my feet and I couldn't help but grin at the latest additions to my wardrobe. September was coming to an end and as we drew closer to winter, I knew I'd be relying on warmer clothes to stave off my least favourite season more and more regularly. Beside my door, a large box of winter outfits sat waiting for me to deliver them to Darcy later on too. She hadn't gotten into this online shopping business quite as thoroughly as I had and I knew she was indulging me by letting me buy for her.

I slid my Atlas into one of the large coat pockets and flicked the lights off before exiting my room. Geraldine had given me a bit of tuition in our Earth Elemental class and I'd grasped the basics involved with moving soil so I was fairly confident that I could manage this without her. I didn't want to ask her to get involved with this again; I knew she wouldn't hesitate to help me if I asked but this wasn't some game we were playing. I'd broken the law and was going up against one of the most vindictive assholes in this school. The less she had to do with it, the better. I didn't want her to end up in trouble on my account.

I slipped out of Ignis House under cover of darkness and trekked across the grounds to The Wailing Wood. The freezing sleet drove over me in a torrent and I played with my air and water magic as I tried to replicate the shields I'd seen other students using against the bad weather. I had varying levels of success, sometimes keeping the rain away, other times seeming to drive it into my face with twice the force. I made a mental note to ask for tuition on it in my Elemental lessons next week.

I moved beneath the dark trees and had to use the marker on my Atlas to locate the buried treasure.

I kept glancing around as I walked, the shadows within the wood setting me on edge and the sensation of eyes on me making my skin crawl.

At least when I'd been up to no good back in Chicago I could rely on streetlights to light my way and walls to conceal me. In this place I could never be entirely sure that I was alone. A more cautious person would probably give up. But I'd always been wilfully stubborn.

I reached the site of the buried treasure and glanced about carefully. The trees were quiet, only the patter of rain on the leaves overhead and the creak of branches in the wind reached me.

With a surge of determination, I dropped down onto my knees and quickly drew on my earth magic so that I could carve a hole into the ground. I had to remove my gloves to guide the magic more precisely and my work still wasn't as smooth as Geraldine's had been. Working with earth was different to the other Elements; it didn't like to be bound to my will in the same way. It was a living thing and to get the best results from it, I had to work *with* it, not against it.

I used the roots of the plants surrounding the treasure to draw the soil aside and coaxed more of it to the surface as gently as I could manage. I was still a blunt instrument when it came to my magic in many ways but I managed to guide the dirt enough to reveal the telltale glint of gold beneath me.

I reached down into the hole and snatched out a handful of coins and some pieces of jewellery. I didn't need much; just enough to screw with a certain Dragon.

I grabbed a second handful and was about to withdraw my hand when a familiar tug of energy resounded from the hole and my fingers skimmed against the cool hilt of the dagger.

The blade almost seemed to purr with recognition as my fingertips brushed it and I was filled with the desire to claim it for my own.

I hesitated. Something about that blade was weird. There was definitely more to it than there seemed to be at first glance. It had a presence, desires...

I meant to leave it behind but when I pulled my hand from the dirt, the dagger was clenched in my fist.

I blinked at it in surprise.

Why shouldn't I just take it? I can use it as part of my plans...

I clucked my tongue, and shoved the dagger into my pocket. I hadn't planned on retrieving it alongside the other treasure but I could still use it.

I coaxed the soil back over the rest of the treasure and encouraged new flowers to bloom above it. I didn't have enough control to remove the dirt from my clothes but I was sure the rain could take care of that before I got back.

I pulled my gloves on again and started to trudge back out of The Wailing Wood as the grey clouds began to grow a little lighter overhead. Somewhere beyond them, the sun was coming up and I needed to prepare myself for my lessons today as well as my plans for Darius.

My mind wandered to the party we were going to attend in the company of the Heirs and their families at the end of the week. It was hard to know what to expect from the Celestial Council but after the less than warm welcome we'd received from their sons, I wasn't holding out high hopes for a warm and fuzzy celebration.

A low howl sounded within the trees as I made it back to the path and I fell still as my heart fluttered in response. The last thing I needed was to run into one of Seth's pack-mates while I was alone out here.

I remained still for a moment, listening carefully until a second howl met with the first, coming from the opposite direction.

Not good.

I swallowed a lump in my throat and turned left on the path, drawing my hood up as I went.

I set a quick pace, wishing I'd worn my running gear. If I started running without it then it would look really suspicious and I didn't want to risk anyone wondering what I'd been doing out here...

I took the coins and slid them into a hidden pocket inside my jacket before zipping it up again, just in case. The dagger was too big to conceal in there so I left it in my pocket and hoped no one would notice it. I wondered again why I'd even taken the thing but I couldn't do much about it now.

The wolves howled somewhere ahead of me and I hesitated before more howling started up behind me, driving me on again. I had the horrible feeling that they were surrounding me but there wasn't anything I could do about it.

I pulled my coat closer around me, my heart pounding a little faster as I searched between the trees for any sign of them.

Movement caught my eye and I spun to the left as a black wolf shot between the trunks before disappearing out of sight.

I chewed on my lip. The edge of the woods was close. I could make it in a few minutes if I ran.

I looked over my shoulder. More howls came from the depths of the forest and a huge white wolf bounded across the path behind me.

I ran.

I cursed my boots as I splashed through the mud at full speed, wishing

I'd worn my running sneakers. But it didn't matter, I was still as fast as the wind when I got going and the path curved downhill to aid me.

The wind whipped my hood back and the sleet drove into my face. I scrunched my eyes up against it and kept going.

The howls had changed in pitch, excited yapping mixing with their baying as the pack took up the chase.

I swore beneath my breath, the edge of the woods coming into view ahead of me. The sound of thundering paws was closing in behind me. I threw a look over my shoulder and spotted six huge beasts in pursuit, their coats a mixture of browns and greys.

Where's the white wolf?

My heart was beating so fast that I was sure it was trying to carve a path right out of my chest.

I looked ahead of me again, digging deep for an extra spurt of speed. I wasn't going to make it.

I reached the edge of the trees half a second before the white wolf pounced.

His paws slammed into my chest and I was knocked flat on my back beneath him, his immense weight crushing me into the mud.

Pain flared up my spine and I cried out in fright.

I wheezed beneath the weight he was exerting on me, trying to struggle out from under him as the rest of the pack circled, yapping and howling with excitement.

"Get off of me, you asshole," I snarled, trying to shove him back. The mud on my hands stained his soft, white fur and he released a deep growl in warning.

I knew that this was Seth, that it was really a man pinning me to the mud and not some wild beast, but my heart shredded at the sound of that growl and fear paralysed me for a moment.

Seth leaned forward, his teeth bared right in my face and I recoiled, mud soaking through my hair all the way down to my scalp.

The wet pad of his tongue ran up the centre of my face and I spluttered in disgust.

The white wolf cocked his head at me before shifting back into his Fae form. The weight pinning me to the ground reduced and I found myself straddled in the dirt by a very naked, very amused Seth Capella.

"Look what came wandering into my territory in the dead of night," he purred excitedly. "Were you hoping for a ride with my pack again, babe?"

"I don't want anything to do with your pack of mongrels," I snapped.

Seth's eyes sparkled with the challenge in my tone and he leaned closer to me, pressing his hips down on mine to keep me in place.

"Your junk is all over my coat," I hissed. "Learn some goddamn boundaries."

"You're the one who came wandering onto my turf," Seth reminded me. "So maybe you're the one who needs to learn to respect boundaries."

"Fine. Let me go and I'll get out of your stupid woods," I said, hoping he might be satisfied by knocking me down in the mud.

He reached out and snagged a lock of my hair between his fingers. "I did say I wanted a matching set," he mused, leaning close to me so that he could brush it against his face.

Anger coiled in my gut at what he'd done to my sister and I yelled a curse at him as I reared forward, slamming my hands into his chest as I tried to throw him off of me.

He reacted quicker than I would have expected, fisting my hair in his grasp and jerking my head to the side so that my face was pressed to the mud.

"You're lucky we need you in one piece for the party on Saturday," he growled.

Before I could respond, he transformed back into a giant white wolf and his weight crushed me once more. He growled, his teeth brushing against my cheek in a clear threat which sent a tremor rocking through my body before he moved off of me.

I scrambled backwards but before I could even try to rise, he cocked his leg and a steaming trail of urine washed over my legs.

"What the hell is wrong with you?" I shrieked, kicking out at him in disgust.

I tried to get to my feet but he slammed into me again, knocking me back down. The rest of his pack circled in, the males cocking their legs over me as well and heat clawed its way through my body as my clothes were coated in a layer of wolf piss.

The stench of it rose up around me, catching in my throat and bringing tears to my eyes. As soon as they were done, Seth barked in command and they all turned and raced away into the trees, leaving me in the mud and the rain and the piss.

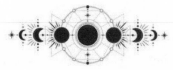

After I had to endure the humiliation of stomping back through the Ignis House common room covered in mud and reeking of wolf piss, I showered for over an hour before I felt even close to clean. I scrubbed my skin until it was pink and burned everything I'd been wearing with a blast of fire magic which helped satisfy my anger a little bit.

FaeBook was filled with posts about what Seth and his pack had done to me so I was the laughingstock of the entire Academy once again. The only thing which was stopping me from bursting into tears over it was the little pile of gold coins and jewellery which had sat by my feet as I showered and the knowledge that Darcy had already set a plan into motion against the Werewolf asshole.

Most of the coins and jewellery now had a new home wrapped in a plastic bag in the cistern at the back of my toilet in my en-suite.

I kept thinking about the damn party I had to attend with Seth and the rest of the Heirs. I had half a mind to back out of the stupid thing but I'd made a deal with Darius and he'd kept up his end of it. If I wanted any hope of him continuing to tutor me with my fire magic then I needed to stick to my word.

My extended stint in the shower to remove the piss from my body meant that I'd missed breakfast and I was dangerously close to being late for my first lesson too but I decided to risk the House Points in favour of setting my plans in motion.

I braided my hair over one shoulder and used a few more hair pins than necessary to secure it in place.

I straightened my school uniform and slid five of Darius's gold coins into my pocket with a little rush of anticipation. I hesitated as I eyed the dagger next, the weird energy emanating from it seeming to want me to take it with me. I placed it in my pocket, took a step towards the door then stopped.

Why the hell am I about to go to lessons with a dagger in my pocket like a damn psychopath?

I shook my head and pulled the dagger back out of my pocket, sliding it beneath the sheets of my bed instead. The stupid thing seemed to call out for me to come back for it but I forced the impulse away with a shudder. I was *not* going to be manipulated by an inanimate object.

At five to eight, I slipped out of my room and headed upstairs with my heart pounding and a determined set to my features. The Heirs may still have been able to push us around but I planned on doing everything in my power to undermine them at every turn. And stage one of that plan required a small break-in to occur.

I made it to the top floor of Ignis House and hesitated as I listened for the sounds of anyone who might be running late for lessons. I had a vague cover story in place in case I was caught up here; I would claim to be looking for Darius to ask about our next Fire Elemental session. It wasn't the best cover. Why would I be looking for him now when he wasn't due to return to the House until tomorrow morning? Why would I have come three minutes before lessons were due to start? Why didn't I just send him a message on my Atlas? But a cover story with holes was better than nothing at all and I was pretty confident I wouldn't need it anyway.

I headed for Darius's room at the end of the hall first, knocking softly just in case he really was back already.

There was no response so I quickly dropped to my knees, pulling the hairpins from my braid and working them into the lock. I was familiar with it from my last foray into his room so I disabled it quickly and a loud click signalled my victory.

The door swung open silently and I was accosted by the smell of fresh paint. His refurbishment had come complete with a brand new TV, luxurious furnishings and plenty of gold adornments. His new bed had a gold headboard with the name Acrux emblazoned on it.

I scowled in disappointment, it seemed that my revenge had ended in him getting upgrades. I really doubted he'd be losing much sleep over the things I'd destroyed in the super-king bed with the plump pillows and dark grey sheets which looked as soft as butter.

His fireplace now had a black fireguard standing before it and I snorted in amusement at that addition.

As much as I'd have liked to set his fancy new room alight for a second time, I imagined the investigation into that would be a hell of a lot more thorough and it wasn't worth the risk.

I tiptoed across his plush new carpet and slipped one of the fat, golden coins from my pocket. I spotted the melted dragon head on the face of the coin and smirked at the fact that I'd plucked this particular coin from the buried treasure.

With a thrill of adrenaline which spilled through me, I placed the coin on his pillow where it glinted, ready to taunt him like the nice big 'someone stole your treasure' message I intended for it to be.

I backed up quickly, tugging his door closed and re-locking it with well practiced moves. *Stage one, complete.*

Next, I headed along the corridor to the last door on the left, my heart thundering a merry tune to a beat of anticipation. I made quick work of that lock too and slipped inside.

I wrinkled my nose as I looked around at the devastation which Milton Hubert called home. There were heaps of dirty clothes, piled up books which lay open with their spines bent and the unholy stench of unwashed teenage male lingering in the air.

His room wasn't as big as Darius's but it was still twice the size of mine. I guessed being part of Darius's posse came with the perks of an upgrade. Shame their friendship was destined to fall on rocky times.

I held my breath as I crept forward, careful not to disturb any of his piles of crap just in case this was actually an organised form of chaos and he noticed the difference. Though I doubted that very much. I reached the double bed and quickly pushed the handful of coins beneath his mattress, making sure they lay flat so he wouldn't notice them.

I backed up swiftly and locked the door again.

Success for stage two.

I pushed the hairpins back into my braid and headed for the stairwell, checking the time on my Atlas as I went. I was already five minutes late but our first class of the day was Cardinal Magic so there was a good chance Orion wasn't there yet anyway.

I sprinted out of the House and up the path toward Jupiter Hall.

As I drew close to the long building, I spotted Orion approaching the doors. He pulled it open and I darted through in front of him.

"Cutting it fine, Miss Vega," he said, thankfully not sounding too angry for once.

"Still made it before you though," I said, offering an insolent smile over my shoulder as I dashed up the stairs.

I ran all the way to class and dropped down into my chair beside Darcy five seconds before Orion strolled into the room, sipping from his mug of coffee like he didn't have a care in the world and wasn't fifteen minutes late for his own lesson. It occurred to me that he could easily use his Vampire speed to get here on time if he wanted to but he clearly chose to be late.

"Did you do it?" Darcy breathed, hiding the words behind her hand.

I smiled widely in response but I didn't reply as I noticed Orion watching us.

"Anything you want to share with the class, Miss Vega?" Orion asked mildly, in that tone which lulled you into believing he wasn't half a second away from launching that boiling hot coffee all over us.

I bit down on my smile, though I couldn't banish it completely, and shook my head at him.

His eyes narrowed with suspicion but he quickly dismissed it, turning to the board where he wrote the title of today's lesson for all to see.

YOU ARE NOT FRIENDS.

I raised an eyebrow at Darcy and she stifled a laugh. It looked like we were in for yet another lesson on the art of becoming an asshole and I opened up my Atlas, ready to learn about what we were lacking today.

Tarot class felt odd without Professor Astrum to teach it but it was even worse having Washer stand in. He was wearing a pair of leather pants today with a lace up fly which was so tight that it was bulging. He'd coupled the pants with a white shirt which clung to his body in a way that made me wonder if it was part Lycra. I could see his nipples through it and he seemed to have forgotten to fasten half the buttons.

A million times ewww.

"Anyone feeling like they want to offload today?" Washer asked as the class walked in. "I'm a little light on power so feel free to come dump on me if you need to. I promise not to bite... unless you ask really nicely."

The wink which followed his offer sent a shudder down my spine and I gave my attention to unpacking my Atlas and Tarot deck from my satchel so that I didn't have to look at him.

He set us to work reading the cards then started moving around the class, peering over people's shoulders to check their work while brushing against them to siphon their magic as he went. Thankfully he started on the far side of the room so we were spared from his attention for the moment.

Darcy shuffled the deck, her eyes alight with intrigue as she held the cards out in a fan for me to pick one.

I waved my hand above them and felt an intense desire to grasp one. I'd never been so sure of my choice when picking from the cards before and I drew the card out with interest, flipping it over to see what it was.

My lips parted as I spotted the card that Astrum had left for us before his death.

"Did you mean to put that in your deck?" I asked Darcy with a frown.

"No," she replied in confusion. "I mean, it wasn't in there earlier, I'm sure of it. I haven't even had the deck out!"

I placed it on the table between us, looking at the mysterious words on the back for the millionth time.

I made a mistake and now my time is up.
The Shadow has discovered me and there is no hope for me to escape their wrath.
The answers you seek are hidden between Leo and Libra.
Don't trust the flames.
Claim your throne.
- Falling Star

As I read the words about Leo and Libra, my head snapped up automatically like a hand had been placed under my chin and lifted it. My eyes fell on the swirling design of the constellations on the wall behind the desk where Leo and Libra sat directly beside each other. As I looked at the wall more closely, I realised that it was in fact lined with tiny drawers which I guessed Astrum had used to store things.

I glanced to my right and found Darcy looking at the exact same thing.

"So I'm getting the feeling that the card wasn't talking about Darius and Orion," she breathed.

I nodded, casting a look at Washer as he leaned right over Tyler's desk with his ass in the air as he inspected the card he'd drawn.

"Knock on the table if he's gonna spot me," I breathed, pushing myself up out of my seat.

Diego and Sofia looked around as I got up too and I pressed a finger to my lips as they watched me move away.

Most of the class were too distracted with their work to notice me slipping around the desk towards the wall. My fingertips were tingling and I could feel the same little tug on my magic that I'd felt the night Astrum had died, right before we'd discovered the Death card. I tried to pull on it but it was like the thing I was yanking on was stuck.

I glanced at Washer again before moving to the wall and brushing my fingers along it. The little drawer between Leo and Libra resisted my first attempt to open it but as I exerted a little magic, the lock clicked open like it had recognised me.

My heart leapt and I quickly grabbed the contents from the drawer just as Darcy knocked her fist against the desk.

I spun around, bumping the drawer closed behind me and concealing the two cards behind my back just as Washer turned his blue eyes on me.

"Why are you out of your seat, Miss Vega?" he asked curiously, taking a few steps towards me which were punctuated by the creak, creak, creak of his leather pants.

"I err, just wanted to..." My mind whirled and in the moment I could only come up with one possible thing to say which would cover my ass, but the thought of it made me want to heave. I really couldn't risk him realising that I'd just taken something from Astrum's drawer so I had to go with it. "To take you up on your offer to... offload some emotional baggage." I cringed internally and Darcy wrinkled her nose in disgust behind his back.

"*Really?*" Washer purred, his tongue darting out between his lips like he could taste my emotions on the air already.

"Yeah," I agreed, my voice sounding about as unenthusiastic as I felt.

"You do look troubled, poor lamb. Why don't we take this somewhere more private? Come on through to the store cupboard." He flicked his hazel hair and creaked across the room to a small door in the far corner, clearly expecting me to follow.

I scampered back to Darcy, passing over the cards I'd grabbed from the drawer with a grimace. "He'd better have left us more than just obscure nonsense this time," I groaned.

"Good luck," she replied, failing to keep the horror from her face as her eyes slipped to the open cupboard door.

"Come on, Miss Vega, I've just thought up a special treat for you!" Washer called from the cupboard and I shuddered as I moved to follow him inside.

Washer smiled widely as I stepped into the meter square cube lined with shelves holding all sorts of fortune telling equipment.

"Are you sure we really need to be in a cupboard for this?" I asked, glancing back at the classroom door.

"It's much nicer to have some privacy for these things," Washer said, either ignoring my discomfort or just not noticing it.

I was about to tell him I'd changed my mind when the call of his Siren gift pulled at me. The sense of unease slid away from me and I found myself walking towards Washer like he was an old friend.

"If you're feeling low, I always find it's nice to relive some tantalising, *exciting* memories," Washer said, reaching for my hand.

He took it and his power increased as I gazed up at his floppy hair, suddenly wanting to brush it away from his eyes so that I could see them better.

He groaned a little as my fingers did just that, sweeping across his brow.

"Let's have a look at some of those *fun* memories then, it'll cheer you right up," Washer urged and lust crept along my limbs, guiding me towards exactly what he wanted.

My breathing hitched as he sorted through my memories like they were snacks for the taking.

After a thankfully brief look, he released me and the lust withdrew as I folded my arms over my chest defensively.

"Tut tut tut," Washer said with a knowing smile. "Mr Altair should know better than to get handsy with his Source in a classroom."

My lips parted, words caught in my throat. I hadn't told anyone about hooking up with Caleb and I'd meant for it to stay that way.

"Our little secret," Washer assured me with a wink.

He showed me out of the cupboard and I scurried away feeling violated. I dropped down next to Darcy and her eyes widened as she looked at me.

"What did he do?" she hissed.

"I... he...." I was so disgusted by what he'd just done that I didn't even have words for it.

Darcy, Sofia and Diego were all looking at me worriedly, waiting for an explanation and I dropped my gaze to the desk as I gave it to them.

"He looked at my memories of me *doing stuff* with guys," I explained, unable to say any more without shuddering.

"What?" Darcy demanded in outrage.

"Pervertido!" Diego exclaimed and Sofia clapped a hand over her mouth in horror.

Washer glanced our way and I hunched in on myself, not wanting him to come over here again.

"Don't worry about it," I said dismissively though half of me wanted to curl up in a ball and die. "What was in the drawer?"

Darcy's mouth fell into a thin line but she obviously realised we were drawing Washer's attention too and let it go. She surreptitiously held out two things to show me. One was a photograph of a man in his fifties. He had a handlebar moustache, bald head and looked absolutely ripped despite his age and smart grey suit. The second was yet another card from Astrum's deck; the deck he'd told us used to belong to our birth mother.

I studied the picture on the card. It showed a man who looked kind of like the pope wearing a red robe and a golden headdress while sitting on a chair and holding a golden staff in his hand. *The Hierophant* was printed at the base of the card.

"What does that one mean again?" Darcy asked, pulling up the meaning for the card on her Atlas.

Before she could find it, Sofia supplied the answer. "The Hierophant stands for convention and tradition. It can be a sign of marriage or arrangement but can also mean a teacher or councillor who will give advice, assistance or aid in learning," she said.

"That last bit would certainly be helpful," Darcy added.

"We could do with someone to give us some answers," I agreed. I flipped the card over and found words written in Astrum's swirling silver script yet again.

Ask him what happened to Clara Orion four years ago...

"I guess he means *this* dude," I said, tapping my finger against the photograph.

Darcy lifted it to inspect it but there were no further words, no name, no way at all for us to figure out who this guy was and I'd certainly never seen him before. She showed it to the others but they both shrugged, clearly having no idea who he was either.

"Do you think Clara Orion has something to do with Professor Orion?" Sofia asked curiously.

"We could ask, I guess..." I frowned, wondering if that would result in any answers.

"Urgh, he probably wouldn't tell us anything," Darcy muttered. "He never gives me straight answers."

I frowned at her, wondering what that was supposed to mean but she went on quickly without elaborating.

"How are we supposed to track down some random guy from a picture alone?" Darcy asked in exasperation, tucking the card and photograph away.

"Maybe you shouldn't," Diego said warily. "The things Astrum knew got him killed. Perhaps it's best you don't go chasing after his secrets."

"He has a point," Sofia agreed, her eyes alight with concern.

"Well it doesn't matter anyway," I said with a shrug. "We've got nothing else to go on, so unless this guy comes wandering in the room at any moment, we haven't got a hope of finding him."

Darcy opened her mouth to reply just as the door swung open.

My heart lurched in surprise and we all looked up, half expecting the mystery man to be looking back at us. Instead Kylie Major was just returning from a bathroom break.

We all released a collective laugh as the tension leaked from us.

I turned to face Darcy again. "Well unless fate decides to deliver him to us, I guess that's the end of that."

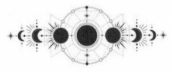

During our last class of the day, I'd received a message to say that a very exciting delivery had arrived and we'd headed straight to Pluto Offices to retrieve it.

We hurried through Earth Territory with the discreetly packaged black box and I had to fight the desire to laugh aloud at what we were about to do.

Darcy was grinning like a Cheshire Cat beside me and I was sure I was too.

As we drew closer to Terra House, we slipped off of the main path and into the trees. They weren't as thick here as in The Wailing Wood but the huge pines and giant redwoods held a kind of majestic beauty to them which took my breath away. Everything in Earth Territory was green and lush and beautiful. The scent of wildflowers and pine hung in the air and everywhere I looked plants of every variety were springing to life.

We'd come here a few days ago with Geraldine to scope out where we needed to go so the path was familiar as we circled around the huge hill which contained Terra House.

Because the House was underground, each of the bedrooms held a window in their ceilings which were cut into the sides of the hill and looked up at the sky.

Caleb's room was at the very peak of the hill so we wound our way between the other windows carefully, making sure we couldn't be seen by any of the students inside.

We had hoped to make it here while the Earth House Captain was still at Pitball practice but there had been a queue at Pluto Offices and it had taken longer than expected to claim our package so there was a chance he'd be back already.

As we drew close to the window, we dropped down to our hands and knees and crawled towards it. The huge round window was split into four quarters by a bronze frame, each of which opened separately.

I smirked at Darcy as we wiggled to the edge of the window and peered down into the luxurious space which Caleb Altair called home. It was like a hobbit hole had had a baby with a penthouse.

I pulled a screwdriver from my pocket and quickly got to work jimmying the closest window open. Just as I heard a telltale click and wedged my fingers into the frame, the door to Caleb's room swung open and we both recoiled as he strode inside.

Darcy's hand landed on my forearm, her grip tightening as Caleb wandered into the space in a filthy Pitball kit. He tossed a sports bag onto the floor and dropped his Atlas on his desk before pulling off his shirt.

I hadn't come here with any intention to spy on Caleb Altair as he got naked but with my fingers stuck holding the window open a crack, I didn't get much choice in the matter as he dropped his pants next.

Darcy blew out a breath of laughter beside me as he crossed the room and headed into his en-suite, giving us plenty of opportunity to check out his ass before he closed the door. The sound of the shower starting up reached us and I relaxed a little.

"He might be a part of the asshole brigade, but that guy is stupidly hot," I murmured.

"No doubt about that," Darcy agreed.

"Shall we get on with ruining his day then?" I asked with a grin.

"Definitely."

I tightened my grip on the window and managed to pull it open an inch before using the screwdriver to release the lock. As I opened it the whole way, I couldn't help but think that Fae really should consider getting better locks on their doors and windows. They were so concerned with intimidating people away from them that basic security didn't even seem to occur to them.

At least it makes our plans easier to execute.

Darcy made quick work of opening the box and I stifled the raucous laughter which wanted to burst from my throat as I caught sight of the huge inflatable as she pulled it out.

She smiled widely as she hung it down into his room, flipping open the plug so that I could blow it up. While she held it tightly, I pressed my fingers to the hole and directed air magic into it, inflating the huge thing within a matter of seconds. Darcy flicked the cap into place to keep the air inside and dropped the monstrosity straight onto Caleb's bed.

She wriggled back out of the window and I secured it quickly, fighting against my desire to laugh with everything I had.

As much as I was desperate to see how this played out, hanging around would have been stupid so we quickly got to our feet and started running back down the grassy roof of Terra House.

Darcy burned the black box with a burst of fire magic while we were hidden in the trees to destroy the evidence.

We didn't slow down until we made it back to The Orb where we fell onto a couch in the corner and laughed so hard that we started crying. I hoped Caleb was enjoying his shower, because he was in for a shock when he got out.

CALEB

CHAPTER SEVENTEEN

I tilted my head back as the hot water raced over my skin, scrubbing my fingers through my curling hair as I washed it with the expensive as hell shampoo Mom had sent me. I complained about her sending me so many grooming products but I still used all of them so I guessed she knew me better than I liked to admit.

As I finished washing the dirt from Pitball practice off of my body, my mind turned to Tory Vega. I still hadn't bitten her since the other Heirs had nearly drowned her and I was currently running high on Darius's power. I'd caught him off guard right after he shifted back out of his Dragon form last night at King's Hollow and even though his nudity made it a little awkward, it was the easiest opportunity for me to catch him unawares.

Seth had been the easiest of them to overpower; his constant nuzzling meant that all it had taken was a moment of Vampire speed and a turn of my head was met with the reward of a long drink of his magic. Now that I'd taken my anger over the situation out on each of them, we could all move on without the need for any more bad feeling between us. That coupled with the fact that our second week of detention was finally coming to an end meant that we should be able to get back to normal again. Last night we'd all truly laughed together for the first time in ages and I was more than pleased to have my relationship with my brothers back on track.

But now that that was done I knew I couldn't keep on giving Tory a free ride. It was time I drank from my Source again and I just had to hope that doing so wouldn't undo the hard work I'd put into winning her around to me.

I wasn't a fool, I knew she didn't trust me and certainly didn't have any reason to want me as a friend. But I hoped she might be open to rethinking the other aspect of our relationship which we'd barely even begun to explore.

I closed my eyes as I remembered that afternoon alone in the classroom with her. The way her kiss had tasted, the way her body had felt as she'd given it to me, the sight of what lay beneath her clothes, the moans of pleasure I drew from her lips... It was making me hard just thinking about it and I half considered indulging in this fantasy a little longer. But I didn't want to jerk off over Tory Vega. I wanted to feel her body writhing beneath mine.

With a grunt of frustration, I flipped the dial around to cold and gasped as the freezing torrent put a dampener on my arousal.

I tolerated it for as long as I could before getting out and grabbing a towel which I ran through my hair before tying around my waist.

I headed out of my en-suite into my room and stopped dead as I spotted a life sized inflatable Pegasus sex doll standing in the middle of my goddamn bed.

My lip curled back with anger. How the hell had someone gotten that in here? And why the fuck was this stupid rumour still circulating about me? I'd tried to laugh it off, I'd tried to ignore it but now it had gone too damn far.

I rushed towards the rainbow striped flying horse complete with gaping butthole and shoved it towards the door.

"Who did this?!" I bellowed, making sure the whole goddamn House could hear me. I was their fucking Captain and a Celestial Heir. What made someone think they could get away with this shit in *my* House??

I was so angry that I kicked my door open using my Vampire strength, causing the wood to splinter around the lock and the thing to fall half off the hinges and into the open hallway outside. A crowd had already gathered to find out what I was yelling about and I snarled at them, baring my fangs before turning back to try and tug the stupid sex toy out of my room.

"Whoever the fuck it is who thinks that this was a good idea had better come forward if you want your punishment to be something you survive!" I yelled, heat clawing up my neck as I tried to force the huge thing out of my room but it's glittering wings were getting caught on the other side of the door. I was face to face with the plastic monstrosity, its horsey mouth puckered into a willing O, waiting hopefully for some sicko to plough their dick into it.

The crowd was growing bigger as more and more people came to see what all the shouting was about and I hoped somewhere amongst them someone was quivering in their little pussy boots as they realised just what level of hell I was going to unleash on them.

I released a string of obscenities as I shoved the plastic Pegasus back into my room and moved to the rear of it to force it out from behind.

There was a tail made of synthetic hair sticking out right above its gaping asshole which tangled between my fingers as I fought with the sordid toy in a bid to get it out of my personal space.

I snarled angrily as I threw my weight against the perverted inflatable and it gave way suddenly, bursting out into the corridor.

I stalked after it, snarling as I noticed some of my House members taking photos and filming me like this was somehow entertaining.

"When I find out which one of you fuckwits did this, I'll drain you of every goddamn drop of power and blood alike, leaving you as a shrivelled husk for the worms to eat!" I bellowed, losing my shit entirely.

I ran at the blow-up Pegasus again, meaning to force it through the door at the end of the corridor but it got jammed once more.

I started swearing, thrusting my weight against it and wrapping my arms around its hind legs to give me purchase.

As I shoved forward, the precarious knot in my towel gave up and the damn thing fell at my feet, leaving me butt-naked just to top off my raging temper.

I shoved it again a few more times, snarling with rage as I failed to get it through the door.

I cried out, losing the plot and sinking my fangs into the plastic monstrosity as I gave up on trying to force it outside and resorted to destroying it.

A high-pitched whistle filled the space as the thing deflated at high speed, its glittering wings flapping feebly as the air rushed out of it and it sank to the ground.

I smirked triumphantly for one fleeting second then turned back to the crowd of assholes watching me.

"When I find out who's doing this bullshit, they're going to wish they were never born!" I bared my teeth at them and was only vaguely satisfied when they recoiled from me. Someone was going out of their way to humiliate and antagonise me but it was only a matter of time before I tracked them down and let them know exactly how powerful I was. Then I'd teach them a lesson in respect.

I stalked back into my room without retrieving my towel and dragged my broken door back into place, securing it with a blast of earth magic which wrapped vines through the gaps to hold it.

I tried to rein my temper in but I couldn't stop myself from driving my fist into the wall, sending lumps of brickwork and dust cascading down onto my bed.

I clawed my fingers into my hair, fighting against the impulse to rip out a fistful of blonde curls as I battled to calm my agitated breathing.

I closed my eyes, inhaling and exhaling deeply as the tremors wracking my body started to slow.

A ping sounded from my Atlas and I stalked towards my desk, hoping that someone was contacting me with good news which might just break through this foul mood.

I snatched it up with a scowl and saw that I'd been tagged in a FaeBook post. I pursed my lips as I tapped on the link. Reading an overly suggestive date offer or even just seeing pictures some of my stalker club had posted of me, gushing about how insanely attractive I was would actually be productive right now. I was in the mood to have my ego stroked a little. But that wasn't what I found when I opened the post.

Tyler Corbin:

@Caleb Altair took his dirty little secret public this evening.
#somelikeithorseystyle #rideemcowboy #secretsout #pullonmytailbaby
#gettingsomepegasass

What followed was a video of me in the corridor after my towel had dropped as I wrapped my arms around the disgusting sex toy's middle and tried to force it through the doorway. I was cursing and grunting and general looked like I was actually screwing the mother fucking thing.

I stared at it for several long seconds, utterly speechless as a rage more powerful than anything I'd ever known grew in my gut.

The Atlas shattered in my grip and I tossed it against the wall for good measure as complete and utter fury consumed me.

I *would* find the person responsible for this and I would make them *pay*.

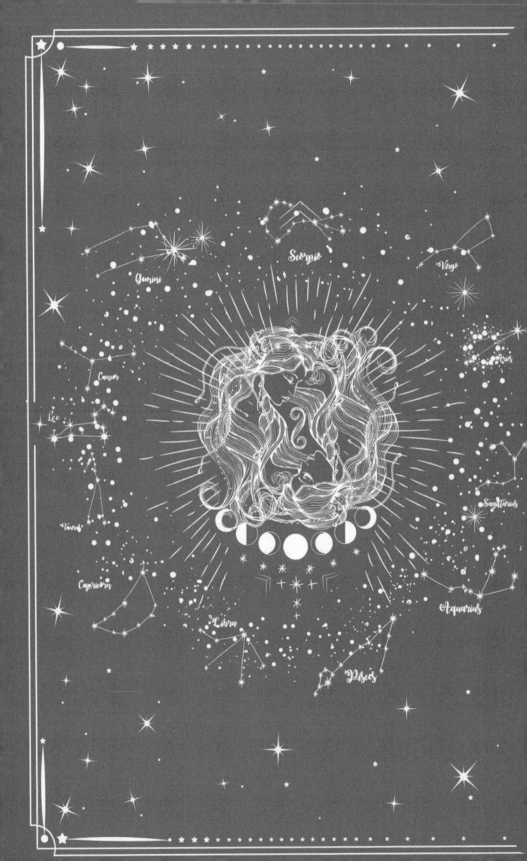

DARCY

CHAPTER EIGHTEEN

The temperature had descended in the night and I hugged my knees to my chest, staying in the warmth of my duvet a while longer with a permanent smile eating into my cheeks. The rain drummed against my window with the force of a hurricane and I shivered knowing I had my Air Elemental class first period. And unless I got the hang of heating the air around me or keeping the storm from touching me, it looked like I had a long winter ahead battling the weather.

I scrolled through the FaeBook feed on my Atlas which was sometimes like playing a game of Russian Roulette. The bullet in this gun was often the latest cruel joke at mine or Tory's expense. After the Nymph attack, there had been a few oh-so-funny jokes wishing her royal highness (AKA me) hadn't been fast enough to escape. But that paled into insignificance now with the wild rumours circling about Caleb and his Pegasus fetish.

After a video of him had gone viral last night, looking like he was actually screwing the life out of that 'Pegasex' doll we'd planted in his room, there wasn't a single other thing students were talking about. We couldn't have planned it better if we'd tried. He was fast becoming the punchline of every joke on FaeBook. And every status I read drew my smug smile wider and wider.

Altair's got the horn for horns!

When he finished, did his winkle twinkle?

Do you prefer a stallion or a mare, Caleb? (asking for a friend)

Is it just Pegasus you're into, Altair, because my Centaur cousin is single?

I soon dragged myself out of bed with vigour, enthused to my core. *Haha sucker! Now you know what it feels like to have the entire Academy laugh at you.*

I showered then dressed in my uniform, pulling on my coat over the top of it and zipping it up. I twisted my hair into a high ponytail, having learned in the past few weeks that wearing my hair down during Air Elemental class was a rookie mistake. I spent a little longer running my fingers through it, pondering Orion›s persistent questioning. Blue or green? I still hadn't answered him.

It seemed less important now. Like Seth taking my hair had been the ultimate reminder of what the blue had stood for. That trust was something I hadn't given for a long time anyway.

Maybe I'll dye it sunshine yellow and it can remind me that I'm a badass.

I headed out of my room, making my way to The Orb through the torrential rain as it swept across campus. I liked the changing seasons, but this rain was a bit much even with my preference for Fall.

When I stepped into The Orb, I immediately knew something was wrong. A commotion had broken out by the Heirs' couch but the large group of people clustered around them made it impossible for me to see what was going on.

Fear pricked my heart and I did a quick sweep of the room, hunting for Tory, Sofia and Diego but I couldn't spot them.

"What's your Order, *amigo*?" Seth's voice rang out and several of the crowd laughed.

My spine tingled with rage as I heard Diego respond. "I don't know yet. Hey - give me that back!"

A hand shot into the air and I spotted Diego's beanie dangling from it.

I set my jaw, knowing I was about as useless as a kitten in a lion fight right now, but I wasn't going to let him stand alone.

"Your Majesty, you mustn't intervene!" Geraldine called to me, climbing onto her chair and jumping onto her table to get my attention.

I ignored her as I pushed through the crowd and people lurched away from me like I was diseased.

I made it to the front of the group where the four vicious creatures who ruled this school were herding their prey. Diego was on his knees, his shirt pulled off of him and his shoulders shaking. Seth stood on the coffee table, dangling the beanie above his head while Max perched on the edge of his seat, his eyes narrowed like a predator's. Darius was lounging on the furthest end of the couch, watching Seth and Diego's interaction with half-hearted amusement, but I couldn't spot Caleb.

"Hey!" I shouted, but they didn't hear me over the clamour of the crowd. I moved to step forward but an arm slid around my shoulders and I found myself in the snare of Caleb's arms. "Tory or Darcy?" he leaned in close, breathing deep. "Different shampoo. You're Darcy."

"Get off of me." I tried to shrug out of his grip but he held on tight.

"I'm in a really foul mood today, sweetheart, so it's best you don't fight back," Caleb growled and the reality of what we'd done to him sank in hard and fast. If he discovered Tory and I had humiliated him, we were worse than dead.

Seth dropped down from the table, his expensive boots thumping against the floor in front of Diego.

"Why is he doing this?" I begged of Caleb and the Vampire pulled me against him tighter, speaking into my ear.

"Your little friend started it."

"He wouldn't," I insisted, my heart rocking angrily in my chest as I tried to break free again. I hesitated to use magic, afraid to bring down the wrath of the four of them on my head. But if I didn't do something, who knew what Seth was going to do to Diego?

Seth put on Diego's hat and my friend's eyes flashed with murder.

"Fight me." Seth wielded the air around him, forcing Diego to bow his head. My friend's shoulders strained against the onslaught of magic. "You wanted a fight, *chico*, now here it is. So fight me like a Fae."

"What did he do?" I demanded of Caleb.

"Seth told him to bow and he didn't. He said he's not his king. This is what happens to your followers," he snarled, his hand sliding up to cup my chin and angle me to watch as Seth aimed a sharp kick at Diego's ribs.

Diego wheezed from the blow, clutching his side and Seth walked around him, placing his foot down on his back.

"Stop it!" I yelled, but if Seth heard it, he ignored me.

Darius glanced at his watch as if he had somewhere else to be as Seth heaved Diego up by the neck and threw him down on the coffee table. A chorus of oohhs sounded from the surrounding students. Max stood up, shifting his weight from foot to foot as if he hoped Diego might hurl an insult his way and give him an excuse to step him.

"You won't fight me like Fae?" Seth snarled, leaning over Diego so his back was to me. "Then fight me like the useless mortal you are."

A round of laughter went up from the crowd and someone started up a chant of, "Kill the mortal, kill the mortal, kill the mortal!"

Diego lifted his palms and Seth's hair danced in a light breeze from the faint magic he cast.

"Useless." Seth rammed his knuckles into Diego's gut and I lost it.

I knew what it would cost me, but I flicked my fingers over my shoulder, casting ice cold water from the tips. Just enough to make Caleb flinch because it did *not* seem like a good time to piss him off even more. The second his grip eased, I jerked free of his hold.

I lunged forward, reaching for Seth's arm as he went to hit Diego again. He whipped it back so hard his elbow caught me in the face. Pain exploded through my cheekbone and I saw stars as I stumbled back. *Ow - dammit!*

Seth's brows raised in surprise as he found me there and a soft whimper escaped his throat.

"Teach her a lesson Sethy." Someone shoved me back toward him and I didn't have to look to know it was Kylie.

In the corner of my eye I spotted Diego scrambling off of the table, snatching up his shirt from the floor and pulling it back on. I couldn't take my gaze off of the fiend before me though, the sharpness of his eyes penetrating right through to my core. Seth stepped forward and I raised my hands, drawing magic to the tips in desperation to hold my own.

I'll fight you with everything I've got.

"Get the fuck to class!" Orion's voice suddenly filled the room. "You're all late. And I'll take ten points from every Fae standing in this room when I reach zero. Ten, nine, eight-"

"We're not even close to done here," Seth said with a smile that planted a seed of fear deep in my heart.

The room was half empty already and Tory suddenly jogged to my side, blurry eyed with rain dotting her cheeks. "What the hell happened?"

The rest of the crowd ran for the door and the Heirs were the last to head toward the exit apart from Tory, Diego and I. I spotted Seth checking his reflection in a mirror beside the door, not seeming in any hurry to leave.

Orion moved across the room with all the speed of a raging bull. Before Seth knew what was happening, Orion smashed his face straight into the mirror and I gasped. He held his head in place while yanking his right arm behind his back cop-style.

"Argh!" Seth roared as Orion stripped the braid of hair from his wrist and applied more pressure to his arm until he whined like a kicked dog. "I'm done with your fucking parading, Capella. This isn't Academy approved school wear." He swiped the beanie hat from his head while Seth nursed a broken nose.

"What da thuck?!" he spat at Orion and my heart leapt with the thrill of seeing him beaten.

His friends lingered outside The Orb and Darius gave Orion a raised eyebrow as if he was questioning his actions.

"Ten points from Aer," Orion snarled, pointing to the door, his hand clenched around the contraband.

Seth squared up to him, growling deeply as if he was about to go full wolf. My gut knotted tightly as I glanced between them.

"Twenty," Orion hissed, moving into a threatening stance. "And another thirty if you dare to lose control of your Order from, Capella."

Seth glared at him for several seconds then backed up, taking his hand away from his face to reveal his newly healed nose. He wiped the blood away on the back of his hand before striding out of The Orb after the other Heirs.

Orion turned his gaze our way and Tory swore loudly.

"Twenty points from Aer and ten from Ignis. Get out." He pointed at the door and we hurried toward it. I threw a lingering glance over my shoulder as we exited, spotting Orion pocketing the band of blue hair alongside Diego's hat.

His eyes met mine for the briefest moment, blazing with a fierceness I didn't understand. But as Tory tugged my sleeve, I turned away and tried not to wonder about the intensity of that look.

Darius and Caleb were still standing outside, but it seemed Max and Seth had headed off to class. I eyed the two of them cautiously as we exited The Orb.

"Hey Altair!" Tyler Corbin waved to Caleb from the end of the path leading toward Fire Territory, surrounded by a group of friends. I spotted Sofia amongst them and my brows jumped up.

The Heirs turned to him as one, like a single beast firing two icy glares.

"What?" Caleb growled.

"Does this turn you on?" Tyler and his friends swiftly pulled off their clothes and burst into their sparkly Pegasus forms, turning around and waving their butts at him.

Tory and I burst out laughing as they kicked their legs and shook glitter from their coats.

"You mother fuckers!" Caleb roared, sprinting toward them with a burst of Vampire speed.

All eight of them cantered away, spreading their wings and launching themselves into the sky. Darius charged forward to assist his friend, tearing off clothes as he went. In seconds, the huge, golden dragon that lay dormant within him exploded into existence and shot into the sky with a powerful roar.

My heart pounded madly as my hair was drawn back by the forceful beat of his wings. He released a spurt of fire at the Pegasuses colourful tails, but their twinkling bodies were already disappearing up into the clouds. *Run for your life Sofia, you rebel!*

Caleb sprinted out onto the grass, following Darius on foot and shaking glitter from his hair as he went, shouting obscenities at the sky.

When Tory and I finally managed to rein in our laughter, I realised Diego was standing there moodily, staring off into the distance.

Tory gave me an awkward look then her eyes fell to my cheek. "Oh shit, are you alright?" she frowned.

I reached up to brush my thumb across my cheekbone and winced at the sharp sting it caused. "Yeah I'm fine."

"Darcy," Diego said, looking to me in despair. "I'm so sorry. You shouldn't have gotten involved."

I shook my head, moving forward to hug him. "Where I come from, people don't stand on the sidelines while their friends get hurt."

"I like the sound of where you're from." He said into my shoulder and I pulled away with a terse smile.

Tory placed a hand on her hip, tutting. "That dog needs taking down a peg or two. I wish we could figure out how to hit him where it hurts."

"How about in the dick?" Diego offered and we started laughing.

"I've still got that Aquarius Moonstone-" I started.

"Now you're extra late," Orion barked as he exited The Orb with a steaming mug of coffee in hand.

"So are you," I countered and I was almost certain he smirked before he turned and headed off down the path in the direction of Jupiter Hall.

"When do I get my hat back?" Diego called after him and Orion answered with his middle finger. I snorted a laugh and Diego shot me a glare but I wasn't paying enough attention. My gaze was lingering on Orion's ass and Tory gave me a pointed look when I finally turned away.

"Come on, stop staring at the teacher, we've got class to get to," she said, giggling as I tried to deny it.

We headed toward Air Territory and Diego started dragging his heels. He kept running his hand through his dark curls as if hoping to find his beanie there.

"You really like that hat," I said gently and he nodded stiffly.

"Mi abuela knitted it for me before she..." He didn't finish that sentence and Tory and I shared a frown as he drew to a halt and hung his head, looking utterly defeated. We stood on the plain of land which stretched toward the eastern cliff. Aer Tower stood tall to our left, the wind beating off of the ocean in a powerful blast and making the turbines spin wildly in the gust.

Diego released a heavy sigh.

"Come on Diego. It's not so bad." Tory nudged his foot with the toe of her shoe - which was affection in her language.

I rested a hand on his arm. "You can't let them grind you down."

"Yeah, I guess," he sighed. Seeing him like that made me want to hug him all over again. "I think I'm gonna skip this class." He looked up, stuffing his hands into his pockets. "You guys are so strong, I don't know how you put up with them."

Before we could object, he headed off toward Aer Tower with his head dipped low. I watched him go with sadness and anger bleeding into my stomach. Seth had been upping his cruelty the last few days. And him peeing on my sister in the middle of the woods, plus beating on Diego got my back up even more than it had when he'd targeted me. It was time we got our revenge on him. Today.

Tory and I headed to Air Cove, walking down the sheer set of steps cut into the cliff wall which led all the way to the beach where our Elemental Class was held. Sand shifted underfoot, the golden colour dulled to a murky brown beneath the dim light of the hanging storm. Although the cove was more sheltered from the wind, we were now closer to the choppy waves and sea spray carried over us like mist.

Professor Perseus was flustered as usual, calling out orders at random as he tried to keep the class under control. He was a slight man with a quaff of hazel hair that constantly changed position in the breeze.

Max was chasing a girl with a piece of seaweed and she shrieked in delight as he caught her by the waist. Several others were wandering off down the beach while a few even looked like they were preparing for a dunk in the sea.

"Please, everybody!" Perseus called out, his voice lost to the wind.

Seth was perched on a rock, his mood clearly sullied by Orion's attack and I noticed his fingers were resting on his wrist where my hair had been. A sweet kind of justice flowed through me as I watched him.

Perseus clapped his hands. "If we could all gather-" Max threw the seaweed at the girl but she ducked it and it slapped Perseus dead in the face. He peeled it off, trying to flick it from his hand as it got stuck there. "Oh bother."

Seth's wolves from Aer House grouped around him, nuzzling and pawing at his hands. He waved them away, resting his chin on his knuckles, but they continued to surround him, one of the girls even licking his face.

I spotted Kylie turning redder and redder as she watched, but she didn't step in. I guessed she had to let him be when it came to his pack.

Tory and I headed over to Perseus, apparently the only ones eager to learn today. Harnessing our powers was a number one priority if we were ever going to be able to truly defend ourselves against the Heirs. And after Seth's run-in with Diego, I was ready to release the storm that had been brewing in me full force.

"Ah, good girls," Perseus said, seeming happy that he had someone to teach. "Today we'll be focusing on wind shields. They can be used for many purposes, but repelling the magic of other Fae is perhaps the most important. I personally like to use them to keep the rain off." He chuckled.

I smiled, eager to learn that particular skill as raindrops gathered in my hair and icy droplets slid down my neck.

"You've both been doing wonderfully with releasing your energy on the sea. This is a slightly more refined technique so you'll have to keep that deep well of power in check. However, once mastered, you'll find this skill is as easy as breathing."

"Can we do hot air too?" Tory asked. "I'm sick of being damp and cold."

"All in time, all in time." He nodded, raising his hands. "Now I just want you to feel the shape of mine first of all."

"I bet you do!" Max called as he ran past, continuing his seaweed game.

Perseus muttered under his breath then gave us a bright smile once again. "Okay have a feel."

I reached out, brushing my fingers against the shield he was casting around himself. It pushed back against my fingers with a gentle pressure. "This is enough to keep away the rain, but a firmer shield feels like this."

"Watch out, it's getting hard now!" Max darted back past us and I tried not to laugh. *Damn fish boy.*

Perseus muttered something about miscreants then gestured for us to feel the shield again. I brushed my fingers over the invisible barrier and this time it was practically solid, pushing back against my hand like a forcefield.

"Yup, I want this," I said eagerly and Perseus laughed.

"I'm going to live in one full of warm air," Tory said wistfully.

Perseus taught us how to push the air out around us and I marvelled at the way it felt to gain more control over my powers. My skin tingled as the wind drifted away from me in a continuous stream, but every time I lost focus, it stuttered and died. The rain beat down on me again and I squinted against the onslaught as a crack of thunder rumbled over head.

"Ay yi yi yi!" Max hollered like an Apache warrior as he stripped off, his Siren form already in place by the time he pulled off the last of his clothes.

"Mr Rigel, this is an Air class!" Perseus called as Max waded into the water, his scales glittering navy and deepest green as they met the sea.

He disappeared under the waves and Perseus sighed wearily.

"Okay girls, I'll leave you to practice, I'd better round up some of these lollygaggers." He headed away and I faced Tory as we started working on creating our shields.

My eyes kept drifting to Seth whose pack were now piled around him like sleeping dogs.

"What's wrong Sethy baby?" Kylie approached, seeming slightly cautious as she neared the group.

Seth glanced our way then shook his head at her in warning.

"What would cheer you up?" She tilted her head to one side and I noticed she didn't have a grasp on shields either, her golden hair glistening with moisture.

Seth stood up, shrugging off his pack and making a beeline for Tory and I without responding to her.

"Oh no." I nudged Tory and she turned, her shoulders stiffening.

I wielded the air around me, making as strong a shield as I could manage and holding onto it with all my might.

He stopped before us, folding his arms, his muscles tightening as he observed us. "Darcy." He pointed at me. "Come here." He beckoned me across the two feet parting us, but of course I didn't move.

"How do you know I'm Darcy?" I asked coldly. "I don't have the blue anymore."

"Not in your hair you don't." He stared at my face and Tory shifted closer.

"Your cheek is bruised," Tory explained and I lifted a hand automatically to touch it, the skin throbbing beneath my fingers. I lost focus on my shield and Seth shot forward.

"*No*." I threw up an arm to defend myself, willing any magic into existence as panic surged. Vines snapped around his throat, closing tight, but he didn't stop coming, reaching out to touch the bruise on my face. I jerked away but I was too late to stop his thumb skating across it.

Warmth spread through my skin and I inhaled sharply as I realised what he'd done. Confusion rattled through me. He'd *healed* it.

He gripped the vines around his neck, releasing a choked noise as he severed them with his own earth gifts.

Tory looked between us, her hands raised defensively. "You okay?" she asked me.

"Yeah," I said with a baffled frown then looked to Seth. "Why'd you do that?" I demanded, weirded out by the strange act.

"My fight was with Diego. Fae to Fae." He hunched his shoulders, seeming uncomfortable about something. "And plus, I have to – fucking -" He growled as if he was trying to stop himself from continuing. "*Gah*." He turned away, marching across the beach, his body shaking as he went. He looked ready to shift and I wasn't surprised when he and the rest of his pack started stripping off.

"If you could all remain in your Fae forms for the rest of the class!" Professor Perseus begged, but the wolves continued to take their clothes off.

"Sethy, what were you doing talking to the Vegas?" Kylie asked, hurrying forward to link her arms around his neck while he wasn't smothered by his pack. Seth released a booming bark in her face and she lurched backwards, her foot slipping on a wet rock. She nearly fell over but regained her balance at the last second.

Seth leapt forward, shifting into his enormous white form and charging off down the beach, leaving huge paw prints in the sand. His pack howled as they tore after him and shock took hold of me.

"Five points from Aer!" Perseus called, but his voice was once again lost to the wind.

"He's in a bad mood," Tory said quietly.

I nodded. "Well he'll be in a much worse mood after tonight."

A grin pulled at Tory's lips. "Just be careful."

"That's code for don't screw it up." I arched a brow and she snorted a laugh.

"Not at all, I believe in you." She gave me a teasing grin.

"Good. Because this is one mission, I am *not* going to fail, Tor."

I'd done a casual wander past the corridor leading to Seth's room three times since dinner. I'd overheard him at The Orb saying he was going into town with his wolf pack and I kept waiting for him to fulfill that promise.

The tower was quiet as most people headed out for Friday night. It was the perfect time for revenge plans as there'd be very few witnesses around.

As I trailed up the stairs once more, I found one of the muscular guys from the wolf pack glaring at me outside Seth's floor. I couldn't turn back, so continued past him and headed up the stairs into the common room as if that was where I'd been intending to go. *Dammit, why aren't they leaving?*

The huge room was empty for once and though it wasn't somewhere I generally spent my time, I figured I'd have to until Mr Tall And Intimidating had vacated the hallway downstairs.

I headed over to a large grey armchair by the furthest window and dropped into it.

Diego hadn't shown his face at dinner and as I curled up in the seat and looked out across the sea, I wondered if I should go and visit him. But maybe he needed some alone time. Besides, I had to spend at least a little while here in case that muscle factory downstairs was watching my moves.

I practised my earth magic as I gazed across the roiling sea, growing a little row of flowers along the arm of my chair. The wind hammered against the pane, the world wild and chaotic beyond it.

Whines and whimpers caught my ear, announcing the arrival of the wolf pack and my heart jolted. I sank lower in my seat, curling my legs up to my chest. With the chair facing the view, no one would know I was here unless they came to the window. I was in the perfect position to eavesdrop and hoped I might overhear what time they planned on going out tonight.

"Come and sit down, Alpha," a girl said softly.

"Okay, Ashanti," he said sullenly and I fought an eye-roll. *Is your life too hard, Prince Perfect? Must be tough ruling the whole school and making everyone else's lives hell.*

"What can we do?" a guy asked, his voice pitching into a low howl like a lament of pain.

"Nothing," Seth sighed. "It's too late."

"Too late for what?" Ashanti asked soothingly.

Seth released a snarl which sounded like a warning.

"Forgive me, I only wanted to cheer you up," Ashanti said warily.

"Nothing can," Seth hissed.

The wolves started whining again and I shook my head. This pack stuff was messed up. No wonder he treated everyone like they were beneath him. He didn't know any different. Not that that made it in any way excusable.

I wish I could cut him off from his pack, make him experience what it's like to be the outcast.

"Let's go out. It will take your mind off of things," a male voice encouraged.

"No, I've changed my mind," Seth growled. "I don't want to go out."

Dammit.

I ground my teeth, frustrated that he was screwing up our plans. And now I was stuck here until they left.

While the wolves started showering Seth in compliments to try and make him feel better, I mulled over whether I should just get up and head out the door. But I'd been sat here too long already. They'd think I'd been listening in on them intentionally.

"Maybe this will make you feel better," Ashanti purred.

A second later, Seth released a low moan of pleasure and I stilled, my heart pinging off the walls of my chest.

Oh God, what's happening?

I curled up tighter in my chair as I heard zippers rolling and more soft, breathy moans from several of the pack.

"Is this better, Alpha?" Ashanti sighed and he groaned again.

Holy crap, I have to get out of here!

I threw a glance around my seat, spotting the wolves surrounding Seth's armchair in front of the fire. Their focus was entirely on him and I spotted a girl's head moving up and down above his lap. *Oh god.*

The common room was empty apart from me and the pack, but anyone could have walked in. They didn't seem to care at all. Another girl in the group leaned down to kiss Seth while a guy massaged his shoulders. A few more of them were starting their own threesomes opposite him so he could watch.

I shook my head, making a solid decision. With my heart hammering, I slid out of my chair and made a run for it. I just simply couldn't sit there and listen to *that*.

No one seemed to notice me and I thanked my lucky stars as I slipped into the stairwell and released a breath.

I hurried back to my room, my mouth dry as I headed inside and pressed my back to the door.

What now?

My eyes fell on my desk and I considered giving up on my task and spending the evening doing some new sketches instead. But as I thought it, my gaze landed on the glistening white stone I'd put on top of my notebook. The Aquarius Moonstone.

They're all upstairs screwing each other, maybe now is as good an opportunity as any?

I grabbed my Atlas, sitting at the desk and finding the screenshot I'd taken when I'd returned to Venus Library the other day.

Aquarius Moonstone:

Often referred to as a 'howling stone'. The Aquarius Moonstone gives off a magical signal which attracts Werewolf fleas to it. The stone can be wielded with a simple earth magic and sends an intense call to many of the lice at once.

Requirements:

One Aquarius Moonstone
One Werewolf Hair from the intended host (from human or wolf form)
Essence of Earth Magic

With the wolf pack thoroughly distracted I figured now was as good a time as any to sneak into Seth's room. I grabbed a couple of hairpins and stuffed them into my pocket, my heart beating a nervous tune as I hurried back upstairs. Tory had been teaching me her lock picking skills in preparation for this and I felt sure I was ready.

I quickened my pace as I turned into his corridor, the sound of moans carrying down from the common room.

As I headed down the passage, I realised it only had one door which made this a whole lot easier. I walked up to it as adrenaline pounded through my blood and Tory's pro tip rang in my ears: *"Don't start picking a lock until you've tried the door handle. I've wasted too many precious seconds believing people aren't stupid enough to leave their doors unlocked."*

With a shrug, I turned the handle on the off chance that – *yes!* It opened and I grinned wickedly as I stepped into his room.

It. Was. *Huge.*

The whole floor was given to him and I guessed his wolf pack too as there were three large beds in the room. The biggest of all sat at the heart of it with red satin sheets. It had the feel of a brothel to it with its black walls and gothic lanterns. Large doors on the left wall presumably led to the bathroom and the opposite wall was nothing but a huge window with heavy-looking red curtains drawn either side of it.

I hurried over to the bed, hunting the pillow for a sign of Seth's hair.

It was spotless.

I sighed, shifting the pillows and searching for what I needed. But with the amount of people who obviously slept in here, even if I did find a couple of hairs I couldn't be sure they'd belong to him. *Crap, this is not going to plan.*

Giggles sounded out in the corridor and I froze. With a swell of panic, I darted into the closet beside the bed just as the pack spilled into the room.

The slatted door gave me a view out and my breathing became choked as I realised I was now stuck in here. There were ten of them in total, all crowding around Seth as they pulled his clothes from his body. He slid his tongue into Ashanti's mouth while reaching out to stroke the chest of the nearest guy. It was the hunk of muscle I'd seen earlier, his hair cropped short and his eyes deepest green. The rest of the pack tore their clothes off, falling onto the central bed, kissing and caressing one another.

Oh my god, I'm going to have to stay here while this orgy plays out.

The closet door was right beside the central bed and I had no chance of escaping without being seen.

Seth drew Ashanti and Muscle Man onto the bed and the pack parted around him as he moved to the centre of it. He pushed Ashanti beneath him and I couldn't draw my eyes away as he claimed her with one powerful thrust of his hips.

My cheeks burned with heat and I moved further back into the closet, the sound of sex clamouring in my ears. More of the pack were groaning, a sea of writhing limbs and naked flesh laid out before me.

Seth's movements were powerful and dominant, every push of his hips eliciting a desperate cry from Ashanti. The muscular male he'd drawn down beside them alternated between kissing Seth and the girl. I was half aware there was no sign of any contraception anywhere and wondered how the hell that was possible if this was a regular occurrence.

Several more minutes passed and I dropped down to crouch on the floor, burying my face in my knees. When a bare ass slammed up against the closet door I nearly let out a squeak of surprise. Seth had a different girl pinned against it and I shot upright, backing into the veil of coats in alarm. His eyes were glazed as he thrust into her again and again, holding her against the door. His usually stern face was set in a mask of pleasure as he stared somewhere off to the right of her head. But the way his face was angled, it was almost as if he was looking right at me and my heart tripled its pace as I clung to the coats around me.

I shut my eyes, trying to block out the loud grunts and slaps of flesh on flesh as I pressed my face into a leather jacket. When they finally moved elsewhere, I lifted my head, wishing I hadn't come here with all my heart.

"Shower time!" someone called and laughter rang out. The pounding of footsteps sounded across the room and hope beamed through me as I hurried forward, gazing through the slats.

The entire group headed into the bathroom and the door swung shut behind them before the sound of falling water rushed through the air. More moans and gasps of pleasure carried from beyond it and I shoved my way out of the door in a surge of motion, making a beeline for the exit.

I'd get the hair another day. Then I'd plant the damn moonstone. Now was *so* not the time to hang around.

I caught hold of the door handle when a voice cut into me.

"Darcy Vega," Seth barked and I stiffened, not moving an inch as my hand remained in place and my heart shattered into a million sharp pieces.

I sensed him moving closer and I turned, pressing my back to the door, knowing I had no choice but to face his wrath. He was soaking wet, his arousal on full display as he closed in on me. "What the fuck are you doing in my room?"

I shook my head, having absolutely no answer. My eyes automatically skimmed down the shining muscles of his body then snapped back up to meet his gaze. Fear was a living thing that coiled through my veins like a snake.

He snatched some boxers from the floor, tugging them on and I sighed a breath of relief.

Seth scowled deeply, stalking closer like a predator. "Explain. Now."

He kept moving, planting his hands either side of me and staring down his nose with an intimidating glare. His body gleamed with water, defining every firmed muscle on his frame.

I cleared my throat, unsure how the hell I was going to talk my way out of this. But I said the only thing I could think of.

"I came to thank you for healing me earlier," I breathed, my mouth overly dry as his wet hair dripped moisture onto my arms. "I didn't realise you-that you-" I nodded to the bathroom door where wanton noises still carried to us.

"So you let yourself in," he growled and a tremor rocked my heart.

"You didn't answer when I knocked and the door was open." I shrugged innocently and he chewed on his lower lip as he surveyed me. The image of him screwing several people was imprinted into my mind with a laser and I prayed it wasn't printed all over my face too.

He released a low groan in his throat then leaned in, nuzzling into my neck. I stiffened in horror, shoving him back and he whimpered softly.

"What the hell are you doing?" I kept my hands pressed to his shoulders, the heat of his damp skin clamming against my palms.

He tilted his head, something overly wolfish about him in that moment. "We have a problem," he said, his voice holding a dark tension to it. He pushed my hands away and nuzzled into my neck again, running the pad of his tongue up to my ear.

"Stop it!" I shoved him again and he backed up like a wounded puppy, beginning to pace.

I realised I was shaking as he weaved back and forth before me, seeming confused and desperate. I was unsure whether to run or fight. But from the way he was acting, I had the strangest feeling that he was about to open up to me. So running away felt like refusing free ammo.

A few of the pack reappeared, dropping down onto one of the beds, not seeming to notice me as they continued their sex fest. Seth didn't pay them any attention either as he moved before me like a pacing lion.

Maybe he wasn't going to open up to me after all.

"I should go," I said, unable to ignore the girl spread across the nearest bed while two guys rubbed, squeezed and licked every inch of her. Heat surged up and down my spine and I gripped the door handle again in an attempt to make good on those words.

"Wait," Seth insisted, catching hold of my wrist. I yanked my hand free but he moved into my breathing space again, his arousal digging into my thigh.

"Back *up*." I pushed him again and he snarled, baring teeth as he began pacing once more. I felt like I was cornered by a wild dog and I had no idea what to do.

"You need to understand something," he lowered his tone, halting his pacing and fixing me in his gaze.

I nodded slowly, my hand still locked around the handle behind my back as a Plan B escape route.

Stay and listen, then run the hell away.

"I made you part of my pack," he spat out, looking furious with himself. "I didn't mean to, obviously." He hounded closer as I frowned, not understanding.

"No I'm not," I said firmly. "And thank god for that."

He growled again and I flattened myself to the door.

"I told you you were an Omega," he said. "Remember?"

I nodded. "But that doesn't mean-"

"I didn't think it did either, but now my instincts are all twisted up, babe." He ran a hand into his hair.

A three-way slammed into the wall beside us and I jumped in alarm. *Nope. I'm out.*

I dragged the door open, darting into the corridor and shuddering as I ran away.

Seth caught my wrist before I made it to freedom and I turned around sharply, slamming my palm into his face.

"Don't touch me," I demanded, but his grip on my wrist hardened as he pulled me into his body.

He ran his hands down my back and I jolted as his fingers came dangerously close to my butt.

"Get your filthy paws off of me this second," I snarled.

"Listen, babe, I can't stop this. I'm an Alpha. And you see all that going on in there?"

I nodded stiffly, backing out of his arms as I tried to remain calm.

"That's how we make this work. They want to please me because I'm in charge. But you're at the bottom of the pack, the newest member. I have to initiate you," he said half of it through his teeth like he wished he could stop himself.

I thought of his twisted initiation into Aer House and shook my head furiously. "I don't want to be in your pack. And I am not going to be *initiated*. Whatever that means."

"It's ingrained in me." He thumped the centre of his chest and I narrowed my eyes.

"Well it's not ingrained in me, so tough luck." My eyes slipped to his hair and I wondered if I could somehow yank a few out before I made my escape.

"I have to protect the weakest in the pack until they find their place," he said in a low voice. "That's why I healed you today. You have to find your position so I can stop feeling like this."

"Well I resign," I said determinedly. "I'm not playing your game, Seth. I don't want anything to do with you or your pack."

He whimpered again, pulling me nearer. "Please just...relax for a second. I'm not going to hurt you."

I placed my hand on his chest as he tried to close the distance between us, but then my gaze landed on his hair. My insides knotted and my shoulders stiffened but if I could put up with this for a few seconds, I could maybe...

It took everything I had to let my body go slack and allow my own personal tormentor to wind his arms around me. He pawed at me greedily, his lips brushing against my temple then moving dangerously close to my mouth as he released a breathy groan. "You have to either please me or challenge me, babe. Pleasing is easier."

I shuddered, but I guessed he mistook it for a shiver of pleasure as he leaned in closer. My throat burned like acid at the idea of him kissing me again. But I'd let him think he could, just for a few seconds longer.

He drew me flush against him so I felt every hard angle of his body. I wrapped my hands around his shoulders, hating the way it spurred him on as he dragged me even closer with a desperate moan.

I reached into his hair, wrapping my fingers in it and tugging sharply. He gasped excitedly and my skin crawled as he rutted against me, pressing his hard length into my stomach.

"Just one night," he begged as I tilted my head back so he couldn't get his mouth too close to mine. "That's all it takes. Then I can forget about you, you'll just be a bottom feeding Omega."

"There's just one problem with that, Seth..." I whispered.

"What?" he asked breathlessly.

I yanked his hair so hard his neck whipped back and he yelped like a beaten dog. A few hairs came loose between my fingers and I shoved him forcefully away with a gust of air. He stumbled into the opposite wall, staring at me in complete disbelief.

"I'd rather never have sex again in my entire life than screw you once." I darted away, leaving him stunned and totally confused.

His hair was clamped between my fingers as I headed into the corridor and ran downstairs. Victory sang a tune in my heart as I quickened my pace to a sprint, tearing into my room and slamming the door behind me. I locked it firmly and rubbed my arms, trying to shake off the feeling of his hands on me. *Ick.*

I headed to the desk, laying out the moonstone with the hair and reading the instructions on my Atlas.

I hope this is worth what I just endured to get it.

A smile pulled at my mouth despite the fact I could still smell that wolf bastard on my clothes. It hadn't gone down remotely how I'd planned, but I hadn't screwed it up either. So mission accomplished.

SETH

CHAPTER NINETEEN

Darcy was *never* going to please me after what I'd done to her at the Fall party. This wasn't how it was meant to go. I was supposed to feel on top of the damn world for destroying one of the Vega Twins. But now I'd somehow initiated her into my pack. Made her a damn Omega. So I was bound to her and my instincts were burning, telling me to go after her and put her in her place for what she just did.

Please me or challenge me, babe. Come on. This is going to drive me insane until you do.

I was sitting on one of the beds back in my room and my pack were running out of steam. I pushed Latisha away as she tried to tug off my boxers again.

"I'm not in the mood!" I snapped and she whimpered, shrinking away from me.

"Come on, Alpha, you're missing out on all the fun," Frank said, dropping down beside me so his bare thigh smashed against mine. He started rubbing my arm and rested his chin on my shoulder.

"No Frank....no," I said half-heartedly as he tried to kiss me. I pushed him back but Latisha reappeared, tugging Alice by the hand. My mouth skewed into a small smile as Alice reached out to cup my chin. She was one of my Betas and always knew how to please me better than most.

She pushed Frank aside and took his seat, leaning in to kiss my neck, brushing my hair away to get closer. Latisha sat on my other side and a stupid grin pulled my mouth wider as they both nuzzled, licked and bit my neck, sending delicious shivers down my spine.

Maybe I don't need Darcy right now.

I dropped back onto the bed, leaning up to scratch my head as something tickled me. Pushing the sensation away, I focused on Alice's large breasts as she straddled me, leaning up to brush my tongue across her peaked nipple. She released a hungry moan but I lost my concentration as my neck began to itch. I pawed at the back of my head, but as I moved toward Alice again, my skin started to crawl like tiny feet were running up and down me.

"*Argh.*" I shoved Alice off of me and she flopped onto the bed. I scratched at my ear, my back, my head again. "Shit's sake."

"What's going on with you?" Alice grimaced and a flare of embarrassment coursed through me.

I'm her Alpha, she can't look at me like that!

"Nothing," I snapped, dropping onto her and pushing my mouth against hers to distract her. While her eyes were closed, I reached around to scratch the back of my thigh as a fiery itch started up there too.

What the fuck is happening? Did the damn cleaning lady use cheap laundry power again? How many times do I have to tell her? Premium wash, once a day.

Latisha ran a hand down my back and I leaned into her sharp nails, hoping she might deliver me from this itchy evil.

"Ah! Flea flea!" Latisha screeched and I jumped upright in alarm.

"Where?" I gazed down at Alice and she pointed back at me. "There!" She rolled away, throwing herself off the bed and the rest of my pack started backing away from me.

I shook my head, but that awful itching started up again and I balled my fists, refusing to scratch. Everyone started pulling on their clothes and a whine escaped my throat. "Hey, wait-"

"I love you Alpha but I can't get fleas just before my mid-terms!" Frank called, racing toward the door.

"I don't have fleas!" I shouted as more of my pack sped after him.

The itching in my scalp became too much and I lifted a hand, raking my nails across my head with a groan of relief.

"See! Get away!" Latisha pulled on a shirt, already halfway across the room.

"It's not true!" I roared. "I'm your Alpha!" I couldn't stop scratching as the itching burrowed deeper and I clawed at myself, scoring red stripes across my skin.

The rest of my pack vacated the room and I released a growl, tearing at my body as the itching became maddening.

"Come back," I said weakly, a whimper leaving my throat as they abandoned me. A hollowness filled my chest as the quiet rang out and the door swung slowly shut.

I can't be alone. I hate being alone.

I threw my head back and howled, the mournful sound filling up my room and reaching out into Aer Tower. But not a single one of my pack replied.

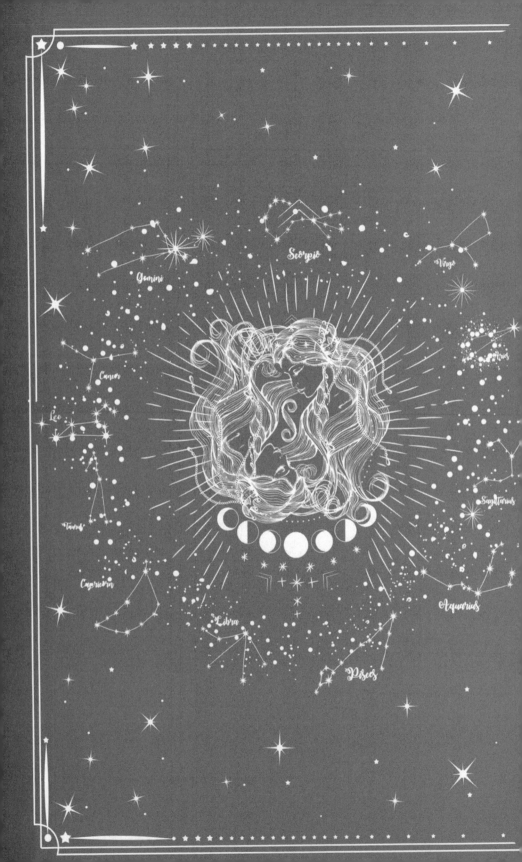

TORY

CHAPTER TWENTY

Because Darius had decided to collect me and Darcy at six for the party from hell, I'd had no choice but to head straight from my Saturday afternoon run to my room to get myself ready with zero time to grab dinner at The Orb. Missing a meal was a pretty touchy subject for me after scraping by in the mortal world and I'd already considered sending Darius a message to make sure we'd be getting fed at this thing. In the end I'd decided against it. I'd promised to play nice tonight and I was going to try and stick to my word. Rich people had to eat too so I was sure I wouldn't be going hungry.

One thing I would not be doing, however, was wearing the dress he'd had delivered for me.

A ridiculously fancy black box tied with a navy ribbon and inlaid with silver stars lay unopened on my bed containing whatever dresses he'd decided upon for Darcy and I to wear. We'd agreed wholeheartedly that that would not be happening. I hadn't even looked beneath the lid. Though I had to admit curiosity was gnawing at me a bit every time I glanced at it. But I wasn't going to budge on this. I'd be showing up at this party as myself and I wasn't going to be dressed up and paraded about like anything else.

Besides, I had my own money and a dress which I didn't mind admitting looked pretty damn good on me. It was midnight blue and clung to my figure in all the right places before falling to the floor. It came up to my neck but was completely backless all the way down to the base of my spine. The four inch stilettos I'd paired with it pushed me close to six foot which meant the Heirs wouldn't be looking down on me quite so much tonight, though short of wearing platforms I'd never actually be able to match their towering heights.

I'd shadowed my eyes and ringed them in black eyeliner and coupled the look with a dark red lipstick. The Celestial Council weren't going to meet a pair of innocent girls who they could push around tonight. I was dressed for war and I was prepared to hold my own.

Keep telling yourself that and maybe it will become true.

I grabbed my Atlas and tapped out a message to Darcy. She was running late and Darius was supposed to be here any minute. She messaged back to say she was on her way and I tossed my Atlas into my clutch as I waited.

A knock came at the door and I stiffened, getting to my feet so that I could open it.

Darius stood outside wearing a black tux which looked like it had been made specifically for him. It fit perfectly and my mouth dried up as my gaze roamed over him. His dark hair was slicked back and the rough stubble lining his jaw ached for me to brush my fingers over it.

No, no, no. Bad Tory.

"Darcy's not here yet," I said in place of a greeting.

"I can see that," he replied.

Before I could lose myself to the spell of his unfairly good looks, I turned away from him, heading back to the mirror which hung on the wall as I applied another coat of lipstick which wasn't in any way necessary.

He stayed by the door, leaning against the frame as he watched me.

"You're not wearing the dress I sent you."

"This might be a good time for you to realise, I don't tend to do as I'm told," I said dismissively.

"I think I like this one better anyway."

I turned to look at him in surprise as his gaze slid over me in a way that made heat rise along my skin.

"Nice to know you can admit when you're wrong," I said. "So you're actually going to stick to your word about being nice?"

Darius flashed me a smile which transformed his face in a way I'd never seen before. "I am. Just try not to fall in love with me though, it could make things awkward when we go back to fighting with each other tomorrow."

I scoffed at that and tossed my lipstick into my clutch just as my Atlas pinged.

Darcy:

I bumped into Orion by The Orb. He says he's coming with us and that you should meet us here...

I raised an eyebrow in surprise and tapped out a quick response.

Tory:

Okay, I'll be there to rescue you from his grumpy face ASAP x

"Darcy says she's going to meet us at The Orb. She ran into your bestie and he told her he can't bear to spend the evening away from you so he's tagging along. I just hope that this party isn't going to be dull, because inviting a teacher has really lowered my expectations for debauchery," I said as I moved out of my room and locked up behind me.

"In all honesty, Lance is more likely to add to the debauchery than detract from it," Darius said, offering me his arm.

"Ooo *Lance* has a first name. Will he want me using that or is it a special right only given to those who get a tattoo in his honour?" I asked, touching my fingers to Darius's forearm where I knew the Libra brand sat on his skin beneath the fancy suit. I didn't take his arm though and started walking down the corridor unassisted.

"What makes you think that tattoo is for him?" Darius asked, falling into step with me easily despite the fast pace I set.

"Oh is it a secret? I thought everyone knew he was your Guardian and you've got that little soul bond thing going on."

"Who told you that?" Darius demanded, his voice dropping an octave.

"You just did." I flashed him a smile and he scowled at me. "Done playing nice so soon?"

He released a long breath as we reached the common room but didn't reply. A lot of eyes turned our way. I guessed the sight of the two of us suddenly hanging out *was* pretty weird.

To the left of us, I noticed Milton Hubert sporting a flashy new gold watch which I'd had delivered to him anonymously. The stipend had taken a hefty hit for that but I'd figured it would be worth the pay off if my plan came together. Besides, I had a whole heap of treasure buried in The Wailing Wood if I ever ran low on cash.

As we passed Milton's table, Darius's little gang all looked up, bobbing their heads like a bunch of meerkats as their leader approached.

"Hey man," Milton said, smiling widely at Darius.

More of the group perked up with greetings, wishing him a fun evening and casting an interested eye over me. I didn't say much as I waited for Darius to finish up with his fan club but I did smile to myself as he noticed the watch. I was counting on him to recognise the value of it instantly and the way his eyebrows drew together made me think he had. Milton was totally oblivious as he sported his flashy new trinket for the whole world to see.

I faked a yawn not so subtly and Darius pulled his attention from his fan club back to me again.

"Sorry," he said. "Shall we go?"

I almost choked on my own tongue at the sound of him apologising and could only raise my eyebrows in response as he guided me towards the door by placing a hand on the bare skin at the base of my spine.

At that exact moment, Marguerite came into the room flanked by three of her friends and her face fell into a mask of absolute horror as she spotted her former boyfriend and me on our way out together.

"What the hell is this?" she demanded, tossing her red hair over her shoulder so violently that it whipped her friend in the eye.

Darius cast a lazy glance in her direction without replying before increasing the pressure of his hand on my back to get me moving. I stepped forward so that he was no longer touching me and began to head for the door despite the livid mean girl blocking our way out.

Marguerite looked like she wanted to set me alight, her hand half raised like she was genuinely considering it. Darius noticed the action and threw an arm around my shoulders which I instantly shrugged back off.

"I'm not your date, dude," I reminded him, not bothering to lower my voice.

"If people see us together acting like a couple they'll give you an easier time," he said, staying close enough to me that I could feel the heat of his body a heartbeat away from mine.

"I'm not a damsel in distress either," I added. Not that he was the Prince Charming type any other day of the week so I really wasn't sure why he was taking this act so far.

Marguerite seemed to think better of attacking while the Heir clearly had me marked as his but the look in her eyes told me the next time she saw me alone I'd be in for some serious shit from her. I threw her a taunting smirk as we passed because, what the hell? She was clearly gunning for me anyway so why not let her bring it on?

"Besides, you'll be back to your usual self tomorrow, encouraging them all to hate me so what's the point of pretending?" I asked.

That remark didn't get an answer and we headed downstairs to the exit in silence. To my surprise, Darius stepped forward and opened the door for me. Apparently the asshole could turn on the charm when he wanted to. That just left me wondering which version of him was the act though. Did he do all of the horrible things he did to maintain his position and keep up appearances for the sake of proving his power? Or could he just pour on the sweetness when it suited him to get his own way? He was so hard to read that I had no idea which version was the real him. But I guessed for one night I could indulge in the fantasy that he actually had a few scraps of decency about him.

"No doubt you won't take my advice," he said slowly. "But I would encourage you not to speak to my father the way you speak to me."

"Pfft, what's he gonna do?" I asked. "Try and drown me? No one's that twisted, right?"

Darius caught my hand suddenly and pulled me around to face him. My heart slammed into my ribs and I tried to pull my hand back but he didn't let go. The Orb was just ahead of us but he held me still instead of letting me carry on to meet with Darcy.

"Who do you think wanted me to do that?" he asked, his voice dangerously low. "I'm warning you, don't push him. He's one of the most powerful Fae in the whole of Solaria and he *always* gets what he wants. Just nod when it's appropriate to nod, say please and thank you and don't let your smart mouth run away with you. I'm not telling you this for *my* benefit."

I looked into his dark eyes for a long moment, sensing that he was being genuine in this but I couldn't for the life of me understand why. What difference did it make to him if his father decided to lay into me? Surely that would be what he'd want anyway?

I shrugged like I didn't much care either way. "I'll behave if he does."

Darius's shoulders sagged a fraction with what I could have sworn was relief and he guided me on again. I extracted my hand from his when he didn't release me right away. I didn't like this new, possibly nice Darius. If I wasn't careful I might just fall for his act.

"What you just said was wrong though," I added as we approached The Orb and I spotted Darcy. She waved as she saw me too and moved away from Orion to join me. Her blood-red dress was held in place with a halter strap and swept to her feet making her look like she was either ready to take on a red carpet or a firing squad of Celestial Heirs and their questionable parents.

"Which part?" Darius asked.

"The bit about him being one of the most powerful Fae in Solaria. Because he's not anymore, is he?" I smirked knowingly and stepped away from him to join Darcy.

"Everything okay?" she asked me, casting a look in Darius's direction.

"Remind me again why we agreed to this," I asked as Seth, Caleb and Max approached us.

They were all wearing tuxedos too and I suddenly felt like I was really out of my depth. This wasn't me. Fancy parties and champagne cocktails were a million miles away from boosting engines and dancing in backwater bars. These guys looked like they were just as comfortable as they did any day of the week. They were the kings of the world and anyone who looked at them knew it. But what did that make us? We were about to step into their world and I really didn't think it had a place for us.

"Still time to make a run for it," Darcy joked and I couldn't help but laugh.

"Good evening ladies," Max said with a wide smile like we were old friends.

"Hi," I replied, not bothering to sound friendly. Darcy didn't even give him that much.

I glanced at Seth, expecting him to crack a joke about the fact that he'd pissed on me the other day but he only offered a pleasant smile before moving to brush his hand along Darius's arm in greeting. He followed it up with a hug, nuzzling against Darius's neck for a fleeting moment while I watched the interaction with amusement. Darius took it in his stride, clapping Seth on the back as they parted and offering him a warm smile. I didn't miss the fact that Seth was scratching himself rather a lot and I exchanged a knowing smile with Darcy.

Caleb was the only one to actually approach us. Darcy stilled as he pressed a kiss to her cheek and he turned to me to offer the same. As he kissed me, his mouth brushed against the corner of mine and I bit my lip to hide my surprised smile. Before he pulled back, he dropped his mouth to my neck and I froze, expecting him to bite me but he only touched his lips to my skin, causing a prickle of energy to run along my spine.

"You're looking delicious tonight, sweetheart," he murmured as he drew back, smiling like we were sharing some great secret.

I could feel the other Heirs watching us and I swallowed the lump in my throat without looking their way. My gaze fell on Orion who looked back at me with a flat stare which made me feel like he'd heard the hitch in my pulse as Caleb had touched me. He looked weirdly at home in his own tux, his youth more apparent beside the Heirs now that they were all dressed the same. I was used to seeing him in a suit while we all wore our uniforms but he didn't even look out of place in our group. It was weird to think of him as a normal guy. I turned my attention from him, glancing at Caleb again as he pushed a hand into his curls.

I stepped toward Darcy as he moved away and she raised an accusatory eyebrow at me.

Damn she can read me like a book. Especially when I'm falling into predictably bad routines.

I shrugged innocently and she rolled her eyes at me.

Point taken. I won't get myself mixed up with the pretty asshole tonight... Probably.

"Is everyone ready to go?" Orion asked, pulling a silk pouch from his pocket and retrieving a handful of stardust from it.

I nodded, eyeing the glittering stardust with interest as we grouped closer together.

The Heirs closed in around us and I was forced to wonder if we were insane to be going along with this. Once we left campus we'd be surrounded by our enemies and trusting them with our fates. The look in Darcy's eyes told me she was thinking the same thing but before we could change our minds, Orion threw the stardust over us.

My gut lurched, the world spun and I was given the distinct impression that I'd just left my stomach contents behind on the ground outside The Orb. Stars sprang to life all around us and it was like we were floating in the cosmos, somewhere and nowhere all at once. As suddenly as they had appeared, the stars winked out of existence and the cool night air brushed my skin as the ground materialised beneath my feet once more.

I stumbled forward a step in my stilettos and Darius caught my arm to steady me.

My hand landed on his bicep which flexed beneath my grip and I bit my lip as I glanced up at him, thanking him before I could stop myself.

"No problem," he said, still holding onto me even though I didn't need him to anymore.

"Sorry!" Darcy gasped behind me and I turned, finding her scrambling out of Orion's lap on the gravel at our feet.

"Predictably clumsy as always, Blue," Orion said but his tone was more teasing than really annoyed. I guessed he wasn't channelling his inner grump so hard tonight. He stood up, casting magic to remove the dust from his pants and I bit my lip to stop myself from laughing.

Darcy's cheeks flushed red and the Heirs failed to stifle their laughter in response.

I looked around to see where the stardust had taken us and found an enormous gothic building sprawling out before us. It looked more like a spa hotel or museum than a home; vaulted windows overlooked the sprawling grounds and pillars stood either side of the biggest door I'd ever seen. There were two towers at either end of the structure which loomed above the rest of it, stone balustrades lining their flat roofs.

Along the rooftop, silhouetted by the setting sun were countless stone dragons who glared down at us with unseeing eyes. A marble porch ringed the front of the building, the steps buffed to a polish which reflected the orange glow of the sky back at it.

"I thought we were going to your house?" I asked Darius with a frown.

He followed my gaze as I stared at the enormous building which spread away from us and seemed to really look at it for the first time since we'd arrived.

"This *is* my house," he replied with a frown like he didn't understand what I meant.

"Shut up," I breathed automatically. I'd seen Buckingham Palace on the TV and this place looked like it could house three of them.

Darius's lips twitched like my disbelief was hilarious but he didn't want it to show.

"If you like this, you should come and see *my* house some time," Caleb offered, moving to stand on my other side. "We've got a dungeon and everything."

"This isn't a house it's a fortress; you could keep a small army in there with room to spare," I countered, ignoring the dungeon comment because I had no way of knowing if he meant that.

Darius and Caleb exchanged a look that screamed of their entitled upbringing and I straightened my spine as I wiped the look of awe from my features. I wasn't going to walk into this place looking like a goddamn tourist at the colosseum, overwhelmed and slack-jawed.

"Technically, your house is bigger than this anyway," Caleb said as we started to walk towards the gigantic door.

"What?" I asked in confusion.

"Well, obviously the Palace is bigger than the Celestial Estates," Caleb supplied. I'd never given much thought to the fact that we had more than just money waiting for us in our inheritance. The idea of us living in a place like this was beyond ridiculous though.

Max shot Caleb a dark look like he didn't like him reminding us about our inheritance but I was glad that he had. I couldn't walk into this place thinking of us as two broke girls from the shittiest part of town, we had to embody the parts of long lost Princesses even if we had zero desire to claim our crowns. If we didn't, I had the distinct feeling that these people would eat us alive.

I stepped away from the two Heirs so that I could walk with Darcy instead. We were in this together, and whatever awaited us within these walls, we'd face it as a united front.

I exchanged a look with my sister which embodied the whole 'holy shit these guys are disgustingly rich' shock before we headed up the steps.

The gigantic door swung inwards as we approached and I looked into a huge entrance hall which I was sure could hold a fully grown Dragon. And as I glanced at the solid gold dragon-head door knocker, I guessed that that was the exact point.

The space inside was spacious and painted white with golden adornments on everything from the door handles to the light fittings to the bannister of the sweeping staircase before us. And I was absolutely sure that that was *solid* gold too.

The servants who had opened the door for us bowed low and stayed in that position as we stepped inside and my high heels clicked on the marble floor.

An elegantly dressed gentleman with grey hair and a neat moustache stepped out of the shadows, offering us a stiff bow as he came to stand at the foot of the stairs.

Is that a butler? Do real people actually have butlers??

"High Lord Lionel Acrux and Lady Catalina Acrux," he announced with a flourish and my attention was captured by the couple who proceeded to descend the stairs like they were goddamn royalty. Which I guessed in this world they kinda were.

Daddy Acrux swept down the stairs with his wife on his arm and captured every inch of my attention in an immaculate blue suit complete with medals pinned to his chest. His blonde hair was styled perfectly and drew my eye to the strong lines of his face. He had a look of Darius about him but his angles looked sharper, more predatory. He was a huge man, at least as tall as Darius, his broad frame packed with muscle in much the same way. His gaze bored into mine as he assessed me and I kept my chin high as I stared right back.

Just when I thought my knees might start trembling from the intensity of his stare, he swept his attention on to scrutinise Darcy, releasing me.

I let out a slow breath, looking at Darius's mother instead.

Holy fake tits!

Mommy Acrux was stunningly beautiful and perfectly put together, her pale pink dress was cut with a sweetheart neckline which revealed *a lot* of cleavage. It was really hard to look away from it. I thought I had a pretty decent rack but beside her curvaceous glory I was a pancake with a face. Real flowers bloomed along the side of her dress, opening and closing their petals in various shades of blue to compliment her husband's attire and I guessed that meant she held the Element of Earth, though I'd never seen magic used in such a pretty, pointless way before. Her face was painted with the exact right amount of makeup to accentuate her beauty. She had Darius's dark hair, bronzed skin and deep brown eyes and she hung on her husband's arm like the definition of arm candy. The men in the room were not so subtly checking her out but I couldn't blame them. *Hell,* I even fancied her.

The butler clearly had more work to do and he stepped forward to announce us to his High Lord and Lady.

"May I present the Celestial Heirs, Max Rigel, Seth Capella, Caleb Altair and Master Acrux," he said.

The Heirs all moved forward to greet the Acruxes and I stifled my surprise as each of them bowed their heads to Daddy Acrux. Mommy Acrux offered out air kisses and embraces which pulled the Heirs against those breasts for a moment. Seth smirked as he moved aside and Darius approached last.

His father barely spared him a glance and his mother didn't offer him one of the hugs but she brushed a hand against his cheek.

"How lovely to see you, Darius dear," she murmured, her tone was sultry and she didn't actually seem to be particularly pleased to see her son.

"I've missed you, Mother," Darius replied, his voice sounding like it was on autopilot even to me.

"Lance Orion," the butler announced next and I got the impression that addressing us last was intentional.

Orion bowed a little lower than the Heirs had as he approached the Acruxes.

"Good evening Uncle, Aunt," he said formally and I frowned. As far as I knew he wasn't related to Darius's family.

He was rewarded with an extra five seconds against the plastic perfection of Mommy Acrux's breasts and I was almost certain his smile took on a forced quality as she released him.

"Ladies Roxanya and Gwendalina Vega," the butler announced last, motioning us forward.

"It's Tory and Darcy actually," I said without taking a step forward and I sure as shit wouldn't be bowing either. This moment was a test of our mettle and I refused to be intimidated into submission.

Daddy Acrux raised a brow at my tone and I could feel Darius glaring at me but I simply held his eye.

"Those are the names we grew up with," Darcy added when no one else took the option to speak. "And we're rather fond of them."

"Mortal names?" Lionel asked, his lips twisting like he found that amusing or disgusting, hard to say which. "Nonsense, the lost Vega twins can't go by any names other than those given to them by the King."

"Well I hear the King was a bit of a whack job," I said mildly. "So perhaps it's better not to live by the way he did things. But if you like the idea of addressing us by those names then why don't I just call you Barry and we'll see how you like it?"

Silence rang out deafeningly and I could feel every eye in the entrance hall pinned on me but I just smiled sweetly and waited to see what would happen. Darcy stood tall beside me, showing a united front against this room of monsters and I was eternally grateful to have been blessed with life at my sister's side.

Mommy Acrux tittered a laugh, breaking the tension as she squeezed her husband's arm.

Lionel flashed us a smile which was more like he was baring his teeth but a beat of laughter came from him too, like we were all just joking around and not actually getting into a pissing contest.

The Heirs instantly joined in with the laughter like they were all programmed to fall into line at the littlest push from their superior.

"Tory and Darcy it is then," Lionel said graciously though he purposefully looked at me as he said Darcy and visa versa. I let it slide though, just glad to have made it through the first test. This was going to be a long night.

"Perhaps we should leave you to your meeting with the rest of the Council," Catalina purred, claiming Orion's arm in her perfectly manicured grasp.

"Yes, we shouldn't keep them waiting," Lionel agreed.

"Come Lance, you can keep me entertained while they talk business," Catalina said, tightening her grip on Orion and pressing her body against his.

Orion dipped his head towards Lionel before leading her away and

I glanced at Darcy to see what she made of our Cardinal Magic Professor curtsying to the Acruxes like a little pet. Her eyes widened marginally and my lips twitched in response. Yep, we were definitely in the thick of crazy town now. No way out but through it though.

"Come," Lionel instructed, turning his back on all of us in a way that I knew was designed to show his dominance. I'd learned exactly how well turning your back on another Fae usually went down but none of the Heirs batted an eye to it this time, clearly accepting their places beneath him in the pecking order. He headed off up the grand staircase and left us to follow.

Darius moved towards me, taking my arm without giving me a choice in the matter.

Much to her disgust, Max claimed Darcy and led her after Lionel with Seth and Caleb trailing after them.

Darius held me back for a moment, leaning down to speak into my ear so that the butler and the other servants didn't overhear what he was going to say.

"Watch yourself, Roxy," he growled, his breath dancing across my skin.

I turned my face towards him, my cheek brushing against his for a brief moment as I looked into his dark eyes. I wasn't sure what I found there but his grip on my arm tightened at the defiance in my gaze.

"Are you deaf, Darius?" I breathed. "That's not my name."

I tried to shrug him off as I moved towards the stairs but he refused to release me, walking at my side instead.

I gritted my teeth in acceptance. I wasn't going to wrench my arm out of his grasp and make a scene but I wasn't just going to roll over for his father or the rest of the Celestial Council either.

At the top of the sweeping staircase, Lionel led us to the left and we followed him along a huge corridor lined with a plush red carpet and huge paintings hanging in gold frames. It was all very grand and ostentatious, more like a museum than a home and I wondered what it would have been like to grow up in a place like this. I just couldn't picture a diddy Darius toddling about the halls with a teddy clutched in his fist.

The butler had somehow made it up here ahead of us and he was waiting outside a set of double doors as we approached. He opened them for us with a flourish.

"High Lord Tiberius Rigel, High Lady Antonia Capella and High Lady Melinda Altair," he said as he moved aside for us to head in.

The room we'd arrived in was a lavish sort of parlour. The kind of room that didn't really seem to hold any purpose. The walls were lined with bookshelves holding thick tomes, deep green curtains hung beside floor length windows which looked out over sprawling manicured grounds with a lake twinkling in the distance.

A huge fireplace took up most of the wall to our right and a fire raged at its centre though the room didn't feel hot with it. There were six plush, cream chairs placed in a wide circle before the fire but no one sat in them.

The other Celestial Councillors were standing to the left of the room, each nursing drinks though they set them down to greet their children as they arrived.

Darius kept hold of me as the other Heirs moved towards their parents and I watched them with interest.

Max's father, Tiberius, was practically his doppelgänger, though his hair was trimmed short in place of the mohawk his son sported. They embraced to an enthusiastic, "Let me get a good look at my boy!" and I couldn't help but remember what I'd seen in Max's mind when I'd been Song-Spelled. This man shielded him from the wrath of his step mother. He'd fought to keep this position for Max despite the fact that he was a bastard and could have more easily been set aside. Despite my particular feelings for the Water Heir, I couldn't help but appreciate the love he shared with his father.

Seth's mother, Antonia, was all Werewolf, pouncing on her son and brushing her hands through his hair as he nuzzled against her with a wide smile. She even dragged a tongue up his cheek in a wolfy kiss and I almost laughed in response. Her hair was a russet brown flecked with copper which caught the firelight and her eyes were pale grey and shone with an intelligent kind of cunning.

Caleb's mother, Melinda, smiled broadly at her son. She shared his golden curls and looked like a fifties pin up girl in a white dress which flared out around her legs. She pressed a kiss to Caleb's cheek leaving a print of pink lipstick behind on his skin which she wiped away affectionately.

Apparently the dismissive indifference that Darius received from his father wasn't a trait all of the Celestial Council shared. I hoped that might mean there was a chance for this meeting not to be a total disaster after all.

Lionel headed straight for a chair beside the fire, the butler placing a crystal tumbler filled with amber liquid into his hand the moment his ass hit the cushions.

Once the Councillors had greeted their sons, they turned their gaze on us. Darcy had moved to stand by my side and we stood firm as they approached.

"Which is Roxanya and which is Gwendalina?" Melinda Altair tittered. "You both look exactly alike."

"That happens with twins," I replied, smiling sweetly to counter the flat tone.

Melinda smiled like she didn't mind the bite in my voice one bit and I found myself warming to her just a little.

"They go by their mortal names, Mom," Caleb supplied so that we didn't have to go through the whole rigmarole again. "Darcy is in red and Tory in blue."

"A pleasure to be reunited with the lost Vegas," Tiberius boomed, offering his hand to Darcy.

She smiled politely as she shook. "Nice to meet you too," she replied.

He claimed my hand next and I was momentarily overwhelmed by the call of his Siren gifts. He wasn't actually using them on me but his mere touch was enough to make me want to spill all of my secrets to him.

I withdrew my hand warily and he gave me a smile which said *clever choice.*

Unsurprisingly, Seth's mother got overly tactile, brushing her hands over our arms, touching our hair, murmuring compliments about our soft skin and generally making me feel like a chew toy. Though her touches were gentle there was something about them that felt claiming, like she was asserting her dominance through them. I guessed that was a pretty accurate assessment of the Werewolf Alpha and politely extracted myself from her grip.

"Shall we get on with it?" Lionel drawled from his chair by the fire. "The evening is drawing on and we have a party to attend."

Melinda Altair chuckled like he'd been joking but his curt tone didn't give me that impression.

Darius guided us over to the fire, directing the two of us towards the chairs to the right. The other Councillors took the remaining three seats and their sons all moved to stand behind them stoically.

"A drink, ladies?" the butler asked and I noticed he'd somehow managed to supply everyone else in the room with a beverage already.

"Sure. I'll take a shot of tequila," I said, not bothering to choose anything with more class to it. This was who I was and I wouldn't apologise for it.

"I'll have a rum and coke," Darcy requested.

Lionel was assessing us like we were something he might just like to eat and I straightened my spine accordingly.

A crystal glass appeared in my hand a moment later and I knocked the drink back in one hit because why the hell not? I was pretty sure I could use the boost to my courage.

Eight sets of very powerful eyes were fixed on us and I was struck with the realisation that if the people in this room wanted to hurt us then we were well and truly screwed. Deader than dead. Beyond the grave. The thought was weirdly reassuring. Here we were, at their mercy, drinking their fancy tequila like it was no different to the piss water version I was used to at Joey's bar and we were still breathing. They wanted something from us. I wasn't sure what yet, but it was clear that they weren't going to hurt us... for now.

"It's such a pleasure to welcome you back into the fold," Tiberius said heartily. "Max tells me you've been settling in well at the Academy, getting up to high-jinx together."

"Is that how he put it?" Darcy asked stiffly and Max offered the barest hint of a smirk from behind his father's back.

"I suppose everything here must seem very strange to you after living amongst the mortals," Melinda said kindly.

"It has been a big adjustment," I hedged. "But I think we're getting the hang of it now."

"I hear you need my son's help to control your fire Element," Lionel added a little scathingly, looking between my sister and I as he tried to figure out which one of us had been getting the tuition from Darius.

"Oh yes, Darius has been a great help," I agreed, not bothering to hide the sarcasm.

"Well so long as you remember he's only screwing you to pass the time and don't get any ideas about marriage, I'm sure it won't be a problem."

"I'm sorry, *what?*" I was damn glad I'd emptied my drink in one hit because I would have spat it out all over his fancy suit if I hadn't.

"I just wanted to make sure you understand that Darius is betrothed. It would be a shame if you got any fanciful notions about him." Lionel watched me as he took a long drink from his glass and I fumbled for something to say that wasn't a flat out insult. Luckily Darcy had my back.

"I'm not sure where you got that idea, but Tory hasn't got the faintest bit of interest in Darius. He can head off into the sunset with his lovely bride and I can assure you she won't give it the slightest bit of thought," she said, her voice saccharine sweet.

Darius apparently had nothing to add to this conversation but his jaw was clenching hard enough to crack a tooth.

"I apologise if I misread the signs." Lionel shrugged, spreading his hands.

"It's fine," I ground out though it really wasn't and I was fairly sure he'd said it just to rattle me. Or maybe he really did suspect that I was sleeping with his son and was trying to call us out on it. Either way, I didn't bother to hide my grimace at the idea and Darius looked pretty pissed about it too.

"You'll have the pleasure of meeting his fiancé at the party," Lionel added. "Mildred flew down especially so that they could spend some quality time together. She may even transfer to Zodiac next term if things go to plan."

Caleb snorted a laugh and his mother swiped a hand at him, smacking his arm lightly to scold him, though she seemed pretty amused herself. Seth looked like he was practically biting his tongue off to stop himself from laughing too. I exchanged a look with Darcy, remembering the conversation I'd overheard in The Wailing Wood when the Heirs were teasing Darius about having to marry his ugly cousin. I looked forward to finding out just how ugly she was once we made it out of this snake pit.

Darius on the other hand didn't seem amused and he looked like he might just be about to turn into a giant, fire-breathing reptile. Max reached over to him, brushing a hand along his arm and he relaxed slightly. I guessed the Siren had just siphoned some of his anger from him and I was a little surprised at the gesture.

"So, tell me girls," Antonia Capella asked. "Have you given much thought to your claim?"

Well at least someone in this room is getting straight to the point.

"We really haven't given it much consideration," Darcy said. "It doesn't even seem real. We have no plans to storm in here and set ourselves up on the throne though."

The Councillors all laughed darkly in response to that.

"I imagine you'd have a little trouble doing that even if you wanted to,"

Tiberius commented and it almost sounded kind but there was a threat there. These men and women guarded the empty throne and they had no intention of letting two girls who had grown up in the mortal world sit on it.

"Well we don't want to," I snapped, my irritation brimming over a little. "We just want to see out our time at the Academy, learn how to use our magic and claim our inheritance - of the financial variety. You can keep your empty throne."

"Just like that?" Melinda asked, arching a brown.

"Just like that," I agreed and Darcy nodded firmly.

"Perfect. Then this meeting has come to a natural conclusion. We should go and join the party." Lionel got to his feet and swept from the room before I even really processed what he was doing.

The other Councillors left too and the Heirs trailed after them.

We rose to follow them and Caleb moved close to me for a moment, his fingertips brushing along my arm.

"Well, that was fun, wasn't it?" he teased. "Shall we go and find something to drink?"

"That sounds like a good idea to me."

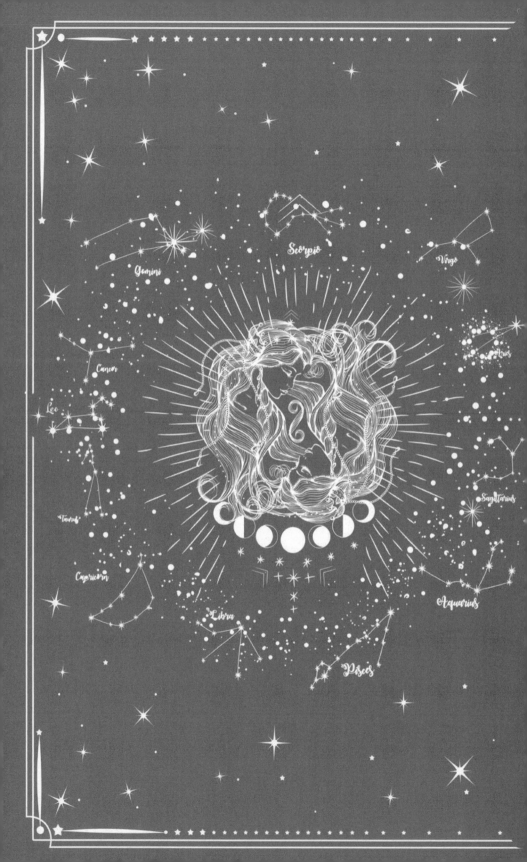

DARCY

CHAPTER TWENTY ONE

We descended into the entrance hall, following Lionel and the other Celestial Councillors through long and winding corridors before emerging in a huge ballroom which was thronging with people. An incredible tapestry encompassing one entire wall depicted four giant dragons in red, gold, green and darkest blue, all sitting atop mountains of treasure. Fire swirled around them and emblazoned at the centre of it was a huge coat of arms with House Acrux stamped on the bottom in bold lettering.

The room was as opulent as the rest of the house with dark wood flooring and three impressive crystal chandeliers spanning the ceiling. At the far end of the hall was a string quartet, strumming instruments made entirely of gold. They played their tune to a dark and ominous rhythm which matched the uneven beat of my heart.

The finery of the party attendees was way over the top; the jewels and trinkets they wore were near blinding. Eyes turned our way as the butler announced Lionel and the other Councillors' arrival, then the Heirs and finally us.

Everyone in the room clapped, straining their necks to make sure they got a good look at the two lost Vega Twins. Though their applause was vigorous, their expressions were calculating, assessing. Whispers were exchanged and sweat began to bead on my brow. I felt like a deer displayed before hunters even though not one of them had spoken a word to us yet. But those eyes said it all. We were a threat.

Someone clapped louder than everyone else in the room, moving through the crowd and parting it with his wide shoulders. My mouth parted as the man muscled his way to the front and recognition poured through me. From his handle-bar moustache, bald head and massive size, it was clear he was the man pictured in the photograph Astrum had gifted us. I glanced at Tory and she gave me a hopeful look.

"Bravo!" he shouted with gusto. "Good show! Great form!"

It was far too generous in response to us simply standing there like a couple of manikins, but he continued to clap while the rest of the crowd stopped applauding and fell into animated conversation with one another.

The Councillors dispersed along with the Heirs, falling into what seemed to be a well-accustomed routine of greeting everyone, shaking their hands and spending a few moments chatting.

Several more people gathered around the enthusiastic clapper, smiling keenly at us and I got the same awkward feeling I did when the A.S.S looked our way.

The man strode forward to greet us and I couldn't believe he'd landed right in our laps.

"Forgive my language, your majesties, but ripen my grapes and call me Talulah, it is an absolute *honour* to meet you both." He reached out a large palm and a laugh escaped me as I realised who this man simply *must* have been related to.

"Do you know Geraldine Grus by any chance?" I asked and he

nodded vigorously.

"My daughter has told me simply everything about you – *everything*. But golly brambles! Where are my manners? You must think I'm an absolute rotter mouth and that I'm terribly impolite for not even giving you my name yet." He bowed low, his hands twirling through the air either side of him and his legs crossed at the ankles. It was kind of impressive how low he got in such an awkward bow. People started laughing and muttering and my heart twitched in irritation. To counter the nasty jibes I heard spoken behind hands and into ears, I spoke my next words overly loudly. "Geraldine is one of the few people in the Academy whose shown us kindness, Mr Grus. We're very grateful to know her."

"Oh my salty sultanas, what a mighty compliment." He flushed red, wafting his hand under his huge square chin. "Please, *please* forgive me, your majesties. My mouth has run away with me again. I'm quite ashamed of myself for speaking so crassly in front of you both. My name is Hamish Grus but do feel free to call me whatever name you desire in response to my lewd behaviour." His friends laughed heartily behind him but not unkindly. They stepped closer, each introducing themselves and we were swept up in a sea of outrageous compliments which were almost as uncomfortable as the glares we were getting from the rest of the crowd.

"Crinkling cucumbers, do forgive me. How rude I am to keep you talking. Please continue with your circle of the room, we have harassed you far too long." Hamish bowed low again, ushering away the other royalists and leaving us practically gasping for air.

"Well at least there's a few people on our side here," Tory said and I nodded, snatching a couple of glasses of champagne as a waiter went by with them, barely stopping for us.

"Hopefully we'll get a chance to ask him about you-know-what later on," I whispered as I passed Tory one of the glasses.

Tory nodded, sipping her drink. "That makes one good thing about this party."

I spotted Orion slipping through the crowd at a fast pace and Lionel's wife, Catalina, searching around as if looking for him. He swept past us, throwing a curt nod our way before heading on and my eyes dropped instinctively to his butt. *Maybe there's two things good about this party.*

"Lionel seems like a charmer," Tory commented.

I nodded, seeking Lionel out across the room, finding him staring right back at me. My heart leapt at his molten stare and I took a quick sip of my drink, forcing myself to hold eye contact with him. It was pretty difficult and my eyes felt like they were about to melt under the intensity of his gaze.

Someone walked in front of him and the second they passed by, he was gone. Like a god-damn ghost.

"Yup," I agreed. "I'm sure he gives great hugs too."

Tory released a wicked laugh, gazing wistfully over at the waiter who seemed to be actively avoiding us.

"Girls." A hot hand slid onto my back accompanied by a wave of excitement. Max wrapped his arms around us both, drawing us closer and though I was aware that his power had a hold of us, the anticipation he was pumping into my blood was too good to ignore. "Let's have some fun."

He steered us across the ballroom and through a door that led into a low-lit room which I could only describe as a smoking room. *Do people really still have those?* Apparently they did because a bunch of cigar stubs sat in a golden ashtray on the nearest table and the thick scent of tobacco hung in the air. Blood red armchairs sat around the space and to the right of them stood Darius beside a large oak writing desk. A row of shots were laid out across it in front of a bottle of vodka and my heart pumped harder as Max released me, his gifts fizzling out of my system.

Darius picked up a shot and knocked it back, releasing a satisfied *ah* after he swallowed it. He grabbed two more, holding them out for Tory and I but neither of us moved.

"I think I'll get my drinks from a less shady room thanks," I said, shaking my head.

"Yeah, I'm gonna decline the date rape." Tory smiled hollowly and Darius scoffed.

"As if I'd need to drug you to get you in my bed," Darius smirked.

"Keep dreaming, Dragon boy." She planted a hand on her hip and I grinned.

We turned to leave and found Seth and Caleb stepping into the room. My heart juddered as they prowled forward, blocking our way out.

"Evening," Caleb said, skirting around us, his eyes lingering on Tory.

Seth scratched behind his ear and I bit my lip to stop myself from laughing.

"Gimme one of those." He moved around us, scratching more vigorously as he grabbed a shot from the desk. He swallowed one then another before pawing at the back of his shirt and scratching his head again.

"What's up with you, man?" Max frowned as Seth started raking under his arm.

"Nothing," he spat, then let out a whine as he scratched himself too hard. I almost lost it when Tory hiccoughed a laugh.

"Almost seems like you've got fleas," Darius said with a teasing smirk and Seth growled deeply.

"I do not have *fleas*," he snarled and I couldn't help the laugh that finally tore free from my throat. He turned, eyes sharpening to slits, but he said nothing.

"Mildred's out there," Caleb spoke to Darius. "Looks like she came dressed as Cinderella's pumpkin carriage."

Darius's shoulders stiffened and he swiped up another drink. "Fuck my life."

"Is that your precious fiancée?" Tory asked as we drifted closer to the door in preparation of leaving.

Darius's lips pursed but he didn't answer.

"He's a bit touchy about it," Caleb mock-whispered to us.

"I am not *touchy*," Darius barked and Caleb backed up a step, but he was still grinning.

"That was convincing," I murmured and Tory giggled.

All four pairs of the beast's eyes slammed into us and I took that as our cue to leave. I caught the door handle but it swung wide again before we made our escape.

"I thought I saw you scurrying in here hubby-kins!" A girl in a vivid orange dress stepped into the room and I had to look up at her towering height and shoulders which nearly matched the breadth of the Heirs'. Her teeth protruded a little from her lower jaw and her eyes seemed to wander, never landing on one spot. Her hair was a massive brown frizz with a pink bow clipped into the top of it, perfectly matching the violently bright shade of her eyeshadow.

She marched between Tory and I like we were made of paper, forcing us aside with her elbows as she charted a direct path for Darius.

"Mildred," he said tersely, his eyes darkening as his bride-to-be reached out to him.

Caleb, Seth and Max sniggered as Mildred leaned in for a kiss and Darius only managed to stop her at the last second by planting his palm on her forehead with a loud clap.

"Not before the wedding," he said firmly and I looked at Tory who was falling into a fit of silent laughter, clutching her side. I tried to smother the giggle that fought its way out of my chest but it floated free and Mildred rounded on us like a hungry animal.

"These must be the Vega Twins," she said coldly. "Well don't waste your time sniffing around my snookums. Daddy says he's saving himself for our wedding night."

Max roared with laughter and Mildred turned on him like a loaded weapon, jabbing him right in the chest. Max's smile fell away as she glared at him like he was her next meal. "What are you laughing at you overgrown starfish?" she demanded, her eyes flashing red and her pupils turning to slits. "I've eaten bigger bites than you before, so don't tempt me because I *adore* seafood."

Max reached out, laying a hand on her bare arm, shifting it slightly as his fingers brushed a hairy mole. "Calm down Milly, we're just having a bit of fun. We want to get to know Darius's betrothed. Why don't you have a shot?" He nodded to Caleb who promptly picked one up and held it one out for Mildred to take.

"Daddy says drinking will grow hairs on my chest," she said, refusing it.

"Too late for that," Seth said under his breath and the others started laughing.

A knot of sympathy tugged at my gut, but Mildred didn't seem to care about their mocking. She stepped toward Seth with a wicked grin and his smile fell away. "Oh and what's wrong with that exactly, Seth Capella? You like your girls hairy, don't you?"

Seth gawped at her in answer. "What the hell does that mean?"

"You like mutt muff," she answered, jutting out her chin and I noticed a few wiry hairs protruding from it.

Seth growled, scratching his stomach as he stepped forward. "I don't screw girls in their Order form, idiot."

"Maybe not, but *you* do, don't you Caleb Altair?" She rounded on him and now I was really starting to warm to Mildred as she cut them all down to size. I settled in for the show, folding my arms and smiling as I waited for her to go on. "My sister's boyfriend's cousin said you like Pegasus butts. He even sent a video to Aurora Academy of you humping a Pegasex blow up doll and it went viral within a day."

Caleb's mouth fell open and his face paled in horror. "I didn't hump it!"

"I didn't watch the video, but everyone told me what was in it. Why would I want to see you screwing a plastic horse?" She shrugged then turned to Tory and I with absolutely no kindness in her eyes.

Oh crap.

"Do you always just stand there gawping like tweedle dumb and tweedle dumber? I thought you were supposed to pose a challenge to the throne of Solaria?"

"Actually we just want our inher-" Tory started but Mildred spoke loudly over her in her baritone voice.

"You do realise the only reason you're at this party is because everyone wants to have a good laugh about how us Dragons are going to use your bony bodies as toothpicks after Darius and I ascend to our rightful place on the throne?" She moved closer, her head cocked and her mouth set into a sneer. "Why would anyone bow to a couple of Orderless, busty airheads?"

My teeth locked together as anger bloomed in my chest.

"I'm kinda fond of the busty part," Caleb muttered and Seth fist bumped him.

"We're not airheads-" I started, figuring I couldn't really deny the other two things - *dammit.* "And the only reason we're at this party is because Darius is helping out Tory in return. It's tit for tat."

"Darius would never give his tat for any of your tits!" she shrieked, smoke spewing from her nostrils.

Tory burst out laughing, but I sensed the danger in Mildred's tone and hurriedly used what Professor Perseus had taught us, forcing a shield of air out around us. Fire streamed from Mildred's open mouth and deflected over the shield in a powerful display of red and gold sparks. My heart hammered wildly as Mildred grunted her fury then stormed past us and exited the room. She slammed the door with a wall-shaking bang and my shoulders dropped with relief.

"Good thinking," Tory said on a breath.

Darius sunk down into a chair and dropped his head into his hands.

His friends grouped around him, their mocking expressions falling away. Seth nuzzled against Darius's cheek and Max reached out, pressing his fingers to the back of his hand while Caleb started pacing back and forth in front of him.

I sensed this was the right time to leave and we both slipped out of the room without a word. We moved away, lingering on the edge of the crowd as I eagerly hunted for another glass of champagne. If there was one way to get through this night, it started with alco and ended in hol.

"This party is a bore, huh?" I turned at the sound of the voice, finding a man beside us who I guessed was in his early thirties. He wore a smart suit, his top button undone and his shining bronze hair swept back stylishly. His eyes glinted with coppery flecks and the smile he gave us was the friendliest I'd seen all night.

"Do we know you?" I frowned suspiciously.

"Not yet," he said, swigging from a glass of champagne in his hand. "Do you want to?" His voice was smooth, not seductive but inviting all the same.

"I'm gonna say no," Tory said.

"Sounds about right," he muttered and I couldn't help but notice how detached he was from the crowd, how he seemed to hover with nowhere to be. Just like us. "Have a fun night then."

He gestured for us to leave but Tory and I shared a look, a decision passing between us to stay for a little longer.

"What's your name?" Tory asked, her tone slightly warmer this time.

"Gustav Vulpecula."

"That's quite a name," I said with a teasing grin and he flashed a bright-toothed smile at me.

"That it is. Handed down from father to son for generations. But do you want to know a secret?" He leaned in closer and the mischief in his eyes made Tory and I lean in too. "I hate it. So most people call me Gus." He winked, stepping back.

"What brings you to the oh so mighty Dragon household?" Tory asked dryly and Gus chuckled.

He turned, sliding something off of his shoulder and I found a large camera in his hand. "I took some new portraits of Lady and Lord Acrux before the ball. You'll all get one before the night is out." His eyes trailed over us. "Well, maybe not you, huh? I hear there's a little tension between you two and the Councillors."

"Who told you that?" I asked.

He rolled his eyes. "The room, Miss Vega. I only need to look around and see the way they're all looking at you."

"Well you're spot on. I'm pretty sure they hate us but they're pretending not to. I'm Darcy," I held out my hand. "This is Tory."

He nodded, clasping our hands briefly. "At least I'm invisible here, I wouldn't want to be on the receiving end of all those sharp stares like you two are." He threw a glance over his shoulder at the door we'd exited. "Are the Heirs in there?"

"Yeah," Tory rolled her eyes. "Being their usual dickish selves."

I glanced at her quickly, unsure if she should mouth off about them in a room full of their supporters.

Gus looked between us with a serious expression, inching closer and lowering his voice. "You don't speak to them like that do you? You've gotta be careful what you say to people with their kind of power."

"Well they usually start it," I said, pressing my lips together. I didn't exactly want to discuss this but I wasn't going to let this stranger make assumptions about us without defending ourselves.

"Like at the Fall party?" he whispered in a deathly quiet voice and I sucked in air.

"You know about that?" Tory demanded, tucking a lock of hair behind her ear.

"Of course. There's nearly two thousand kids at that school. Sure, it was only a third page story instead of a front page due to Ling Astrum's murder but still..." He shook his head, his expression sad. "You two have been through the mill. Did they really cut your hair off?" he asked me, eyeing my full locks in disbelief. "Or maybe that bit was exaggerated?"

"No," I said sullenly. "Seth did it. And then he wore my hair on his wrist as a trophy."

"He didn't," Gus breathed in shock. "How did he get so close to you?"

I hugged my arms, embarrassed as I whispered, "Well I stupidly kissed him."

"Seth was acting nice all week," Tory added. "Like he really cared about Darcy. It was vicious, just like them."

"Shitting stars," Gus said under his breath. "So they did try to drown you?" he asked Tory in horror and she nodded stiffly.

"In Lunar Leisure; they Coerced me to jump into the pool then froze the surface. Professor Orion had to get me out."

Gus let out a low whistle. "Sounds like it's been hell. I'm sorry." He frowned sympathetically. We fell into a discussion about that night and it felt kind of good to open up about it. Even Tory and I hadn't really spoken about it since. And I was starting to feel like we had at least a few people on our side here.

Orion bowled through the crowd like an oncoming storm and grabbed both of Tory and I's arms.

"What are you doing?" I gasped as I tried to pull my hand free.

He bared his fangs at Gus, his eyes flaring with rage. "Get the fuck out of here."

Gus released a dogish bark then scuttled off into the crowd, disappearing in an instant.

"*Shit*," Orion hissed, glancing around as people looked our way. He tugged us closer, his eyes flitting between us and my heart hammered violently in my chest at his expression.

"That guy is a Teumessian Fox and a damn reporter," he hissed.

"A reporter?" I echoed in alarm.

"Yes and he used his Order gifts on you. Foxes are sly, they get under your defences, befriend you then draw the truth from your lips. Why Lionel thought it was a good idea to let..." He trailed off, glancing over his shoulder and drawing us further into the corner of the room. "Dammit, Lionel set you up. *Fuck*. What did you tell that guy?"

"We told him about the night of the Fall party," Tory said in horror.

Orion nodded stiffly. "Most of that has been leaked anyway, so you'd better count your lucky stars that he didn't get anything more damning on you. If anyone else starts asking about that night or your time at the Academy run the hell away, got it?"

We both nodded and he rolled up his sleeves, turning away.

I caught his arm. "Where are you going?"

He gave me a dark smile that set my pulse racing. "Fox hunting." He shot off into the crowd and my hair was pulled forward by his momentum.

"Shit, I hate these people," Tory hissed and I nodded, a scowl pulling at my face.

"The sooner we're taught to defend ourselves against other Orders, the better."

"Grain-free granola, these champagne bubbles are going right through me. Which way to the bathroom?" Hamish Grus called out in his booming voice, appearing further along the ballroom.

"Let's go after him and make this party worthwhile," I whispered and Tory nodded, her mind clearly on the same track.

"We'll corner him outside the bathroom," she said.

We hurried after him as someone gave Hamish directions through a door and along a vast corridor. We held back as we followed and Hamish strode off ahead, humming to himself as he went. He soon turned through a door and the scent of potpourri carried from within it.

We stopped beneath a painting of a Dragon who appeared to be eating a

Pegasus whole, its yellow legs protruding from the beast's jaws.

Nice.

Hamish reappeared and we pretended to be admiring the painting as he approached.

"Well bless my goslings, a solo audience with the Royal Heirs. How the stars are shining on me today." He bowed low and we smiled kindly, patiently waiting for his display to end.

"It's quite the piece, huh?" Tory jerked her chin toward the painting and Hamish looked at it, his eyes darkening to pitch.

"It's a filthy insult to the Solarian Orders. Dragons are not better than any other, they just like to think they are." He moved nearer, waggling his finger angrily at the picture. "They're a bunch of slippery wangadoodles if you ask me." He cupped his mouth in disgust at what he'd just said. "*Do* forgive me, your highnesses, I don't normally have such a dung tongue, but I just get so wound up when it comes to equality." He shook his fist.

"You're honestly not offending us," I promised. "And I totally agree with you." I grimaced at the picture. "If this is what all the Dragons are like, I don't want anything to do with them."

"Professor Orion seems very close with Darius," Tory said airily and I assessed Hamish's reaction closely.

He pursed his lips, nodding stiffly. "That grizzly gherkin and his family have always worked closely with the Acruxes." His brows knitted together sharply. "Unfortunately, that relationship doesn't always work in the Orions' favour." He sighed sadly and I sensed we were getting closer to what we wanted to know.

"Mr Grus...do you know someone called Clara Orion?" I asked tentatively.

His spine straightened and he glanced up and down the hall. "Gravy balls, where did you hear that name?"

"Just from one of the students at school," Tory said quickly and Hamish nodded slowly.

He smoothed down his large moustache, his lips twitching as he seemed to decide what to say. "This is entirely classified, but as you are the true rulers of my kingdom, I will divulge to you what I know on the subject. You see, after your poor mother and father were murdered, my gifts as a Royal Constable were better served in the FIB. I joined them for many years but the last case I worked for them four years ago..." He shifted uncomfortably, looking up and down the hall again. "It was the disappearance of a young woman called Clara Orion."

"Did you find her?" I breathed.

He shook his head, his expression grave. "No, things got very shady indeed while I conducted my search. My investigation led me to the door of the Acruxes. The last time she was seen alive was here, you see, in this very house."

My heart thundered in my ears and a cold ball of ice formed in my stomach.

"I pushed for a more thorough search of his grounds and for Lionel to give more information about why Clara didn't make it home that night. But between him and Clara's mother, Stella, I could get nothing from them. The bond between their families is iron clad. Even Stella wasn't forthcoming with information about her own daughter. In fact, the only one who seemed devastated by the loss of Clara, was her brother, Lance Orion."

A pang of sympathy pulled at my heart for Orion. Whatever had happened to his sister, I had the feeling it was something terrible.

Hamish glanced along the hallway back toward the ballroom. "I fear the Acruxes have ears everywhere in this place," he said ominously. "Come, let us return to the party." He marched off down the corridor and Tory and I headed after him.

Questions whirled in my mind, but the moment we stepped back into the ballroom, the crowd descended on us. We were showered with false compliments and dragged in two separate directions as the vultures took their pieces of meat at last.

Behind their smiles was a calculating gleam which unsettled me to my core. And I wondered if any of them were keeping wicked secrets for the Acruxes that involved Clara Orion.

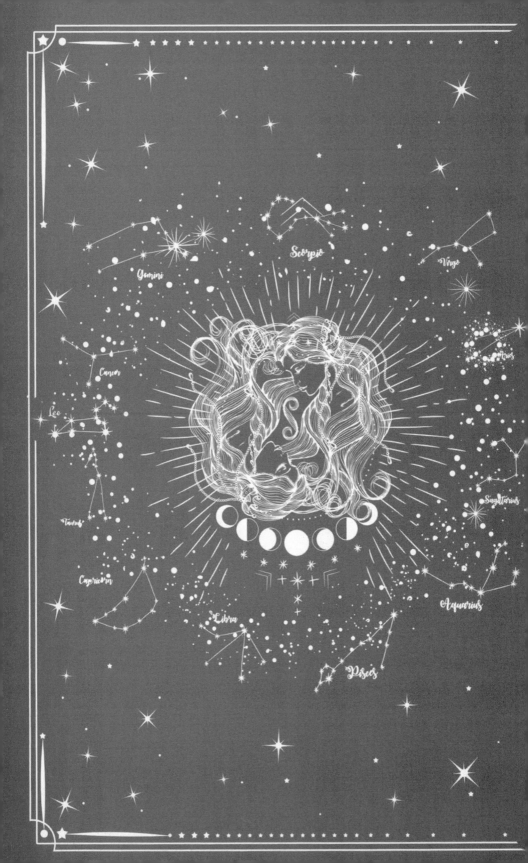

TORY

CHAPTER TWENTY-TWO

I didn't think I'd ever been to a party that was less about fun and more about rules, honour, respect, keeping up appearances... in short it was dull as all hell. If this was what it took to rule over Solaria then I was doubly sure I didn't want anything to do with the throne.

The Councillors had all been cornered by supposed party-goers who were all in the process of pushing their own agenda in one way or another. I caught snippets of conversation about things like taxes, land claiming, Cerberus hunting rights and even one particularly shrewd looking bastard who was complaining about his desire to take mortal slaves despite the fact that it was outlawed. I gave him an extra wide berth as I moved throughout the lavishly decorated room.

More than one eager man or woman tried to approach me. Some of them gushed about the joy of the Vega Twins returning, others seemed to be sizing me up. I didn't allow any of them to snare me into conversation for more than a few moments. Now that we knew the one seemingly friendly guy at this party had really just been a reporter on the hunt for a story, I wasn't going to risk getting snared in another trap.

Caleb's mother, Melinda, had her eyes on me from across the room. She was engaged in conversation with her handsome son and from the looks he kept shooting my way, I was fairly sure I knew what the topic of conversation was.

The string quartet played some beautiful, classical music and couples swirled across the dance floor in perfectly synchronised moves. They looked amazing but the lack of dim lighting and thumping bass counted me out when it came to the idea of dancing tonight.

Waiters swept around the room with silver trays perched on outstretched arms, sporting all kinds of fancy bite-sized bits of food which didn't count as a real meal in any way. I'd tried a few of them but the flavours were so rich and overpowering that I'd quickly decided against eating any more. My stomach was pitifully empty and I wished I'd eaten something before we'd left. Rich people might have had the right idea when it came to some things but they didn't know how to enjoy food.

I snagged my fourth flute of champagne as a waiter swept by, drinking it in one go and adding to the fizzy party in my belly. One thing they did seem to get right was the alcohol and it would have been rude of me to refuse to drink it when they'd gone to so much effort to provide it for me.

I felt Darius approaching me before he arrived and turned to face him as his shadow fell over me.

"I'm not sure I've ever seen anyone look so bored at a party," he murmured, leaning close to me so that his words didn't carry. His scent coiled around me, smoke and cedar and danger, or simply put, temptation of my particular variety. I fought against the effects of it and turned my gaze from him to inspect the room again.

"I'm not sure I've ever been to a more boring party," I countered. Though that wasn't strictly true. It was definitely interesting to see the Celestial

Council at work and to put some faces to names but this didn't really seem like the best way to learn anything real about the Fae elite. It felt like a production, staged a little bit for our benefit but more tailored to suit the Councillors than anyone attending.

"Well you wanted to see how the other half lived. Now you know, it's frightfully dull."

A smile tugged at my lips. "Who says frightfully?" I teased. "You wear your mask tighter here than you do at the Academy."

Darius's eyes darkened a little. "Who says it's a mask?" he asked. "I was born to this. This is who I am, who I'll ever be."

I leaned a little closer to him, tiptoeing to speak in his ear. "Well, that seems *frightfully dull* to me," I breathed. "Don't you ever want to just rebel against all of it?"

Darius caught my gaze and fire seemed to burn within the depths of his eyes. "All the time," he replied, his voice a low growl.

I smiled conspiratorially at him. "Prove it," I dared.

Darius straightened, looking around the room until his gaze caught on Daddy Acrux and the mischief in his expression spluttered out. Lionel was watching our interaction with just enough zeal in his gaze to make my heart flutter with anxiety. There was something about the head of the Acrux family which set all of my instincts screaming warnings.

"Do you want to dance?" Darius asked, his tone returning to its formal setting.

His hand brushed across the bare skin at the base of my spine and butterflies spilled through my stomach before I could stamp them out.

"You've danced with me before, Darius," I said slowly, reminding him of the drunken evening we'd spent grinding up against each other on the dark dance floor of a bar. "And it doesn't look like *that*," I pointed out as the glamorous couples swept across the dance floor in perfect time with each other.

"I know the moves," he replied. "And you're a quick study."

I blinked at the almost-praise from him then laughed it off. "But I don't want to dance to your tune," I said before turning away from him and slipping into the crowd again.

My back mourned the loss of contact with his fingers as I walked and I could feel his eyes trailing over me but I didn't look back. Darius Acrux was a brand of poison I really shouldn't taste.

On the far side of the room, I spotted a table laid out with more drinks and made a beeline for them.

I snagged another delicious glass of champagne and took a large gulp.

"I don't think I've ever seen a girl ditch Darius like that," an amused voice came from behind me and I turned to find a guy looking at me from a seat at a table in the corner.

He had dark hair that curled in a messy kind of way, looking like it had broken free of his attempts to tame it. His green eyes sparkled with restrained laughter and I couldn't help but stare at his strong features; he looked almost familiar but I was sure I'd never met him before.

"Well, even Dragons can't just get their own way all of the time," I said, moving closer to him.

Apparently that had been the right thing to say because he smiled widely in response to it.

"What's so great about Dragons anyway, right?" he asked, though a strange tightness came over his posture as he said it.

"Who'd want to be a big old lizard with anger management issues?" I joked. "I think I'd rather be a rabbit shifter - at least bunnies are cute."

"You don't have a very rabbity aura about you," he replied with a smile which lit up his face.

"I'm not sure if that's a compliment or not."

"It is. Although a rabbit might be exactly the kind of ruler we need; shake it up from all these predators."

"Maybe that's why I can't get on board with this fancy food. It's just not meant for someone of my Order... although I'm really looking for a sandwich rather than a carrot," I said wistfully.

He snorted a laugh. "Yeah I had a pizza before I came to join the festivities. I'm only supposed to stay for an hour or so anyway... show my face, sit in the back, avoid emotional triggers..."

He didn't seem to want to elaborate on that weird statement so I didn't push him but I did wonder why he'd come if that was all he was going to do.

"Well, I didn't really want to come at all so maybe I can just hide out back here with you?" I finished the rest of my drink and placed my glass on the table as I drifted closer to him. Aside from Hamish, he was the first person I'd met at this party who seemed at least halfway genuine.

"Sure. If you don't mind missing out on all the fun," he said. "I'm sorry but am I talking to Roxanya or Gwendalina? You're a little hard to tell apart."

I rolled my eyes at those stupid names. "I believe I originally went by Roxanya but my name is Tory."

"You haven't taken back your royal name?" he asked in surprise.

"I haven't taken back my royal anything. Though I won't say no to the money when it comes time to inherit that. You didn't give me your name either," I prompted.

"You don't know?" he asked in surprise.

"Oh sorry, dude, are you famous? Must be a bummer to meet someone who isn't a fan then," I teased.

He snorted a laugh. "I'm Xavier," he said. "The Dragon's younger brother."

"Oh," I said. *Well that was a quick end to what had seemed like a pleasant conversation.* "Actually... I should probably go... mingle or something." I started to back away, searching the crowd for Darcy. I spotted her on the far side of the room, engaged in conversation with Hamish and a few of his friends. The smile on her face was genuine enough so I was at least confident she didn't need rescuing.

"You really don't like him, do you?" Xavier asked in surprise.

"Who?" I asked innocently.

"Darius," he said, his gaze moving over my shoulder.

"This is the part where I insult him and he's right behind me, isn't it?"

Xavier's eyes sparked with amusement and he nodded.

Well far be it from me to disappoint.

"In that case, I happen to think he's a vindictive, pretentious twat-waffle who really needs to pull the stick out of his ass and let loose more often," I said.

"I thought we were being nice this evening?" Darius murmured behind me and I stifled a flinch at just how close he was.

"You said *you'd* be nice. I made no such promises," I pointed out, turning to look up at him as he moved to my side. Although now that I thought about it, maybe I had... the champagne tequila cocktail taking place in my digestive system was wreaking havoc with my memory as well as my manners.

Now that he and Xavier were so close to each other it was obvious they were brothers, though Xavier didn't seem as intense as Darius. But they shared the same jaw, the same colouring, even though Xavier's build was a lot less stacked.

"Well you're making Xavier smile so I'll forgive you this once," Darius said.

"Poor Tory is starving to death," Xavier said, though his smile fell a little in response to his brother's words. "Maybe you can find her something good to eat while I take my leave of this party."

I followed his gaze and noticed Lionel looking our way. He didn't seem pleased about something and Xavier got to his feet hastily.

"It was nice to meet you," I said.

"You too, Tory. See you later, Darius." Xavier tucked his chair back into place and quickly left the room.

I glanced at Darius as we were left alone together. Apparently my attempts to avoid this particular Heir were doomed to fail tonight.

Darius looked over my shoulder and his face dipped into a scowl. I followed his gaze and spotted his fiancé Mildred barrelling through the crowd towards us with a frown on her face which melded her eyebrows into one bushy line.

"Come on then," Darius said hastily, leading the way to the door Xavier had taken out of the room.

"Where to?" I asked in confusion. The party was in full swing and I was fairly sure we weren't supposed to be leaving it. Not that I'd ever cared much for rules but it seemed odd that he'd gone to so much trouble to get me here just to sneak me away again. Plus it was probably a good idea for me to get the hell away from him before his toothy bride arrived and tried to snap me in half with her brawny arms.

"Xavier said you want some real food," Darius said suggestively, heading on out without bothering to make sure I was following.

I hesitated. I didn't really want to go anywhere with him but I couldn't deny the draw I felt to him either.

The champagne probably isn't helping with that.

My stomach growled impatiently and I sighed as I gave in to its demands. I snatched another glass of champagne on my way out, quickly drinking it in one gulp before hurrying after him. If alcohol was going to make this decision for me then the least I could do was make sure I consumed plenty of it. I glanced back at Darcy as I left but she was laughing at something Hamish had said and didn't notice me. Mildred on the other hand looked like she was primed for murder and I hurried out of the room as she began to battle her way across the dance floor with me locked in her sights.

Darius led me down corridors with gilded decorations at every turn. Dragons *really* liked their gold and it was obvious they had plenty of it to spare.

"Thank you for cheering Xavier up," Darius said as he opened the door onto a narrow corridor and led me inside.

Thankfully there was no sign of Mildred catching up and I had to hope we'd lost her. A few serving staff squeezed past us carrying trays as we walked, bowing their heads as they spotted the infamous Acrux Heir.

"Why did he need cheering up?" I asked curiously.

"No reason."

I rolled my eyes at his back.

At the end of the long corridor, he opened another door and we stepped out into a huge kitchen filled with bustling staff who were refilling champagne glasses and making up more of the fancy bite-sized bits of food.

Darius skirted the madness and I followed him, careful not to get in anyone's way.

He approached a woman who was working on a tray of creamy puff things and leaned close to ask her something. She instantly stopped what she was doing and headed away with a bow.

Darius beckoned for me to follow him and I gritted my teeth as I did, wondering why I'd even come down here with him. The drink was making my head swimmy and apparently it was affecting my judgement too.

He led me through a door to a darkened room with a few soft chairs by the far window and a small table in the centre of the space.

Darius headed for the chairs but I ignored him, taking a perch on the table instead.

"Do you ever do as you're told?" he asked me, noticing the fact that I'd stopped following him.

"Nope. Do you ever stop telling people what to do?" I asked.

"I think I might just miss your smart mouth when you fail The Reckoning," he muttered.

I didn't validate that with a response.

He removed his black jacket and I eyed his fitted white shirt appreciatively before pulling my gaze away. I did not need to fall under the spell of Darius Acrux's stupidly hot appearance. Darius tossed his jacket down on the closest chair and moved to stand beside me. I could feel his eyes on me but I gave my attention to the room, studying portraits of old men in stuffy clothes and dragons soaring across the sky. Their choice in decor was boringly repetitive.

The door opened and the kitchen maid came in carrying two plates with subs for us.

I smiled at her as I accepted mine. "Thanks," I said and she stared at me like I'd just slapped her before heading out of the room.

"What was that about?" I asked before taking a bite of my sandwich.

Holy hell that's good.

"Serving jobs are generally taken by Fae with negligible amounts of magic," Darius said as I ate like a woman possessed. "Thanking them for their work is kind of like the sun thanking a daisy for blooming. Just having a position in our household is beyond what they expect in life."

I paused, my food suddenly tasting like soot in my mouth. Of course that was how they viewed people with less than them. They were the elite, top of the pecking order, why would they waste time thanking those beneath them?

If we'd met in the mortal world he never would have looked at me at all... and I'd have robbed him blind while he pretended not to notice my existence.

I ate the last few bites of my food in silence and put the plate down beside me as soon as I was done.

"I'd like to go back to the party now," I said coldly.

Darius eyed me over his own sandwich which he'd barely touched.

"Because I don't thank servants for doing their jobs?" he asked with barely concealed ridicule.

"Because you're boringly predictable just like everyone else here. You're all more concerned about what everybody else thinks and sees than you are about enjoying life. What difference does it make if someone's the most powerful Fae in the room or the least? I'd sooner have the time of my life with a powerless nobody than stand about posturing with a guy who doesn't even know how to have fun." I shrugged and got to my feet, intending to make my own way back to the ballroom but Darius moved forward a step, boxing me against the table as he placed his sandwich down.

"I want to show you something," he said, his voice dropping a little lower than usual and causing a shiver to run down my spine.

"What?" I asked.

"I said show, not tell. You have to come with me."

Curiosity nagged at me and the champagne urged me into recklessness. He'd promised to be nice after all, so why not? And even though I'd said I wanted to go back to the snooze fest party, I didn't really. Given the choice, I'd just head back to the Academy.

"You'd better not be about to whip your junk out again," I warned. "Because I've seen way too much of you for my liking."

"Oh I think you liked it just fine," he countered and the heat that flooded my cheeks at his tone stopped me from raising any further argument on the subject.

He stepped a little closer to me and I fought against the impulse to lean in.

"Come on then, don't keep me in suspense," I demanded though a little voice in the back of my head wondered if I meant something else by that statement.

Darius's mouth hooked up at one side and he inclined his head to yet another door on the other side of the room.

I followed him as he led the way through the manor to a grand atrium before opening the door onto a dark stairwell which led down to what must have been an underground chamber.

I eyed him warily but at this point I was pretty sure he'd have attacked me already if he was going to. Darius Acrux may have been a lot of things but it seemed he was a man of his word; he'd promised to be nice to me tonight and that was what he was delivering. I'd have to keep an eye on the time though, at midnight his Cinderella spell might come undone and he'd turn back into an asshole shaped pumpkin.

Lights came on automatically as we descended and at the foot of the stairs, he opened another door and led me out into into an underground parking lot.

I eyed the row of flashy sports cars in every make and model imaginable but he didn't pause by them, instead leading me to the far end of the lot.

A smile tugged at my lips as I spotted the lineup of super bikes. They were all top of the range, ultra-sleek, ultra-beautiful speed machines. My fingers tingled with the desire to touch them as the tempting allure of adrenaline called to me.

"You said you could ride," Darius said, offering me a genuine smile. "So I thought maybe you'd like to see my collection."

Damn, the way he said 'my collection' made me want to punch the entitlement right out of him but I didn't miss the fire burning in his eyes as he looked at the bikes. That was a passion I knew well. He was a sucker for my kind of temptation too.

"Have you done any modifications on them?" I asked, reaching out to brush my fingers along the saddle of the closest red beauty.

"They're top of the line," he said dismissively like I didn't know what I was looking at. "They don't need any mods."

I snorted derisively. So he liked to ride the pretty speed machines but he didn't know how to work on them. "Figures pretty boy wouldn't know how to get his hands dirty," I teased.

"Maybe the kinds of bikes you're used to riding need work to make them perform better but this kind of quality doesn't require any extras. Besides, I could just pay someone to do it for me even if they did."

"Of course you could. That's not really the point though." And he was wrong about the kinds of bikes I was used to riding. I spotted four models amongst his collection which I'd ridden within the last six months. The others could easily be mine with a little bit of time and a tool or two. Not that I felt the need to tell him that.

"You wanna take one for a ride?" he offered. "You can test your supposed skill against mine; there's a circuit to the west of the estate."

My eyes widened at that offer. I'd missed riding since coming to the Academy and I hadn't really thought I'd be able to get out again any time soon. But I wasn't sure I wanted him to know quite how much this meant to me. Every other piece of information the Heirs had gotten on me up until now had been twisted against me in some way and I didn't want them trying to take this from me too.

"I'm not really dressed for it," I said slowly though in all honesty I had no issue with tying my dress in a knot around my waist if that was what it took to get me out on the road.

"I'm sure I could lend you my shirt if you want to take it off," he replied.

"That would require both of us taking off rather a lot of our clothes." There was a dare hanging in the air between us and I was afraid that I wouldn't be able to resist it much longer.

I eyed the line up of bikes, my heart beating a little faster as I tried to decide which one I'd choose.

In all honesty I was too drunk to ride, although the sandwich *was* mopping up some of the excess alcohol and I was feeling a little less dizzy... It still wouldn't have been the best idea though.

"Why do you have the same bikes that that they have in the mortal world?" I asked as I began to wander between the immaculate machines. Some of the badges were different, I read names like Yamaharpy, Sphinxzuki, Hondusa, Harley Dragonson and I couldn't keep the smirk from my lips but the actual bikes were definitely mortal models.

"There are several permanent rifts between our world and the mortal world where we import all sorts of goods like these. The importers like to change the names as a kind of in-joke but a hell of a lot of our products come straight out of Taiwan or China, direct to Solaria," Darius explained.

"Why?" I asked. "Can't Fae invent their own bikes and cars?"

"I guess we could... but why bother? We've got better things to do with our time and it makes sense to use the mortals like our own personal goods suppliers. The Fae they deal with even manage to Coerce the best prices for everything we import. No Fae vendor would create any of the things we desire so cheaply." Darius folded his arms and leaned back to perch on the saddle of a stunning green bike as he watched my exploration.

"So you basically abuse the mortals with your power?" I asked.

"We use our power to take what we want from them," he agreed. "Just the same as we do with other Fae."

He had a point there; Fae were equally asshole-like to their own kind.

The sound of a door opening and closing drew our attention back to the stairwell which led to the house and we both looked around as Lionel Acrux strode into the parking lot.

Darius straightened instantly, unfolding his arms as he looked towards his father guiltily.

"I thought I told you to stay at the party, Darius?" Lionel asked, his voice low as he prowled closer.

Darius dipped his head a little before he replied. "I was just showing-"

"If you're going to screw the Vega girl at least do it on your own time. Tonight, your responsibilities should be taking precedence."

That was the second time he'd implied that I was looking to sleep with his son and my hackles raised in response at the fact that he thought he had the right to speak to me like that. Earlier I'd been too flustered to defend myself but this second snide comment didn't hold the same shock factor and I'd had enough to drink to loosen my tongue.

"First of all, *ew*. I'd sooner have ants in my pants than let Darius get into them," I snapped. "And secondly, what the hell makes you think you can talk about me like that? I'm a person, not some plaything to be used and dropped just as soon as your precious son has to marry his cousin."

Lionel Acrux stared at me like I'd just pissed in his cornflakes and ground them into his hair while he slept. The fury in his eyes was punctuated by them shifting into an emerald green colour complete with a slit for pupils.

"Do you think that because of your royal blood you can come crawling out of the gutter and just speak to me however you please?" he hissed. "Who do you think you're talking to?"

I surveyed him through narrowed eyes, pushing my shoulders back as I fought the urge to run screaming for the hills and stood my ground instead.

"Well I *think* I'm talking to an oversized iguana with a superiority complex, wrapped in an expensive suit. But its hard be sure beneath all the bullshit," I snarled.

Lionel growled low in the back of his throat, advancing steadily as his Dragon eyes locked on me with deadly intent. Panic gripped me but through some miracle or possibly just fear paralysing me, I managed to hold my ground.

Darius took a step between us. "I told you, Father, they're totally uncivilised. I don't even think they had proper schooling in the mortal world and they've never learned how to respect-"

"Get back to our guests, Darius," Lionel hissed and the cold rage in his voice made my tongue stick to the roof of my mouth.

Darius opened his mouth to say something then closed it again. He glanced at me, his eyes flashing with anger and possibly something else too, though I didn't dare put a name to it.

He started to step back, moving aside so that his father would have a clear view of me again but his brow furrowed and he held his ground instead.

"Just leave it, Father. She'll fail The Reckoning anyway and there's no point risking a scandal-"

"I told you to leave, *boy*," Lionel growled. "Roxanya and I need to *talk*."

Darius hesitated again then shook his head. "She's not worth it."

An actual snarl left Lionel's lips and I half considered running.

The two Acrux men stood their ground and I held my breath as I tried to figure out what was going on between them. One thing I had quickly realised though was that I should have listened to Darius's warning about his father because I'd just waved one hell of red rag at this big bastard of a bull.

"No, she's not," Lionel agreed finally, his gaze narrowing on his son. "And it would seem she isn't the only one looking for a lesson in respect. Come with me."

He turned and strode across the garage, heading back towards the stairs which led into the house. Darius followed a few steps behind him, his shoulders tight and his eyes on the ground. He didn't look back at me and they left me alone in the parking lot.

When the sound of the door closing again reached me, I sagged back against one of the bikes and tried to focus on calming the frantic beat of my heart.

It was cold in the parking lot and I hugged my arms around myself as I tried to steel myself to go back to the party. One thing was for sure, I was going to spend the rest of it avoiding every Dragon in sight.

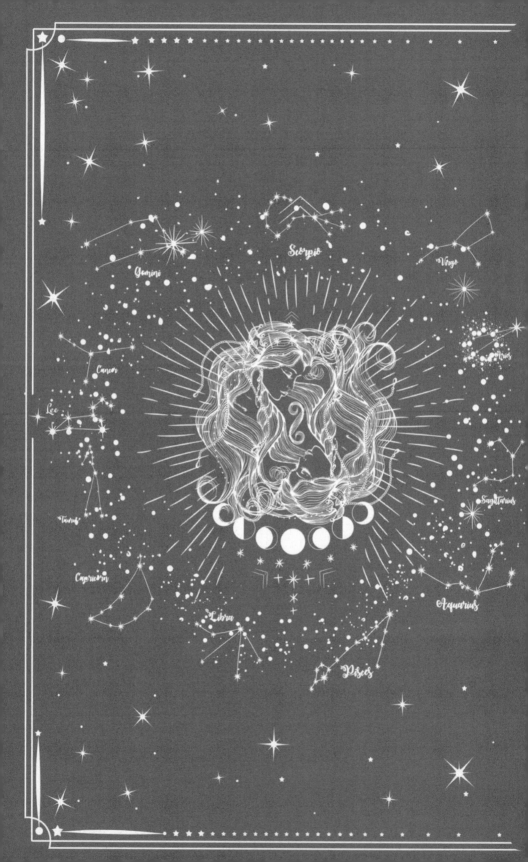

DARCY

CHAPTER TWENTY THREE

I wound through the expansive hallways of the house, hunting for a way out. I needed some fresh air. I couldn't find Tory and spending another minute in the company of people who questioned me on how I might rule their kingdom and destroy everything the Celestial Council had worked for was a special kind of hell.

As I continued my search for an escape, I got the feeling I was in Hotel California, turning left and right down endless beautiful hallways.

For crap's sake where is the exit???

"-well if you learned to behave appropriately for once, we wouldn't have to keep going through this cycle would we?"

Lionel's voice rocked a note of terror through me and I knew without a doubt I should *not* be wandering around the halls of his house.

I darted into a shadowy alcove beside a huge statue of a dragon - *of course* - and squeezed myself further in behind it. Not even a scrap of dust lay in the recess and I had to marvel at the efficiency of their cleaning staff.

Lionel stepped out of a door across the hall and I peered through a gap in the circling tail of the dragon with my heart in my throat.

He rolled down his sleeves, buckling up his cuffs and my gut churned as I spotted flecks of blood on them. "Oh for fuck's sake," he snarled as he spotted the marks. "Now I have to go and change as well!" he roared back into the room then stormed away down the corridor and veered onto a staircase, practically spitting fire.

My heart bashed against my ribcage, my breathing heavy as I remained there for a minute, making sure Lionel was well and truly gone. When I was confident he was, I wriggled forward to try and make a run for it. The door reopened and I shrank back quickly, my lips parting as Orion and Darius stepped out of the room.

"Drink," Darius said gently but Orion shook his head.

"I'm fine, I've hardly cast tonight. You need to get back to the party. You'll only end up here again if you don't."

Darius clapped Orion on the shoulder, "I'm sorry-" he started but Orion cut over him.

"Don't. I'll stand with you every time he lays a finger on you. I can't always stop him, but I'll be there."

"You shouldn't have to be," Darius sighed heavily.

"It is what it is," Orion said, then lowered his tone. "And it won't be forever. You'll be able to wield the shadows yourself soon."

I frowned, unsure what he meant by that but it seemed to cheer Darius up as he nodded.

"Come on," Darius said, but Orion shook his head.

"I'm going to get some air. You know I don't like crowds."

"Me neither, lucky for you no one forces you to stand in the middle of them."

Orion scowled, resting a hand on Darius's shoulder. "One day this entire estate will be yours. Hopefully sooner rather than later, huh?"

Darius ran a hand over the back of his neck, stepping away from him. "I'll remember that the next time Father beats the shit out of me." He didn't let Orion answer, striding off down the corridor, glancing warily up the staircase his father had taken as he walked past it.

I held my breath as Orion remained standing there, my stomach all twisted up in knots. Lionel beat Darius? It was just awful. And why did it sound like Orion was often there when that happened?

My clutch slipped from under my arm and a soft clap sounded as it hit the floor, making my heart shatter as I snatched it back up. Maybe a normal person wouldn't have heard it but a Vampire? No chance.

"Who's there?" Orion snarled, his tone holding a deadly warning. *"Come out this second."*

His Coercion dominated every muscle in my body and I lurched out of my hiding place like someone had tied a leash around my neck and pulled. His eyes widened as he discovered who had been eavesdropping on him and I bit down on my lower lip, trying to think up some reason why I might have been wedged in behind a stone dragon for the past five minutes. Nope; there was literally no reason in the world that warranted that.

His eyes were scalding hot and his jaw was pulsing with rage.

"Hello my shining star!" a female voice rang out. "What in Solaria are you doing down here with one of the Vega Twins?"

My gaze whipped down the corridor to take in a sleek woman who must have been in her fifties. She had a dark bob of hair which sharpened to longer points by her chin. Her skin was dewy and the fitted black dress she wore was elegant yet sexy at the same time. She walked toward us on high heels, using a burst of speed that could only have meant one thing. She was also a Vampire.

My heart lurched as she came to a halt before me, head tilted and eyes roaming. She was an inch taller than me even in my heels and that gave her the advantage of staring down her nose at me. "Hello pretty girl, I'm Stella."

"Darcy," I said, trying not to show my discomfort as she breathed in deeply before my face.

"Mmmmm," she hummed. "All that power." She bared her fangs. "Just a little taste..."

"Hey - wait!" I raised my palms in a panic, magic thrumming in my hands as I prepared to try and fight her off.

Orion was at my side in a heartbeat, his arm sliding possessively around my waist. "She's my Source, Stella," he snarled, baring his own fangs back at her.

"Oh my, you have been busy since I last saw you baby boy," she teased. *Baby boy?*

She licked her lips as she eyed my neck again and I took a step back. "What a terrible crime it would be for a mother to share her own son's Source. How selfish of me to think I could ask such a thing of my own flesh and blood." She toyed with her hair, a pout pushing out her lips as she tried to manipulate him. But I didn't get the sense it was working.

"Don't start," he said wearily. "What are you doing down here anyway?"

"I could ask the same of you." Her eyes flashed to me and she swayed a little as she inched closer.

"You're drunk," Orion sighed. "Go back to the party."

"You don't mind if I stay a little longer do you, cherub?" she asked me and I wriggled out of Orion's arms.

"Actually, you two stay, I've got somewhere to be anyway." *Specifically: anywhere but here.* I started walking but Orion caught my wrist and yanked me back against his hip.

I looked up at him in alarm as he held me firmly in place.

Stella licked her lips, weaving her head as she laughed. "Do it again. But let her go further this time. I love the hunt."

"Go back to the party," Orion said forcefully, his voice reverberating through his body right into mine.

Stella started circling us, sighing dramatically. "Oh Lance, you're so disappointing. I miss having a child who enjoys my company. Clara-"

"Don't you utter her name," Orion spat. "You lost that right a long time ago."

Stella tutted, still circling us, plucking at my dress, trying to take my hand, but Orion kept swatting her away. "I miss your Daddy. He was such fun. Always up for chasing, hunting, playing. You're so boring ever since you became a teacher at that drab Academy." She leaned in to pat Orion's face and he had to let her or else let go of me.

Her eyes dropped to me. "The apple never falls far from the tree though, cherub. Just like The Savage King's blood runs in your veins, so does a predator's in my baby boy's. If he wasn't bound by so many rules and consequences, he'd chase your pretty neck all around this house and drain you dry when he caught you."

"Stop it," I snapped, anger climbing in my chest. I despised the way I was being handled. Like a mouse in the paws of cats. I wanted to get the hell out of here. "Let me go," I demanded of Orion but a low noise in his chest told me he had no intention of obeying.

Stella nodded eagerly. "Yesss let her go, let her run." She snapped her teeth together and I suddenly realised I was probably better off where I was. I clutched onto Orion's shirt with one hand and with the other I aimed my palm at her. "Go. Away. Or I'll make you." The amount of alcohol I'd had was loosening my tongue and I was kinda proud of myself for embracing my inner Fae.

She gawped at me, stepping back and holding her heart in shock. She was still swaying, but I couldn't smell any alcohol on her even though Orion seemed to think she was drunk. "Are you going to let The Savage King's daughter talk to me like *that*?" she demanded.

Orion glowered at her. "I don't control her, she can say what she damn well likes."

"Gah! What a child I've raised. I'd swap you for Clara any day."

Orion stiffened, his arm beginning to tremble where it was locked around me. "And I'd trade you for Dad in a heartbeat."

Her eyes glowed like nightshade then glimmered with tears. Thick, wet droplets splashed down her cheeks. "How could you say such a thing? How can you hurt me like this, after all I've done for you?" Her tone had changed to a melodramatic begging and I had to pity Orion for having to deal with this crap.

Orion said nothing and Stella barrelled on, practically wailing. "This is why your Daddy's gone, he couldn't bear the son he'd raised. You had such promise. But you had to go after your own heart and you broke his in the process. *That's* why he killed himself."

"He didn't kill himself. Stop acting like a child," Orion said coldly and his tone said this was a game he was used to. Like he was the parent in their relationship.

"He might as well have!" she shrieked, heading off down the corridor in a flood of tears.

Orion released a long breath. "I'm sorry you had to see that. She's...got some issues."

"Is she alright?" I breathed, unsure how to feel as her sobbing carried back to us.

"It's all an act. Don't buy into it. The second she sees you're affected, she'll sink her claws in and never let go."

I glanced down at his hands which were still locked tightly around me. I was flush to his side and the burning heat of his body seeped into mine. "Speaking of not letting go." I cocked a brow and he released me, though I found myself lingering against him for half a second before I moved back.

I glanced over my shoulder and pointed. "Is this the way out?"

His face skewed into a devilish smile. "Aren't you forgetting something, Blue?"

"Err." I shrugged. "No?"

"Why were you hiding behind that statue?"

I folded my arms. "You never let me get away with anything. For all you know I like wedging myself in dark corners."

A laugh burst from his throat and I grinned in response.

One point to me.

"Come on, I'll show you the way out and you can give me the real story while we walk." He stepped to my side, placing a hand on my back to get me moving and sending white hot sparks flying out from the base of my spine. I nearly stopped breathing when his arm slid around my waist and remained there.

"So?" he prompted when I said nothing.

"I heard Lionel and decided I didn't want to be found wandering his home like an enemy spy."

"Good call," he commented. "And I suppose you figured out why we were all in that room?" he asked darkly.

I dropped my eyes to the shiny wooden floor beneath us. "Yes," I whispered.

"So you know the way Lionel treats his son?"

I nodded, my gut tightening uncomfortably. "I know the way Darius treats *us* too," I murmured.

Orion fell quiet for a long moment, seeming to be thinking. "Darius is just doing what he thinks is right."

"It doesn't excuse-"

"I know," he said firmly then sighed. "Let's not talk about the Heirs. They give me a headache most days of the week."

I nodded and quiet descended on us, seeming to thicken the air and make it harder to draw breath. All I could feel was his hand on my waist, and all I could smell was cinnamon and his manly musk.

For a moment, it felt so natural to walk there like that, side by side with him. But the second we turned a corner and he released me, the spell was broken. He was my teacher and there really wasn't anything more to it than that. Half the girls in school swooned over Professor Orion in class. But he was the look don't touch variety of guy. Which made him enticing even before his villainous good looks were factored in.

"So...your mother seems interesting," I said lightly and he shot me a grim look.

"That's being polite. She's a black-hearted woman and I advise you to stay away from her. Anything that comes out of her mouth tends to be a lie devised to manipulate."

"What she said about your father-"

"Like I said, it's not true. My father died in a magical accident. I would know. I was there when it happened."

"Oh," I breathed, my heart breaking for him. I may have lost two sets of parents and never known the embrace of a mom or dad, but I'd never been old enough to mourn them. "That's awful, I'm so sorry."

Orion drew in a long breath. "It's in the past. That's where I tend to leave it."

We reached a long hall lined with floor length windows which overlooked an incredible courtyard. Stretching through the middle of it was a glimmering rectangular pool, illuminated by blue lights at its base. Orion opened the door and I followed him out into the beautiful place. Every wall was lined with potted trees and ivy climbed the walls, all highlighted by strings of golden fairy lights. Several sun loungers lay in a row to the right of the pool and to the left was a pool-side bar complete with barbecue.

"This place is ridiculous," I half laughed as I took it all in.

Orion threw a grin back at me as headed to the bar, ducking behind it. "What would madam like?" he asked in a formal tone which was a damn good impression of the Acruxes' butler. I giggled hurrying over to take a stool in front of the bar and placing my clutch down, relishing the cool breeze against my burning neck.

"Hmm...a Manhattan?" I teased and he cocked his head.

"I'm afraid we're fresh out of bullshit, how about a white wine spritzer with a tiny umbrella in it?"

I laughed, nodding eagerly as he made up my drink then poured himself a measure of bourbon.

He held it out for me and I leaned across the bar to take it. As I took hold of the glass, he didn't let go and I gazed up at him under my lashes questioning why.

"Have I told you how exceptionally beautiful you look tonight, Darcy?"

Darcy.

He'd said my name. For the first time ever. And why did it sound like so much more than a name when he spoke it? It was like he'd fired an arrow and it had punctured a flesh wound in me at the exact same moment.

Hell. I needed to get over this guy. Why was I so caught up on him?

Unavailable, that's what it was. We always want what we can't have and Professor Orion was off limits. Simple as that. And those muscles. And the beard. And the dark eyes. And the dimple. But that was it.

"That's the first I've heard of it, Professor," I whispered, unable to make my voice rise any louder.

"Don't do that," he grunted, releasing the drink.

I eyed him curiously as he walked around the bar with his bourbon in hand. He took the stool beside mine, his arm butting up against me.

"Do what?" I asked, swivelling around to face the pool and taking a sip of my spritzer. It fizzed on my tongue and sent a deep kick of heat through my chest.

"You know what."

"You're very presumptuous, Orion. You think I'm far more aware of your chaotic way of thinking than I really am." I sipped my drink again, spying on him from the corner of my eye.

He took a swig of his own drink and the familiar waft of bourbon drifted over me, tingling my senses. It was becoming a trigger, like the moment I walked into his office and he uncorked a bottle, it made me want to taste it on his mouth. And then that led to me wondering whether his fangs would brush my tongue when we kissed, and *that* always led to me mentally undressing him, then me conjuring an image of what those muscles looked like beneath that shirt...

"I have something for you," he said and I turned, blinking out of my dark fantasy.

"You do?"

He nodded, reaching into his inside pocket and taking out my coil of blue hair. My heart combusted and a choked noise escaped me. I reached for it and he slid it onto my wrist.

He kept my hand in his, his eyes downcast as they remained on the band of hair. "I want you to know, I believe you would have gotten this back yourself when you were ready. But I took a lot of pleasure in retrieving it for you all the same."

I stared at him in complete shock, unsure what to say, my tongue tied in knots. "But Fae don't fight battles for other Fae," I blurted, completely astonished that his actions that day had been to take this back from Seth. For me. And nothing else.

He finished his drink and planted the glass on the bar, rising to his feet. He didn't reply to what I'd said and I barely even remembered what it was as he started pulling his clothes off.

"Err, what are you doing?" I half laughed as he shed his jacket and kicked off his shoes, pulling off his socks. *Oh my god.*

"I hate parties, but I like swimming." He started undoing the buttons of his shirt and though his back was to me, I was still captivated as he dropped it to the floor like a silken sheet. My eyes scraped down his skin to where his muscles etched an upside down v into his lower back, disappearing beneath his waistband. His shoulders were tanned and heavenly broad, making me long to explore all of those muscles with my hands.

He dropped his pants and my mouth grew wetter as he stepped up to the edge of the pool in nothing but black boxers.

Heat rode a wave in my belly and I clenched my thighs together as desire took hold of me. He leaned forward then dove into the water like a pro, disappearing under the surface with complete grace.

I finished the end of my wine, placing the glass down and twirling the little umbrella between my fingers. When Orion didn't resurface, an uncomfortable feeling plucked at my gut.

I dropped the umbrella, hurrying to the edge of the pool and searching for him. I couldn't see him anywhere and my heart started to race at the amount of time it must have been already. One minute, two?

I knelt down, leaning further over the edge.

Hang on a second, he has the power of air so maybe that means-

He breached the surface right beneath me, catching hold of my arm and dragging me into the pool. My scream was swallowed by the water as he pulled me down down down to the deepest part of the pool.

My chest was ballooning already and the panic of him yanking me under so fast meant I'd barely taken a breath. He suddenly pushed me from behind and I crashed onto my knees, air somehow flowing freely around me. I stared up in complete awe as I found myself in a large, rectangular pocket of air carved out by magic against the wall of the pool. I stood upright, pushing my sopping hair from my eyes as I caught my breath.

I was alone in the space as I stared at the water rippling above me, the blue pool lights reflecting off of the surface. I was soaked through and I'd lost my heels on the way down, but I didn't care, the party had sucked anyway and this moment was too incredible to be ruined by smeared make-up and damp clothes.

I stared out into the gleaming water to my right just as a shadow emerged from it. Orion walked through the wall of water as easily as if he'd been walking above ground.

"This is amazing," I laughed, my voice echoing back to me.

"You're not mad I dragged you to the bottom of a pool then?" he teased.

"This makes up for it," I said with a slanted smile, gesturing to the beautiful magic he'd cast.

I hope I can do things like this one day.

His shining skin drew my attention and I became enslaved to the need to explore every inch of his flesh. His body brought on an ache in me I hadn't known for a long time. Since my ex had dumped me after I'd given him my virginity, I hadn't done more than fool around with guys. The desire to go further had never really risen again. Not until Orion. And I had never, in all my life, wanted anyone like I wanted him.

His beard had been trimmed even shorter for the party, revealing the powerful cut of his jaw and that divine dimple in his cheek. He'd brought me here, alone, cordoning me off from the world. And the blazing intensity in his gaze made me hope that maybe he was about to drop the teacher act for one night and admit he was drawn to me too.

He glanced above us and his brow furrowed heavily. "Up there are a thousand reasons why we can't be together."

I swallowed thickly, goosebumps rushing along my skin in response to his words. I pressed my back to the cool tiles of the pool and the goosebumps spread deeper, evoking a shiver across my body.

"I'm bound by so many rules I could waste the rest of your evening telling you them," he said.

"Skip them then, sir." A smile played around my mouth as a thrill danced in my chest.

He moved closer and rested his hands either side of me on the wall. "I think the time for sirs and professors is over, don't you?"

No answer came from my lips, but my body gave it to him as I reached out and did the one thing I'd dreamed about the most since this all-consuming crush had first started. I brushed my fingers across the stubble on his jaw, resting my thumb over the dimple in his cheek, feeling the tiny rivet in his skin.

The distance parting us suddenly felt like too much; the air was racing over my exposed flesh, chilling me to the core. I needed the heat of his hands, the red hot press of his stomach and chest.

"Lance," I breathed and his pupils dilated as I met his gaze.

He devoured the space between us and I experienced pure sin as his mouth crushed against mine. It was gunpowder meeting fire and the result was an all-consuming blaze which burned me up from the inside out.

A desperate noise escaped me that would have made me blush if I'd had any scrap of self-awareness left. But that was all it took for him to slam into me full force, hitching my legs up around his waist so fast it made my head spin.

My hands finally got their deepest wish and roamed down the plains of all that gloriously golden skin. But it wasn't enough just to feel the flex of his muscles, I needed more and I took it by scratching against his beautiful shell, wanting to break beneath flesh and bone and burrow my way deeper.

I need more.

One of his hands tangled in my hair, tugging it to tip my chin back and eliciting another moan of pleasure from my lips. He swallowed it up, his tongue sinking into my mouth and making my heart find a rhythm it had never beat to before.

He kissed me like he wasn't allowed to kiss me, but if he didn't he'd die. I tangled myself around him with equal desire, the well of magic in my body spilling over and flooding my veins. A profound and unknown energy hummed within me, drawing to the edges of my skin. Orion seemed to sense it too as the hairs raised along my arms and static energy crackled everywhere our flesh met.

I was entirely lost to the deepest and most carnal desire I'd ever felt.

His hand found the slit in my dress and his fingers trailed onto my bare leg, making me gasp in response. Fire surged down my spine only to bounce back up again as he gripped my thigh and squeezed.

With so little clothes parting us, I felt every inch of his arousal pressing between my legs and I started to wonder how far this kiss was going to go. My fingers slid into the verge of his hair as I ground against him and my thoughts scattered again. He released a rumbling growl filled with nothing but need and his hand shifted between us, roaming deeper beneath my dress until he found the top of my panties. I nearly lost my mind as his fingers brushed the sensitive flesh there and skimmed the line of my underwear. My back arched as I tried to bring his hand closer to fulfil the promise of ecstasy I knew he could bring me.

Instead, he pulled his hand free and placed it on my hip with a heavy breath. It took everything I had, but with his fingers firmly away from the area of my body which was trying to run the show, I could think a little clearer.

He pulled back almost the same moment I did and I swallowed hard as I felt the lasting sensations of that kiss everywhere. My mouth tingled and my cheeks stung from the scrape of his stubble. My thigh muscles throbbed where they were still locked tightly around his waist and my heart seemed to bleed from the loss of contact with his mouth.

We remained breathless and silent, staring at each other like the reality waiting above us wasn't about to rip us apart. But I knew as well as he did, this was a one time only thing. Now I just had to convince my body of that.

I unwound my legs from him, bracing my hands on his shoulders as I dropped down. He steadied me for a moment then the air between us changed. His eyes darkened and he didn't need to speak to let me know what he was thinking. A vow hung solidly around us. *This won't happen ever again.*

He opened his mouth to speak but I spoke before he could, not wanting to be commanded into eternal silence. I already knew what would happen the second we left this magical place behind, I didn't need to be told. "Let's go."

"We can stay a little longer...if you want." His expression was that of a wounded man but I knew whatever pain lay in his body, would never be mine to heal.

I shook my head, lifting my chin to gaze up at the surface of the pool. "No, I think we should go back to reality now." *The longer I stay, the harder it will be to leave.*

"Are you angry with me for bringing you here?" he asked and I was compelled to look down, falling into the intensity of his eyes as a strained line formed on his brow.

"No."

He reached out to skate his fingers across the line of my jaw, feather light. "You know how it has to be."

I nodded, leaning away from his touch which felt like forcing two magnets apart. "I know."

What happens at the bottom of the pool, stays at the bottom of the pool.

"Come on then, Blue." He held out his hand.

I took a shuddering breath, placing my hand in his. "I think it might be best if you don't call me that anymore." I tugged at a lock of wet hair. "It's not blue anyway."

He glanced at me with shadows in his eyes, but nodded all the same. He stepped into the pool, tugging me after him and I took a breath before pushing through the magical wall. I felt it drawing in behind me, the water filling that private space which would never exist again.

I pulled my hand from his grip, swimming to the surface and taking a breath as I breached it. I swam to the edge of the pool, pulling myself up onto the tiles and shivering as the night air blew around me.

Orion resurfaced a second later, placing my shoes beside me before hoisting himself out and rising to his feet. I got up too, hugging my arms around my chest and trying to will heated air to my fingertips. It was like trying to get fire going in a storm, the kindling was there but the flame wouldn't take.

"Here," Orion said stiffly, moving closer and opening his palm. Hot air wrapped around me and he left me in it as he scooped up his own clothes and had himself dry within a few seconds. I turned away as he started to dress, a sinking feeling weighing in my gut. I'd stepped out of a blissful dream into a darker reality and I so wanted to go back to sleep.

My dress dried out and my hair fell around me in loose curls. I slipped on my shoes which Orion must have dried already then moved to pick up my clutch from the bar, taking out a pocket mirror and checking my makeup. I looked miraculously okay. My mascara was waterproof and hell was it proving its worth right now. I used the powder in my bag to touch up the rest then placed it back. I eyed the damp band of hair on my wrist with a tug in my heart then slid it from my wrist and tucked it into my bag.

I took a breath then turned to Orion, knowing I couldn't put it off any longer. He was fully dressed, his back to me and his hands in his pockets.

"My sister loved this place," he said, surprising me.

I moved to his side, gazing around the beautiful courtyard. "Oh yeah?"

"We used to come here as kids. Back then things were so simple. We didn't see anything but the good in the world."

"What happened to her?" I asked gently, stealing a glance up at him.

His brows were drawn and the darkness in his eyes was back in full force. He didn't answer for a long moment. "She got caught up with some bad people."

"The Acruxes?" I guessed and Orion looked at me for the first time since we'd left the pool.

"Don't go looking for trouble, Miss Vega." His tone was formal and I was unsettled by how much it hurt considering I'd already known it would be this way. I said nothing and he released a low breath. "Would you like to see her?"

"Clara?" I asked and he nodded, giving me a ghost of a smile. "Yes, I'd like that."

He headed back toward the glass doors and I followed him inside, relishing the warm air that heated the place. It was as if a constant fire burned behind the walls of this house, like we were deep in the belly of a volcano.

Orion walked ahead of me, never looking back as we wound through the huge halls, the only sound between us the click of my heels and the pounding of his footfalls.

He soon drew to a halt beneath the staircase Lionel had disappeared up earlier and a deep pressure weighed down on me. Photographs were dotted along the wall rising to the next level. Orion walked up the steps and plucked one of them from its hook. I followed him and he passed me the picture in its golden frame.

My fingers tingled with expectant energy as I gazed at the formal photograph. It was a group portrait taken on the vast porch steps at the front of this house. The four Acruxes stood at the centre of it and from the looks of him, I guessed Darius was around fifteen. To their left was the other Councillors and Heirs standing in front of them. A few more people I didn't recognise clustered beyond them.

To their right was Orion's mother, Stella, and beside her was Orion himself looking bored; he could only have been a few years younger than he was now. Beside him was a girl with hazel hair and stunning features and it was obvious who she was even before Orion leaned forward and pointed her out. She was leaning against her brother with a serene smile on her face that didn't suggest anything was wrong in her life.

"This was the night she...vanished," he said tersely, his eyes flashing with some memory. I glanced up at him in horror, pain stroking my heart at the broken look in his gaze.

"What happened to her? Didn't you leave the party together?"

Orion's mouth pressed into a tight line and I sensed he wasn't going to tell me anything more. But that meant he knew something.

"Lance?" I whispered and he stood up straighter in response to that.

"If I can't call you Blue, you're not calling me that." He snatched the picture and placed it back on the wall. Something about that cut deeper than any other promise we'd made tonight. But maybe that was the way he felt about his nickname for me.

"Go back to the party," he sighed, his gaze firmly on the picture. Before I could respond, his head twitched and he looked up the stairs, his face transforming as he clearly heard something.

"What is it?" I asked, but he shook his head.

"*Go*," he growled then shot up the stairs, disappearing around the corner.

I stood there, a little in shock at being left so abruptly, but I quickly regained my senses and climbed up a step, taking the picture from the wall again. That same burning energy rolled through me and my hands seemed to move of their own accord. I turned it over, removing the back pane.

My heart hammered with excitement as I discovered what I'd somehow known would be there. One of Astrum's Tarot cards lay beneath it with a horned red beast sitting upon a throne. The Devil was printed at the base of it and fear crawled into my gut as I turned it over to read the inscription on the back.

Do not underestimate the beast who shadows you.
He is the ultimate power, ruling over your lives and the lives of many others.
Beware of his lies.
The answer to your question will be revealed on the lunar eclipse.
But when finding the truth, don't let the shadows take you.
- Falling Star

My chest constricted and I hurriedly pocketed the card before rearranging the picture and placing it back on the wall.

I turned and headed downstairs, walking back to the party with fear licking up and down my spine. I needed to find Tory and show her this card. The lunar eclipse was just a week away and coincided with The Reckoning. So whatever was waiting for us on that day, we had to be ready for it.

ORION

CHAPTER TWENTY FOUR

My thoughts were in turmoil as I raced up the stairs, leaving Darcy Malone and knowing that the next time I saw her things would be back to normal. And by normal I meant I'd be smothering the fiery pit of longing that raged inside me every time I was around her and she'd be back to thinking I was the asshole teacher who treated her just like everyone else: a piece of shit.

I rounded onto the landing, focusing on what I'd heard and trying to force the girl with blue hair from my head. *It's not blue anymore, idiot. Wake up and smell the goddamn roses. This was never meant to happen.*

I slowed to a halt, entirely silent as I approached Lionel's rooms. No one was allowed in there. Not unless they were getting beaten or fucked. Luckily for the male gender, Lionel's tastes were firmly female.

The voices that carried to my superior hearing made my gut writhe. It wasn't news to me that they were screwing each other, but it still made my skin crawl.

The seductive purr of my mother's voice made me want to twist knives into my ears just so I wouldn't have to hear it, but I remained there because of what I'd heard Lionel say when I'd stood with Darcy on the stairs. *"It's only a week until the eclipse."*

My heart thumped an unsteady rhythm and I knew what it would cost me if Lionel found me here. But the one thing he hadn't banked on when he'd bound me to his son, was that I had to protect him from *everything*. Including his sadistic bastard of a father. So if standing here listening to *Uncle* Lionel nail my mother could help me protect him, then that was exactly what I had to do.

"We chose poorly last time," Lionel's harsh voice followed a grunt of pleasure that made me shut my eyes to try and wipe that noise from my memory. His words awoke a raging creature in my chest who wanted him dead and bloody at my feet. *And mark my words, I'll see that day come, Lionel.*

"We should have used Lance," Stella said bitterly. I'd stopped calling her Mom a long, long time ago. Mothers looked after their children, and she'd proved herself worthless in that department. The dismissiveness in her voice told of how little she cared for me these days. Back before I'd enrolled at Zodiac I was once her rising sun, now I was just a dog she kicked occasionally. Not that I had any regret over why she didn't like me anymore. If she wanted me dead, then I'd stay alive to spite her. Amongst other reasons.

"You don't really mean that," Lionel growled. "He's got some use and at least he's fulfilling his purpose without complaint these days. My son fights me at every turn."

They both fell silent and the tell-tale thump thump thump of a headboard drilled into my head.

Stella giggled excitedly. "You're such a bad man. You know how to put a Fae in their place, don't you Lion?"

Arghhhhh.

More heavy breathing and wall-banging followed and I wondered if it was actually worth me eavesdropping on my mother's sexcapades for information or if I was just torturing myself for no good reason.

Were they really planning what I suspected on the lunar eclipse, or were they just discussing old times? I had to know. Because if they were going to do it again, we were in deep shit.

"I won't make the same mistakes again, this time we'll pick the right Fae," Lionel growled. They fell into a crescendo of bangs and moans and I stormed away from the room, figuring I'd heard enough. My heart thumped painfully hard as I sped through the halls of the Acrux manor back toward the ballroom.

With the approaching lunar eclipse, I'd feared this would happen. But now it was confirmed, that fear spread like a disease, gnawing into my bones.

This can't be happening again.

Clara's face came to mind, the sprinkle of freckles across her nose, her slanted smile, the way her shoulders had trembled just before she'd died...

Bile rose in my throat as I reached the doorway to the ballroom. I drew to a halt, resting a hand against the wall and trying to fight off the rage, the tearing panic, the seizing grief of losing her. Of that awful fucking night. I wanted to claw my way back through time and stop it all from happening. I'd make better decisions. I'd tear off Lionel's head before he could place this bind on me which forced me to guard his son. I'd save Clara from her suffering and the shadows which had consumed her.

My brain rattled against the inside of my skull and my fangs sharpened to deadly points, begging me to kill the ones responsible for this.

I took an even breath then shoved my way through the door, hunting the ballroom for Darius. I found Darcy first and my gaze wouldn't shift from her for several seconds. She was speaking with Grus and his pompous royalist friends and my spine prickled with unease.

You kissed The Savage King's daughter you moron.

A vein pulsed in my temple as I clenched my jaw too tightly. I'd given in to temptation and though I vowed never to lay a hand on her again, I still couldn't undo what I'd already done. My Libra instincts were screaming at me like a disappointed parent, telling me I'd acted unfairly by offering her a ray of hope then stamping on it just as quickly. The scales of my inner compass were well and truly tipped and the only way to right them again was by ending this before it started. But something cut into me, forcing me to acknowledge it like a blade spinning in my gut. *Alright so maybe I can't forget about her right away. But I'll damn well force her out eventually.*

I finally dragged my eyes elsewhere and found Darius across the room. His expression was distant as he stood with the other Heirs, a war contained within his eyes. As if he sensed me, his gaze flitted my way and I jerked my head to beckon him.

He didn't say a word to his friends before he strode away to join me and we moved in tense silence back out of the ballroom and further down the corridor. I soon guided him into an empty lounge and sank into an armchair.

He remained on his feet, his mouth flat. "What's going on?"

"It's happening again," I growled. "I just overheard your father and my mother discussing the lunar eclipse." I left out the part about them screwing each other. Darius knew full well his father wasn't a loyal man to his wife, but I didn't think it was worth mentioning. Darius had had a rough enough night as it was.

His jaw ticked with rage and he shut his eyes for a long moment. "Who have they chosen?" he asked eventually and I shook my head.

"It didn't sound like they'd picked yet."

Darius started pacing, his hands flexing as he drew fire into writhing balls in his palms. "This night is just getting better and better," he muttered. "Do you think there's any chance of them actually succeeding this time?"

I considered that. "It's impossible to say. After what happened last time, I would have thought they'd never want to attempt it again." A tense pause passed where breathing became a bit harder. *Fuck, Clara why did you have to get wrapped up in their world?*

Darius went to say something as he noticed my expression but I barrelled over him, not wanting his sympathy. "If they succeed this time who knows what hell they could unleash."

Darius sighed heavily. "I'll have to come home more often, see if I can get Father to tell me anything or trust me some more."

I gave him a look of disbelief. "Do you really think he'd open up to you? He hasn't shown any inclination to trust you with his plans so far and now that he's gotten it into his head that you're chasing after Tory Vega-"

"I'm not chasing after her," he snarled. "I saved her from herself. She insulted him right to his face, if I hadn't stood between them fuck knows what he would have done to her."

Anger pulled at my insides and I didn't know if I was angry at him for softening towards a Vega or if I was angry at myself for the exact same thing. I stood up, too furious to remain in place. "Well maybe you should have let him, now he only has more reason to mistrust you." I started pacing, my shoulders tight as I let those words settle over the room. The worst thing was, I knew I didn't mean them. And that was a serious problem.

"I know," Darius said wearily, his eyes following me as I paced. "I don't know what the hell came over me. That girl just knows how to push my buttons. The sooner her and her sister are gone, the better."

My throat tightened and I stopped walking, facing a bookcase at the end of the room. "Agreed," I said quietly. I glanced over my shoulder and Darius shifted, turning away and my brows lifted. *Shit are we in the exact same boat here?* "Maybe you were thinking with your dick and not your head."

Darius kicked at the floor, looking away from me. "That's not the point. We still need them gone."

I nodded firmly. No girl had ever turned my head enough to make me an idiot. I'd already made it clear that that kiss was a one time thing with Darcy. *It should have been a never time thing but here we are.*

Tonight was just one long series of mistakes that the stars were definitely laughing about. My horoscope had told me I'd be ruled by Venus today. And that was the horniest fucking planet in the solar system. I should have been prepared to deal with it. I was a Professor at Zodiac Academy, dammit, and I couldn't even ward off Venus when it shoved me in front of The Savage King's daughter.

Mercury was moving into retrograde soon too, maybe that was why my decisions were all over the place. But this was the worst possible time for me to lose focus. There was too much at stake.

I released a low growl, my fangs sharpening as my anger rose. I had to get this dilemma under control. Now. "We *will* get rid of them. But I'm concerned about where they'll go with the Nymph situation becoming more volatile every day."

Darius nodded, his brow creasing. "We'll have to make sure they go back to the mortal world. The Nymphs have no way to travel there so they'd be about as safe as we could hope."

"Not as safe as if they stayed where we could keep an eye on them," I muttered and I hoped that that wasn't a Venus-fuelled comment.

Darius folded his arms, setting his jaw with some decision. "The longer they stay, the more control they'll get over their magic and the more threat they pose to me and my brothers. If we don't watch out, we could end up with two naive savage princesses on the throne and give the Nymphs exactly the kind of unbalance they need to tip the scales of this fight in their favour."

I sniggered at that. "So you think they could overthrow you if they stay then?" I baited him.

Darius's eyes flashed gold with rage. "That's not what I said. But I felt Roxy's power and I almost lost myself in it. She didn't tire in over two hours of wielding a constant stream of powerful fire magic. We've got four years of experience over them but if it came to brute force they could pose a challenge. It seems like a stupid risk to take if we can just get rid of them now instead."

I rolled my neck, vaguely looking around the room in hopes of finding something to drink. It was a habit I'd formed after Clara's death. A drink a day made that familiar ache stop. Sometimes it needed three, or four. But I drowned it eventually. This night felt like a solid six.

"I don't want to argue with you," I said, marching across the room as I spotted a likely place for Lionel's stash. I yanked open the cabinet, busting the lock – *shame about that* – and found a bottle of port inside. Not really my drink of choice but when in Rome. I snatched it out with a couple of glasses and Darius gave me that look that said *you drink to much*. Except he'd stopped actually saying that a long time ago. And tonight he stepped forward and took a glass himself.

"Tomorrow we can deal with this," I said firmly, knocking the nectar down my throat and willing it to take away this stress. "Tonight I have some forgetting to do."

TORY

CHAPTER TWENTY FIVE

I hadn't seen either Lionel or Darius since my return to the party and I was hoping that would continue to be the case until we could get out of here.

I skirted the edges of the ballroom, sipping from a glass of champagne and trying to avoid attention. It was a little easier to do while Darcy was nowhere to be seen; one Vega Twin alone could pass as just another girl at a fancy party.

"You don't look like you're having much fun," Caleb murmured in my ear and I flinched as I turned to find him standing beside me.

Damn sneaky, speedy Vampire.

"I'm getting the distinct impression that Fae just don't know how to party," I said, faking a yawn which turned real half way through.

"I'm sure I can liven things up for you," he purred.

"I've already had that offer from one of your friends and it ended with his psycho father laying into me. So I think I'll pass." I started to walk away but Caleb caught my arm and pulled me towards him.

"Sorry sweetheart, but your little reprieve from our arrangement has come to an end," he said with a smirk which revealed his growing fangs.

I opened my mouth to protest but he whirled me around, using his Vampire speed to move us until he had me pressed against the wall in a shadowy corner.

He brushed my hair away from my neck gently and leaned in without any further hesitation.

"Wait," I breathed, my heart pumping a little faster from his proximity.

He hesitated an inch from my flesh. "Why?"

"Because... this is too easy," I said, thinking quickly.

Caleb laughed, his breath dancing over my skin. "Why would I have any complaints about that?"

"Aren't you supposed to be a big, bad predator? Wouldn't you prefer to work for your meal?" My mind was whirling with an idea which might be a little insane but also just might result in me keeping all of my blood and power in my body tonight.

"Go on," he offered, inching back so that he could look down at me, interest lighting his navy blue eyes.

I placed my palm on his chest to hold him away. "Let's make it a game. I'll run from you and hide. If you can't find me within fifteen minutes you don't bite me tonight."

A smile hooked at his lips. "But I could just bite you right now," he said. "What else do I get for winning your game?"

"Are you afraid you'll lose?" I taunted.

His eyes flashed and I knew I'd hit the right button with that one. Of course he wouldn't be able to resist the urge to prove himself able to beat me in another way.

"You're just delaying the inevitable," he teased.

"We'll see. But you can't use your Vampire speed," I added, prodding him in the chest.

"Alright," he said with a grin. "No Vampire speed."

"I get a two minute head start."

Caleb's smile widened and I couldn't help but smile back. The champagne was buzzing in my veins and my magic was sizzling with the excitement of this game. He was probably going to catch me anyway but at least this way I had a chance to escape.

Besides, I had some tricks of my own up my sleeve which he didn't know about. I'd been slinking through the shadows and hiding from the cops for years; finding me wouldn't be an easy task.

"What are you waiting for then?" Caleb asked, stepping back to release me from the prison of his arms. *"Run."*

My heart leapt with excitement and a laugh escaped my lips as I turned and sprinted out of the room, ignoring the few party goers who noticed me. My stilettos clicked loudly on the marble floor so I paused for half a second to pull them off and carried them as I fled.

I ran down several long corridors and found myself back by the huge door which led out to the cool night air and the grounds beyond. I took a step that way then paused. That was where he'd expect me to go. I glanced up at the wide stairwell which curved away to my right. Sneaking around the private rooms of Daddy Acrux's house was probably a terrible idea but there was a good chance Caleb would think I'd be too chicken-shit to do it.

With a surge of madness I turned right and pounded up the stairs. My hand landed on the golden bannister as I hauled myself up and up faster. I fisted my long skirt in my hand and turned left at the top of the stairs, heading down the corridor we'd taken earlier to meet with the Celestial Council.

I took a left, hit a dead end, whirled around then took a right instead. I kept running, winding through hallways at random before snatching at a door handle and pulling it wide.

I found a huge office awaiting me, the scent of smoke and hard liquor hanging in the air. I hesitated and for a moment I was sure I could hear footsteps coming this way from somewhere out in the corridors.

I quickly pulled the door shut behind me and scampered into the room. Another door stood ajar in the far corner and I ducked my head inside but only found a little closet stacked high with old, leather bound books. They had titles like Beating the Acursed, Advanced Predictive Charting and Binding a Strong Will.

I backed up and the sound of footsteps reached me from beyond the door.

My breath caught in my chest and I scrambled back across the wide room before ducking under the huge oak desk.

My heart raced as I pressed my back to the underside of the desk and heavy footsteps entered the room.

I bit my lip as adrenaline surged through my veins, sinking deeper into the space beneath the desk and willing my thundering heart to slow.

The footsteps drew closer and I fell deathly still as I spotted a pair of legs clad in a deep blue suit. That wasn't Caleb; it was Lionel Acrux and if he discovered me here I would have a lot of explaining to do.

He took a seat in the wing backed chair behind the desk and I shrank aside as he crossed his ankles three inches from my hiding place. The sound of him cracking his knuckles broke the silence and he let out a huff of irritation.

"Is it done?" he asked suddenly and it took me a moment to realise he was on the phone. "No. I don't want excuses on this, if you're not capable of executing the plan then there are plenty of people ready to take your place. I've already had to deal with a disrespectful Heir tonight and I warn you I'm in no mood to tolerate further failure."

In the silence that followed, I could just hear the tinny voice of someone replying but I couldn't make out any of the words or even whether it was a man or a woman on the other end.

"I trust you to see to this as a matter of priority," he snarled. "Contact me the moment you've got something productive to tell me. And don't keep me waiting long unless you want to feel the wrath of my Dragon Fire."

Something slammed into the desk above my head and I flinched, my heart jolting violently.

Lionel released a long sigh laced with a growl before getting to his feet again.

I didn't move. I didn't even dare to breathe as he prowled around his desk and headed for the door.

He hesitated on the threshold like he sensed something wasn't as it should be and a shiver of fear fled along my spine.

Lionel left, pulling the door closed with a sharp snap and I finally released my bottom lip from its hold between my teeth. I'd bitten down hard enough to draw blood and the metallic taste of it filled my mouth.

I inched along, meaning to get the hell out of there but the door opened again, this time remaining open as someone else stalked in.

I leaned forward to get a look out from beneath the desk and relief filled me as I recognised Caleb's black tux and polished black shoes.

"One minute to go," he murmured and I stilled. "You almost got away."

My heart pounded in response to his words. Did he really know he'd tracked me down? Or was he just hoping that he had?

Magic tingled through my fingers as I considered my options. If I really only had to escape him for one more minute then I should probably run for it. I was fast and without his Vampire speed I could probably outpace him for long enough to win this game.

Caleb moved around the desk to the back of the room and I shifted forward on my hands and knees. The door was in sight but I'd lose a few precious seconds as I got to my feet.

At the far end of the room, the door that led into the little library space still stood ajar. I called on my air magic and sent a gust of wind towards it.

The door closed with a sharp snap and I leapt to my feet as Caleb was distracted. I ran for the exit and raced out into the corridor.

Caleb laughed as he took chase and I couldn't help but laugh too.

I shot down the long corridor, the marble floor cold against my bare feet. I could hear him gaining on me and I threw a glance over my shoulder.

"No cheating!" I cried as I spotted his lengthening fangs.

He laughed as he ran faster but he didn't use his Vampire speed.

I rounded a corner and grabbed the closest door handle, wrenching it open as I tumbled inside. I found myself in a small room with a round mahogany table at the heart of it. Decks of cards and gambling chips were stacked neatly in the centre of it and four chairs were tucked beneath it.

I ran to the far side of the table, putting it between me and the door just as Caleb burst in.

He was smiling widely, his golden hair a mess of curls which caught the light from the corridor outside as he stalked towards me in the darkened space.

"Got you, sweetheart," he announced, pausing on the opposite side of the table.

"Not quite," I countered. I placed my free hand on the back of the closest chair, still holding my stilettos in the other. "And you're almost out of time."

Caleb smirked as he took a step to the left and I shadowed him, keeping the table between us.

He laughed darkly and my heart thudded in response.

"I almost couldn't find you," he said and I could tell he was surprised by that. Each time he took a step to circle the table I mirrored it to keep him away.

"Next time you won't," I said confidently. "This house is stupidly big. I took a wrong turn."

Caleb moved left again and so did I. I was getting closer to the door and I couldn't help but glance at it. Caleb noticed.

"You're not running again," he growled before pouncing up onto the table.

I shrieked, stumbling backwards as he leapt towards me. I threw my shoes at him and they bounced off of his chest making him pause in surprise.

He barked a laugh then lunged at me, faster than was humanly possible.

He caught my waist and I squealed as he pushed me back against a heavy bookcase which stood along the wall. My hands landed on his shoulders like I was going to push him off of me but I didn't.

"Cheat," I breathed as my heart pounded.

"Only a little," he admitted.

Before I could say anything else, he leaned forward and kissed me. My heart leapt, my skin tingled and my traitorous body gave in to his demand. I was supposed to hate him. I was supposed to be shoving him off of me and slapping him and telling him to stay the hell away from me.

I definitely shouldn't have been pulling him closer, my hands fisting in the material of his shirt, my lips parting to admit his tongue.

I could still taste blood from where I'd bitten my lip and he obviously could too, a groan of desire escaping him as I felt a soft tug on my magic from the welt on my lip.

Why am I always a sucker for the bad guys? And why does it always feel so good?

The heat of his kiss lit me up and I gave up on any thoughts of pushing him away. It wasn't like I was giving him my heart anyway. Just a kiss... or maybe two...

Caleb's hands slid into my hair and I arched my back, pressing my body against his.

His grip tightened in my hair and he dragged my head backwards, breaking our kiss as he moved his mouth down my neck, teasing with the idea of biting me, his fangs flirting with my flesh.

My body was alight with his proximity and I moaned, urging him on. I didn't want this to stop even if I really should have.

Caleb withdrew just enough to look into my eyes and the heat I saw in his gaze made my toes curl.

"You wanna play another game, sweetheart?" he asked, his voice deep.

"What do I get if I win?" I breathed.

"I think this game will have two winners," he promised.

My gaze roamed over his face hungrily but then I glanced at the open door. This really wasn't the best place for us to be making out... or doing anything else either.

"I can sort that," he said, taking one hand off of me and casting magic at the door. A long vine curled across the carpet before pushing the door closed and winding itself around the handle to lock it. An orb of orange light flickered into existence overhead as we were plunged into darkness, casting shadows over his stunning features. He aimed his palm at the ceiling next and I felt a wave of magic wash over me. "Silencing bubble, so we don't have to hold back," he explained.

I looked into his eyes, wondering if I was really going to do this with him. Heat was curling its way through my body, lighting me up with desire for this beast before me and I decided to act on it before I had the chance to question my decision.

I caught his mouth with mine and shifted my hands to start unhooking his shirt buttons.

I could feel him grinning as he kissed me harder, driving me back against the bookshelf and shoving his knee between my thighs.

I pushed his shirt off of his broad shoulders and looked at the perfection of his muscular torso for a moment, running my hands down his chest.

He drove me back against the shelf more firmly, kissing me again. I devoured the taste of him, his hands sliding over my breasts through the thin material of my dress and making my nipples harden in response.

I placed my palms on his chest and pushed him back, propelling him around so that he was pressed against the shelf instead of me and a dark laugh left him.

"Do you wanna be in charge, sweetheart?"

"Well, I *am* more powerful than you," I teased.

His eyes lit with the challenge in my tone as I took a few steps back and pulled on the knot at the back of my neck. My dress fell from my body like a spill of oil and pooled at my feet, leaving me in nothing but my black panties.

"Holy shit, Tory." He gazed at me hungrily and I stepped back again biting on my bottom lip as I looked at him.

"Take your pants off," I commanded.

Caleb's smile deepened and he held my eye as he kicked his shoes off and unhooked his belt. I twisted my fingers through my hair as I watched him, my pulse rising as he revealed more of his muscular body to me.

When he was down to his navy boxers, he advanced on me again.

I smiled, backing up as he stalked towards me until the backs on my thighs met with the games table.

He was upon me in a heartbeat, his hands gripping my thighs as he lifted me up and sat me on the table. His mouth pressed to my throat, stubble grazing across my skin in the most delicious way.

His kisses moved lower, passing over my collar bone before making it to the swell of my breast. His mouth landed on my nipple, his tongue flicking against it and making me moan in pleasure. His hand found my other breast while he spread his other palm across my lower back to hold me in place.

I locked my ankles around him, pulling him closer so that I could feel the full length of his arousal grinding against me through the lacy fabric of my panties.

His mouth found mine again and I pushed my fingers into his golden curls as my breasts skimmed against the firm lines of his muscular chest.

My muscles were tightening, my heart pounding and my body aching for more of him.

I grazed my fingertips down his chest, feeling every ridge of his abdomen before reaching the waistband of his boxers.

I pushed my hand beneath the soft material and wrapped my fingers around the hard length of him.

Caleb groaned against my lips as I began to move my hand up and down, a tingle running along my spine as I felt just how much my touch affected him.

His hands made it to the sides of my panties and he peeled them down as his heavy breathing broke our kiss. I lifted my ass to let him remove them and he stepped back, forcing my hand off of him as he tossed my underwear aside.

I watched as he pushed his boxers off revealing every inch of him and my mouth dried up with desire.

He shot forward with his Vampire speed, scooping me up and moving me backwards as he lay me beneath him on the games table. Poker chips and cards scattered all around us and a surprised laugh left my lips.

He grinned as he kissed me again, hard enough to bruise my lips but still not enough to tame my desire.

My hands explored the curve of his shoulders and I arched my back off of the table so that my nipples skimmed his flesh.

Caleb shifted, moving between my legs, our kiss breaking for the briefest moment as he looked into my eyes and pushed himself inside me.

A moan of pleasure escaped me as he filled me and I tipped my head back, my eyes falling closed as I absorbed the feeling of his body merging with mine.

"*Fuck*," Caleb breathed as he started to move, slowly at first but building in speed as I urged him on.

My nails were digging into his shoulders and I was glad that he'd cast the silencing spell because I was making enough noise to be heard in the party downstairs.

Caleb kissed me again then pulled back, pressing his palms to the table on either side of my head as he looked down at me. I reached out between us, exploring his chest with my hands for a moment before he snatched them into his grasp and pinned them above my head.

I writhed beneath him as he smiled darkly and increased his pace, pushing me towards the edge.

My body flexed and tightened beneath him, my back arching as he drove me on and I cried out as he wrung a wave of pleasure from my flesh.

He slowed down a little as I caught my breath, releasing my wrists and kissing my neck.

I panted beneath him for a moment before rearing up and rolling him beneath me so that I could sit on top of him instead.

Caleb groaned with desire as he looked up at me and I changed the pace again, riding him towards his climax.

One of hands reached out to caress my breast while he pushed his other thumb down on the spot at the apex of my thighs, exactly where I wanted him.

I tipped my head back, my hair brushing along my spine as my muscles began to tighten around him again.

I could feel him losing control too and I bit my lip as I moved a little faster.

Pleasure rode through my body and I cried out just as he came apart beneath me, my name spilling from his lips. I collapsed forward onto his chest and lay panting in his strong arms for several long seconds as he trailed his fingers through my hair.

"You don't know how much I've been wanting to do that," Caleb breathed in my ear and I smiled as I turned to press a brief kiss to his lips.

"I think you made it pretty clear," I teased.

I climbed off of him and retrieved my clothes from the floor, pulling them back on again as Caleb followed me and did the same.

He kept his eyes on me as he pulled his pants back on and moved forward to retie my dress again for me, his fingertips brushing across my neck and sending a shiver along my sensitised skin.

He buckled his belt and located his shirt while I ran my fingers through my hair in an attempt to tame it. Caleb waved a hand through the air and I felt the silencing spell dissolve around us.

I pushed my feet back into my stilettos and we stood looking at each other with our clothes back on and a secret between us.

"I like playing games with you, Tory," Caleb said as he moved towards me.

"I didn't entirely hate it," I admitted. "Sorry I'm not more... horsey," I added with a smirk, unable to help myself.

"That fucking rumour," he growled, but there wasn't really any anger in his tone after what we'd just done.

"I heard you like it when they shove their horn up your-"

"Shut up. I just showed you exactly what I like." He snorted a laugh.

"Mmm... Maybe I'll let you show me it again some time."

Caleb's eyes twinkled with amusement and he caught my cheek in his large hand, kissing me again. There wasn't as much heat in it but it still made me feel a little weak at the knees. Maybe making nice with one of the Heirs wasn't the worst choice I'd ever made.

"Caleb?" a harsh voice came from the doorway beside us and fear darted through me as I pulled away from Caleb in surprise.

Darius stood in the hall, the vine which had secured the door burned to a crisp on the ground from his magic. He was scowling at the two of us and seemed even more intimidating than usual. His gaze took in the cards and poker chips all over the floor alongside the less than perfect state of my hair and I was endlessly grateful that he hadn't turned up five minutes ago.

Caleb didn't release his hold on me but turned to look at the other Heir with a hint of irritation in his gaze.

"I'm busy," he said flatly, a clear demand for Darius to leave.

"My father and the other Councillors want to speak to all of the Heirs before we leave. They sent me to look for you," Darius said, ignoring his friend's irritation. "Your sister and Lance are already waiting outside for you," he added to me, his tone dismissive.

Caleb sighed and turned back to look at me but I couldn't tear my eyes away from Darius. He looked my way, meeting my eyes and I almost flinched from the anger I found there.

"I haven't finished yet," Caleb said, his eyes roaming over me but I was still trapped in Darius's gaze.

"Well stop playing with your food and get on with it," Darius demanded.

Caleb growled in response to the command but he leaned in to brush his mouth against my neck. I didn't bother to try and fight him off but I released my hold on his shirt so I was no longer pulling him towards me.

"We can pick this up later, sweetheart," Caleb murmured. "But I need my strength if I've gotta face the Councillors." His teeth slid into my neck, and his hand pushed into my hair as he held me in place.

The strange sucking sensation pulled at my gut as he tapped into the well of power that lay within me, drawing it into himself.

Darius's gaze stayed fixed on us the entire time and I couldn't help but look back at him. His eyes were like two burning pits of rage and I wondered briefly if Caleb was breaking some rule of theirs by being less than awful to me.

Caleb withdrew his fangs from my skin and brushed his fingers over the wound, healing it for me. I looked up at him in surprise and he smiled ruefully.

"See you downstairs, sweetheart," he murmured, leaning forward like he was going to kiss me again.

I ducked aside with a taunting grin. "Not if I see you first," I warned playfully.

He chuckled darkly. "I look forward to catching you again then."

Caleb moved to join Darius and the two of them turned and walked away down the corridor without another glance at me.

"What the hell was that about?" Darius asked him in an undertone.

"Lighten up, Darius. We were just playing a game. And you have to admit I got a damn hot prize for winning it."

Darius grunted in response and the two of them turned a corner, leaving me alone.

I turned the other way and headed back towards the stairs to find Darcy and get the hell away from the Acrux Manor. Hooking up with Caleb Altair had not been on my list of things to do tonight but it hadn't been the worst thing I'd ever done either.

I tried to wipe the smirk from my face as I remembered the way his hands had felt on my body and navigated my way back through the sprawling manor. The place was seriously massive and I hadn't realised quite how far I'd run in my bid to escape from Caleb. I took a few wrong turns before finally finding the stairs and heading down to the huge door that led outside.

Darcy and Orion were standing out on the gravel drive, looking in opposite directions to each other.

"Hey," I called as I moved to join them, wrapping my arms around myself against the chill of the evening.

Darcy glanced at Orion then hurried toward me with a taut expression. I raised a questioning eyebrow at her and her cheeks heated a little in response.

"Where have you been?" she asked, eyeing my hair with her mystical twin senses tingling.

"Oh, I erm-"

"With *who*?" she demanded, her eyes widening.

I glanced at Orion awkwardly and he rolled his eyes before stalking away from us further down the drive.

"It's not a big deal," I said as Darcy waited for her answer expectantly. "Seriously, it was just a bit of fun."

"Well I'm guessing this bit of fun has a name," she teased.

I sighed in defeat, ready to admit to yet another Tory's bad choice in men moment. "Caleb."

Orion turned to look back at me with a raised eyebrow and I cursed his damn Vampire ears. I should have realised he'd still be listening in. *Nosey asshole.*

"But Tory, he's an Heir!" Darcy spluttered before she could stop herself.

I dropped my eyes guiltily and she quickly reined in the saucer eyes and battered down the judgement.

"I mean, I get it, he's stupidly hot and everything," she hedged quickly. "I'm just worried about you. What if he's up to something?"

I snorted a laugh. "Don't worry about it Darcy, I'm not falling for him. It was just a mutually beneficial moment of madness."

"Okay, good," she said with relief. Then her eyes sparkled with mischief as she dropped her voice. "So how was it?"

Orion cleared his throat and I scowled at him.

"I'll tell you later when there are less *nosey* Vampires using their bat ears around us," I said.

Darcy giggled in response, looking over at Orion who didn't even bother to pretend he hadn't been listening to us.

We were interrupted as the four Heirs spilled out of the house and I looked around to find Caleb smirking at me. I returned his smile for the briefest of moments before looking back at my sister.

"Can I have a word for a moment, Roxy?" Darius asked as he drew closer to us. The other Heirs kept going and they moved past us to join Orion as he started walking further down the drive.

Darcy looked between us uncertainly and I gave her a reassuring smile before she hurried after the others.

"So?" I asked, unsure whether he was pissed at me or not. It was nearly midnight after all so his nice guy act was about to go pop.

He took my hand and pulled my arm around his as he glanced back at the manor. He started walking, drawing me along with him and I let him as curiosity prickled at me.

"You shouldn't have spoken to my father the way you did," he said slowly and I geared myself up to go on the defensive.

"Well he didn't really give me much choice."

"What was it you called him again?" he asked.

"Ummm, I don't really recall..."

"I think you said something about an oversized iguana," he prompted and I snorted a laugh.

Darius tried to resist laughing too but he couldn't really hide his smile.

"You're lucky he didn't kill you for that. I don't think I've ever heard anyone insult him in all my life," he added.

"Well, maybe they don't... to his face," I hedged and his smile widened for a moment before falling back into a frown.

Darius slowed me down before we could get any closer to the others who were waiting by a huge water fountain which stood beyond the drive. I glanced up at him and the look in his eyes pulled me up short as he gripped my arm tighter.

"Don't ever do anything like that again though," he warned. "I diverted his attention this time but he won't ever take that kind of attitude from you a second time."

I wanted to make some snide comment but he was looking at me so intensely that I only nodded. I had no intention of ever seeing Lionel Acrux again anyway. I certainly wouldn't be accepting anymore invitations from him.

He stared at me for a long moment as if he was trying to figure me out and I dropped my eyes before he could. I didn't want Darius Acrux in my head.

My attention snagged on a deep red stain on the sleeve of his pristine white shirt and I pointed it out.

"Are you bleeding?" I asked.

"No," he replied forcefully before looking down at the offending stain and waving his hand to clear it away with his water magic.

"Well that was obviously blood so-"

"I said *no*, just drop it," he snarled.

I flinched back but he didn't release me and my heart started beating faster.

He sighed heavily and shook his head before letting me go. "Sorry, I just... I'm not bleeding now. It's not an issue."

"Okay..." I took a step back, wondering why I was even talking to him. This was the guy who had tormented me for weeks and he was clearly going to snap right back into asshole mode after tonight. But something about this nice version of Darius kept drawing me in despite my reservations.

"Come on, let's catch up with the others and get back to the Academy," he urged, offering me his arm again.

The anger which had risen in him a moment ago seemed to have gone so I tentatively accepted his arm and we started walking down the driveway and away from his family.

"Careful," I teased. "Someone might think we don't even hate each other if you don't release me soon."

We made it to the edge of the pooling light which lit up the front of his house and he drew me into the darkness beyond it.

"I never said I hated you," he murmured, his voice deep as he tugged me around to face him.

I looked up at his striking face, the moonlight highlighting his strong jaw and pulling my attention to his mouth for a moment.

"Well I really feel sorry for anyone you *do* hate," I muttered, pulling my arm out of his grip. He resisted for a moment like he wanted to keep hold of me but gave in when I tugged a little harder.

"The things I've done to you... you know it isn't personal, right?" he asked.

I looked up at him for several long seconds, wondering if he seriously bought into that horse shit or if it was just what he was trying to sell me. I wasn't really sure what I saw there but I definitely didn't buy his excuses.

"Is that how you justify it to yourself?" I asked bitterly, our little bubble of peace well and truly burst now that we were standing in the cold air of the night.

Darius hesitated and I gave him an eye roll dramatic enough to fell a small tree. I turned away from him, looking for Orion and the stardust which would take us back to the Academy but his fingers curled around my wrist before I could escape.

"Do you hate *me*, then?" he asked quietly and for some strange reason it sounded like the idea of that didn't sit well with him.

I forced myself to reply in a steady tone, holding his eye as I spoke. "No," I said and a glimmer of relief spilled through his eyes, almost halting me there but I wasn't quite so blinded by him as to give him a free pass for all his bullshit. "To hate you, I'd have to care about you. And I don't give one shit about you," I said coldly.

I shook his hand off of me for the second time and stalked away towards Darcy and Orion. He didn't follow me and I was glad. Because I had the horrible feeling that that might just have been a lie.

DARCY

CHAPTER TWENTY SIX

Good morning Gemini.
The stars have spoken about your day!
With an event bringing many people together around you, you'll soon be caught up in the excitement. And rightly so too, after so much effort has been put into a project you've been working on, you'll finally find yourself reaping the rewards.
If you tread carefully things will flow smoothly, but one wrong move could incur the wrath of your enemies.

I groaned sleepily as I turned my Atlas over, not really absorbing its message. I squinted toward the window, finding the dark sky staring back at me. After the party last night, my head was pounding and I'd had *many* dreams about Lance.

Professor Orion, I corrected sharply in my head. I had to forget about that kiss, but holy shit it felt like it was permanently branded on my lips.

I slid out of bed, combing my fingers through my hair. I'd stayed up late discussing Astrum's latest card with Tory. But all we could conclude was that we had to be careful drawing closer to the lunar eclipse and hope that our questions really would be answered on the day. In all honesty, the cards seemed like a way to drive us to madness. If Astrum knew something we needed to hear, why had he set up this convoluted game to tell us? Why not just spell it out plainly?

As I came to my senses, I pushed away my negative thoughts and excitement started up a fanfare in my heart. There was a reason I was awake so early. And it was one of the best reasons I could think of to be awake at the butt crack of dawn.

I showered and dressed in jeans and a cream sweater, pulling on the navy blue Pitball jacket that had been hanging in my closet since day one. It was lined with silver stripes up the sleeves and Zodiac Academy was printed across the back in the same colour. Kneeling down, I pushed aside the coat I'd folded at the bottom of the closet and took out the paper bag I'd wrapped the Griffin poo in.

A wide smile pushed at my cheeks. *Time to take down another Heir.*

I stuffed it in my satchel, hanging it over my shoulder and grabbing my Atlas on the way out of the door. All was quiet in Aer Tower and my anticipation grew as I sped down the stairs, rushing through the exit. Luckily it wasn't raining but a thick fog hung over the grounds, making it difficult to see as I made my way toward Earth Territory by the light of my Atlas.

Though it chilled me a little to do so, I took the route through The Wailing Wood and cut a direct path to the centre of campus. I jogged past The Orb and made my way into the north western corner of campus. I hadn't often come close to the Pitball Stadium but I'd seen it a few times and been drawn to its shining exterior.

It rose up high above me; rectangular in shape with curved metal walls. On top of it was a huge silver dome which covered the entire pitch. I jogged around to the back entrance and found Geraldine waiting there for me with a key as we'd arranged.

"Holy raincoats, your majesty," she said as I slowed to a halt in front of her. "It's a misty morning indeed."

"It is," I laughed softly. "Thank you for doing this."

"Not at all, it's my absolute star-given pleasure to assist you and Tory. How was the party last night? My father says you were both the shimmering shellfish of his evening."

"Yes, it was great to meet him," I said earnestly.

"I know he can seem a little goody-two-shoes at first. He's not like me with my rebellious ways and cockamamy mouth. I do hope he wasn't too proper. I know you and your sister prefer the company of scallywags like me."

"No er...he was very um-" I had no idea how to respond to her mad assessment of herself.

"Oh begonias!" Geraldine gasped, looking over my shoulder. "Good morning, you're looking most majestic on this blessed day, your highness."

I turned to find Tory trudging along with the hood of her new coat pulled up and a scowl gripping her features. She pushed her hood back, tugging off her headphones and shivering. "It's cold and I'm dog tired and hungover but this is so worth it," she said through a long yawn.

I beamed. "Once we get this done, we can go grab some coffee."

"No no no." She shook her head. "The match isn't until one. So I'm going back to bed for another six hours."

I laughed, turning to Geraldine as she unlocked the door and we slipped into a dark corridor which led under the stands. Adrenaline trickled through me and I found myself prancing along behind Geraldine as she guided the way, switching on lights as she went.

"Have you got the griffin turd?" Tory asked, jogging to my side with another yawn.

"Obviously," I said, taking it from my pocket it and waving it at her.

She wrinkled her nose, wincing away from it. "You can do the crumbling."

"I will be most honoured to do the crumbling," Geraldine said before I could argue. "And I also brought a special gift for one of the other Heirs with me." A dark glimmer entered her eyes as she glanced back at us and I squealed in excitement.

"I love targeting these assholes," Tory said with a grin.

We followed Geraldine into a huge locker room and she headed straight for a row of lockers at the centre where a wide space was divided by a long bench. Hanging from a rack were a row of ten shiny bags in the same blue and silver colours of my Pitball jacket, each with a surname blazing on the side of it.

"Normally I'd never get access to the other player's kits. But these were delivered just yesterday. They're brand new for the match against Starlight Academy today." Geraldine brushed her fingers over the bag marked Rigel with a visible shiver. "Smell that?" she breathed and I glanced at Tory.

"Um...no?" Tory said.

"It smells like the Heirs' lives falling apart," she said dramatically.

"Oh good," I chuckled, hurrying forward with the Griffin poo.

Geraldine produced some plastic gloves from her pocket and I had to admire how prepared she was for this. "I am happy to do it alone."

"I want to actually," I said keenly, taking a pair and Tory plucked the other from her grip.

"Yep, I'm in so long as there's gloves. You got us in here Geraldine, you've done plenty."

Geraldine's eyes brimmed with proud tears for a moment and she bowed low, stepping back to watch as I unzipped the bag and pulled out Max's navy and silver kit. It consisted of a large shirt with *Waterguard* printed above his surname, a pair of long shorts, socks and steel capped boots. We first turned each item inside out then I took out the solid lump of poo and broke it in half, handing one bit to Tory.

We started rubbing it on the inside of his clothes and were soon laughing madly as we layered every inch in a fine powder of Griffin shit. This kit was going to make his whole body turn purple and lumpy from the toxic poop and he'd be forced to quit the match to go and soak it off.

We stuffed the poo back in the bag and I tossed it into the trash before we carefully hung the kit back up and returned it to his bag.

When we were done, we stripped the gloves off and high fived, grinning wickedly.

"I can't wait to see his face," Tory said and I nodded excitedly.

A glint caught my eye and I glanced over Tory's shoulder, spotting Geraldine rubbing glitter into the crotch of Caleb's shorts.

"Geraldine!" I gasped. "That's genius."

She beamed, folding the shorts away and zipping up the bag. "Those nincompoops won't know what hit them."

"Hurricane Geraldine hit them," I said and she fell into frantic laughter, snorting intermittently.

"Blazing ballerinas, that's the funniest thing I've ever heard." She snorted again and I couldn't help but join in with her laughter.

"We'd better get out of here," Tory said with a smirk and we headed after her.

We made sure there was no trace of our attack left behind as we hurried back out of the stadium, finding the dawn starting to seep into the sky.

We headed toward The Orb and I tempted Tory inside before she disappeared back to her bed as the scent of freshly baked pastries sailed from inside.

"Okay five minutes," she said hungrily as we walked through the empty space.

I grabbed a still-warm cinnamon swirl then filled up a mug of coffee while Geraldine hovered around me, trying to do everything for me instead.

"It's fine, Geraldine, really. I'd rather do it myself," I promised and she darted toward Tory, nearly scalding herself as she tried to push a mug under the coffee machine before my sister could.

We soon sat down at our usual spot at the centre of the room and all at once, our Atlases pinged loudly. I took mine out as the others did the same, frowning as I read the notification on the screen.

Zodiac Academy has been mentioned in The Celestial Times!

I clicked the button with a note of dread resounding through me, finding exactly what I feared. An article entitled *The Return of the Lost Heirs* by Gustav Vulpecula was on the first page of the site, headed with a photograph of Tory and I at the party which I had no recollection of him taking. We stood apart from the crowd with drinks in our hands and a general air of discomfort about us.

United, the Vega Twins entered the Acrux ballroom like they were born conjoined and were yet to be severed. Upon meeting everyone in the Celestial Council, Roxanya (left) and Gwendalina (right) asserted that their names were in fact Tory and Darcy. Though many laughs were had, it seemed this was not in fact a joke, but the mortal names the twins now insist on going by. However, it is very puzzling to some, that they have adopted the Vega surname without complaint. This does indeed appear to be an acceptance of their inheritance and therefore their claim to the Solarian throne. So are we to fear an upheaval of the Celestial Council if they graduate from Zodiac Academy?

The answer, we hope, is no.

From my extensive discussion with the two twins, a few unsettling things became clear to me. Firstly that Roxanya ('Tory') is crass in both tone and manner. Upon asking her about her time at the prestigious academy where they have graciously been accepted (despite obvious lack in training and decorum) she started listing her many sexual conquests at the Academy instead. As the sharpness of champagne on her breath sailed over me, I had to admit, I was starting to become worried about the mental state of the girl as she rested a hand on my arm and seductively licked her lips. Had I not been a man of better taste, I may have fallen prey to her overt display. From the way her eyes roamed the room, I fear more than one man fell for her tricks that night and do hope she will soon seek counselling for the sex addiction which clearly ails her.

With my nerves a little on edge, I turned to the second twin in hopes of finding a more suitable figure for the Solarian throne. Quieter, at first I enjoyed the polite discussion I shared with Gwendalina ('Darcy') but the way her eyes glazed between questions and the several seconds it took for her to come up with short, blunt answers, alerted me to the fact there was something hindering her mentally. I was patient with her, drawing out answers as best I could but it seemed the girl had had many delusional episodes during her time at the Academy. She spoke of ravens whispering to her through her window at night and of a mystical mountain hare who lives under her bed. It was soon difficult to believe anything that came out of Gwendalina's ('Darcy's') mouth, and when I asked her about her relationship with the Celestial Heirs, she proceeded to dribble on my shoes and stare off into the distance – no doubt departed to one of her delusions. It is also worth mentioning, that all the while her wild stories had continued, her sister had made efforts to slide her hand down the back of my suit pants and I had to sternly remind her that I was a married man. To that, she'd scoffed and continued her abrasive assault.

Taking a short break from their unsettling company, I spoke with the Celestial Heir, Max Rigel, who had this to say to them, "We ask only that the Vega Twins respect our position as Heirs to the Solarian throne and that they rescind their claim for the betterment of the kingdom."

When I put this quote to the Vega Twins for a response (rather nervously), Roxanya ('Tory') slurred a sexually abusive comment at me, stumbling under the influence of the many drinks she'd consumed while Gwendalina ('Darcy') remained vacant, muttering quietly to a raven I could neither see nor hear.

As a kingdom, it is time we asked ourselves who we wish to see sat on our throne. The four Celestial Heirs, the proud and handsome boys born of our world and nature, or the two odd and slightly bizarre twins who were born to The Savage King. A man who killed thousands during his reign, who himself was rumoured to be impaired by many destructive mental illnesses and who brought our kingdom to its knees before his death.

Only time will tell which party will claim the throne. But I for one, hope the Vega Twins do us all a favour and step out of the running.

I looked up, horrified that that asshole would have lied about us so viciously.

"I do *not* have a sex addiction," Tory balked, slamming her Atlas down as she looked up.

Geraldine opened and closed her mouth like a fish out of water. "Fiery balls!" She sprang to her feet. "I'll speak with my father and see if I can have this drivel retracted! I am outraged that my Queens have been so deeply insulted." She marched from The Orb with fury in her posture and I looked to Tory with my heart sinking in my chest.

"Everyone's going to think we're completely insane."

"I'm sorry did you say that to me or to the raven on my shoulder?" Tory asked.

I broke a laugh and she cracked a smile, glancing down at the article and shaking her head.

"Screw what they think," she huffed.

I nodded firmly. "You're right. In the next few hours, Max Rigel is going to taste what it's like to cross us. So if this Vulpecula guy wants to make an enemy out of us too. Then more fool him."

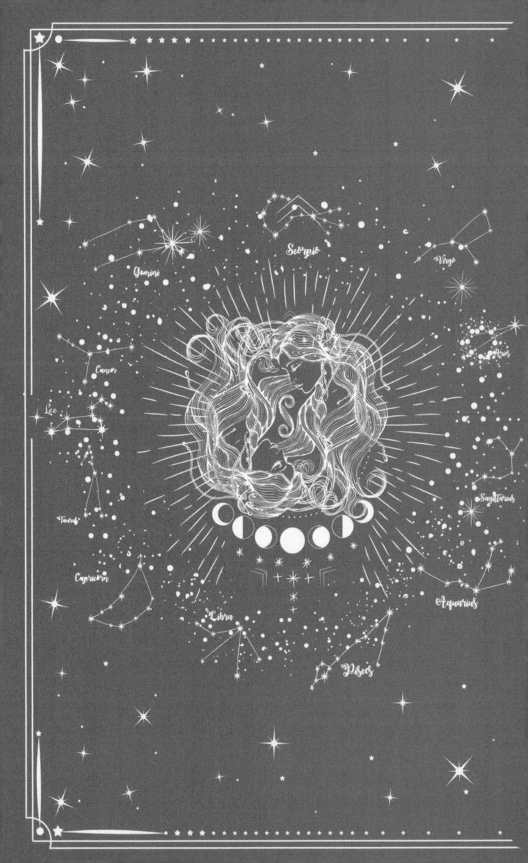

TORY

CHAPTER TWENTY SEVEN

As I snuck back into Ignis House with the light of dawn following me inside, I headed straight upstairs to the top floor. I slid my headphones down to hang around my neck as I listened for the sounds of anyone waking. There were a few scuffling footsteps, the odd hum of a shower running and the faint sound of an alarm clock leaking through the doors which surrounded me but it didn't seem like anyone was actually out of their rooms yet.

I tiptoed towards Milton Hubert's door and pulled the thin envelope from my pocket which contained a rather recognisable gold ring set with a row of black onyx through its centre and a love note from a secret admirer. The note had urged him to wear it today for luck in the match with the added promise of a hook up with the very promiscuous mystery woman who'd written the letter later on as a reward. I'd even taken a tip from Darius's fan mail and sealed it with a lipstick kiss.

The real genius of the note was in the spell Sofia had found to cast on it though; once unfolded, the letter would be readable for two whole minutes before it would burst into flames and destroy all evidence of its existence. She may not have held a lot of power but the tricky little spells that she was able to master already astounded me.

I smiled to myself as I pushed it under his door before jogging back down to my own room on silent feet.

When I made it inside, I quickly peeled off my running gear and jumped into the shower. My heart was pounding with adrenaline at the thought of today. It was beyond time that we saw Max suffer publicly and with a bit of luck, Darius would fall into my trap too.

By the time I emerged, dried and styled my hair, applied my makeup and got dressed in a crop top and ripped jeans, I could hear a lot of people up and about.

I pulled on thick socks but didn't bother with shoes as I headed out of my room and down to the common room. The moment I stepped into the wide, comfortable space Darius appeared in front of me.

"You're up early, Roxy," he commented, his gaze trailing over me inquiringly.

"You take way too much interest in my routine, dude," I replied lazily as I attempted to side step him. I didn't want to be drawn into a conversation with him, all I wanted was a front row to the drama which was about to explode just as soon as Milton Hubert dragged his sorry ass out of bed.

"Moved on to your next conquest already? That sex addiction of yours must be quite difficult to maintain," he teased, clearly hoping to get a rise out of me.

I leaned closer to him, the scent of cedar and smoke overwhelming me for a moment. "Well the real challenge is finding someone who can keep up with me," I said.

"I'll pass your complaints on to Caleb," Darius replied, though his jaw tightened as he said it, making me believe my hook up with Caleb pissed him off far more than trying to taunt me with it would.

"Oh no," I replied smoothly. "No complaints there from me."

Darius seemed to have something else to say to me but I didn't wait around to find out what, heading for the coffee machine in the corner of the room. After my early start, I was going to need a lot of caffeine to fuel me today but I was confident it would be worth it. He didn't give up that easily though and followed me across the room.

I was tempted to tell him to take a hike but I was in a good enough mood to let his stalking slide.

I tossed a cup into the machine and hit the button for a mocha before turning to Darius with a raised eyebrow.

"Can I help you?" I asked.

"I'm just waiting to get a coffee."

"Let me guess, flat white?"

"Why do you say that?" he asked.

"Because it's the most boring coffee you can get. Maybe you're an espresso guy though, to go with that whole intense thing you've got going on... but the idea of you holding one of those teenie tiny cups in your massive hands is kinda ridiculous so I think not." I pulled my coffee from the machine and added three heaped spoonfuls of sugar to it as Darius hit the button for a flat white.

"Whereas you prefer your coffee with a bucket of sugar added because you're just so damn sweet?" he asked sarcastically as he watched me.

"No. I like my sugar with a dash of coffee added because I'm bitter." I gave him a false smile then walked away.

The early start gave me my pick of the room so I chose an armchair opposite the huge couches where Darius and his posse always sat so that I'd have a front row seat to the show.

I took my Atlas out and stuck my headphones on as I started scrolling through FaeBook posts without really looking at them. There were plenty of people quoting that ridiculous article and tagging both me and Darcy in their posts but I shrugged it off and tucked my feet up onto the chair opposite me.

I laughed as I spotted a notice for all Werewolves to report to Uranus Infirmary for a flea dip by the end of the week.

Slowly but surely, Darius's little fan club all emerged from their pits and moved to join him on the couch. There was no sign of Sofia and I guessed she'd taken the chance to have a lie in. Every now and then I'd feel eyes on me and glance up from my social media perusal to find Darius looking my way. I didn't like it. What did he want with me? It couldn't be anything good.

Marguerite appeared wearing pyjamas which could arguably be called underwear and positioned herself in Darius's line of sight with a few of her friends. He didn't even blink at her as she tossed her red hair about and laughed too loudly in response to any joke one of her brain dead cretins came up with.

Her performance made me smirk into my coffee, especially when Darius looked my way again and stared long enough for her to jump to her feet in outrage.

"Enjoy it while it lasts, *whore,*" she snarled at me before stalking away.

"It's sex addict, not whore," I called after her. "And it's not cool to mock people for medical afflictions."

Marguerite whirled on me, her eyes blazing with fury as I casually flipped her off.

"Go and get dressed, Marguerite," Darius said lazily before she could do anything in response. "You're ruining the pre-match vibe in here with your shrieky voice."

If looks could kill then Marguerite would have just impaled me on a bed of nails before feeding me alive to a hoard of bloodthirsty ants. But as they couldn't, she only succeeded in turning her face the same beetroot shade as her hair before she burst into tears and ran from the room with her friends trailing behind.

I could feel Darius looking at me again but if he was waiting for a thank you then it'd be a hell of a long time coming. I dropped my gaze to my FaeBook feed and pointedly ignored him while I continued to wait.

After what seemed like hours, a monobrowed lump of muscle swaggered into the room sporting a fancy new ring alongside his flashy gold watch.

I perked up, straightening in my chair and trying not to be obvious about the fact that all of my attention had fallen on the arrival of Milton Hubert.

A preemptive smile came for my lips and I lifted my hand so that I could chew on my thumbnail to hide it.

Milton crossed the room to get his own coffee and I waited... and waited... and holy crap the anticipation was freaking killing me but I waited some damn more.

Milton collected his coffee, his eyes scanning the room as he held the cup in the hand which sported the ring from Darius's treasure haul. He was showing it off, hoping the mystery girl would see it. Little did he know his mystery girl was a six and a half foot Dragon asshole with the shortest fuse I'd ever come across and a temper to rival a hurricane. I almost felt bad for Milton Hubert. Then I remembered the fact that he'd taken naked photos of me and shared them around the school on my first day at the Academy and my pity whipped away on the wind.

Milton headed for Darius's fan club, still looking around hopefully as he lowered his ass into an armchair opposite Darius on the couch.

He said hey. Darius stayed silent. I should have been subtle but I was full on staring now and I couldn't help it.

Darius frowned at Milton just a little, his brows pulling together and his eyes narrowing.

"Where did you get that?" he asked and his voice was so low and dark that almost everyone in the room fell silent instantly.

"Huh?" Milton lowered his coffee carefully, registering the threat in Darius's voice without taking in the words.

The House Captain kept his gaze fixed on his prey as he leaned forward slowly, resting his elbows on his knees as he pinned Milton with a deathly stare.

"That ring," Darius reiterated and I had to give Milton credit for not pissing himself.

He cleared his throat, tilting his hand as he looked down at the offending piece of jewellery. "I err... it was left in my room-"

"By who?" Darius snarled. He wasn't moving. At all. He wasn't even blinking.

My heart started thumping an uneven rhythm in my chest as excitement mixed with what was undoubtedly fear. I began to go over every step I'd taken in laying the foundations of this trap. I'd taken everything into account, there was no way to trace any of this back to me. But if Darius didn't believe that Milton had been the one to screw him over then he'd be hunting for an alternative suspect. And realistically, how many people in this Academy could he even count as his enemies? Maybe he didn't believe that me and Darcy were brave enough to do something like this but last night I'd looked his father in the eye and insulted him. I was showing him my true colours more and more often. He could see he hadn't beaten me when he'd tried to drown me. So maybe me pulling off a stunt like this wouldn't seem like such a stretch anymore.

"I don't know," Milton breathed, placing his coffee down on the table and flexing his fingers uncomfortably. "There was a note though-"

"Show it to me."

"It... it's gone. It burned up. Does this ring mean something to you?"

"It was in my room, before it burned down," Darius snarled. "Which means someone stole it."

Milton ripped the ring from his finger as if it had scalded him, tossing it to Darius with a flick of his wrist. Darius made no attempt to catch it and it bounced off of his chest before hitting the floor.

The rest of the posse seemed to smell blood in the water and they all started getting to their feet, shrinking away from Milton and moving to stand behind Darius.

"Look, man, I didn't know. You know I'd never... I love you, I-"

Darius got to his feet in one swift motion and Milton fell to his knees on the floor in front of him, lowering his head as fear wracked through his body.

It didn't matter that I was staring now, everyone in the common room was and you could have heard a pin drop. I slid my headphones from my ears to hang them round my neck, my lips parting in surprise as Milton trembled before the Heir he'd pledged his loyalty to.

"Where did you get that watch?" Darius asked slowly.

Milton quickly unbuckled the watch and tossed it at Darius's feet too. "Someone sent it to me, I don't know why-"

"Let me guess, no note either? No proof that you didn't buy it after coming into a shit load of Dragon gold?" Darius asked.

The room was growing hotter the longer this interrogation went on and it took me a moment to realise that it was heat pouring from Darius as his rage grew.

"I didn't, I swear I didn't-"

"Then you won't mind if I check your room." Darius turned and swept towards the stairs, the crowd of students scrambling out of his way like he might just eat them alive if they didn't.

I got to my feet, shallow breaths passing my lips as I drifted after Darius with the rest of the Ignis House students, though no one dared follow him up the stairs.

My gaze slid to Milton who was still kneeling on the floor, a wide space left empty all around him like he was some kind of pariah and no one wanted to be associated with him.

A huge crash sounded from the top floor followed by the roar of a Dragon. I flinched but then so did everyone else. Darius's rage was a tangible thing, coiling in the air and threatening to consume everyone within sight.

He strode back into the room and everyone scrambled out of his way.

A rolling wave of heated energy slammed through the centre of the common room, crashing into Milton Hubert and sending him cartwheeling across the space before throwing him into the wall.

Darius advanced on him with his teeth bared and his eyes transformed into golden reptilian slits. His power burned through the air and more than one person ran for the exit.

"What the fuck is *this*?!" he bellowed, launching a handful of gold coins at the floor beneath Milton's feet.

The heat pinning him to the wall fell away only to be replaced with ice which crawled over Milton's body, fusing him to the wall and making his eyes bulge with panic.

"I don't know, I swear I've never seen those before," he breathed, shaking his head again and again.

Darius yelled out in rage, the ice shattering and releasing Milton to fall sprawling at his feet where he landed a solid kick to his gut.

"You are a liar, a thief and a fucking traitor!" he snarled. "I can't even trust my own people in my own House! From this day forward you are nothing." Darius turned away from Milton as if he didn't even warrant his rage, his gaze sweeping over the rest of the students. "As far as I'm concerned Milton Hubert is shunned. He doesn't bear relevance. He doesn't matter. He doesn't exist at all. If you're with me, then I suggest you all see him the same way."

No one dared speak but heads nodded all around me and I recoiled from the way these people behaved. They were so willing to shun someone they'd called their friend just five minutes ago. All because some bigger, badder, meaner jackass told them to.

Darius prowled through the room and once again everyone scurried out of his way, desperate not to be the next victim of his rage.

Silence fell and Milton whimpered where he lay on the floor. I actually felt kinda bad; I'd known Darius would lose his shit but I hadn't quite been prepared for the level of it. Guilt twisted at my insides and I wrung my fingers together uncomfortably.

A huge crash sounded upstairs and a few people screamed. The next sound to come was the echoing roar of a Dragon intent on burning down the whole world.

I looked out of the window and spotted Darius wheeling through the sky breathing a gigantic fireball into existence.

A shiver ran down my spine at the raw, unbridled power of the beast before me. If he ever found out what I'd done then I was sure I'd meet a worse fate than what he'd just dished out to Milton Hubert. But despite the fear that that invoked, as I watched him running away from the place he'd called home, his faith in the unwavering loyalty of his fan club well and truly shaken, I couldn't help but bathe in the glow of satisfaction it gave me.

Too bad Darius Acrux, you really should have realised who you were dealing with before you declared war on us.

DARCY

CHAPTER TWENTY EIGHT

I headed to the Pitball stadium clustered together with Tory, Diego and Sofia. We moved along with the sea of students and Professors all heading up the path into Earth Territory. Everyone was dressed in the navy blue and silver colours of our team and anticipation rolled through me at what awaited us in the towering dome ahead. Tory had fashioned an oversized Pitball shirt into a dress by tying a knot in it where it hung to her mid-thigh and I had my Pitball jacket on over my favourite blue playsuit.

A small flutter of fear accompanied my excitement over the match. What would happen to Max when he broke out in a full body purple rash? How long would it take him to withdraw from the game? A twisted satisfaction filled me at the idea. To lose out on something that meant so much to him was the perfect way to get back at him, even if it was nothing in comparison to what he'd done to us. As much as I hated the Heirs though, I'd never drown someone for revenge. We weren't like them. But I was ready to see another one fall from grace.

"Hey Tory, if you need someone to help you through your sex addiction, PM me on FaeBook!" a guy hollered back at us followed by raucous laughter from his friends.

"My addiction only involves sex with attractive guys, so no thanks!" Tory yelled back, though her shoulders tensed and I scowled, knowing that this was getting to her deep down even if she did front it out like a pro.

"Ignore him," Diego said gently, glaring at the back of the guy's head.

Another of his friends turned around, walking backwards and pulling a gormless face at me. "Look she's talking to a raven again!" She pointed at Diego who glowered back at her.

I pursed my lips, glancing at Tory as we both mentally agreed we weren't going to rise to it. From the looks of them, they were seniors so we'd have no chance if we started throwing magic around.

One day suckers.

"Sorry Diego," I said but he just shrugged, seeming in a brighter mood today. I was glad; we all deserved to have some fun.

We filed into the huge arena and my anger fell away, awe swiftly taking its place. The shining silver dome above glittered like stars, twinkling with an array of lights which were directed down onto the pitch and stands. We were bumped and jostled along as students split away down the sloping seats, spreading out deeper into the huge space while another crowd filed in from the other end of the stadium. I squinted across the expansive pitch, figuring they must have been from Starlight Academy as they were dressed in red and white.

The pitch itself was nothing like any I'd ever seen. It was the shape of a football pitch but that was where the similarities ended. In each corner was a large bronze pyramid around five feet in height with a football-sized hole at its peak. In the four corners of the pitch, the turf was painted in the colours of the Elements; blue, green, red and white. At the very middle of it was a huge, circular bronze plate and dead centre of that was a large pit almost ten feet in width.

"How does this game work?" I asked Sofia over the clamour of noise.

She grinned excitedly at me which lifted the Z and A she'd painted on her cheeks. "I'll explain as it goes along."

"Miss Vega and Miss Vega! The two of you! Roxa- I mean Tory and Darcy!"

We turned, finding Principal Nova in a smart dress and a Pitball cap wading through the mass of students, smacking them on the heads with a rolled up programme as she forced her way through. "Move, move move." She struck someone every time she said the word then finally arrived in front of us with a flustered smile. "You both have Pitside seats reserved for you with the Celestial Councillors and other prestigious attendees."

"Thanks but no thanks," Tory said quickly.

"We'll stay with our friends." I gestured to Sofia and Diego and Nova glanced at them like they were a disappointment to her in every way.

"Oh...really?" Nova frowned. "Fine. Just bring them with you if you must." She ushered us along and Sofia let out a squeal of excitement as Nova led us down the steps all the way to the front row.

We filed alongside the pitch and I noticed a faint shimmer around the very edge of the grass. "What's that?" I pointed and Sofia immediately answered.

"It's a force-field to protect the crowd from any rogue magic which might fly our way."

"Oh that's comforting," Tory said, gazing up at the roof as she drank in the place.

The sound of the crowd was a constant buzz of excited chatter and I was totally infected by it as Nova led us to seats front and absolute centre of the pitch.

"This is amazing!" Diego whooped, slinging his arm around Sofia as they dropped into a couple of seats. We were about to sit beside them when Nova grabbed both of our arms and turned us to face the row above; it was cordoned off and covered by a dark glass shelter. Sat within it were the Celestial Councillors with fancy looking drinks in their hands. Seth's mom, Antonia, wore a Zodiac Academy cap and Max's dad, Tiberius, wore a jacket with Rigel stamped on the breast. Lionel and Catalina were the only ones who didn't wear any of the Pitball regalia and I was kind of surprised to see them there at all. What surprised me a little less was Lionel's butler standing two feet away with a tray of ice water and glasses. His expression was formal but his eyes kept whipping to the pitch and I wondered if he cared more about Darius's game than his parents did.

Nova announced our presence and they all looked to us, some with more enthusiasm than others. None less than Lionel. I was grateful when Nova's sharp talons released my arm and I could drop into my seat.

She moved further up the row, sitting beside a bald man in red and white Starlight colours who was waving a flag; I guessed he was the other Academy's principal.

Dramatic music filled the stands, a heavy drum pounding through the air to a quickening beat. My knees bobbed as the lights dimmed across the crowd, narrowing entirely onto the pitch.

The drumming grew louder and louder until it was all I could hear then spotlights fell onto the front centre of the pitch and the beat dropped to a familiar dance song.

A large group of Zodiac Academy cheerleaders appeared in tiny skirts and crop tops, waving their pom poms, doing cartwheels and flips. Heading the group was none other than Marguerite and I noticed Kylie and Jillian amongst their ranks of powdery make-up and big doll eyes.

I might have disliked them but damn their routine was impressive. Two girls shot up into the air almost fifty feet, propelled by air magic before tumbling back down in perfect synchronisation, ready to be caught by the waiting group below. They all lined up across the pitch and Marguerite cartwheeled past the line; every time she passed someone their pom-poms burst into blue and silver flames, eliciting a huge roar from the crowd. I found myself clapping and cheering along, unable to help it. They were dazzling, their magic making their routine almost unbelievable to watch.

They ended in a huge pyramid with Marguerite balancing atop it, one leg pulled above her head and her other hand firing colourful sparks into the air.

They headed off the pitch to booming applause from the Zodiac fans, and even Starlight Academy students clapped with enthusiasm.

The Starlight cheerleaders were next, rushing onto the pitch in a blur of red and white. The magic they used was tamer than the Zodiac team's, but their routine was just as slick, the girls hitting every mark. They ended it by casting a shower of sparks into the air that wrote out *Starlight* which flashed several times before scattering away on the wind.

The cheer squads returned to their seats at the edge of the pitch and the drums started up once more, announcing the beginning of the game. The tension in the stadium made me sit forward in my seat, snaring all of my senses at once. The scent of the turf, the excited murmuring of the crowd, the pressure in the air.

A fierce looking woman appeared on the opposite side of the pitch, leading the ten members of the Starlight team up from a passage that led under the stadium. She wore a black t-shirt with the four Elemental symbols printed on it in white.

The students of Zodiac Academy applauded but those from Starlight went wild, standing up and bashing their hands together, crying out to their team with pure energy.

My stomach clenched as Orion appeared in the underground passage and led our team out, wearing the same black kit as the other coach. His brow was taut but his expression was full of anticipation, his mouth set in a way that told me how much he adored being on that pitch.

My heart pattered wildly as I took in his biceps bulging against his shirt sleeves and the defined muscles of his legs.

I can't believe I kissed a teacher.

I can't believe I can't tell anyone.

I can't believe I'll never get to do it again.

I finally shifted my gaze to the ten Zodiac players behind him, all lining up opposite the Starlight team. The four Heirs were centrally placed and on either side of them I recognised Darius's friend, Damian Evergile, with his dark hair and harsh features, and the beautiful Ashanti from Seth's pack with her surname, Larue, printed across the back of her shirt.

The two Keepers were dressed completely in silver; one was the fair-haired Justin Masters from the A.S.S and the other was a tall girl with thin lips and the surname of Badgerville on her back. The final two members of the team were Geraldine who was playing the position of Earthbacker (whatever that meant) and someone called Jones who was in the position of Waterback.

"I'm confused already," I said, leaning in to speak to Sofia.

"*Well,*" she piped up excitedly. "There's ten players on a team, the two Pit Keepers guard the Pit from the opposing team to stop them getting any balls in. The easiest way to remember the other players is that there are two of each Element, one plays defence to keep the other team away from the ball, the other plays offence to get the ball into the pit. For example, there are two Earth players on every team. Our Earthbacker, Geraldine, is defence and Caleb is the offensive Earth player called an Earthraider."

"What's Darius?" Tory asked, leaning forward to speak to Sofia as she pointed him out at the centre of the team.

"He's defence for fire which is called a Fireshield. The fire offence is called a Fireside." She pointed. "Damian Evergile is playing but it's normally Milton Hubert." She gave us a look to say he must have been replaced and I bit my lip on a grin.

A female referee jogged out onto the pitch dressed in white with a large, metal ball under her arm.

Tory perked up. "Oh it's my Liaison, Professor Prestos."

Her legs were a deep tan beneath her shorts and as she turned to glance back at the crowd, weaving her fingers into her high ponytail I noticed how pretty she was.

"Do you even go to your Liaison classes?" I teased.

"We have an arrangement which works mainly via email. You should try it with Orion, see if he'll let you out of them," she said airily.

My mouth dried out at her words. "Oh well...he'd never let me." *And I don't want to stop them.*

"Maybe you should ask."

"Na," I said, waving her down and she shrugged, turning back to face the match.

Maybe I should try and get out of them though. How awkward is it gonna be when we're next alone in a room together? And how will I stop myself from thinking about that earth-shattering kiss?

Oh god. I'd better be ready to deal with that.

Orion and the Starlight coach shook hands and my gut writhed madly as they both spoke to their teams, clapped some of them on the back then jogged to join us in the sectioned off area of seats.

Orion's eyes fell on me for half a second before shooting in the opposite direction, leaving my stomach in shreds. He sat a few seats down with Nova and I relaxed a little, drawing in a deep breath.

Prestos moved between the two teams, standing in the middle of them and placing the ball down between them. The Pit was nearly twenty yards away beyond them and my fingers curled up as I wondered who was going to score first. Even though I hated the Heirs, I still kinda wanted to see our team win.

Come on Zodiac.

I kept an eye on Max, noticing him shifting foot to foot, rubbing the back of his neck then his stomach, his thigh. Seth was only a few feet away from him, his hair tied up in a bun and the word Airstriker in silver on his back above his surname. He kept lifting a hand to scratch his head then curled his fingers up and balled them at his sides, refusing to do it. Caleb was rubbing surreptitiously at his crotch which was glittering under the intense spotlights on the pitch. And Darius looked like he wasn't even slightly over his anger with Milton Hubert as he clenched his jaw so tightly he must have been in danger of cracking a tooth.

I descended into giggles, sharing a look with Tory as she fell apart too.

"Team Captains, step forward!" Prestos instructed and her voice rang out around the stadium from a microphone she must have been wearing.

A tense silence fell over the entire crowd and my whole body knotted with tension as Darius stepped up from Zodiac and a tall guy with a ripped body and deep green eyes stepped forward to meet him.

Prestos jogged back to the edge of the pit, lifting a whistle to her lips. A huge timer appeared high up above, glittering with magic as it readied to count down from five minutes- *was that all?*

Before I could ask Sofia for more information, Prestos's whistle screeched and Darius swung a fist right into the Starlight Captain's face. As he lurched sideways I saw the name Quentin on the back of his shirt alongside the position of Earthraider.

"Oh my god," I gasped as Darius lunged to pick up the ball, only to receive a knee right to his chin. Darius was ready, lurching back and throwing a kick while the entire stadium bellowed in encouragement.

Quentin took the blow to the stomach, stumbling away and Darius grabbed the ball which looked pretty damn heavy. The second he had it, the two teams charged forward. Geraldine roared like she was going into battle, magically tearing up the ground beneath the feet of the Starlight team so they stumbled wildly, unable to get their hands on Darius. He made a beeline for the Pit as the four Keepers grouped in around it.

"Go on!" Orion roared from my right, rising to his feet as more and more people stood up all around us.

Darius was charging along, devouring the ground between him and the Pit. He was going to make it. He was right out ahead and the rest of the Zodiac defence were bringing Starlight's team members to the ground with fierce tackles, blasts of fire, gusts of air-

A vine whipped out and caught Darius by the leg and as he fell, he turned, launching the ball into the sky with all his might. He sent a blast of fire out to propel it forward, sending it cascading down toward the two teams like a meteor on a collision course.

Seth jumped high above the two teams with a propulsion of air, but the Starlight Airstriker had the same idea, flying up beside him. They smashed into one another, hitting the ground hard and Seth started throwing wild punches at him without hesitation. He jammed his knee into his chest and held him in place.

"You're out, Cubin!" Prestos shouted and her voice resounded throughout the whole stadium.

The Starlight Airstriker hobbled off the pitch to a bench where a row of substitute team members were sitting.

My eyes whipped back to the match and Starlight's Earthbacker now had the ball, racing for the Pit at the centre.

Max tried to knock her aside with a blast of water, but stumbled to a halt before he could cast it well enough, clasping onto his neck and rubbing like mad. "Ahhh it burns!"

Tory and I fell apart into laughter as I noticed his skin was turning blotchy with violent purple patches. "Ahhhh!"

"Rigel! What the fuck is going on?" Orion bellowed just as a blaring BUZZZZZZZ announced Starlight getting the ball into the Pit.

A scoreboard lit up above the stands, showing Starlight had scored one point but then words in red flashed beside it.

Cubin OUT = -1 point.

The scores returned to zero and the Starlight crowd groaned collectively.

The clock reset to five minutes and the teams split up so they were scattered between the four Elemental corners with the Keepers still ringing the Pit.

"What happens now?" I asked Sofia.

"Now it's round two. Every round lasts five minutes. After an hour, it'll be half time then they play for a final hour. Just watch, it's about to get seriously intense." She pointed to the four corners of the pitch. "There's only one ball in play per round, it'll be fired into the pitch randomly from the four Elemental Quarters. A Fireball is scorching hot, an Earthball is seriously heavy, an Airball is light and will be shot far up toward the roof and a Waterball is freezing to touch. If no one gets the ball in the Pit before the five minutes are up – *boom!*" She mimed an explosion with her hands and my mouth fell open.

"Holy shit," Tory breathed and I nodded in absolute agreement of that.

"If the ball is dropped at any point in the game, including just before it explodes, the team loses five points. So everyone on that pitch is prepared for the injuries they'll get if it goes off," Sofia explained.

"That's insane," I breathed.

"Nope." Diego leaned forward from his chair with a manic gleam in his eyes. "That's Pitball."

MAX

CHAPTER TWENTY-NINE

I bounced from foot to foot as Prestos lifted the whistle to her lips and the second round was about to begin. I eyed the other team's Waterguard as I prepared to block her moves. She was big for a girl but I still had at least sixty pounds on her and I'd be using that advantage to tackle her if the ball shot out of the Water Hole in our Quarter.

The whistle blasted and the ball shot from the Air Hole instead, racing up towards the silver dome overhead as Seth leapt after it, propelling himself higher with air magic.

I started running as fast as I could, the Starlight Waterback keeping pace for a while until I threw an elbow into her face and sent her rolling through the mud behind me.

I had my sights on the ball but as I ran, the material of my shorts was bunching between my legs and I suddenly doubled over as the burning raced over my balls.

"What the fuck are you doing Rigel?!" Orion yelled from the side of the pitch but I was near blinded from the burning pain in my left testicle.

I howled like a newborn baby for a moment before regaining the clarity of mind to draw on my water magic and flood my shorts to wash the burn away. It looked like I'd just pissed myself but it helped. As a moment of relief came for me, I swept the water over my entire body and sighed in satisfaction. It hadn't completely doused the flames across my skin but it had definitely taken the edge off.

I looked up to see Caleb sprinting down the midfield with the lightweight Airball beneath his arm and a determined snarl on his face. The Starlight players were racing to intercept him but even without his Vampire speed, which he couldn't use in the game, the boy was born fast.

"Take it home Cal!" I bellowed, throwing my arms out as I shot a jet of water at the Starlight Pit Keeper closest to him as she made the mistake of stepping out of the no-magic zone around the Pit.

Heavy footsteps announced the arrival of the Starlight Waterback three seconds before she tackled me and I grunted as she threw her shoulder into my stomach, driving the air from my lungs.

I stepped back to brace myself but my foot slid in the mud of my own damn puddle which I'd created while trying to stifle the burn.

My boot twisted beneath me, her weight dislodging me instantly and I went down hard beneath her.

I had every intention to throw her off of me with a blast of air but as my back was pressed firmly to the ground, the burning erupted across my flesh once more and I yelled out as stars burst before my eyes. I couldn't concentrate on my magic and for an achingly long moment she held me pinned to the mud.

A whistle blew and then the most horrifying words sounded. "Rigel! You're Out!"

The Waterback was gone before I even made it back to my feet and I cursed loudly as I clawed my way upright, flooding my skin with water again in an attempt to stop the fire which was licking across my skin.

I looked back just in time to see Caleb slam the ball home but with the point we'd lost for me getting knocked out, it still left us in a draw with no points scored.

My ass hit the bench as I was forced to sit out a second round before I could return to the game but I yelped the moment it did, lurching upright again as the pressure caused my ass cheeks to burn with hell fire.

A dark shadow shot towards me from my left and before I could blink, Orion was in my face.

"What the hell are you playing at out there?" he snarled, snatching hold of the front of my shirt and pulling me nose to nose with him.

"Ah, shit!" I cried as his grip increased the burning along my back. "Someone's done something to my goddamn kit!"

I lifted my shirt to show him the purple welts which lined my skin and his eyes narrowed as he looked me over before reaching out to heal me.

Green light slid from his palm as he pressed it to my stomach but it was no good, the burning persisted.

Orion hissed between his teeth as he pulled his hand back and quickly washed it off with a blast of his own water magic.

"You stink," he said as he shook his hand out. "That's Griffin shit."

"What?!" I cried. No wonder I was burning up, that stuff was practically toxic. "Those Starlight assholes must have sabotaged me!"

"Well unless you can prove that you can't start throwing around accusations. The only cure for that rash is bathing in a potion which you'll need to get from Uranus Infirmary. I'm pulling you from the game-"

"No," I snarled before he could make the call official. "My father came to watch me play." My gaze slid to the stands where my dad's eyes were on me, filled with concern. Behind him, my step mother watched too and though she hid it from the world, I could see the pleasure she was taking in seeing me fail. I couldn't let that stand.

"If you're going to keep playing then you need to suck it up," Orion demanded. "Head in the game, work through the pain." His favourite catch phrase had never seemed so literal.

"I'm in," I growled, forcing my thoughts away from the constant burn.

I looked back at the pitch just in time to see an inflatable Pegasus sex toy floating over the Starlight crowd with Caleb's name scrawled along its side and an arrow pointing at its open ass.

Cal noticed it too and he fumbled his throw, his aim way off as he passed the ball to Darius who dove forward to try and save it. His fingertips brushed it but the Starlight Airsentry threw a gust of wind at the ball and it fell to the ground with a wet thump.

My lips parted with horror as the scoreboard lit up with a -5 score to Zodiac and the Starlight crowd went wild.

Darius snatched the ball back up and managed to hook it to Seth who slammed it into the Pit but that only brought us up to -4.

"What the fuck is happening?" Orion murmured in disbelief.

My time out of the game was up so I raced back onto the pitch to await the next ball without another word. I moved from foot to foot, trying to ignore the burning agony which had now firmly found its way between my ass cheeks.

The whistle sounded, a flaming ball burst from the Fire Hole and once again the game was on. I just had to force my way through it until the end.

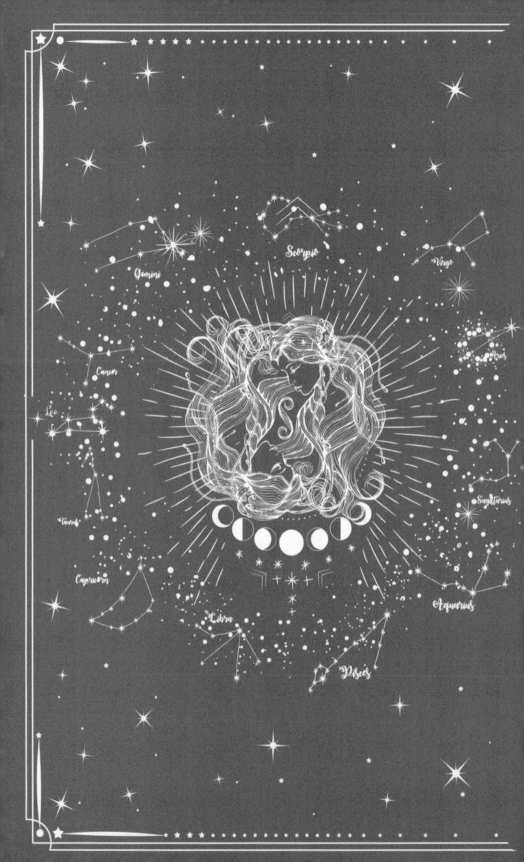

TORY

CHAPTER THIRTY

I watched the game with wide eyes and laughter bubbling in my throat. As if watching the Heirs completely fall apart wasn't enough to make my day, I had a front row seat to Lionel Acrux and the rest of the Celestial Council falling prey to humiliation too. It was just too damn good. Too damn poetic.

Ah sweet justice.

And even though this mild form of torture only really came down to embarrassment, it still went a good way to making me feel powerful again. After what they'd put me and Darcy through, this was the very least of what these jerk-offs deserved and I hoped they were enjoying the dish of karma they were tasting.

Laughter fell from Darcy's lips and I followed her gaze to see Seth scratching at his ass like he'd lost a ferret up there. I couldn't help but burst out laughing too and I could feel the death stares it was earning me from the Councillors in response. Their faces were the perfect masks of the well-to-do proud parents they were embodying here today but the tension in their posture told the true story. They were mortified by the display that was being put on here. Reputation was everything to people like them and right before a whole swathe of cameramen and reporters, their precious Heirs were losing the plot.

Swift footsteps drew my attention to the row behind me and I turned my head from the game for a moment to see Washer squeezing between the crowd, calling Principal Nova's name.

The Principal turned irritably as he reached her and he shouted to be heard over the crowd, allowing his words to carry to me.

"The cards gave me a vision, Headmistress!" he said urgently, the usual lecherous tone to his voice missing for once as his eyes bulged, revealing way too much of the whites.

I elbowed Darcy to draw her attention to him and she tilted her head to listen too.

"Not now, Washer," Nova said, trying to wave him off as the Starlight Academy Principal looked around curiously.

"But there was terror and fire and death!" Washer insisted, his voice trembling on the last word. "It isn't safe here, this place has been marked-"

"Trying to find a way to forfeit the game?" The Starlight Academy Principal mocked as Nova's brows dipped with concern. "Just because you can see that Starlight is going to win?"

Washer's eyes were wild with fear but Nova's cheeks flared at the implication from the other Principal. "Certainly not," she snapped. "No other predictions have been made like this about today and let's be honest, you have made very inaccurate predictions in the past, haven't you Professor Washer? Remember the time you were convinced your nephew was going to be eaten by a Nemean Lion on his birthday?"

"That was different," Washer implored.

"Or the time you told Professor Perseus he was going to catch the Faeonic Plague? He wouldn't come to work for a week!"

"I know but-"

"I will discuss this with you *after* the match has concluded, Professor Washer," she said firmly.

"But I-"

"Enough, I'll have no further distractions from the game," she commanded.

Washer backed up like she'd struck him and his gaze landed on my sister and I as he started to move away. Before the crowd could swallow him, he mouthed one, single word to us, sending a shiver tracking down my spine.

Run.

I exchanged a loaded glance with Darcy. "Do you think he really does know something?" I breathed, looking around for some sign that something was about to go horribly wrong here.

"I don't know," she said slowly. "But it sounds like he often makes wrong predictions."

I shrugged at her. We both knew I was the more skeptical of the two of us and if Nova didn't feel the immediate need to flee then maybe there was nothing to worry about. What were the chances of something happening while we were surrounded by so many people anyway?

Before I could give it too much thought, my attention snagged on Darius as he charged across the pitch like a stampeding rhino, tackling a member of the other team so hard that I heard something crack.

My breath caught in my throat as the Starlight player groaned on the ground while Darius snatched the ball from him and launched it across the pitch with the force of a torpedo.

A timer was counting down as the Starlight player failed to get up and Darius raced away from him without a backwards glance. I knew it was part of the game but it was insanely brutal. Although if I was being totally honest, watching all of them brawl like that and seeing the power they exuded even while they were losing, was totally hot too.

Darius's muscles pumped fiercely as he sprinted away from me and I found myself staring at his legs which were splattered with mud and somehow looked even better because of it.

"Olef you're Out!" Prestos yelled but the Starlight player still didn't move. A pair of medics jogged onto the pitch and gave him a quick inspection.

"Broken back!" one of them yelled. "This is a long heal, call in a sub once his time out is up."

My lips parted, I stared on in shock and I couldn't quite believe what I'd heard.

"Did he just say that Darius broke that guy's back?" I asked in disbelief.

"That's the risk you take when you play," Orion said darkly as he walked past me to regain his seat.

Darcy raised her eyebrows at me and I returned my gaze to the match just as Geraldine tore up the pitch with a rumble of writhing earth magic, knocking the Starlight Waterguard off of her feet and forcing her to drop the ball. A huge -5 flashed into place on the Starlight scoreboard and I leapt from my seat in excitement to applaud my friend.

"Go Geraldine!" I screamed and she flashed me a smile as she somehow managed to hear me.

Seth almost missed the ball as it was thrown to him next while he was distracted by scratching his head. He managed to wrangle it with a gust of air magic and started sprinting for the Pit as the timer above us ticked down to ten seconds.

The crowd started counting down, "Nine! Eight! Seven-"

Seth leapt into the air, propelling himself forward with his magic but the two air Elementals on the opposing team threw their own magic up to counter him.

"Three! Two-"

Seth gritted his teeth as he threw even more power into his propulsion but he was out of time.

The ball in his arms exploded in a blast of pure air which snapped his head back and sent him tumbling out of the sky. He hit the ground hard as the crowd *ooohed* in disappointment. For three whole seconds my heart didn't beat at all as I stared at his prone body in the mud, wondering if he was dead.

Seth coughed, pushing himself into a sitting position just as Darius appeared to offer him a hand up. He shook his head to clear it and my eyebrows rose all the way into my hairline.

"This game is crazy," Darcy breathed, her eyes wide with the thrill of it.

"I think I love it," I agreed.

ORION

CHAPTER THIRTY ONE

"**W**hat the fuck is going on out there?!" I roared, pure fury dripping through my body like melted plastic.

It was half time and the team were sitting on a bench before me in the locker room, looking defeated already. Caleb hid his face in his hands while the other three Heirs tried to comfort him after the chants of 'Did you get a BJ from a horsey? Did you get a horn stuck up your ass?' had chased him out of the stadium.

Max was patting his lumpy, purple skin and Seth kept scratching his head and frankly, they were falling the shitting hell apart.

No one answered me. Real surprising.

"Starlight Academy are a second rate team. You are *elite*. Your parents don't pour their not-so-hard-earned money into this place for no reason!"

Silence.

"ANSWER ME!" I bellowed.

Geraldine Grus trembled as she stared up at me. "Suffering sausages,

Coach. We'll do better, I'm sure we can if we all-"

"Quiet," I commanded and she nodded obediently. I pointed at her. "*You* are the only player out there working your ass off. And you're supposed to be playing defence not scoring Pits." I glared at the other team members. "Grus is picking up all of your slack out there. If you don't win this match, you'll be starting the season at the bottom of the league and the matches only get harder from here. You were lucky to draw Starlight so early, this match should be child's play!"

I looked to the Heirs again, my jaw tightening as Max groaned, pawing at his body and Caleb still didn't look up as Seth rested a hand on his shoulder. Darius was glaring at the far wall like it had taken a shit on his dinner plate.

"You four. Up. Now," I ordered.

They moved toward me, dragging their heels and I shook my head at their morose display.

I jabbed Caleb under his chin, forcing him to look at me. "Altair, fuck what the crowd thinks. I don't care if you're into bondage with leprechauns, leave that shit off the pitch, you got it?"

He took a heavy breath then nodded. "Got it," he said with a little more enthusiasm.

"Rigel." I snapped my fingers at Max and he stepped closer, lifting up his shirt to show me the raised purple rash now covering almost all of his body.

"Hell, it's getting worse." I released a low whistle.

"Healing it doesn't work," he moaned. "I need to go to Uranus Infirmary-"

The rest of the team started laughing and I shot them a glare to silence them as Max hung his head.

"Well it's your call. I can sub you for someone else," I said, cupping the back of his neck to make him look me in the eye. "But so help me Rigel, if you choose to stay and you play like the turd on strings I've just witnessed for the first half, I will make sure this rash lasts the rest of the damn term, understand?"

"Yes, sir. I want to play on," he muttered and I released him, snatching Seth by the collar and yanking him closer. I was maybe one percent rougher with him than the others. But he had cut off Blue's hair and I just couldn't fucking forgive it. End of story.

I fisted my hand around his man bun, pressing my forehead to his. "Do we have a problem, Capella?"

"No," he gritted out.

"Then why are you scratching every corner, every nook, every damn orifice of your body in front of four thousand people?" A vein was popping somewhere in my temple and my heart was slamming itself against my ribcage with such vigour it was a genuine concern. Maybe I needed this win more than they did. Maybe they weren't driven with all the desperate passion of a guy who'd lost his chance to play for the Solarian Pitball League. But so help me, in all the years I'd either played for or coached the Zodiac Academy Pitball Team, we had never come last in a tournament. So we weren't going to start this year.

"I've got fleas!" Seth lamented and I shoved him away from me on instinct. He sank down to his knees and clung onto my legs, seemingly in the midst of a nervous breakdown. "My pack won't sleep with me or run with me or spend any time with me and I'm not meant to be alone. And it itches so much, Professor!" He stared up at me in desperation and I scowled down at him, shaking him off of my legs. *This is pitiful.*

"Get up. Try and bring your dignity with you. Every Werewolf in the Academy is getting flea dipped next week. So until then, suck it up. I'll give you the same choice I gave Rigel. Are you in or are you out?"

He glanced at his friends, seeming to draw strength from them. "I'm in," he sighed. "I'll do better."

"Good." I smacked him overly hard on the shoulder so he stumbled forward and I tried not to acknowledge the fact that that had anything to do with Darcy. Because it didn't, dammit.

"Darius." I beckoned him and he moved toward me, splattered with mud as dark as the scowl on his face.

"What's gotten into your head?" I asked, softer than I was with the others.

He shrugged his huge shoulders and I raised an eyebrow, waiting for him to drop the act.

"It's fucking Milton Hubert," he snapped. "He was the one who broke into my room, stole my shit and burned my goddamn room down. He was supposed to be my friend."

By the stars, could all of these issues have occurred at a worse time?

I sighed heavily. "Are you sure?" It hit me suddenly that if Hubert had done that, he might have the draining dagger we'd been looking for. But I'd searched all of the students rooms...where would he have hidden it? - *shit I can't think about this right now.*

"Yeah," Darius snarled. "I'm sure. The guy had the gall to wear one of the gold rings in front of me."

"That seems moronic," I commented.

"He's not exactly the brightest spark." Darius shrugged though his teeth were still clenched hard.

"Alright." I rested a hand on his shoulder. "I need you to put this aside for the last half. Then if you want to, you can go full Dragon asshole on him later. I'll even bring a flame thrower and help you do it to make sure we get back *every* item he stole. But your friends need you on point right now. Look at them." I gestured to Seth who was sticking wet toilet tissue to Max's rash as if that would be any help at all and Caleb who was wiping at the glitter which was still stuck to his crotch no matter what magic he used to try and remove it. It was pathetic.

"They need you, man." I shook Darius a little and he nodded, seeming to see that at last. He moved to join his friends and they looked up hopefully as he arrived.

"Right team." I clapped my hands to get their attention. "Go out there and destroy Starlight Academy like you were made to do. You were trained by the best, so be the best." I gazed across the lot of them as they lined up. The Heirs pulled ranks, clapping each other on the shoulders but some of them still looked miserable.

A familiar chant carried from the crowd back in the stadium and hope burned through my chest. *Perfect timing!*

"You can't scare the Heirs, the Heirs don't care. You can't scare the Heirs, the Heirs don't care!"

The rest of the team took up the chant, grouping together and locking their arms over their shoulders in a circle, though I noticed Ashanti Larue kept her distance from Seth. The Heirs soon joined in, jumping up and down and pumping their fists.

I folded my arms, grinning as I watched. The funny thing was, that chant was the biggest lie I'd ever heard. Because I'd never, in all the years I'd known them, seen the Celestial Heirs look so rattled.

DARIUS

CHAPTER THIRTY TWO

As half time finished, we grouped together and prowled back out onto the pitch like we were the kings of the goddamn world. Rage still coiled in my gut, hot and bitter but I couldn't let it rule me again; I had to channel it into this match.

We were eighteen points down. *Eighteen!* I didn't think we'd ever come into a second half at such a disadvantage before. Hell, I wasn't sure we'd ever come into a second half at a disadvantage at all.

The other team were already back on the pitch. There was still ten minutes to go before the second half was due to start and they were spending that time riling up the crowd.

To my right, the Starlight students were still bellowing a song about Cal hooking up with a Pegasus and I gritted my teeth as I looked towards my friend.

The moment of weakness he'd caved to in the locker room had given way to cold, hard fury and he glared up at the Starlight stands with venom in his gaze. There were now four huge blow-up Pegasus sex dolls drifting back and forth amongst them, and my scowl deepened as I spotted my own name scrawled across one of them with Seth and Max's on the other two.

The Zodiac crowd roared yet another chorus of 'The Heirs don't care!' and I wished in that moment that it was the goddamn truth. I'd never really experienced this kind of mocking before. Sure, we'd all had more than one scandalous or scathing story printed about us but we'd never had to stand and listen to this kind of abuse before.

It occurred to me that I'd inflicted this kind of humiliation on people countless times and for half a second, my mind snagged on the Vega Twins and the way they'd looked after Lance had pulled Roxy from that pool. But this wasn't the same. I'd *had* to do that. It was for the good of Solaria and I stamped down the little voice in my head which was trying to question that fact with a vengeance.

I turned to look at my teammates but my eyes were really on the other Heirs as I spoke.

"How is your power doing? We need to smash them with our magic this half," I said, reaching into my core to assess mine. Despite the fact that I'd been using magic since the start of the game, the well of power within me still burned fiercely, especially after sitting with the bag of gold I'd brought to the locker rooms for most of half time.

"I'm three quarters full," Seth announced. His hands were fisted at his sides as he fought against the urge to scratch again. He was the only one of us who couldn't replenish his magic during the halftime allowance due to his need for a run beneath the moon to do it but he always held back on using too much in the first half for just this reason.

"I'll go and get my fix now," Max announced, striding away towards the Starlight cheer squad as he fought a grimace at the pain of his purple flesh.

"I should top up too," Caleb added, his gaze drifting over to the edge of the pitch where the Vegas were standing by their seats, talking to their friends.

He didn't actually move though and I got the feeling that he didn't want Roxy to see him shaken.

"Come on, let's show these Starlight assholes who they're dealing with. You've got fucking royalty for a Source," I urged, clapping a hand on his shoulder and guiding him towards them. Orion had already gone ahead of us and was just slipping through the forcefield to take his seat close to the twins. His shoulders were tight with tension and his jaw locked as he glared straight ahead.

We prowled across the pitch and Roxy looked around as she saw us coming. She pursed her full lips but didn't show any other sign that our arrival bothered her. I gritted my teeth, wishing she'd just flinch so that my father and the other Councillors could see that they were afraid of us at the very least but of course she didn't. Her sister stood beside her and the look of disdain directed our way sent a wave of anger through me. Who the hell did these girls think they were?

To make matters worse, the Starlight Captain, Quentin, got to them before we could and he offered them a teasing bow and a smile which made me want to knock his teeth out. Which I intended to do as soon as the second half started. The girls both laughed at something he said, smiling like he was the funniest fucking dipshit they'd ever met.

Roxy's dark eyes moved to mine and I felt a lurch right in the centre of my gut for a half a second as it seemed almost like she was directing that smile at me. She'd made a dress out of an oversized Pitball shirt which skimmed her thighs and made her look like she'd just crawled out of my bed and pulled it on. The idea of that excited me way more than it should have but as she turned to whisper something to her sister, I saw the name printed across the back of her shirt wasn't Acrux, it was Grus.

Of course it is. Stop thinking with your dick and get your head back in the game!

The Starlight Captain noticed us approaching and made himself scarce

485

but I noted the lingering looks the twins gave him as he jogged away.

"Enjoying the game, sweetheart?" Caleb asked as we drew close enough to speak with them. I didn't miss the way Roxy's eyes trailed over him and the fact that there was considerably less hatred in her gaze when she looked his way than what she directed at me. I guessed he hadn't half drowned her but it still pissed me off.

"We are," she admitted with a wide smile. "Isn't Geraldine amazing?"

"Yeah she's the fucking cat's pyjamas," I growled, wishing I could actually aim an insult the Cerberus's way but that girl was single handedly saving our asses from total annihilation at this point so I couldn't even pretend to do it. Without her we would have been royally screwed.

"Maybe she should be the Captain," Gwendalina suggested with a taunting smile.

"Maybe she should," Lance agreed loudly and I scowled at my friend. There was no way he'd offer me any loyalty when it came to Pitball. If I wasn't the best then he'd say it to my face. I just wished he'd hold his opinion back in front of the Vegas.

"I just need a quick top up," Caleb said and Roxy didn't even fucking flinch at that. She sighed like him biting her was a goddamn inconvenience and pulled her long hair over her shoulder to offer him access to her neck.

"You'd better hurry up," she added. "Only two minutes of half time left."

I glanced around at the board to confirm what she'd said and by the time I looked back, Caleb had her in his arms and his teeth were in her throat.

She didn't even have the decency to look horrified, her fingers twisting into his hair as he held her in place. His fucking hand was on her thigh, skimming the hem of that shirt and for a moment I actually wanted to rip his arm off.

I shook my head and turned away from them. This anger with Milton was spilling into everything I did today. I just couldn't believe that he'd done such a thing to me. He was one of my most loyal followers, I'd never even sensed an inch of defiance in him let alone a betrayal of this magnitude and I couldn't get it out of my head. If I couldn't trust someone as devoted as him then who the hell *could* I trust?

My gaze skimmed over the box above the twins where my parents were sitting but I didn't let it linger there. If I saw the look of frustration and disappointment I knew would be on my father's face then I really would lose the plot.

Caleb released Roxy, leaning close to whisper something in her ear which made her fucking laugh while I ground my teeth. He spared a moment to heal the bite on her neck and we turned back to the pitch.

"I hope you do better this half!" Gwen called after us.

"You can't do any worse, right?" Roxy added and I clenched my fists to stop myself from rounding on them.

Max was approaching from the other side of the pitch, jittery with the excited energy he'd just drained from the Starlight cheer squad who were now all cheering in a less than enthusiastic way. A dark smile filled my face at the sight of that and I imagined the Starlight fans hadn't loved watching their cheer squad paw at our Waterguard while he drained all of the pep from them.

The team lined up on either side of me as the final minute started counting down and Prestos appeared with a metal Starter Ball.

Quentin stood opposite me and I snarled in his smirking face. I'd happily teach him a lesson in why we were destined to rule over Solaria and he was headed toward a middle ranking position in some backwater town.

The crowd were counting down the seconds but I blocked them out, my whole world zeroing in on the Team Captain opposite me. He tried to hold my gaze but his smirk slipped and his eyes flickered with concern a moment before the whistle blew.

I bellowed as I charged straight towards him, wrapping my fist in ice half a beat before slamming it into his face. Teeth met with my knuckles and he was thrown back into the mud to a huge *ooooh* from the crowd.

I snatched the twenty pound ball into my arms and started running, throwing fire magic out in an arc before me as I sprinted straight for the Pit.

Every member of the opposing team leapt into my path but I battered them aside with the strength of my charge and the heat of my fire.

The two Starlight Pit Keepers were waiting for me as I made it to the bronze plate surrounding the Pit and my magic spluttered out as I crossed the no-magic zone. I was running with the charge of a stampeding elephant though and they didn't stand a chance as I collided with them, knocking one of them to the floor on my left and knocking the other straight back into the Pit just as I slammed the ball down on top of him.

I turned back to the Zodiac crowd, pumping my fist triumphantly as they went wild.

To add to my victory Prestos yelled, "Parker, you're Out!", as the Pit Keeper I'd knocked into the Pit failed to get himself back out of it in time.

We were two points up already and I was determined to claw back every point we needed plus some. I wasn't going to lose this fucking match.

The next round started up immediately and I grinned as the flaming ball shot out of the hole in my zone. Damian, our backup Fireside who'd taken Milton's place when I banned him from playing, raced forward to grab the ball and I charged at the two fire players from Starlight.

Their Fireshield tried to intercept me but I slammed into her full-force, knocking her to her ass in the mud. Their Waterback shot Damian with a blast of water and the ball was thrown from his arms before being snatched by their Earthraider Quentin.

Seth was sprinting into position ahead of me close to the Pit and Max made it to my side as we charged towards the ball.

A wave of earth magic tore across the ground before us, throwing Max into me and sending us both crashing to the ground. Max screamed as the pressure of my weight on him increased the burning in his skin. *These Starlight assholes are going to pay for sabotaging him like this!*

Lance was bellowing obscenities at me and I leapt to my feet, racing after the ball again but it was too late. Starlight scored and to make matters worse, Prestos announced Max Out again.

My lips parted in horror as he hobbled away and I scrambled back to the Fire Quarter in anticipation of the next ball.

Typically the ice ball shot out of the Water Hole where we were one player down. Our Waterback was instantly tackled by their Waterguard who pinned her to the ground long enough to knock her Out. Meanwhile their Waterback managed to surround herself with their Airsentry and Earthbacker as she raced for the Pit.

I threw a blast of fire at them, knocking all three to their asses but somehow the Waterback managed to hook the ball into the hands of their Fireside as she fell and he slammed the ball home in the next breath.

I shook my head, unable to believe what was happening as we resumed our positions and my rage built into a tangible thing.

The next ball shot out of the Air Hole but Seth was scratching his damn ass and missed the play. Caleb ran to intercept Starlight's Airstriker who instantly started glowing a sparkling yellow as he ran.

"Look he's after some Pegasus ass again!" someone shouted.

The Starlight crowd started up a new chant at Cal's expense. *Altair loves Pegasex! He's horny for the horn!* Over and over the words came from the crowd and Caleb stumbled as it got to him, missing his chance to tackle the Airstriker and giving him the opportunity to score again.

My heart was pounding out of rhythm, I was losing a grip on my anger and I was filled with the awful fucking possibility that we might actually lose this game.

DARCY

CHAPTER THIRTY THREE

As we drew closer to the end of the match, Zodiac had managed to claw their way closer to evening the score though they still had a way to go if they wanted to win.

Geraldine used a sea of vines to throw a ball over the heads of the Starlight Pit Keepers. She skidded through their defences, entering the no-magic zone and caught the ball out of the air to a chorus of cheers. I was off my seat, yelling for her to score the point with adrenaline surging and she threw it into the Pit to a deafening cheer.

The round ended with Starlight with ten points and Zodiac with five. The final round was about to start, but Orion called for a huddle, drawing the soaked, muddy, distressed looking team to the edge of the pitch. I strained my ears as they grouped around him in a crescent. My gut tugged a little as Max rubbed at his sore arms, purple welts beginning to rise there. I didn't want to feel bad, but I couldn't help it as he groaned in pain. I'd thought that he'd quit the game to go get help, but he was persevering through his agony and it made me feel like crap.

He deserves this, dammit.

Geraldine had a fire in her eyes but she looked exhausted, her kit smothered in mud and bruises shining on her arms. Sofia had mentioned the players weren't allowed to replenish their magic during a game aside from half time so every ounce they had had to be saved for tactics on the pitch.

Orion gave them a tense look. "We're five points down, you know what that means."

They all nodded.

"Do what you've gotta do to win. I believe in you," Orion spoke mostly to Darius then grouped the ten of them together in a circle, starting up a chant that bled into the Zodiac audience until the entire stadium shook with the ferocity of it.

"Zodiac will not be beat! Zodiac can take the heat!"

It was so catchy that I was soon joining in and a band far up in the stands took up the tune too. Nearly every single student, professor or parent there to support our school clapped in time with the rhythm. It was an ear-splitting cacophony which drowned out the cheers of Starlight and it was the first time I'd ever witnessed Fae being so united in one cause.

My heart pounded in time with the tune as the Zodiac team raised their arms in the air, jogging back onto the pitch. Orion hovered at the edge of the turf, his head tipped low and his hands stuffed in his pockets. His shoulders were like a wall of tension and his jaw was set in stone.

"Come on Zodiac," I whispered, looking to Tory.

"I hate the Heirs but I kinda want our school to win," she said, echoing my thoughts.

"Plus Geraldine will be a hero after this if they pull it off," I said excitedly.

"It's about to get brutal," Sofia said seriously as if the entire game hadn't been one long, violent brawl. "The only way Zodiac can win or draw is if

Starlight get minus five points or more. So they have to get the opposition to drop the ball or get six of their team struck Out of the round."

"Shit on a brick," Tory breathed, curling her hands into fists on her knees.

I chewed on my lip desperately as I looked across to where the two teams were moving into their Elemental Quarters. Seth's eyes were set on the Starlight Airsentry, Olef, while his hands curled up, forcing himself not to scratch. Max swung his head side to side but kept his hands away from his burning skin too. Darius looked like he was about to murder someone and the way his eyes were set on Quentin, I suspected he was going to tackle him the second the whistle blew.

Geraldine dug her heels into the ground like a bull about to charge and I pitied anyone on the Starlight team who was about to face the wrath of Zodiac.

The whistle peeled through the air and a ball burst out of the Fire Hole, blazing through the atmosphere in a burning trail of fire, glowing red hot. Starlight charged toward it, their Waterback shooting a blast of liquid up to cool the ball before it was caught skillfully by the Fireside.

The four Heirs ate up the ground, speeding ahead and plowing into four of the Starlight team, trying to take them to the ground as fast as they could.

The ball was tossed to their Airstriker who blazed a trail toward the Pit.

"No!" I yelled, my heart tumbling in my chest as he cast a powerful gust of air at the Zodiac Keepers.

The Badgerville girl was blown aside but Justin stood his ground, teeth clenched as he sent a fiery blaze back at the air Elemental. Damian Evergile slammed into the Airstriker at the same moment, snatching the ball and running for the opposite end of the pitch.

"What's he doing?" Tory gasped.

"They can't Pit the ball!" Sofia cried over the roaring noise. "The round will end and one point isn't enough to win the match."

Three of the Starlight team chased after Damian at high speed while the

Heirs and Geraldine tried to wrestle five of the opposition to the ground.

"Benson, Tulissa, Quentin, you're out!" Prestos announced and Zodiac cheered wildly as Max, Darius and Seth stood up to let them go. Only Tulissa walked herself off the pitch while the other two were carried away on stretchers.

"Oh my god," I breathed, completely stunned by the brutality playing out before me.

The guy Geraldine was trying to force to the ground kept throwing heavy punches at her, forcing her back and I winced every time she took a hit. Darius sprinted forward to help followed closely by Caleb and they dove on top of Geraldine to hold the Starlight player down.

Prestos's whistle blew shrilly and my eardrums nearly burst with the noise that sounded from the Zodiac crowd. "Avery you're out!"

Four of Starlight were Out. They only had six members left in play, but they were working their assess off to get the ball from Damian who was circling the pitch as fast as he could. He looked exhausted and as he ran past Caleb, he tossed him the ball. Caleb let out a burst of speed, racing away from the three members of Starlight who were still in hot pursuit.

Darius and Seth charged toward their Keepers, seeking out easier prey while Caleb distracted the remainder of their team. The two of them fled, leaving the goal wide open, but they clearly knew the tactic Zodiac were playing. Our team didn't want to Pit the ball, they wanted to force two more Starlight players out of the game to secure their win.

The Keepers were fast and I wondered if this was a tactic they were well accustomed to in the final round. Darius and Seth were like predators chasing down gazelle, their eyes set on the slowest of the two players. They collided with her full force and a horrible snapping noise filled the air as they took her to the ground. She lay eerily still and when a few seconds passed, Prestos's whistle blew. "Ling, you're out!"

The boys got off of her and two medics raced onto the pitch with a stretcher to peel her off of the ground. *Oh shit.*

"It's a draw," Diego gasped. That was five players out. There was no way Starlight could bring it back so close to the end of the round. The clock was counting down ten seconds and the entire school roared as Caleb raced for the Pit.

"We can still win!" Sofia screamed as Caleb tore toward it, a victorious grin pulling at his mouth.

No one saw the Starlight Airsentry coming. He forced a blast into Caleb's side that sent him crashing into the mud, his arm twisting awkwardly beneath him. He fell on top of him, snatched the ball and tossed it into the Pit with a yell of exertion.

A collective gasp of absolute horror dragged in around me.

Starlight Academy went completely crazy as the timer hit zero and the scoreboard flashed with the final scores. *Zodiac: 5 Starlight: 6*

I shook my head as the Zodiac team fell to their knees on the churned up ground. Orion turned and kicked his seat so hard it snapped in two. Nova dropped her face into her hands as the Starlight Principal did a victory dance next to her.

I stared at the pitch in utter disbelief.

Holy shit, we lost.

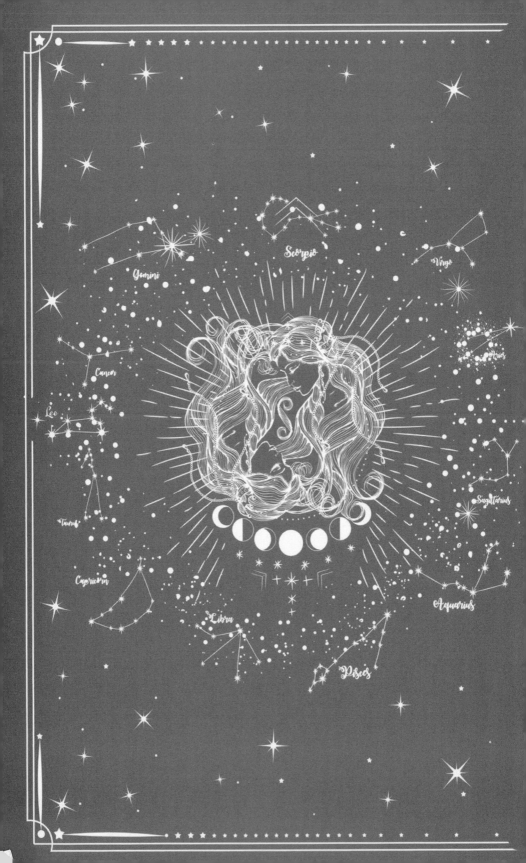

TORY

CHAPTER THIRTY FOUR

I was strangely disappointed by the fact that our team had lost the match and that feeling was compounded by the look on Geraldine's face as she crossed the pitch. She looked truly crestfallen and guilt stirred in my gut at the knowledge that we had caused this downfall.

Max ripped his shirt off and the purple welts all over his skin glowed beneath the light of the silvery dome overhead. My gut twisted guiltily again. I hadn't really thought he'd stick out the game with that stuff on his skin and end up so badly burned by it but he'd clearly made the choice to stay. I was kind of impressed by his dedication, even if he was a total jackass.

A huge crash sounded Darius kicking one of the pyramids which released the balls and I couldn't help but be a *little* satisfied with how upset this had clearly made the Heirs.

A faint vibration rumbled through the ground at my feet and I looked up as the huge, silver dome above our heads started to retract, allowing a view of the blue sky beyond.

"What's going on?" I asked.

"The dome holds the magic which powers the no-magic zone around the Pit and the forcefield protecting the stands," Sofia explained. "They lower it at the end of the match to turn them off. It makes it easier for the maintenance staff to re-set the pitch and retrieve the balls from the Pit."

"Are you ready to go, girls?" Nova asked loudly behind us and I felt her taloned hand land on my shoulder.

"Go where?" Darcy asked in confusion.

"Oh, did I forget to say? We thought it would be a nice touch to have the Vega Twins presenting the medals."

"What? No, I really don't think-" I tried to protest but she was already steering us both out onto the pitch and the students from Starlight Academy were cheering raucously.

Darcy caught my eye and I could tell she was about as keen as I was to stand up in front of all these people but it was clearly too late to stop it from happening.

I looked around and noticed the Celestial Council and their spouses grouping around Lionel as he produced a pouch of stardust from his pocket. Clearly none of them wanted to stay and watch the other team claim their victory and with a flash of light, all eight of them disappeared.

The two teams had lined up either side of a low podium and were waiting for us, with all members now fully healed.

The Heirs hardly even glanced our way, their eyes on the ground as they sagged with disappointment. I wondered if they'd ever lost at something like this before and I had the strong sensation that they hadn't. If they were experiencing even an ounce of the humiliation that they'd caused us, then I was sure that it had been worth it.

A smile was fighting for control of my face though I fought against it. I was sure the rest of my classmates wouldn't appreciate it if I grinned like a moron while presenting a trophy to the competition, but as Seth twisted his toe in the mud like a disappointed three year old I found it pretty hard to stop myself.

Nova clapped politely and pushed an envelope into Darcy's hand before giving me a golden medal which hung from a red ribbon. She waved a hand at Darcy who opened the envelope nervously.

"Fae of the match," she said and I flinched in surprise as her voice rang out over the whole stadium. "Goes to Geraldine Grus."

I could finally let my smile free as I looked around to see Geraldine leaping out of her spot in the line up, her eyes glimmering with emotion.

"Oh sweet onion balls!" she gasped as she rushed towards us.

"Congratulations!" I said enthusiastically as I placed the medal over her head.

She crushed me in an embrace, lifting me clean off of my feet as she celebrated. Darcy wrapped her arms around us too and we laughed as Geraldine descended into happy tears.

"And congratulations to the winners of the match: Starlight Academy!" Nova added loudly when we didn't seem likely to break free of Geraldine any time soon.

The crowd from Starlight went crazy, their applause deafening as the team jumped up and down in ecstatic celebration.

A low growl caught my attention and I glanced to my right where Darius stood almost close enough to touch. His jaw was locked tight, his spine rigid and his eyes burning with rage. I looked away from him quickly, though I couldn't help but feel glad that this was upsetting him.

Poor little Darius lost his favourite game. Imagine how bad you'd feel if someone tried to drown you though? Not that I'm bitter at all...

Nova passed Darcy a bunch of flowers and gave me a medal on a green ribbon as the Starlight Airstriker stepped up to claim them.

The guy pulled both of us into an exuberant hug as he claimed his prizes and I couldn't help but feel a bit pleased for the team as we worked our way through the line, handing over flowers and medals to each of them as they approached. I imagined beating a team filled with the Celestial Heirs was something that none of them would ever forget.

I could feel heat radiating off of Darius beside me as he fought to maintain his composure while the line worked its way past us but I didn't look his way again.

The last Starlight player to approach us was the Captain, Quentin. He smiled widely as he accepted the flowers from Darcy, tossing her a wink. As I placed the medal around his neck he pulled me into a tight hug, his hand skimming my ass less than accidentally. I pushed him off with a laugh, his excitement infectious in a way that made me think he was a Siren but it didn't feel invasive like the way it always did with Max. Maybe because he wasn't trying to force any emotions onto me, just sharing his own.

"Why don't you two girls come back and party with us at Starlight tonight?" he offered and I didn't miss his suggestive tone.

"Why don't you fuck off while you've still got some teeth left?" Darius said before we could respond.

I frowned at him but his gaze was locked on Quentin.

To my surprise, Quentin laughed tauntingly. "And to think, we were worried about facing off against the Celestial Heirs," he said, aiming his comments at me and Darcy. "Turns out they really aren't that impressive after all. It would be a shame if Solaria ended up in their loser hands. Maybe the two of you should reconsider the idea of taking up your crown?"

I laughed at his brazen behaviour, wondering how much more it would take for Darius to snap.

"Yeah," I replied jokingly. "Maybe we should take our crowns back after all."

Darcy laughed too, flicking her long hair. "Oh yeah," she agreed. "I think a crown would suit me actually."

Quentin yelled out in surprise as a shot of heated energy slammed into him like a freight train and he was catapulted halfway across the pitch before falling into a heap on the ground.

Before I could react in any way, I found a severely pissed off Dragon Shifter snarling in my face. My breath caught in my lungs and I blinked up at him as he growled at me.

Seth moved in on Darcy beside me, his face set with the same enraged scowl while the other two drew close behind them.

"Do you want to say that again?" Darius asked, his voice low, the threat in it sending a tremor right through my core.

Darcy caught my hand and I almost tugged her back a step but as our palms met, I felt a well of power brewing like a tempestuous storm between us. This wasn't like when I power shared with Darius during fire Elemental training. My magic and my sister's didn't need any encouragement to merge with one another. They were born of the same womb, trusted each other implicitly, longed to be together.

Somewhere deep in the base of my soul, a warrior was crying out to be set free. I hadn't meant to lay claim to the throne, but why the hell shouldn't I? That throne had belonged to our father. Our veins held the blood of The Savage King and in that moment I felt pretty damn savage myself.

"You heard us," I snarled right back at him.

"Unless losing affected your hearing?" Darcy added.

"Are you saying you want to try for your claim after all?" Seth asked, his tone laced with surprise.

"It's not our claim," I countered darkly.

"It's our birthright," Darcy finished.

A ripple of energy raced through the four Heirs like they were somehow communicating with each other despite the fact that none of them took their gazes from us and they didn't utter a word.

"Alright then," Darius said darkly. "If you want it then you'll have to fight for it."

"And crawl up out of the gutter to claim it," Max added.

"Then strive to keep it every, single, day," Caleb growled.

"So you'd better be ready," Seth hissed.

Darius and Seth moved so quickly that we barely had time to react. We both flung our free hands up and our combined power shot from us in a wave of energy which managed to combine all four Elements.

The four Heirs were thrown away from us and the whole stadium fell into stunned silence as they crashed into the ground on the far side of the pitch.

For a moment, none of them moved and Darcy and I stepped off of the podium as we advanced on them, still hand in hand with raw power writhing beneath our skin.

Everyone in close proximity scattered as we advanced, even some of those in the stands began to turn and back away now that the forcefield was down and there was nothing to protect them from the magic we could unleash.

The Heirs regained their feet, moving together for a moment as they regarded us. Max and Caleb stepped back and for a second, I couldn't figure out why until Seth and Darius stalked towards us, power surging around their open hands. This was the Fae way, one on one and as Darius's gaze locked on me I knew what he was waiting for.

I exchanged a look with my sister and she nodded as our hands parted. My own power tumbled back into the well within me and I fought for control of it again as Darius advanced.

We hadn't had a single class that even discussed using magic in combat but I knew without doubt that Darius didn't give two shits about that.

He flicked his fingers at me and a fireball with the head of a dragon shot towards me with open jaws.

I gritted my teeth, calling on water as I threw a deluge his way, dousing the dragon and losing sight of Darius as the torrent concealed him. Before I could figure out what to do next, Darius leapt through the downpour, protected by his own water magic as it parted mine like a tide.

He launched a javelin made of ice straight for me and I screamed as I leapt back, tripping as I fought to escape it and falling in the mud on my back.

I caught a glimpse of Darcy as she was swept up into a vortex of Seth's creation and my heart leapt with panic.

Darius advanced on me quickly and I drove my fingers into the soil on either side of me, guiding vines up out of the ground to bind him. Hundreds of the vines slithered around him, working to lock him in their grasp but they were burned from his flesh as soon as they met with it.

I rolled aside, scrambling to my feet just as Darcy fell in a heap beside me, dumped from Seth's magical whirlwind unceremoniously. She wheezed out a cough but drove up a hand in the same motion, engulfing the Werewolf in a fireball. Before it could do any damage, Seth stole the oxygen from the blaze, extinguishing it instantly.

I launched another wave of water at Darius to slow him down as I caught Darcy's hand and yanked her to her feet.

She threw me a desperate look as she directed more water at Seth but he created a wall of soil to protect himself from it.

Darius broke through my water attack again with a vicious swipe of his hand and the two of them advanced on us like predators with cornered prey.

I backed up but my foot slipped over the edge of a hole and only my grip on my sister stopped me from falling.

I looked down to see the Pit opening up beneath me, countless balls resting in the depths of it alongside the shadows.

"We gave you the chance to bow to us willingly!" Darius shouted loud enough for the whole stadium to hear him. "But it seems you have to be brought to your knees before you learn!"

As one, he and Seth threw their hands out at us and I had no chance to defend myself before a blast of icy water slammed straight into my chest just as Seth threw a gust of air at Darcy.

We fell back with a scream, falling, falling, then *splat*. The air was driven from my lungs as I landed flat on my back in the thick mud at the base of the Pit. Pain flared through my body and tears swam in my eyes as the stadium beyond us erupted into cheers and laughter.

Darcy groaned beside me and I blinked as my eyes adjusted to the darkened space.

"If you want to get out of there, you'll have to fight your way through our magic," Seth called as he moved to stand over the hole above us with Darius at his side. "Which should be easy for someone as powerful as the two of you."

Panic bled along my limbs as he and Darius started casting magic over the roof of the hole above us. Glimmering colours lit the air as they placed spells overhead to keep us trapped and I shivered as I scrambled to my feet.

Darcy moved close enough for her arm to brush against mine as we waited for them to stop.

When they'd finally finished, Max and Caleb moved to stand beside them, the four Heirs looking down on us, united as one.

Max spat at us and I flinched but the wad of spittle just hit the magical shield above us before slowly sliding down the side of it. "Catch ya later, little Vegas," he purred before turning and walking away.

Seth followed next and Caleb held my eye for a moment before he followed too. Darius lingered the longest, his jaw tight as he stood over us. He lowered his gaze slowly, dropping his head before turning and abandoning us to the Pit.

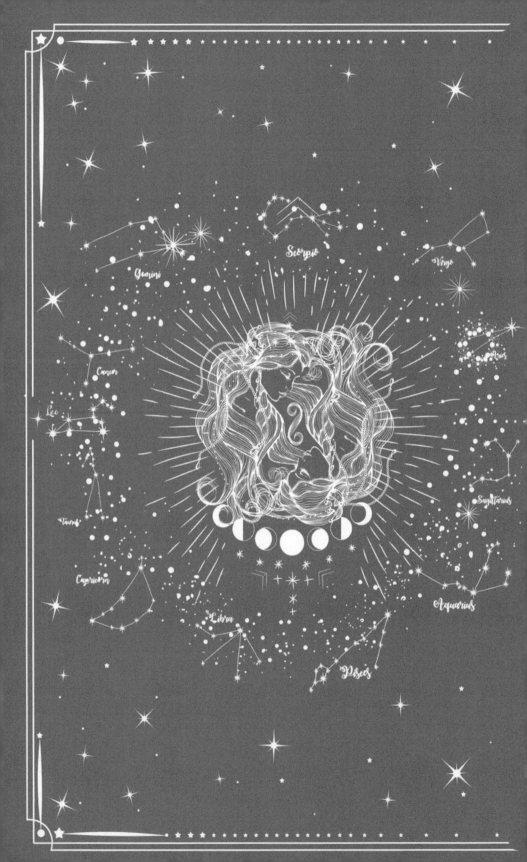

DARCY

CHAPTER THIRTY FIVE

I shivered in the Pit surrounded by mud and damp, staring up at the bright sky and listening to the collective laughter and cheers that boomed around the stadium.

We tried to force our way out, throwing as much magic as we could at the forcefield the Heirs had cast over the top of it. But it was no good.

Jackasses! Why had I ever felt sorry for them? They didn't care how far they took things with us so long as we remained at the bottom of the pecking order. But I was so done taking their shit. When we got out of here, I was going to make it my personal mission to destroy their lives.

"You know what, we should *really* take the throne," I said bitterly, throwing a rock so it skittered across the soft earth and bounced off of a Pitball.

"Yeah, that would wipe the smirks off of their faces once and for all," Tory said, casting fire up at the forcefield. The heat emanated from it and I shielded my eyes, lifting a hand to guide my own fire up to help her. The air became suffocating and we soon had to extinguish the flames and think up another tactic.

Another round of, "The Heirs don't care!" started out in the stands and I ground my teeth.

Yells and laughter clamoured together and I scowled up at the sky. There was no chance of anyone coming to help us. This was between Darius, Seth and us. Fae against Fae.

I scooped up a Pitball, throwing it at the forcefield with a blast of air so it slammed into the magical barrier. It ricocheted off of it and smashed back into the mud, sinking in an inch.

A fanfare started up and the sounds of thousands of people moving signalled everyone was leaving.

No no no! We're gonna be left down here like rats in a hole.

"Dickwads." Tory kicked a Pitball then swore as it happened to be one of the heavy earth balls. She shook out her foot, calling the Heirs every vicious name in her vocabulary - which was a damn lot.

A pitchy scream in the distance made my heart jolt and I frowned, listening hard, but the crowd continued to chatter and the music played on. I blew out a breath, gathering a storm of air in my hands as I prepared to pummel the forcefield once more. Tory was building a fireball and she nodded to signal she was ready to release it.

Screams echoed across the stadium and the air fizzled out of my hands.

"What the hell?" Tory breathed as my heart pounded a frantic tune.

"Back back back!" Nova's voice sounded close by.

"Hey – hello?! What's going on out there?!" My voice echoed off the walls and no reply came in response.

I hurried to the curved edge of the Pit, wondering if I could claw my way up and poke my head out. Tory joined me, but we both froze as chaos broke out above. The rush of footsteps, people shouting orders, hundreds of feet pounding across the pitch. More screams raked against my eardrums and my lungs compressed.

"What's happening?" I gasped but Tory shook her head, having no answer to offer.

"Give me a boost," I asked and she nodded quickly, bending down and cupping her hands together. I stepped into her palms and she propelled me up to the top of the Pit with a gust of air. I cast vines along the edge to catch myself, haphazardly grabbing onto them and trying to get a purchase. I lifted my head just enough to see out without getting too close to the dangerous energy of the Heirs' magic.

A swarm of feet raced past the Pit, obscuring my vision. "Hey!" I shouted, trying to catch someone's attention, but everyone seemed too frantic to look my way. People were changing into their Order forms left right and centre and those with wings took off toward the sky, seeming desperate to escape.

I couldn't hold onto the vines any longer so I dropped to the ground with a wet thump. Washer's warning flashed through my mind and I drew magic to my fingertips as fear danced through my veins.

"What's going on?" Tory demanded as flames flickered in her hands.

"I don't know, everyone's panicking."

We both flinched as a Griffin leapt overhead then took off toward the sky with several powerful beats of its wings.

"Evacuate! Shift into your Orders – don't let them get close!" Nova cried.

A fireball bloomed above us and panic wrapped around my heart, making it hard to breathe. "We've got to get out of here."

"Our magic was stronger together." Tory snatched my hand and the keen wave of her power swept into mine. "Ready?"

I nodded and we raised our free hands. I drew air to my fingertips, a powerful storm swirling around us and sending our hair flying out in tendrils. The fire in Tory's hand flared blue with the intensity of the heat and as one, we released the blast at the shield. It slammed into the centre, creating a ripple of colour over it, but it didn't give.

"Shit!" Tory snapped.

"Again," I encouraged but my breathing faltered as a thick pocket of darkness seeped across the forcefield above, swallowing us up in its shadow. It moved like a living thing, the thickening cloud crackling with a strange energy. Adrenaline pushed through my veins, my muscles tensing, urging me to run. But there was nowhere to go.

A dreadful rasping, sucking noise filled the air and my worst nightmare came true.

"Tory- it's a Nymph! The Academy must be under attack," I exclaimed, the smothering feel of its horrible power settling over my insides.

"It's okay, it can't get through the Heirs' barrier," she breathed, but she didn't look too confident about that as we backed up to the furthest corner of the Pit.

The shadow spread out against the forcefield and lights flashed where it touched. In a horrifying instant, I realised it could immobilise the magic in the very air.

The shield stuttered out and something hair-raisingly terrifying dropped right out of the darkness. The Nymph landed before us, impossibly tall, its body a twisted, gnarled knot of long limbs, serrated teeth and curling horns. Its probing fingers extended towards us and fear slammed into me full force.

"We have to get out!" I screamed, grabbing Tory's arm and stumbling as the full strength of its influence sucked at our magic, draining our energy by the second. The moment it locked down our power, we were doomed.

I clawed my way up the far edge of the Pit with Tory at my side, using the last of my strength to cast vines into existence and tug ourselves higher.

Something brushed against my ankle and I kicked sharply, releasing a yell of determination. It curled tighter around my foot and a scream escaped me as I lurched backwards. Tory scrambled over the edge, grabbing my arm and hauling backwards with all her strength.

I clung to her with fear scraping at my ribcage. She shot a spear of ice over my head and a shriek behind me made me wince.

The Nymph released me and I scrambled away in relief. Tory yanked me upright and we stumbled forward. Before we made it three paces, she slammed to a halt and I staggered away to avoid colliding with her.

Terror strummed every nerve ending in my body as I took in the churned up pitch spreading out ahead of us, the chaotic crowd tearing past us in a mixture of Order and Fae forms. At every exit were Nymphs, standing tall, blocking everyone's escape paths. Their shadowy creatures were like wraiths as they released their rattling call, immobilising the Fae surrounding them before descending on them in their weakened states.

A sea of red, white, blue, and silver shirts massed around them as students from Starlight and Zodiac fell prey to their malignant power.

"Oh my god," I breathed, counting more and more of the monsters around the stadium. Several at the verges of the pitch, one in the Pit and an uncountable amount up in the stands. Thirty...forty? More?

A group of Harpies swarmed across the stands like bees, casting powerful blasts of magic at the Nymphs from a safe distance.

A baying howl cut through the air and I spotted Seth high up on the stairs directly ahead of us, cupping his hands around his mouth. His howl was echoed by hundreds of students and the Werewolves burst into their Order form, the gigantic beasts charging up the aisles to take on the Nymphs. They relied on the brute force of their teeth, diving onto the tree-like creatures and ripping them apart.

I hunted for our friends amongst the masses, for Orion. But I couldn't spot them in the surging crowd. As a Nymph was brought to its knees before one of the exits, a stampede of students headed that way to get out, soon crushing each other in their bid to escape.

My throat was tight, my lungs even tighter. Shock held me in place but I knew I had to move. And not just move, I had to fight.

The rattling, rasping pull of a Nymph's magic behind us made me lurch around, raising my hands as power coiled into my veins.

The beast was dragging itself out of the Pit and I propelled a jet of water from my hands, forcing it back down. Tory hurried forward, freezing the water as it cascaded over the vile creature, holding it in place at the bottom of the hole.

"Tory!" I gasped as a Nymph burst through the crowd beyond her, its blazing red eyes seeming to lock onto her as it knocked students aside to get closer. Its arms raised and its twisted, pronged fingers were ready to strike as its rattling cry paralysed the Fae surrounding it.

Terror threatened to overwhelm me as my limbs weakened and my insides hollowed out. They just had to get near and we were finished. No more Academy, no more Heirs, or dreams, or thrones. No more Lance Orion.

I ran toward Tory, snatching her hand and urging that powerful energy to roam between us. It flickered at the edges of my skin and I lifted a hand barely in time as it exploded from my body. Tory's magic combined with mine, twisting into a tight coil of fire and water. It slammed into the Nymph, holding it off. But it wasn't enough.

I shouted out in effort as we continued the onslaught, desperate to keep it at bay. But the Nymph's power fell over me and my knees quickly weakened. It tugged at my insides, halting my magic and as we turned to run, I found it impossible. My legs nearly gave out and Tory groaned in fury as she fell under the same spell.

The students close by had scattered, leaving us alone with the terrifying monster. I felt its hold on my magic right down to the marrow of my bones.

Fear drilled through to my core and panic threatened to overwhelm me. *We can't die here like this!*

A bellowing roar shook the foundations of the stadium and a huge beast swooped down from above, casting a thick shadow over us. Hellfire rained out of the Dragon's mouth and with a jolt of recognition I realised the magnificent golden beast was Darius. A surge of hope filled me as he swooped low to the ground, releasing a furious blaze over three Nymphs on the pitch.

As he banked hard, careering our way, Orion leapt from his back and fell onto the Nymph before us, slamming a shining dagger into its spine.

Black shadows burst from the wound and the creature wailed a horrible moan as it shuddered and died beneath him.

Darius landed on all fours with an almighty crash, drawing back his wings and releasing a spiral of fire which circled around one of the Nymphs at the nearest exit, consuming its body in the blaze. The heat of it rolled over my cheeks and smoke tingled my senses.

Students ran for the exit while a group of Pegasuses shifted beyond them. I spotted Sofia amongst them with a wave of relief just before a glittering sparkle washed over her and she took off into the sky as a beautiful flying horse. Instead of racing for freedom as I expected, she and the other Pegasuses turned in perfect formation, targeting a Nymph in the stands and blinding it in a cloud of thick glitter. One by one they each took it in turns to smash and kick their back hooves into its head before circling around to do it again.

Three more Nymphs stepped out onto the pitch and Orion cast a wall of air at them to hold them back. His muscles strained as he dug in his heels and Tory and I threw up a huge wall of energy to join his. I immediately felt the creatures' power fighting to stifle our magic and knew this couldn't go on for long.

"Hold the wall!" Orion commanded, dropping the power of his shield and racing toward them with his Vampire speed. My heart stumbled as he used the propulsion of our air power and dove toward the Nymph on the far left, driving his blade deep into its heart. It released a horrible shriek that raked at my eardrums, tumbling to the ground and bursting into nothing but smoke and dust.

Darius roared furiously and I turned to watch as a deep shudder rolled down his spine and his tail flicked out in a deadly swipe. Seats in the stands were shredded as the lethal appendage cut a path through them and several Nymphs. He released a swirling ring of fire which engulfed the two Nymphs still held back by mine and Tory's power then snapped his teeth together in satisfaction.

Four more descended onto the pitch to take their place, one of them knocking the blade from Orion's hand and sending it skittering across the mud.

"Lance!" I yelled in panic as he fell to his knees under the powerful onslaught of two Nymphs at once. He extended one hand our way as he cast a swirling shield of wind around us in a final effort to protect us.

"No," I gasped in complete, desperate panic as a Nymph moved toward Orion, reaching down, aiming its probing fingers for his chest. I was moving before I could stop myself, charging toward him in a desperate act to help. I managed to hold onto the very last inch of magic I had in my grip and that would have to be enough.

Orion was on the verge of death and I simply couldn't see it happen. Every fibre of my being was begging me to save him.

Darius released a powerful blast of fire which billowed overhead, unable to attack the Nymphs without also catching Orion in the blast.

Orion buckled forward, his hands braced against the ground and something shifted within me. A burning energy filled me up with the heat of a million stars, burrowing into my core. My body felt as though it was about to lift off of the ground with the sheer power of it as a rippling sensation raced across my shoulder blades.

The Nymph lunged forward, ready to slice its razor sharp claws into Orion's heart and I knew that mere seconds parted him from death.

I threw out my hands with a yell of pure rage, letting that fiery energy burn right out of me. A line of fire exploded from my body like a writhing, winged creature of sharpest blue and darkest red. It hit the Nymph square in the chest and its wails echoed around the entire stadium before the beast exploded into a coil of black smoke right before my eyes.

I didn't know what it meant, all I knew was that I couldn't stop unleashing it. Not until every one of these monstrous creatures were dead at my feet.

I let the fiery behemoth within me take over, willing it to wrap the Nymphs near Orion in a swirling inferno of death. They disintegrated as the fire fizzled out and black smoke twirled up toward the sky in their wake.

I sprinted to Orion and pulled him to his feet, pawing at his arms as if to reassure myself he was alright.

"What the hell was that fire?" he asked in disbelief, his eyes trailing over me in awe.

I shook my head. "I was hoping you could tell me."

I searched for Tory but I couldn't see her. More of the crowd had spilled onto the pitch and I realised why as a wall of Nymphs marched down the stairways, their arms extended in a bid to immobilise their magic.

Max was high up at the peak of the stands with Caleb at his side, the two of them battling a group of Fae as magic collided between them. Horror tangled with my blood as I realised they weren't Fae. They were Nymphs disguised in Fae form, their stolen magic rogue but powerful, blasting huge holes in the stadium as they tried to hit Max and Caleb. They were one wrong move away from death, but I couldn't focus on them any longer as I turned and started running across the uneven ground with Orion at my side.

An errant blast of magic shot up toward the sky, slamming into the edge of the open roof. A groaning, tearing noise wracked my ears as a huge plate of metal tumbled from the structure.

A scream burst from my throat as it plummeted right toward us. On instinct, I forced air out from me in the way Perseus had taught me and Orion grabbed my hand, his energy flooding into my veins in an instant. It pushed the shield out around us, feeling like a solid, unbreakable wall. *But was it?!*

I flinched, snatching onto Orion's shirt and wincing sharply as the huge panel crashed into the top of my shield with an ear-cracking boom. It split into two before falling on either side of us and I looked up at Orion in shock.

He stared at me for half a second, his mouth parting. "Lucky you trust me," he growled and my eyebrows shot up. *Do I?*

Orion dragged me on towards the exit with a spurt of his Vampire speed. He slammed his shoulders into the crowd to forge a path through, but I pulled back, snatching my hand from his grip. "I'm not leaving without Tory."

He tried to grab hold of me again, but I ducked away, refusing to let him take me from this fight.

Horror sizzled in my blood as a huge Nymph towered at the back of the crowd and immobilised its nearest prey, making the students around me fall into a panic.

Orion caught my hand and I dragged his magic into my own on instinct, the rush of his added power filling me up like jet fuel. I unleashed the burning giant inside me and it erupted from my body in the shape of wings, speeding toward the Nymph and folding around it. The creature stumbled back as it burst into flame, its body burning up from the inside out before tumbling into a shower of black dust.

The students stared at me in complete shock as they got to their feet and ran for the exit.

Orion pulled me around to face him and my heart faltered as he clutched onto me.

"I'm not going anywhere," I demanded and he nodded, a strange smile pulling at his mouth despite the absolute madness descending around us.

"Go on then." He gestured to the raging battle. "Show me what you've got, Blue."

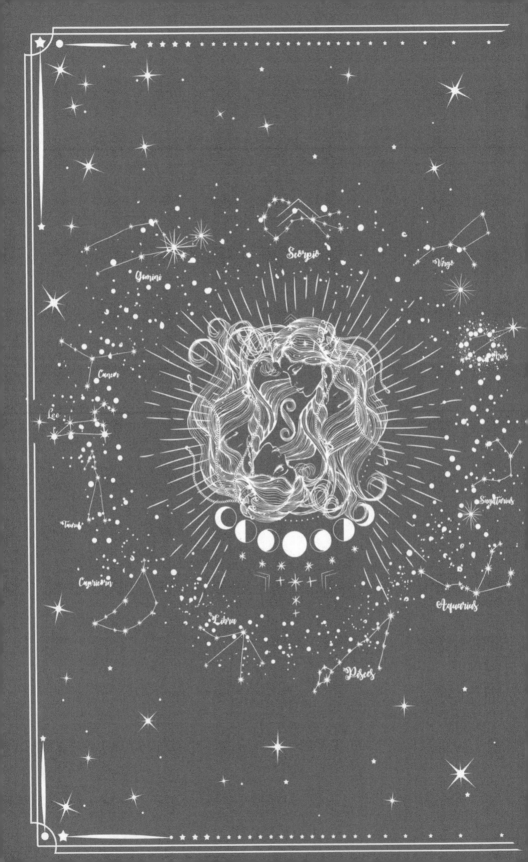

TORY

CHAPTER THIRTY·SIX

My heart pounded an uneven rhythm as I took in the chaos surrounding me. Throughout the stands students were shredding through their clothes as they shifted into their Order forms to escape the carnage.

Harpies, Griffins, Manticores, Dragons and Pegasuses flew for the open roof, many of them with their friends still in Fae form riding on their backs.

A red Dragon who I recognised as Geraldine's friend Angelica swooped overhead before blasting a Nymph with fire and destroying it in one precise hit.

A Sphinx and Medusa bolted for the exit and I belatedly recognised Marguerite and Kylie.

I caught sight of Darcy with Orion between the panicking bodies around me and relief spilled through me.

I started to run towards her but a surge of air magic slammed into me and I was tossed aside as a Nymph with stolen power aimed at me again. I tumbled across the mud and threw a wave of water back at my attacker, knocking the creature to the far side of the stadium with its force.

My hands sank into the mud beneath me as I pushed myself upright and a huge roar laced with pain echoed right through my body.

I turned my gaze towards the enormous golden Dragon in the centre of the pitch as eight Nymphs rushed towards him at once. Darius swung his reptilian head around, bearing a row of razor sharp teeth at the creatures as they charged him.

Dragon Fire blasted from his mouth, destroying four of the monsters before the tail end of it blazed overhead, warming me in every way. My own power burned hot within me as one of the Nymphs managed to leap onto him, driving the sharpened probes of its fingers straight into his flank.

Darius bellowed in agony again and I started running towards him as a desperate ache built in my chest. It didn't matter that I hated him and he hated me, in that moment it was only us and them. And I couldn't bear to let them take him.

I cried out as my power pooled within me, begging to be set free.

Flames licked their way out of my body, swarming over my flesh until they danced right before my eyes in a mix of blood red and lightning blue. The feel of them on my skin was electrifying and they pulsed with some deep magic which answered my call like it was the most natural thing in the world.

The flames burst from me like a living creature, slamming into the Nymph whose claws were deep in Darius's flesh before burning it alive. The creature shrieked in an agony so intense that I could feel it echoing back to me through my magic.

Darius roared again, his huge head swinging above mine a moment before his jaws snapped closed on a Nymph who was running up behind me.

The grinding and crunching of bones mixed with the screams of the creature as Darius bit down viciously until it stopped moving. He launched its broken body away from us and it collided with the stands on the far side of the stadium which had almost emptied out as the Starlight students fled in panic.

More of the Nymphs were trying to circle closer to us and Darius swung his golden tail, the huge spikes on the end of it swiping the legs out from beneath one of the creatures.

I blasted it with red and blue flames before it could get up and the fire danced through my veins like pure ecstasy.

Darius released a torrent of Dragon Fire over his shoulder before wheeling around, his wings tucked close to protect them.

I ducked low as he moved, dancing between his feet and shifting beneath his stomach before ending up on the other side of him. Somehow he didn't step on me even though he was thrashing about, breathing fire and swiping his claws at the monsters who came for us.

A chorus of rumbling growls announced Geraldine approaching in her Cerberus form, all three of her giant dog heads bearing poisonous fangs at a Nymph as it raced to escape her.

She pounced, slamming the creature into the dirt and for a moment my heart leapt in panic as it reached for her with probing fingers. In the next heartbeat, she ripped its head from its body, shattering its skull in her tremendous jaws before bounding after her next target.

Nova's voice boomed out across the stadium. "All students untrained in combat are commanded to flee to the safety of your Houses! Take to your Order forms and RUN!"

My heart leapt as I realised that meant me and Darcy but I'd lost sight of her in the madness again and we still hadn't discovered our Order forms even if I'd wanted to try and do as she'd said.

I looked around wildly, trying to locate my sister. Max and Caleb were fighting back to back at the far end of the stadium; Max wielding water in sweeping arcs as his navy scales shone wetly. Caleb darted between his magic as if they'd choreographed their attacks, finding holes in the water the moment they appeared and bursting through them to strike the Nymphs with a combination of physical attacks enhanced by his Vampire abilities and earth magic.

A high pitched scream drew my attention and my heart leapt with panic as I spotted Diego being thrown to the ground before a Nymph who was over eight feet tall. Blood blossomed across his cheek and Sofia dove from the air in her Pegasus form, landing in front of him as she shifted back into Fae form. She stood over Diego, casting a flickering flame between her hands in an attempt to help him.

The Nymph drew in a rattling breath and my chest seized as I sprinted towards them. Sofia fell to her knees beneath the power of its spell.

I screamed a battle cry like a damn Viking warrior as I flung my palms out, aiming for the nightmare creature and sending blue and red fire to consume it on blazing wings. The Nymph shrieked as it burned before bursting apart, leaving a trail of black smoke hanging in the air where it had been.

Diego's eyes were wild with panic as he stared between the black smoke and me.

"Shift!" I commanded, my voice unintentionally thick with Coercion as my worry for my friends compelled me to make sure they got to safety.

Sofia's eyes widened a moment before a pale pink Pegasus burst from the confines of her skin once more. I skidded to a halt in the mud beside her, reaching down to heave Diego back to his feet. He swayed unsteadily and I shoved him towards Sofia without wasting time on being gentle.

"Climb on," I said. "And fly as far from here as you can get!"

I tried to turn away as Diego clambered onto her back but he caught my wrist.

"Come with us, chica, it's not safe for you here either-"

"I'm not leaving Darcy," I replied dismissively, pulling my arm back. "But the two of you need to *go.*"

Sofia flapped her sparkling wings as my Coercion gripped her and my heart twisted at the concern in their eyes.

"Don't worry about me," I added as they took flight. I watched for a moment as they sped towards the sky then turned back to my hunt for Darcy.

Darius roared behind me as his flames took out another Nymph but a second leapt around the blaze and onto his back. I sucked in a sharp breath, drawing on the well of power within me as I started running back towards him.

Darius spun around, the razor sharp spines on his tail swiping within inches of my face as he tried to dislodge the creature but it clambered all the way up until it was lodged between his wings. He swung his head around, snapping at it as he tried to rip it off of him but he couldn't twist his head into that position.

The Nymph released its rattling breath and my knees buckled as it weakened me.

I staggered forward, my hand landing on Darius's front leg as I tried to steady myself.

The Nymph shrieked excitedly and drove its probes into the flesh between Darius's shoulder blades. A roar filled with pure agony escaped him and he fell forward onto his chest as pain wracked through his body.

Where my hand still rested against him it was like I could feel that pain within myself. I felt like I was tearing in two, my soul ripping free of my body and the deepest sense of dread filled me.

Darius swung his head around to look at me, one huge, golden eye reflecting back the image of a girl who was breaking in half.

He snarled at me, striking his nose against my chest to knock me back a step. As I stumbled away from him, he struck me again, a deep growl echoing from his throat as he urged me to run.

I stared at him in shock for a moment and he trembled as more pain tore through him.

"So fucking bossy," I snapped, shoving his big Dragon face aside as I moved closer to him instead. "You probably *are* stubborn enough to die here rather than let me help you."

Darius growled at me but I ignored him as I leapt up onto his leg and started climbing up the side of his big ass Dragon body.

His scales were smooth and hot beneath my palms but I managed to gain purchase by grabbing hold of his wing and hoisting myself higher.

His body was trembling beneath me and he bellowed in pain again, urging me on faster.

I reached up, grabbing a thick spine which ran down the centre of his neck before coming face to face with the creature from my nightmares.

The Nymph shrieked, lunging at me faster than should have been possible and I almost lost my grip on Darius as I fell back.

My heart lurched violently but I managed to catch the top of his wing, swinging myself around as that paralysing rattle juddered through my core, halting my magic in its tracks and stealing my energy from me.

Fear shot through me as the Nymph pounced, its probes aimed right for my chest.

I screamed, throwing my fist out even though I knew it was no good. As my knuckles connected with the bony ridges of its face, pain exploded through my hand swiftly followed by a flood of red and blue flames.

The Nymph shrieked so loudly that I threw my hands over my ears as the flames consumed it, a wisp of black smoke sweeping up towards the sky where it had been moments before.

I fell forwards, my palms meeting the warmth of Darius's blood as I braced myself against him.

More Nymphs were running straight for us and with an echoing roar which vibrated right through my body, Darius destroyed all five of them with a torrent of Dragon Fire.

His head fell forward as he used the last of his energy and I cried out, grabbing hold of his wing as he tilted sideways beneath me. He crashed to the ground on his side and through some miracle, I managed to keep hold of his wing before falling against his neck. I wrapped my arms around him, scrunching my eyes closed as a tremor tore through his body and the golden colour of his scales seemed to shine with inner power and heat.

My stomach lurched and I released a scream as I found myself falling over ten foot down to the ground as Darius retreated into his Fae form.

I kept hold of him as I fell, crashing down into the mud of the Pitball pitch on top of him with a cry of fear.

All around us the fight raged on but beneath my hands, blood was pulsing from his chest and he was lying deathly still.

"Darius?" I demanded, shaking him while still trying to press down on his wounds. It wouldn't be enough though, his back and legs were bleeding too. A bloody gouge shone wetly on his neck and his breaths were far too shallow.

"Help!" I shouted, though my eyes stayed fixed on Darius's face and my heart was pounding the rhythm of a war drum in my chest.

The hairs were rising along the back of my neck, a strange sensation prickling in my chest. This moment felt eternal and fleeting all at once, like we were hanging between two great points and everything could change on the turn of a coin.

"Wake up!" I demanded, pushing my magic towards him in hopes of being able to do *something*.

Instead of stopping the blood or healing him, my magic spilled into his body, merging with his in the reverse of what we'd been doing when he helped me with my fire magic.

His power welcomed mine instantly, drawing it in, blending with it completely like it had been waiting for this moment. The feeling took my breath away and though it didn't slow the blood, I felt the tension ease from his muscles and the fear loosen its grip on his heart.

My hands were shaking as they ran slick with Darius's blood and silent tears tracked down my cheeks.

His heart was slowing down, his power flickering like a candle in a breeze. If someone didn't get to us soon, Darius Acrux was going to die.

And though it seemed like he should have been the last person in the world for me to care about after everything he'd done to me, I wasn't sure I could bear it if I lost him here.

DARCY

CHAPTER THIRTY SEVEN

Seth sped in front of me as a huge white wolf, knocking me back as he dove onto a Nymph. His coat was flecked with blackish blood and more joined it as he ripped the Nymph's head from its shoulders in one powerful bite.

An echoing Dragon roar billowed up to the sky and I felt it right down to my bones.

"Argh," Orion hissed, clutching the crook of his elbow and I turned to him in alarm.

"Are you alright?" I begged.

"Darius," he growled, then shook his head. "Just keep moving and take out any Nymphs you can. Go that way." He pointed across the pitch and I nodded.

Orion had retrieved his silver blade and we worked as an unstoppable unit as we made our way in that direction, my eyes ever-roaming as I hunted for signs of my sister.

Heat blazed over me from one side and I turned sharply, throwing out my hands just in time to block the stolen fire magic cast by a Nymph, releasing a torrent of water. The hiss of the two powers colliding filled my ears and steam spurted out in every direction.

Orion sprinted past me in a blur of motion and the Nymph's magic died in a wave as he skewered its heart with his silver blade. He ripped it free and we ran to meet each other once more, racing on toward the other end of the pitch.

I ducked as Geraldine bounded over us, chasing a Nymph down and finishing it with her toxic bite. As we hurried to carry on, my foot caught on something soft and I glanced down. Horror thickened in my stomach as I found a body in a navy and silver kit. Ashanti's lifeless bronze eyes gazed up at me, her limbs awkwardly twisted and a single line of blood leaking from her mouth.

"Fuck," Orion hissed, drawing me away and I tried to smother the shock of it, a strange ringing filling my head.

As we continued across the field of hell, my shock gave way to a burning fury like nothing I'd ever known. I was Fae. These were my kin. And they were falling prey to the hands of our enemies.

With a yell of defiance, I fell into a frenzy as I made my way forward with Orion, striking at any Nymph who got too close. He helped me guide my power every time I blasted one into oblivion with the monstrous fire I'd been gifted and together we carved a path forward.

As a plume of smoke lifted ahead of me, I realised the crowd was thinning and hope dared to raise its head in my chest.

The few Nymphs still standing released a wailing cry and started to flee.

"Are they leaving?" I gasped as Orion moved closer to me, his blade coated in black Nymph blood and his arms flecked with it too. He was breathing heavily but he assessed the battle with complete control as the students and professors chased the last of them to the exits.

"It's over," Orion said with a breath of relief. "For now at least."

My gaze fell on the bodies strewn in the stands and fear overwhelmed me. *Where's Tory?*

Panic raced through me and I pulled away from Orion, desperate as I hunted for my sister.

"Tory!" I screamed, but it felt like screaming into a void. There was no way she'd hear me over the shouts and wails of the Fae surrounding us.

She has to be alright.

With the way ahead clear, Orion dragged me into his arms and my stomach lurched as he sped across the pitch at a fierce speed.

As we made it across the field, my heart jolted with relief as I spotted Tory kneeling over Darius. My relief was quickly swallowed by fear as I saw the blood pooling out around the Fire Heir from multiple wounds.

"Heal him!" Tory begged as she spotted us. Her eyes raked over me as Orion put me down and her shoulders sagged a little as she realised I was okay before her gaze fell back on Darius beneath her. Tears had tracked lines down her cheeks and her hands were stained red with his blood as she fought to help him. My lips parted in surprise as I noted the fear in her gaze, wondering what could have happened in that fight to make her look at Darius that way.

Orion fell down beside him, looking distressed and I hurriedly knelt down too. He pressed his fingers to a bloody wound on Darius's side and it slowly began to heal.

"He's survived worse," he growled bitterly as Darius groaned, coming to.

I sagged forward, beginning to tremble as exhaustion took hold of me.

Orion nudged Tory's hands away from the wound on Darius's chest so that he could heal it next and she shifted forward, pressing her bloodstained palm to his cheek instead.

Orion's jaw tensed and I noted the pale colour to his skin as he threw his magic into healing his friend. His gaze slid to me imploringly. "I need more power to-"

"Take mine," Tory said, offering him her free hand without looking away from Darius for a moment.

Orion snatched her hand without a moment's hesitation, the green glow in his palm gaining intensity instantly.

Darius coughed, his eyes flickering a few times before snapping open. His gaze fell on Tory as she continued to look down at him. Her hand was still pressed to his cheek and he frowned slightly.

"You..." he began but he didn't finish what he'd been going to say.

His hand moved over hers for a moment, holding it in place against his cheek as he held her eye.

I shifted uncomfortably beside them, feeling like I was laying witness to something private.

"Good as new," Orion muttered, releasing Tory and Darius in the same movement.

Tory blinked, snatching her hand away from Darius's face before scrambling off of him and getting to her feet. She turned her back on him, moving to my side and pulling me into a hug.

"You're alright," she whispered, pushing back to look at me and I nodded, tears stinging my eyes as I stared at her ash-smeared cheeks. It was such a relief to find her alive that my heart could hardly take it.

"Thanks to some insane blue and red fire I cast," I said and Tory's eyes widened.

"You used it too?" she asked in surprise, gazing down at her palms as if searching for an answer. "It was nothing like our usual Element."

Tory looked to Orion for an explanation and I rested my shoulder against hers, adrenaline still making my body shake.

He shook his head, seemingly lost. "I don't know what it was, but it was powerful enough to kill Nymphs. It was nothing like anything I've ever witnessed..." He trailed off as he pulled Darius upright and the Fire Heir looked between Tory and I, his eyes flickering with some dark emotion.

"You just proved your worth." Darius didn't say it with any kindness, in fact he sounded genuinely threatened for the first time since I'd met him. And though I was overwhelmed by this power, it felt more natural than anything I'd ever known. Like it had always lived within me.

I gazed around at the devastation, embers tumbling through the air and the wails and moans of those in pain carrying from all around us. Who knew how many were dead and how much magic the Nymphs had taken for their own?

The need to find my friends and make sure they were all okay enveloped me like ice cold water.

"Why did they attack us?" I whispered, ready to do anything I could to help.

Orion looked around, his jaw locked tight and his eyes as dark as ink. "They attacked the children of the most elite Fae in Solaria, so my guess is, the Nymphs just declared war on our kind."

ALSO BY

CAROLINE PECKHAM

&

SUSANNE VALENTI

Brutal Boys of Everlake Prep

(Complete Reverse Harem Bully Romance Contemporary Series)

Kings of Quarantine

Kings of Lockdown

Kings of Anarchy

Queen of Quarantine

**

Dead Men Walking

(Reverse Harem Dark Romance Contemporary Series)

The Death Club

Society of Psychos

**

The Harlequin Crew

(Reverse Harem Mafia Romance Contemporary Series)

Sinners Playground

Dead Man's Isle

Carnival Hill

Paradise Lagoon

Harlequinn Crew Novellas

Devil's Pass

**

Dark Empire

(Dark Mafia Contemporary Standalones)

Beautiful Carnage

Beautiful Savage

**

The Ruthless Boys of the Zodiac

(Reverse Harem Paranormal Romance Series - Set in the world of Solaria)

Dark Fae

Savage Fae

Vicious Fae

Broken Fae

Warrior Fae

Zodiac Academy

(M/F Bully Romance Series- Set in the world of Solaria, five years after Dark Fae)

The Awakening

Ruthless Fae

The Reckoning

Shadow Princess

Cursed Fates

Fated Thrones

Heartless Sky

The Awakening - As told by the Boys

Zodiac Academy Novellas

Origins of an Academy Bully

The Big A.S.S. Party

Darkmore Penitentiary

(Reverse Harem Paranormal Romance Series - Set in the world of Solaria, ten years after Dark Fae)

Caged Wolf

Alpha Wolf

Feral Wolf

**

The Age of Vampires

(Complete M/F Paranormal Romance/Dystopian Series)

Eternal Reign

Eternal Shade

Eternal Curse

Eternal Vow

Eternal Night

Eternal Love

**

Cage of Lies

(M/F Dystopian Series)

Rebel Rising

**

Tainted Earth

(M/F Dystopian Series)

Afflicted

Altered

Adapted

Advanced

**

The Vampire Games

(Complete M/F Paranormal Romance Trilogy)

V Games

V Games: Fresh From The Grave

V Games: Dead Before Dawn

*

The Vampire Games: Season Two

(Complete M/F Paranormal Romance Trilogy)

Wolf Games

Wolf Games: Island of Shade

Wolf Games: Severed Fates

*

The Vampire Games: Season Three

Hunter Trials

*

The Vampire Games Novellas

A Game of Vampires

**

The Rise of Issac

(Complete YA Fantasy Series)

Creeping Shadow

Bleeding Snow

Turning Tide

Weeping Sky

Failing Light